When she did not face him again, when she stood there in tense silence, her back to him, her slender spine rigid, Griffin slowly, tenderly, placed his hands on her shoulders. He heard her soft intake of breath, felt her fine bones quiver as his palms settled lightly atop her arms. Her head tipped back as he caressed her, tentatively at first, scarcely touching her, almost afraid that if he moved too boldly, that if he clutched her too tightly, the sweet illusion would dissolve like mist in the morning sunshine. He feared that if she knew how badly he wanted her, how tormented he was becoming by the very thought of her, she would pull away and run.

But she did not pull away.

God help him, she did not run. . . .

By Tina St. John
Published by the Ballantine Publishing Group

LORD OF VENGEANCE
LADY OF VALOR
WHITE LION'S LADY

WHITE LION'S LADY

Tina St. John

IVY BOOKS • NEW YORK

An Ivy Book
Published by The Ballantine Publishing Group
Copyright © 2001 by Tina St. John
Excerpt from *Black Lion's Bride* copyright © 2001 by Tina St. John

This book contains an excerpt from the forthcoming book *Black Lion's Bride* by Tina St. John. This excerpt has been set for this edition only and may not reflect the final content of the forthcoming edition.

www.ballantinebooks.com

ISBN 0-804-11962-7

Manufactured in the United States of America

First Edition: August 2001

10 9 8 7 6 5 4 3 2 1

For J.C.G. and C.S.G.,
and anyone else who's ever been lost and
searching . . . May you find hope. May you find
happiness. May you find home.

Prologue

England, 1179

Mocking laughter rang in Isabel de Lamere's head as she fled the enormous outdoor gathering, trying to escape the scene of her humiliation. To think she had actually been excited to attend the summer feast at Droghallow, a demesne held by a friend of her father's. Eight-year-old Izzy had looked forward to the event for weeks, eager for the chance to don her finest kirtle and make new friends of the children from surrounding shires.

It might have been a fine day indeed, if not for Drog-hallow's odious young heir. Sent reluctantly by his father to see that Izzy enjoyed herself, the lad had made mean sport of her instead, ridiculing her awkwardness in front of the other children. Before long, they were all making fun, finding fault in everything about her: her pudgy limbs, her plain face and freckled cheeks, her unruly red hair. Izzy had fled the group before her tears could further condemn her.

Sucking in great gulps of air, she ran down the motte and across the wide plain in no particular direction, stopping only when she found herself utterly breathless, waist-high in the tall grass of the outlying gully. She collapsed to her knees in the cool, shifting reeds, fighting to choke back the sobs that stung her throat and trying to focus on anything else but the knot of hurt the children's gibes had left in her heart.

Her search for diversion led her teary gaze to a patch of blossoming weeds but a few paces before her. There a butterfly had paused, its pretty yellow wings beating as it drank from a wild daisy. Perhaps she could capture it for a pet, she thought, watching as the pretty insect lit softly on another of the sunny flowers. She got up and crept toward it, but as if it sensed her stalking dangerously near, the butterfly took flight, fluttering off on a zigzagging path toward the edge of the woods.

It took little coaxing for Izzy to follow. She chased after without so much as a backward glance or a thought for her previous troubles, single-minded now in her determination to catch her prize.

The shade of the forest cooled her skin as she stepped into the dense glade, the great oaks and towering conifers sealing her off from the bright light of midday at her back. The rich scents of moss and moist sweet earth surrounded her. Birds rustled in the treetops high above, their trilling chatter drowning out the din of celebration taking place on the castle hill. A woodland creature scurried unseen in the bramble near Izzy's feet, fleeing from the intruder's path.

As if being led to another world, Izzy followed her butterfly guide deeper into the thicket, her eyes trained on the tiny beacon of color dancing amid the shadowy gloom of the forest. It hesitated some distance in, alighting on a tall orange flower, drinking in the nectar while Izzy stole up from behind. She sunk her teeth into her lip in utter concentration, so close she could smell the pungent perfume of the bell-shaped bloom. Very slowly, she brought her hands up from her sides, cupping her palms as she homed in on the feasting insect, eager to hold the iridescent beauty if only for a moment. Alas, it flitted off once more.

Izzy gave chase in earnest now, following after on a mad trail that led her first in one direction, then another, but ever deeper into the cool dark woods. Determination made her reckless, made her oblivious of the scrapes her bare ankles took as she lifted her skirts and crashed through the thickening underbrush. She ducked under spindly outstretched branches and waded into large patches of dew-kissed ferns, pursuing relentlessly until, at last, she lost sight of her quarry.

But it was far worse than that, Izzy realized suddenly. She had completely lost track of where she was.

She stood there for a moment, pivoting her head in search of a path out or some means of getting her bearings. Nothing looked familiar in these woods. The dense foliage swallowed up both sound and light from outside, making it impossible to discern the direction of Droghallow's castle. Izzy's heart, which was still pounding hard from the chase, now picked up a more urgent beat.

Heaven help her, she was lost.

I am not afraid, she told herself. She would simply follow her tracks out of the woods and head back safely to the gathering. Turning, full of new resolve, Izzy took the first step.

It was then that she heard a rustle in the bramble a few paces ahead of her. Twigs snapped under a heavy gait, followed by an animal grunt and a deep snort. Izzy knew she was in danger even before she saw the boar's wild-eyed gaze and sharp ivory tusks. The bullish, hairy beast blocked her path, sniffing at the air. Evidently deciding she was foe more than friend, the boar curled its lips back and let out a throaty squeal of warning.

Izzy swallowed hard. She had nowhere to go. The trees were thick and many here, knitting her in from both sides; behind her was a sea of tangled underbrush that would surely slow her flight.

The boar advanced, head low, eyes trained on her.

Izzy stood unmoving, staring wide-eyed as the boar inched closer. It sniffed at the ground, growling and snorting. Some subtle movement nearby caught the beast's attention and for an instant it looked away. Her body tensed, every fiber urging her to flee regardless of her dubious chances of escape.

It might well be her only hope . . .

"Don't move."

The firm command seemed to whisper from out of the very trees themselves, instantly rooting Izzy's feet to the ground. "Stand very still," the voice instructed her. "The slightest motion could make him charge."

Izzy stood frozen, scarcely able to breathe. She watched the boar's snout twitch, its beady eyes searching for signs of this newest intruder. She tried not to let her gaze linger on the sight of those awful tusks: curved, lethal slashes of gleaming white against the beast's swarthiness.

"That's it. You're doing very well." The gentling voice sounded again, closer this time. "Tell me your name."

"Iz-Izzy," she stammered in little more than a tremulous whisper.

"I am coming up behind you now, Izzy. Be still. Don't be frightened."

But Izzy was terrified. The boar bared its teeth, tossing its head and shrieking in a deep murderous pitch. The horrible noise chased a shiver up Izzy's spine, leaving her entire body trembling. "Oh, please," she sobbed quietly. "Please, help me."

There was a crunch of movement behind her. Did her rescuer near, or was he instead deciding to make his retreat and save his own hide? Izzy could not be sure. In front of her, the boar pawed the mossy ground with a cloven hoof, snout down, the hairs on its back standing up like a bristly, coal-black fin. It gave a quick snort.

Then it charged.

Izzy screamed. She squeezed her eyes shut, waiting to feel the certain, savage impact of the boar's tusks at any moment. She waited, but death did not come. Instead, she heard the sharp grate of a blade being unsheathed from its scabbard. She felt a rush of cool air as someone leaped in front of her, sweeping her out of harm's way with a strong, sure arm.

Twigs snapped under the boar's enraged attack. A cry rang out, then cut short suddenly. The ground beneath her feet reverberated with a heavy thump, the sound of solid weight hitting soft, moist earth.

Then all went utterly still in the forest.

It took several moments before Izzy dared open her eyes. When she did, she saw the beast that might have killed her lying lifeless on the ground. Standing over it in silent contemplation, bloodied sword in hand, was a golden-haired, lanky boy. He glanced over his shoulder as Izzy approached. Striking green-gold eyes met her astonished gaze.

"You saved my life." Izzy came up beside him, finding it difficult to keep from staring at the felled beast, which was frightful even in death. "That was the bravest deed I've ever seen," she whispered. "You might have been killed in my place."

"A man must be willing to face danger," he told her as he cleaned and resheathed his sword. He turned a solemn gaze on her. " 'Tis a knight's duty to protect a lady in need, whatever the risk."

Izzy blinked up into his youthful, sun-burnished face and felt herself warm from within. She had never been called a lady before. Nor had she ever seen such chivalry demonstrated outside the realm of her imagination. Awestruck and utterly speechless, Izzy took in her champion's features, from his mane of shoulder-length, wheat-colored hair and leonine green eyes, to his blunt nose and proud, finely cut chin. He was still a youth, perhaps a half-dozen years her senior, but to Izzy's way of thinking, he possessed all the courage and honor of ten grown men.

He was wholly magnificent, this golden stranger who had just saved her life, and Izzy fell just a tiny bit in love with him.

"Come," he said, holding out his hand to her. "The woods are a dangerous place for a young maiden alone. I will see you safely out of here and back to the gathering."

He guided her along an obscure path through the bracken, his warm hand engulfing her fingers, his every step as sure and capable as his strong, steadying arm. "What possessed you to venture so far into the forest unescorted?" he asked her when they had gone some distance. " 'Tis one thing for a lad to prefer running wild in a dark glade over the stuffiness of a noble gathering, but quite another for a maid to feel likewise."

Izzy did not want to admit to him the shameful cause of her flight from the celebration. "I was chasing a butterfly," she said, a half-truth, and a foolish-sounding one at that. "Before I knew it, I had lost my way."

"Be thankful you did not lose any more than your way," he scolded dryly, though Izzy could see a grin tugging at the corner of his mouth. They reached a spot where the growth was thick and tangled, clawing branches blocking their way. Gallantly he swept it aside, allowing her to pass freely beneath. "After you, my lady."

Beaming, she ducked beneath the mass of briars, then bobbed a quick curtsy to him. "Why, thank you, Sir . . . ?"

"Griffin." He returned to her side, smiling, then offered her a courtly bow. "Griffin of Droghallow, at your service."

"Droghallow?" Izzy paused, feeling a sudden tug of disappointment. "Surely you cannot be kin to Dominic of Droghallow?"

The lad gave her a quizzical look. "Do you know him?"

Instantly the jeering image of her chief tormentor's face sprang into Izzy's mind. "His father and mine are acquainted, but I assure you, I have no wish to know Master Dominic. Just this afternoon he was making terrible fun of—" Izzy frowned, unwilling to finish the thought. "I think he's an awful bully," she amended.

"Aye, Dom can be unfairly cruel," Griffin said, almost apologetically. Then he leaned forward, lowering his voice to a conspiratorial whisper. "If he troubles you again, just tell him how you have heard he is deathly afraid of the dark. Remind him that he cannot sleep a wink unless a torch burns beside his bed all night long. Once he knows you have his secret, I doubt he'll be eager to bother you anymore."

Izzy grinned up at him, grateful for this further kindness. It seemed the boar was not the only beast her golden champion would slay for her this day.

"Dom and I are not blood kin," Griffin added as they continued walking, following the light that marked the edge of the woods. "His father and stepmother took me in when I was a babe, orphaned and abandoned at Droghallow's gates some five-and-ten years ago. To my knowledge, I have no living relations."

"None at all?" Izzy whispered in frank sympathy. Her parents were so dear to her, it was impossible to imagine not having them in her life. "Do you know nothing of your family?"

"Only this," Griffin said. He paused to withdraw a pendant from beneath his tunic and held it out to her. It was a small half circle of enameled bronze—a medallion, embossed with the image of a white lion rampant in its center. "Lady Alys, Dom's stepmother, found it in my swaddling the day she brought me in. It's all I have of my true parents . . . whoever they were."

"I'm sure they were fine, noble people," Izzy told him, hearing the note of sadness in his voice and feeling a sudden need to fix it. "They would be very proud of you today, Griffin."

He glanced at her, then let the medallion fall back against his chest with a shrug and started walking once more. "Sir Robert—Dom's father—says I have the mak-

ings of a fine knight. He is training me as his squire, and
one day I shall be made a member of the garrison here at
Droghallow."

"You'll be his best, I have no doubt," Izzy declared, trotting along to keep pace with his long strides.

Griffin chuckled. "I mean to be better than that," he said,
staring distantly ahead at the path, his brows drawn together in thought. "I mean to be a great knight one day. A
man of my own means. A man of honor."

Izzy blinked up at her champion in total admiration.
"Then so you shall," she said, matching his declaration
with the instant, inexplicable faith that he could do anything he set his mind to. "You shall be the greatest, most
noble knight in all the realm, Griffin of Droghallow!"

"Do you think so?" He paused to regard her with that intense stare of his.

She smiled, fully confident. "I have never believed anything more."

Her fervent avowal hung between them for several long
moments, filling the silence of the glade. Then Griffin
smiled, too, his slow, spreading grin dimpling his cheeks.
"You are an odd girl, Izzy. An odd girl, indeed, given to
chasing butterflies and believing in a stranger's dreams."

She glanced away from his green-gold gaze, frowning
down at her slippers, suddenly embarrassed. When he
reached for her hand, she did not know what to do. She
could only stare, astonished, as he lifted her fingers to his
lips and pressed a chaste kiss to her palm. "It has been my
great pleasure to meet you, my lady."

Grinning, he started to back away from her, edging
deeper into the woods. Izzy watched him, too dazed to ask
him where he was going. Her pulse was beating so fast and
loud in her temples, she scarcely heard the angry shout that
sounded from some distance behind her in the field. It
sounded again, closer now.

"Isabel de Lamere! Where have you been?"

It was her nurse, come to fetch her. Izzy knew without looking that the large old hen of a maid was huffing her way across the plain, not at all pleased to have been dispatched from the celebration on her present errand. But despite the threat thundering up behind her, Izzy could not tear her gaze from her golden champion's handsome face.

"Sir Griffin," she whispered, but then he was gone, vanished into the shadows of the trees. She looked down at her palm, to where her champion's lips had touched her, and as her gaze fell, she noticed something glittered in the loamy ground at her feet. His white lion medallion. The chain was severed, evidently lost to him by a break in one of the links. "Griffin, wait!" she called as she picked up the pendant and scanned the forest for any sign of him.

A moment later, her nurse was upon her, seizing her by the wrist and dragging her in tow away from the forest and farther afield, to rejoin the gathering. Izzy trotted along, clutching the medallion in her fist, happy if only for the chance she might have to see Griffin again, to return his pendant and thank him once more. Griffin of Droghallow had saved her life today. He had called her a lady, kissed her hand . . . and stolen her heart.

Izzy felt the fires of a thousand romantic musings stir to life within her when she thought of him. Never would there be a man more noble nor more honorable than her brave hero, her chivalrous White Lion, Griffin of Droghallow. She believed it with all her heart.

Chapter One

Autumn, ten years later

"Have ye no heart, Griffin of Droghallow? 'Tis death ye
deliver upon us today!"

Of the score of grubby-faced peasants assembled in the
village for the surrender of the rents, only the miller's wife
dared to speak out. Heavy with child and with another
clinging to her skirts, the matron waddled forward bearing
murder in her eyes. It was a look Griff had seen often
enough in his line of work as captain of the Droghallow
guard. He scarcely bothered to pause as the woman approached the place where he stood, securing the straps on a
cart laden with grain sacks and wool. Several livestock had
been tethered to the wagon, as well, and the bleating com-
plaints of sheep and lowing of cattle did little for Griff's
patience in his present task.

This was only the first of a half-dozen villages he and
his men would see today in their duty of securing the
month's rents for Droghallow's coffers. It had been a hard
year for the country, made worse with the new king's relentless demands of his vassals and allies to show their loyalty by sending funds to support the burgeoning war in the
Holy Land. Everything of value in England now had its
price. Royal manor houses went up for bid; noble titles inherited through generations had to be further secured by
huge tariffs to the crown; and in courts across the land,

10

lawsuits were settled in favor of the party offering the largest bribe.

Richard Plantagenet had just been crowned, but already he was preparing to leave London. He and his army were soon to be away, fighting to win back the Holy Sepulcher for Christendom. It was a noble mission, but some wondered if England's price would prove too steep. Some wondered if the king's brother, Prince John, would show more interest in England's welfare were he in power instead.

Granted a fair share of English titles and properties upon his brother's coronation, John kept a close watch over the country he was certain would soon be his. And while some noble vassals collected funds to support a Holy War, others collected in secret for war of a vastly different kind: a royal war that might well pit brother against brother.

With England's fiefs pressed from all sides, it was the villagers who suffered most, Droghallow's among them. They were overworked and tired, in an uproar over the news that in his greed to purchase more lands and titles, their lord, Dominic, Earl of Droghallow, was seeking higher rents than ever before. Most of the holdings would be unable to pay. Foodstuffs and animals would be taken for trade instead, dooming the peasants to a long, cruel winter.

But their suffering was not his cross to bear, Griff told himself as the miller's wife drew up two paces before him, angry tears in her eyes.

"What manner of beast are ye, Griffin of Droghallow, that ye would take food from our children's mouths and wool that would warm the little ones in the cold months to come?"

The woman's daughter, a waiflike creature, stringy-haired and impossibly thin, came out of hiding behind her mother's skirts. "Don't cry, Mama," she said in a small voice, hugging her close. "Please, don't cry."

Griff glanced away quickly and yanked on one of the

wagon straps, pulling it tighter than needed, concentrating on the burn of braided rope against his palm rather than looking for one moment longer at a child who would likely be dead by springtime.

"Does a serf's life mean so little to a knight? Can ye not see that we need every cow and fleece and sack of grain that can be had? Do ye not care—"

" 'Tis not my place to care, madam." Griff harshly tied off the strap and turned to stare down at the miller's wife. "I've been sent to collect what is due Droghallow's lord. Now stand aside and let me finish."

"Animal!" she railed at him, her round jaw quivering. "Soulless beasts, ye are! May the lot of ye rot in hell!"

Griff felt moisture hit his face and he paused, momentarily stunned. The woman had spit on him. The gathered crowd, which had been watching the entire exchange in rapt attention, now stood wholly mute and unmoving. Silence reigned in that next moment, as if no one dared even to breathe. The miller's wife held Griff's stare, but her entire body shook with terror and she clutched her daughter a little tighter.

"P-please," the woman stammered. "M-my lord, I beg pardon."

Griff said nothing. With the back of his hand he wiped the spittle away, too surprised to be angry, too indifferent to be offended.

The focus of his attention was now drawn past the circle of peasants to the mill, from where his men were emerging. Treading along before the pack of knights was the miller, head bowed, hands tied at his back like a criminal.

Odo, Griff's lieutenant, led the group, grinning proudly. "Just like a miller, skimming a bit off the top of everything he grinds. Swore up and down that he was keeping nothing from us, but we found three more sacks hidden behind a false board in the storeroom."

"Add them to the wagons and let's be on to the next village," Griff ordered, eager to be done with the day already.

Seeing the rents collected and delivered was only the first part of his mission for Dom. There was another task awaiting him at Droghallow, a task that had occupied his thoughts continually since Dom first discussed it with him a few days ago.

During a trip to the royal court, Droghallow's enterprising earl had come into the knowledge that a young heiress, recently inherited and since betrothed at the king's order, was soon to be en route from a London convent to her new home some leagues north of Droghallow. In one month she was to be wedded to Sebastian of Montborne, one of King Richard's most powerful—and wealthy—vassals. That this man also happened to be one of Dom's most hated political rivals only made the opportunity for treachery all the more tempting. Dominic wanted the lady captured and brought to him. He had promised Griffin his pick of Droghallow knights to aid him in the task and a handsome reward upon his successful return.

Griff mentally added the crime of kidnap to his long list of past sins and skulduggery performed at Dom's behest. He had never considered himself the bride-stealing sort, but the lure of so much silver was potent bait. And Griff did not mind dirtying his hands as long as it was worth his while.

Buoyed by the thought of a rich boon soon to be his, Griffin walked around to his waiting mount and stepped into the stirrup.

"What about him, Griff?"

Odo gestured toward the miller, who now stood huddled together with his wife and daughter. From where he sat, high atop his destrier's back, Griff stared down at the couple, who waited in dread for his decision. The man would surely see severe punishment at Droghallow, too severe, when his crime had been done in part with the intent to help feed a hungry village. Still, the transgression demanded some manner of recompense.

"There are no more bags of grain or flour left in the mill?" he asked Odo.

"Not a one. The place is empty, I made sure myself."

Griffin nodded. With the harvest taken some weeks past, the mill would remain unused throughout the rest of the fall and coming winter. Looking past the dozens of watchful faces gaping up at him in fear and smoldering contempt, Griffin considered the idle wooden outbuilding. He slid a glance at Odo, then coolly jerked his chin in the direction of the mill.

"Burn it."

Chapter Two

The old Roman road leading away from London was crowded that morning and filled with the unmistakable sounds of despair. A nobleman was being laid to rest that day; his funeral procession had slowed travel to little better than a crawl as those making their way out of the city paused to let by the group of mourners.

Streamers of smoke from the burning candles and oil lamps carried at the front of the cortege trailed on the breeze, floating over the sober, bowed heads of the attending nuns and clergy and the dead man's bier, which was draped in black silk and borne on wooden slats suspended between two poles. The nobleman's family followed directly behind, two proud sons holding onto their wailing mother's arms, helping her remain upright when grief seemed determined to collapse her in the street.

From within her own conveyance, a well-appointed litter flanked by half a dozen armed escorts now halted at the side of the road, Isabel de Lamere parted the silk curtains that canopied her from the sun's glare and watched in sympathy as the sorrowful parade passed.

Behind the widow and her sons walked a little girl. Garbed in black, her cheeks tearstained and red, the child clutched a small bouquet of flowers in her fist. Her quivering jaw and trembling hands brought a flood of sadness to Isabel's eyes, for in a way, she knew that little girl. Indeed, she had once been her, deprived of a father at an early age and all but forgotten by a mother who could not shoulder the loss of her husband.

Isabel offered the child a gentle smile as she passed the silk-veiled litter, communicating her sympathy in a warm glance and a hopeful, silent prayer that, in time, the hurt would heal and everything would be all right. The little girl seemed to cling to Isabel's gaze, blinking through her tears and finally returning a wobbly half smile as she continued on up the road toward the churchyard. Isabel watched the child's retreating back until the trailing crowd of mourners swallowed her up.

"What an irritating inconvenience," groused Isabel's traveling companion, a maiden of similar age who was also on her way from London to be wed to a nobleman of the king's choosing.

Cloistered at the abbey of St. Winifred for nearly as long as Isabel had been there, at eight-and-ten Lady Felice had suffered the dissolution of two previous betrothals and was clearly impatient to see her present arrangement through to fruition. She seemed to be of the mind that if she did not make it to her betrothed's estate with all due haste, the man would suddenly have a change of heart and beg release from his obligation.

Isabel wondered if he might be more inclined to do so once he finally met his bride-to-be. While the petite blond was fair enough of face and respectably dowered, at her best Lady Felice was a charming conniver; at her worst she possessed the disposition of a shrew. Isabel would be only too glad to see the end of their journey and bid farewell to the spoiled, complaining young woman.

"For pity's sake! How long must we delay here?" Felice huffed, leaning forward to peer around Isabel at the crowded street. "Who is dead?" she demanded of a passerby. "I do hope it was someone of import to warrant all of this bother."

"Hush, Felice!" Isabel chided, appalled by the girl's insensitivity. "A father and husband has died. He was of import to his family; show them some respect."

Felice rolled her eyes. She sat back against her cushioned seat with a petulant pout. "You're a fine one to talk about respect," she snipped acidly. "Or do you forget your own father died a branded traitor to the Crown?"

Isabel kept her face turned away so Felice would not see her pained wince. No, she had not forgotten the sad fact of her father's dishonor. Far from it. His shame haunted her every day of her life, ever since the morning, six years ago, when he was hauled away from Lamere Castle in chains, convicted of a years-old treason against the previous king of England, Henry II.

Isabel's beloved father, along with a score of other barons, had been found guilty of participation in a rebellion against the king and executed. He had not even tried to deny the wrongdoing, claiming with his last breath that he did only what he felt was best for his country at the time, and that given the chance, he would do so again.

As a result of his betrayal, everything he owned was deemed forfeit to the Crown: his lands and titles, his wealth, even his marriage to Isabel's mother, which was annulled, illegitimizing Isabel and her infant sister. She and little Maura were declared bastards and sent to live in separate convents as wards of the king. Their mother, a distant relative of the royal family, was allowed to retain the rights to her dower lands, but was returned to her homeland of France in supreme disgrace. Six years had passed without a word from her, but rumors circulated that the noble lady had gone quite mad with grief and humiliation. Then, less than a month ago, a missive arrived conveying the regretful news that Isabel's mother had succumbed to an illness.

Isabel was now inherited of the château in France and several other estates that bordered the northern kingdom of Wales. She was a landed heiress and, King Richard decided, prime for marriage. He had matched her with the

Earl of Montborne, a man Isabel had never met and knew
only by reports of his sterling reputation.

It had been some years since she had trusted in the
honor of men—trusting her father's honor had taught her
that bitter lesson—but Isabel hoped she would be able to
convince her new husband to allow her to send for Maura
once they were wed. If she could do nothing else in this
life, she prayed for the chance to be reunited with her sister
and the opportunity to look after her until she was old
enough to start her own life.

"I vow I cannot credit why the king saw fit to betroth
you, of all people, to Sebastian of Montborne," Felice continued once the funeral procession had gone ahead and the
horses were guided back onto the road to resume the trek
north out of London.

The lurching of the litter as it moved forward upset the
beads in Felice's elaborate hairstyle, a plaited and coiled
crown of flaxen locks veiled in pink silk and held in place
with a circlet of twisted gold. She reached up to make certain nothing was amiss on her head, then brushed irritably
at the wrinkles in her traveling gown, a stunning kirtle the
color of a maiden's blush that fit her slender form to perfection. The fashionable garment, with its long, pointed
sleeves draping nearly to the bottom of her skirts and its in-
tricately beaded bodice, easily outshone the pretty, pale
green gown and veil Isabel wore for the journey. Indeed,
not even the fine dress Isabel had packed for her wedding
could rival Felice's rich attire.

"Imagine," the young woman continued, shaking her
head, "a traitor's bastard wedding one of the king's most favored vassals while I, grand-niece to the royal chancellor,
am relegated to becoming the wife of a mere baron. It
hardly seems fair."

Isabel bit back the urge to remind Felice that until
he was appointed chancellor by King Richard, her uncle
William de Longchamp was a veritable unknown in noble

circles, a commoner. To those left with no choice but to abide him in his present role for the crown, Longchamp was now considered no better than a commissioned thief, liar, and cheat. Isabel had the distinct impression that the Longchamp fruit did not fall far from the tree.

"Don't despair of your situation too soon," she advised Felice with a reassuring pat of her hand. "After all, you're not yet wed. Perhaps this betrothal will fall through just as the other two have."

Felice sighed heavily and gave a little nod before she registered the subtle barb in Isabel's comment. Her belatedly insulted gaze snapped up to Isabel, who had since returned her attention to the passing countryside.

The forest grew thick not far out of the city and continued to hug the sides of the road for some long hours into the journey. Chin propped in her hand to hold her head upright, Felice dozed while Isabel remained awake and far too pensive for sleep. She watched as fellow travelers and pilgrims passed on the narrow road, headed, as she was, to points north. She listened to the songs some of them sang to pass the time, wondering at the people's various futures and destinations almost as curiously as she wondered at her own.

With her past falling away by leagues, what lay ahead of her?

Isabel tried to picture Montborne, a place she had never been but had heard of often, the place that was soon to be her home. She closed her eyes and easily imagined its vast rolling meadows and fertile fields, the thriving villages and glorious stone castle that presided over it all. She pictured the joy on her little sister's face when Maura would arrive at Montborne, delivered from life at the convent and brought to live with Isabel and her husband as a family.

As she had tried numerous times since first hearing of her betrothal, Isabel tried to picture Sebastian, the Earl of Montborne, her fiancé. She tried to envision herself meet-

ing him, marrying him . . . and here is where she failed.
For although she had heard many accounts of the youthful
earl's dark good looks, somehow, whenever Isabel tried to
imagine the man who would be her husband, her mind con-
jured the image of a brave, handsome knight with tawny
hair and flashing green-gold eyes.

She pictured Griffin of Droghallow.

In truth, she had never forgotten about her childhood
hero, the boy who had rescued her from certain doom a
decade past and left her with a token of his courage and
honor—the white lion medallion that Isabel carried with
her every moment of every day. She had drawn on it for
strength the day her father was arrested, and she had relied
on its power to see her through each painful night that she
spent at the abbey, frightened and alone, separated from
her family and all she loved.

With a glance at Felice to make certain the woman still
slept, Isabel withdrew the medallion from within the
bodice of her gown and held it into the light coming
through the litter's curtains. Lovingly, she smoothed the
pad of her thumb over the enameled metal, knowing the
careful embossment by heart: fashioned out of a disc of
bronze that had been cut in half vertically, the medallion
contained the heraldic representation of a fierce white lion
rampant, a majestic creature of great courage that Isabel
had always likened to Griffin of Droghallow himself.

Not a day passed when Isabel did not think about Griffin, wondering what had become of him and if she might
ever see him again. She included him in her prayers without fail, asking God to keep him safe and happy. Isabel
dreamed more frequently than was seemly that she would
see Griffin again, that somehow their paths would cross
and she could return his medallion and thank him personally for all he had given her with his kindness those ten
years ago. She had dreamed of other encounters with him

as well, encounters vivid enough to bring a blush to her cheeks just to think on them in the bald light of day.

Isabel shook her head as if to sweep her sinful thoughts away, the same way she must learn to sweep aside her girl-ish fascination with a man who was little more than pleas-ant memory to her now.

She was to wed Sebastian of Montborne. She would honor that vow in all ways starting this very moment, she decided as she put away the medallion and shifted in her seat, closing her eyes and settling back against the cush-ions with a sigh.

She must have nodded off for a while, for she woke with a start when she heard one of her escorts shout an impa-tient hail to someone ahead on the road.

Felice roused at the sudden bark of command as well. "What is it? Are we finally arrived?" she asked through a groggy yawn.

"We have stopped for some reason," Isabel answered, peeking out of the curtains.

It was nearly dusk outside, though the encroaching for-est made their surroundings seem darker than twilight. The road this far north would be more accurately described as a path, the narrow, ambling trod now deserted save for the ladies and their convoy of attending guards. And a shep-herd with his flock, Isabel noted upon closer look. The old man stood about a furlong up the road, directly in the way of the traveling party, his sheep seeming to be hemmed in from the front and back, unwilling or unable to vacate the road.

"Get those beasts out of the road, graybeard, and let us pass," one of the armed escorts ordered.

The shepherd merely stared, wide-eyed, unspeaking and uncooperative. Isabel wondered if he was deaf, for she could plainly hear the impatience in the knight's voice. She could also hear the jingle of arms and gear; she could sense the nervous anticipation of the horses as their riders waited in wary silence.

Something felt queer about this delay. Something was frightfully wrong here. Isabel tried to lean farther out to get a better look at the situation up ahead.

"Back inside now, my lady," one of the guards advised in a low, even voice. "There is no cause for concern."

But there was. Isabel knew it by the schooled calmness in the man's tone. She swallowed hard and sat back as she was told, praying she was only letting her imagination get the best of her. " 'Tis nothing, I'm sure," she told Felice, who was scowling across from her. "A shepherd and his flock have blocked the road. We'll be off as soon as they've gone."

"I will tell you only once more," the leader of the guards said to the shepherd. "Clear the road and let us pass."

"Oh, for pity's sake," Felice grumbled, loud enough for all to hear. "Trample the imbecile if he won't make way!"

The toe of Isabel's slipper connected sharply with Felice's shin, silencing the woman at the very moment that the true cause of their delay became horrifyingly clear to all. From out of the surrounding trees, an arrow flew. It hit its mark with lethal accuracy, claiming one of the guards and plunging the rest of the traveling party into chaos.

Isabel and Felice could only listen in terror as an ambush ensued outside over the bleating of frightened sheep and the surprised shouts of the guards. There was the whoosh of more arrows, the pained cries of the men and horses, and soon thereafter, the metallic clash of blades. The horses carrying the litter shifted nervously amid the skirmish, making the veiled conveyance sway and lurch frightfully.

"We're being attacked!" Felice wailed, bursting into tears. "Dear God, we're going to die!"

Isabel wanted to calm the woman, but there was nothing she could say. Fear robbed her of her own voice. She braced her outflung hands against the framework sides of the shifting litter, struggling to keep a grip on her surroundings, as well as her sense of reason. She did not have to see the battle taking place outside to know that unless they took action, all too soon she and Felice would find themselves thrust into the fray.

"Felice," she hissed to the screaming young woman. "We can't stay in here and wait for these brigands to find us. We will have to try to escape."

"Escape?" Felice hiccupped, her eyes wide and filled with tears. "But I'm afraid!"

"So am I. Take my hand and let's jump out the back of the litter."

Outside on the road, there was a clash of metal on metal, then a man cried out in agony. A horse gave a shrill whinny and sidled into the litter, nearly tipping it.

"Felice," Isabel whispered fiercely. "We must go now."

She reached out with one hand, but the sobbing girl would not take it.

"We'll be caught!" she croaked in protest. "We'll never make it!"

"It's our only hope," Isabel argued, scarcely harnessing the urge to shake Felice out of her mounting hysteria. "We have a good enough chance of escape, but we must go now."

Felice shook her head and sobbed. "No! I can't go out there, Isabel! Please don't make—"

Stones crunched as heavy boots drew up beside the litter, cutting short Felice's further whining. It was too late to escape their attackers' notice. The sheltering curtain was ripped away like the flimsiest spider's web. It fell to the ground, laying open the litter and revealing the leering, grizzled face of a huge bear of a knight. "Good eve, ladies. Lovely night for a kidnapping, don't ye think?"

They both screamed. Holding onto each other and trembling with panic, the two women shrank back as far as they

could from the hulking brigand whose grasping, beefy
arms reached easily more than halfway inside the narrow
conveyance. He swept the small space and caught Felice by
the ankle.

"Nooo!" she shrieked, eyes wide with terror as he
started to pull her toward him. Felice's dainty hands scrab-
bled for purchase in the litter, to no avail. "Oh, Isabel,
please! Help me!"

Isabel held on to her and tugged with all she had, while
Felice worked to kick and squirm and twist her way out of
the man's clutches. He lost his hold and Felice was suddenly, miraculously, freed. Then, without the slightest
warning, she latched onto Isabel's arm and jerked her forward, shoving her at the man.

"Take her, you stinking beast, not me!" Felice cried,
slipping behind a stunned Isabel to make her escape out the
other side of the conveyance. She tumbled out onto the
ground and ran off screaming into the woods.

"Felice!" Isabel cried in horror and stark disbelief.
Abandoned and terrified, she struggled against her attacker. Thrust into his arms by Felice's betrayal, Isabel now
found herself seized about the shoulders, unable to put up
much of a fight as the man began to pull her forward.

"Behave now," he told her. "We mean ye no harm."

He dragged her out of the litter and set her feet on the
ground, retaining his iron grip on her arms. Isabel stood
there and took in the calamity of her traveling party with
one quick glance. Her stomach threatened to revolt. Four
of the guards and two of their horses were dead, lying
where they had fallen in the road, bodies gashed from combat, arrows protruding from blood-soaked points of impact. The remaining two escorts must have taken to the
woods, either in pursuit of their attackers or, as Felice had
done, out of fear for their lives. Isabel could only guess,
and at the moment she did not much care.

From the corner of her eye, she caught a glimpse of the rest of their attackers, armed with swords and crossbows, stepping out onto the road. Some yards away, Isabel spied a hooded figure on horseback dressed all in black. He came out of the woods and paused in the road, staring at the carnage.

Isabel's captor saw him, too. He turned his head and chuckled, hailing the man with a jerk of his chin. "Look here what I found!" he called jovially.

It was all the opportunity Isabel needed.

She stepped forward and brought her knee up as swiftly and as hard as she could. It was a useful tactic she had learned in Lamere's bailey and had all but forgotten in her time at the abbey. If her skill was rusty, she was relieved to find that it had lost none of its effect. Her assailant immediately released his grasp on her, clutching instead a part of his own wounded anatomy. He dropped to his knees with a curse and a strangled groan.

The leader of the band of rogues, the grim knight in black, saw what happened—indeed, he had attempted to warn his man but Isabel's knee had proven faster. Now he gave his horse his spurs, barreling toward her and his sputtering accomplice. "Don't let her get away!" he shouted to the others, his deep voice booming against the silence of the forest.

Heart fluttering with panic, Isabel ducked down and scrambled under the horses and the litter they carried, making her escape in the same direction Felice had fled. She hitched up her skirts and tore off into the woods, panting and breathless with terror, her legs fueled by sheer determination to survive.

Behind her, she could hear the brigands give chase, crashing into the thicket. She could hear their curses and the metallic jangle of their armor, knew they were now equally determined to find her. It was nearly dark. If she could find a hiding place deep enough within the woods, perhaps she could wait them out. Perhaps they would tire of pursuing her and give up.

Or perhaps they would find Felice first and take her instead, she thought with a decidedly un-Christian brand of hope.

Skidding down into a leaf-strewn ravine, Isabel ran along the bottom of the deep gully, searching for anything—a cave, a large rock, a hollow old tree—that might serve to conceal her for a while. When nothing availed itself, she simply kept running, plunging deeper and deeper into the ever-darkening forest.

At least she no longer heard evidence that she was being pursued. In fact, the woods had grown quite still with the rising of the moon. Isabel slowed her pace as the ground began to slope upward. She was tired and thirsty; a stitch in her side made it hard to draw more than shallow breaths. She had to rest, she decided, leaning her back against the black trunk of an ancient gnarled oak.

How wise was her plan to flee into the woods? she wondered now. She had no food, no water, no blanket to ward off the night's chill. And if she escaped capture by the men who attacked her on the road, how long could she expect to remain safe from the outlaws and vagabonds who peopled England's dense forests? Would she survive at all? How could she look after little Maura's welfare if she never made it to Montborne?

It was that thought more than any other that spurred Isabel on when exhaustion sought to consume her. Squaring her shoulders with renewed resolve, she pushed away from the tree, prepared to crawl to Montborne if she had to. She took a determined step forward, then paused, shocked to find that another large tree now blocked her way.

Except it was not a tree, a fact she realized too late.

It was a man. The leader of her attackers, the knight she had seen in the road, garbed from head to toe in black.

Gloved hands fisted on his hips, legs spread shoulder-width apart, he stared down at her from within the deep hood of his mantle. Isabel had to tip her head all the way back just to find his face; all she could make out of his features was the hint of sandy colored hair falling in a wild mane about his shoulders, and his smile, a cruel slash of white in the darkness.

He was a menacing presence, unmoving and grinning like the devil himself.

"Going somewhere, my lady?"

Chapter Three

Griffin had followed the young woman personally from the road, tracking her progress into the wood with the same stealth and patience that a wolf would employ to stalk a hare. Now as she blinked up at him, panting and effectively ensnared, he watched as first fright, then flight, registered in her flashing eyes. Barely a scant heartbeat passed before she pivoted on her heel, intent to bolt in the opposite direction. Griff seized the woman around the waist before she could take the first step.

"Unhand me!" she gasped, the breath whooshing out of her as Griff easily lifted her off her feet.

With her hands pinned at her sides, he dragged the lady to him and proceeded to carry her under his arm like a sack of grain. A rather disagreeable sack of grain, for she made every effort to squirm and buck her way loose. She managed to work one arm free and began pummeling his thigh, a bit too aimlessly for his peace of mind.

"Have a care with that flailing hand of yours, my lady, unless you mean to lose it. You may have left my man wheezing in the road, but I warn you, deliver like to me and you'll find that I will recover much faster and my wrath will be severe."

Evidently she did not think it prudent to test his threat, for she all but gave up her fight as he brought her to his waiting mount and pushed her up onto the steed's back. Griff followed quickly behind, settling her into the saddle before him. With one arm wrapped around her slim waist, he then guided his mount back out to the road.

Griff's company of men were working with haste to clear the path of bodies and any other evidence of struggle. All that remained of the caravan now was the tattered litter, its delicate canopied frame smashed, torn pale curtains wafting like ghosts on the night breeze.

"Unhitch the wreck and toss it in the ravine," Griff instructed the knights. "The horses are of fine enough flesh; round them up and we'll take them with us."

"Ignoble thieves," Griff's hostage hissed under her breath.

A nearby female shriek punctuated the lady's cool epithet, drawing Griff's attention over his left shoulder. The second of the women, a disheveled blonde in a dirt-stained pink silk gown, was being led none too happily out of the woods by one of Droghallow's soldiers. Her hair, which had no doubt enjoyed a rather impressive coif at the start of her day, now hung limply in her face, a jumbled mess of unraveled braids and dripping beads. She swore an oath as the man pushed her into the road, her unladylike curse so vivid it raised even Griff's brows.

"Take your filthy paws off of me, cur!" she railed, struggling against her captor. "Who do you beasts think you are? By my vow, I shall see you hang for this—all of you!"

Griffin had not been expecting to find two women in the caravan from London. Was this spitting viper the Montborne bride, he wondered? She was bedecked as a princess, with the haughty demeanor to match. A sharp contrast to the quiet beauty seated ramrod straight in the saddle before him.

Of the pair, Griff figured that she, and not her foul-tempered companion, would prove the more cunning quarry. Even now he could feel the coiled tenacity in the lady's slender form, the silent contemplation of her situation, the calculating calm. She had felled Odo easily enough, a man three times her size. Griff did not trust for one moment that her apparent lack of resistance meant anything less than a measured wait for an ideal opportunity to gain her freedom from him.

To let her know she would not be getting that chance, Griff tightened his arm around her waist, pulling her toward him until her spine pressed flush against his chest. She gasped at the contact and tried to arch away, an unwitting move that settled her pert breasts quite nicely on his forearm, while her fingers dug into his muscled flesh as if to test the strength of her bonds.

Enjoying the squirming warmth of her body a little more than he likely should be, Griff called a curt order over the top of her veiled head. "Mount up, men. We'll ride for a couple of hours, then make camp for the night."

They were careful not to use each other's names or mention Droghallow specifically, understanding that the less their captives knew of their abductors, the better. Dom had made it clear that if there was any trouble along the way, he wanted there to be no possibility of linking him to the crime.

Riding to the front of his assembling company of soldiers, Griffin paused beside Odo. The big knight was recovered of his galling injury, even if the glare he slanted his petite assailant betrayed that his pride still sorely pained him.

"Take the other woman with you on your horse," Griff instructed, marshaling a chuckle when the guard looked less than eager to mount up with the venomous lady. "Bind her if you like, Lieutenant, but don't take your eyes off her for a moment. And beware her fangs, lest you feel their bite."

They set up camp roughly a league away from the scene of the skirmish, in a forest glen about a half day's ride from Droghallow. They could have pressed on and made the rest of the journey that night, but the men were tired, as were their horses. As for their two hostages, the women had been through quite an ordeal; it seemed of little harm to afford them a few hours' rest.

A fire was built out of fallen timber providing ample warmth from the autumn chill that permeated the night air. Griffin instructed the women to gather close to the flames, he and Odo taking up a seat next to them, well within reach should either lady think to flee. The blonde's mind seemed more fixed on finding blame for her circumstances and imagining what might befall her than it was attuned to thoughts of escape.

"I cannot believe this is happening to me," she complained, sniffling as she brushed at the dirt that soiled the torn sleeve of her gown. "This was supposed to be a pleasant journey for me—I was on my way to be wed, for pity's sake!"

" 'Twill be all right," her companion soothed in a discreet, but firm tone of voice. "Upsetting yourself will do no good and likely will only serve to amuse these men. Try to be calm."

"Calm?" the blonde choked. "How can I be calm when I am sitting here alone and helpless, certain to be ravished at any moment by this band of common thieves and rapists!" She turned her ire on Griffin. "You won't get away with this, I promise you! I am very well connected, and fully capable of seeing that you and your men pay for this—with every one of your miserable lives!"

"Is that so?" Griff asked in mild challenge, curious what Dom might be getting him involved in with this scheme. "And how do you aim to do that?"

The shrew's friend shook her head as if to silence her from divulging any useful information to would-be ransomers, but the attempted warning went wholly unheeded.

"I'll have you know," the noble brat declared, blowing an errant tangle from out of her eyes, "that I am Felice of Rathburn, grand-niece to William de Longchamp, King

Richard's royal chancellor. When he hears what you have done to me, he'll have your churlish head skewered on a pike at the White Tower! When he finds out that I have been abused by the basest of criminals, ruining my chances to wed, he'll scatter your entrails to the vultures and feed your heart to the palace hounds!"

She went on, colorfully describing the various penalties he was certain to suffer at her uncle's hands, but Griffin was not listening to a word of it. His attention was fixed on the auburn-haired beauty who stared at him through the wavering glow of the small campfire. She was stunning in her quiet scorn, regarding him with a level stare, her delicate chin held proud.

"That must make you the Montborne bride," he said, registering her slight flinch of surprise when he mentioned the name of her betrothed.

"What do you want with us?" she demanded softly. "You did not attack us on the road for the purposes of ravishment or you would have likely done so by now."

Griffin acknowledged her logic with a slight curl of his lip.

"You have been hired to take us somewhere," she surmised rather astutely. "Someone has paid you to abduct us? Who—and why? Was it worth the lives of our escorts? Is it worth yours?"

"You ask a great deal of questions, my lady. Perhaps you should first consider whether or not you are prepared to have the answers."

She stared at him in haughty disdain, but Griff could see the flicker of uncertainty in her amber-brown eyes. An unwed innocent cloistered past the marrying age of most girls, per Dom's description, the Montborne bride was not the plain, overripe plum Griffin had been imagining. Nay, this lady was a rare peach, fresh-faced and tart, with the fiery coloring to match.

Beneath her gossamer veil of pale green silk, Griff

could see that her hair was the burnished hue of rich copper, thick strands of silk that rebelled against the plaits and covering that held them in place. The lady was noble born and gentle bred, that much was clear, from her delicate brow and creamy skin to the aristocratic line of her nose and the slim, slightly mutinous, curve of her jaw. There was a cool, reserved quality about her features that seemed to clash with the spark of fire in her eyes, with the lush sensuality of her mouth. He found himself staring at her rose-colored lips far longer than was seemly, wondering what other delicious contrasts he was obliged to leave undiscovered.

"I am prepared for any answer, so long as it is the truth."

Her quiet statement jolted him out of a rather wicked musing. He glanced up and met her steady gaze. "Is that so, my lady?"

"Yes."

That her reply was little more than a whisper was proof enough of her trepidation despite her efforts at this show of bravery. Griff saw no point in frightening her further with the details of her abduction or his suppositions over what Dom might plan to do with her once she was delivered to him. She would have those answers soon enough.

"It's late," he said, dismissing her questions as he rose to his feet and motioned for Odo to come. "Untether the reins from the spare horses and bring them to me. I wager they'll make a sufficient binding for these fair ladies. We can secure them to that tree over there."

"Oh, God! No!" the blonde wailed in a renewed fit of hysterics. "Oh, please, help me! Anyone, please! Help! Help me!"

Her shrill cries shot through Griff like the sharp pain of a raw nerve. It was enough to wake the dead, not to mention any forest outlaws lurking within a league of her senseless caterwauling. Griff had no intention of listening to her for a moment longer. He drew a dagger from a sheath on his belt, then walked over to her. He knelt down at her level, weapon gleaming beside her face.

"No, please! I don't want to die!" she sobbed, her plea cutting off as Griff took hold of her diaphanous veil and freed it from her head with one efficient swipe of his blade. He wadded the fabric into a ball, then stuffed it in her mouth.

"Be quiet," he said pleasantly.

She obeyed. Within moments, he and Odo had secured her to the base of a sturdy oak. Next Griffin turned to the Montborne woman. She faced him with dignity and a good amount of stubborn determination, as if daring him to show her the same humiliation. He did not see the need. Nor did he think it wise to afford her even a meager distance from him while he tried to rest for a few hours. She would find a way to escape him, he could see it in her eyes.

He tied one end of the leather reins to her wrist, knotting it so securely it would likely need to be cut from her arm upon their arrival at Droghallow. Then he grabbed the other end and fastened it around his own wrist.

"What are you doing?" she gasped, staring in wide-eyed confusion at the tether that now bound them together.

"You will stay at my side for the night, my lady. I won't have you and your friend plotting an escape while I sleep."

"Why, you arrogant—" Her eyes narrowed on him as if incensed that he had voiced her very intention. She tugged against the offending cord, huffing in frustration when the knot held firm.

While his men prepared their own sleeping arrangements around the waning fire, Griffin led her away from her sniffling, but now considerably more docile, companion to a mossy spot of ground he thought would suit well enough as a makeshift pallet. He unfastened his mantle with his free hand and let it fall like a blanket on the forest floor. He sat himself on the warm swatch of wool, giving the lady a persuasive tug when she seemed reluctant to join him.

"Relax," he instructed her as she scrambled to extricate herself from where she had sprawled, practically atop him. "We'll be leaving before dawn. You'd do well to get some rest while you can."

"Not so long as you are breathing beside me," she scoffed.

Griff chuckled at her tenacious spirit. "Then do as you please, my lady. But be warned, I am a light sleeper. If you so much as jostle this tether, I will know it."

Stubbornly, Isabel remained sitting for some hours longer, even after her captor had settled onto his side facing her, his eyes closed, breathing slowed in sleep. She stared at him, scowling, wondering what sort of mercenary rogue was attached to the other end of the slim leather line that held her prisoner. More to the point, where did he mean to take her, and for what purpose?

Whatever it was, Isabel did not intend to sit there, waiting until the morn when she would find out. She had to get away. She had to find her way to Montborne. But how? She wondered, staring down at the thick, tight knot at her wrist. She would never get it untied.

Through the canopy of oak and pine trees over her head, the slimmest shave of moon glow provided an answer. The milky ray of light poured down from the night sky to wink against the hammered steel grip of her chief abductor's dagger—the very same weapon he had drawn to help silence Felice's blathering.

It was sheathed on his belt, scarcely an arm's length away. Closer, if she could dare to put herself beside him. That short distance was all that separated her from freedom. Could it be so simple? Her conscience hastened to remind her of his warning: he did not sleep heavily. Could she even hope to steal his blade and cut loose her bond without his notice?

It was a fool's gamble, to be sure. But she had to try.

Slowly, without a sound, Isabel eased herself down, stretching her limbs out as if in sleep. She hardly drew breath, heedful of the silence and praying not to wake him as she got into position at his side, facing him. This close, waiting some long moments to make certain he still slept and watching his face in repose, it was difficult not to take into full measure the harsh attractiveness of his features.

His wide brow was nearly hidden beneath a forelock of sandy hair. The mane of long silky waves framed the striking lines of his tanned chiseled cheeks and square, stern jaw, giving him an air of wildness even in slumber. A silvery scar cut into his chin, a vicious arc of colorless skin that should not have added to his rugged appeal, yet somehow did. His eyes, thankfully still closed, concealed their color but were fringed with thick dark lashes that any lady would envy. His nose was prominent and bold, its straight line marred only by a faint jag that bespoke of his violent living. If his sculpted, sensual mouth bespoke of anything, Isabel had to guess that it would whisper of wicked, sinful encounters and pretty, seductive lies meant to charm a maiden out of her senses.

He looked like heaven in the moonlight, a fallen angel, heartbreakingly handsome yet undeniably dangerous—and oddly familiar to Isabel in some shadowy, inexplicable way.

She weathered a queer chill that had little to do with the autumn air and focused her attention back on the task at hand. Holding her breath, she slowly inched her fingers forward on the mantle, pausing halfway between their parallel torsos. Nervously, keeping her eyes trained on his, she crept her hand a little farther. His chest and abdomen expanded as he drew each long breath, brushing the tips of her fingers.

She was almost there.

Biting her lip in concentration, she reached down to touch the belt at his waist. Only a few finger lengths and she would have the handle of the dagger. She could almost taste freedom.

Not much farther now.

She stretched her arm, rolling not even a hair's breadth closer to him—and nearly jumped out of her skin when he stirred. Her hand flew back to her breast. She froze, staring at him in mute terror as he sighed and shifted slightly on the mantle.

But he did not wake.

Heart pounding in her throat, Isabel waited until her fear passed and she could breathe again, then started her quest anew. This time, she was bolder, knowing time was of the essence and that the real test would lie in pulling the dagger from its sheath without rousing the dragon. Praying for stealth and courage in equal measure, she reached out and went straight for her prize. She followed the smooth line of her captor's sword belt, pausing only when her fingers encountered the cool grip of the dagger. Swallowing past her trepidation, she seized the blade and began to slide it carefully out of its sheath.

The next thing she knew, her arm was pinned beneath a firm, unyielding weight.

She cried out in surprise, a small yelp of shock that she could do nothing to bite back. Even worse was the shock of glancing up and finding her captor's eyes open and fully alert, staring at her, his face nearly nose-to-nose with hers, his mouth quirked in a lazy, sardonic grin.

"You'll find nothing but trouble there, my lady."

"Get off of me!" she cried in desperation, scandalized by the position in which she suddenly found her hand.

Hard-hewn muscle and the ridge of his slim hipbone pressed her arm to the earth, while her palm—dear Lord, her palm lay open beneath him, her fingers splayed across something that she could only pray was the hard outline of his sheathed dagger. Heaven help her, but she had never been so familiar with the area of a man's groin and she had no desire to be so now, particularly not when the scoundrel pinning her so awkwardly beneath him seemed to be so devilishly enjoying it. "Get off," she sputtered. "I beg you, get off!"

He eased up only enough to avail her the retrieval of her hand, but neatly hemmed her in with an arm braced on either side of her. Imprisoned by the presence of his powerful body, Isabel could only blink up at him, uncertain what he would do with her now. She had blatantly defied him. Felice had merely annoyed him and she now sat bound and gagged. What degradation would she herself suffer for her brash actions? She mustered a cool expression despite the fact that inside she was quaking, terrified to think on what her brazenness might have earned her from this man.

"I warned you to give up any thoughts you had of escape. What was your plan, lady? To kill me while I slept?"

"No!"

His eyes narrowed on her. "For a lady who professes to relish the truth, I would think you'd be disinclined to stretch it so thin."

"I would have done you no harm," she swore, surprised—and somewhat disappointed—that the idea had not even occurred to her. "I only wanted to free myself. I simply meant to cut my bonds and be away."

"To Montborne?"

"Yes!" she gasped. "Please, you must let me go! I have to get to Montborne!"

"Your passion overwhelms me, demoiselle." He stared at her for a long moment; she prayed that in his prolonged silence, he considered her plea. Prayed that he would show her some speck of mercy and let her loose. His lazy, spreading smile seemed to indicate otherwise. "Am I to understand that yours is a love match, my lady?"

"I don't expect you to understand anything, least of all my reasons for wanting to marry."

His gaze bore into her. "Do you love this fiancé of yours?"

"Would it make a difference to you if I did?"

He exhaled a slight laugh. "Alas, no. I find I am merely . . . curious."

"Well, then, speculate on it all you wish," she hissed up at him. "My feelings are none of your affair." She tried to pry his arm loose from its position beside her, growing increasingly desperate to put space between her and this overbearing rogue. He did not budge, indeed, he only seemed all the more intense.

"Nay, you scarcely know him," he said as if he could read the truth in her eyes. He seemed to take some brand of wicked delight in the notion, his rakish grin deepening, setting off twin dimples in his beard-grizzled cheeks. "I would wager you've never so much as met the man. Have you?"

She refused to answer, for all the good it did her.

"You've never met your bridegroom and yet you would risk your life and limb to go to him. Why is that, my lady?"

"It is my duty, sirrah," she told him in an imperious tone. "The king himself has decreed that I wed."

"Somehow, you do not strike me as the sort to blindly follow orders, no matter who they might come from." His head dipped a bit closer to hers, so close their breath mingled, their faces almost nose to nose, sharing the same air. "Try again, demoiselle. The truth this time."

She thought about the many reasons she had for marrying Sebastian of Montborne—Maura's welfare, the restoration of her family's name, a good match to reestablish some of her house's former honor—each one compelling enough in its own right to make her risk the fires of hell itself to see it through. She thought of all the deeply personal reasons she had for wanting the arranged union with the Earl of Montborne, but in the end she settled on the one that would expose the least of her pain to this coldhearted stranger.

"I made a vow before God," she said, her voice sounding very small, her chest rising and falling between the too-close press of their bodies. "I made a vow, and I am bound by my oath."

The rogue looked less than convinced. "Honor is a foolish master, my lady."

"Honor, sirrah, is all that separates man from beast," she informed him tightly.

"Indeed," he relented, "so it is."

He chuckled as he said it, lifting one tawny brow and baring his teeth in a decidedly wolfish grin, leaving no doubt in Isabel's mind as to which of the two categories this scoundrel subscribed. She bucked against him once more, testing his hold on her even though she knew it was futile to fight him. He would let her go only when he was through toying with her, so much like a predator taking sport with his helpless prey.

"So, tell me, my lady," he said, watching her with those unnerving leonine eyes, "how did you come to be left so long in the convent? Were you a tax on your poor papa? Too willful for your own good, perhaps? After all, most women of your advanced age have been wed, bred, and widowed twice over by now."

"I am not willful and eighteen summers is hardly old," Isabel retorted hotly. She saw his amusement deepen and took a calming breath, annoyed that she had let him goad her into defending herself. "As if it is any of your concern, I was sent to the abbey after my father . . . died."

Heaven help her, but though she tried to say it without choking, the word still caught in her throat and drew her captor's attention. She waited for him to pounce on the show of weakness, certain that having smelled blood, he would take this opportunity to tear her emotions to ribbons, but instead he merely stared at her, saying nothing. There was no mockery in his gaze now, no amusement on his lips. Rather, there was a queer sort of empathy in his hard features, a distant look in his eye that said he knew what she was feeling. That, somehow, he understood.

Isabel squirmed under the weight of his silent consideration, thinking herself mad for believing this rogue could know anything of heartache. Like as not, he was merely tiring of his game of cat and mouse. Perhaps in his boredom, he would decide to release her.

"Please," she said, "won't you just let me go?"

He studied her for a long moment, his gaze drinking her in as he brushed aside her skewed veil and stared at her face. "I can see why he chose to take you," he said at last. "Any man with eyes in his head would surely pay a king's ransom for a woman such as you."

His unsettling appraisal shocked her, but her mind locked onto his other confusing disclosure. "Who chose me? Are you telling me that you were sent to kidnap me . . . *specifically?*" It made no sense to her at all. Especially not when Felice, as beautiful and favorably connected as she was, had been taken alongside her. "I don't understand," Isabel said, confused. "Who would want to take me prisoner? I am no one of import. The daughter of a . . ." She bit back the ugly word that had come to describe her fallen father. It still burned so painfully to admit it. "I am no one."

Her captor shrugged. "Mayhap you do not appreciate your worth, my lady." He brushed her cheek with his knuckles then, an unexpected and startlingly gentle caress that should not have made her pulse skitter for anything more than fear or revulsion.

"If 'tis money you seek," she managed to whisper, "I will see that you are rewarded. I give you my word. Just let me go now. Release us both, Felice and me."

"I cannot," he said, whatever tenderness he might have

shown her before suddenly gone. He backed off of her then, rising to his knees and reaching out to grasp her about the wrist and pull her to her feet.

"What could my capture possibly mean to anyone?" Isabel persisted. "What could it mean to you?"

He paused for the slightest moment, his strong fingers swallowing her hand, those hard green eyes meeting and holding her worried gaze. His smile was anything but reassuring. "What you mean to the man who wants you is anyone's guess, demoiselle. What you mean to me, however, is a fat bounty. Fat enough to start my life over—far away from all of this."

He spat the last word like a curse, jerking his chin toward her. Isabel was not sure if his scorn was aimed at her or at himself and the crime he was committing. She had no time to consider it further, for in the next instant she was being dragged along with him as he barked an order to his men to wake, rousing the camp and setting them about the task of remounting with cold, efficient command. In a matter of moments, the party was off, making their way on a trail he seemed to know well.

A trail that came to its end far too soon for Isabel's comfort.

Only a handful of hours later, their destination loomed ahead, a large castle perched on a high hill. The forbidding place rose out of the morning mist like out of a dream, a nightmare vision of dark stone walls and cold shadows. A feeling of bone-deep fear gripped Isabel as she, Felice, and their hired abductors approached the soaring curtain wall. She had to batten down a shiver of pure dread as they were admitted within the massive gates and rode into the center of the wide inner bailey. The party dismounted; Isabel and Felice were left to stand like chattel on the block before the soldiers who took them.

She took in the sight of the tower keep and its outlying

buildings, feeling that this was not the first time in her life she had stood in this very space.

In a far corner of her mind she heard children laughing, taunting. She heard a little girl crying, felt the sting of her humiliation. A name whispered in the back of her memory, elusive, too many years distant for her to discern it now. She tried to coax the name forward, but then a dark-haired man emerged from out of the keep and said it for her.

"Well, well," he said, smiling as his gaze swept the group, lighting with interest on the two women. "Welcome to Droghallow, ladies."

Isabel's heart lurched. Of course she knew this place. *Droghallow.*

How could it be? She stared at the nobleman standing before her in his rich attire, a man of slight frame beneath the lush fabric of his fur-trimmed mantle and dark blue tunic and hose, his leering smile and wicked eyes recalling now the bully she had encountered on this very spot ten years ago. Dominic of Droghallow. What did he want with her?

But a more alarming—some hundred times more distressing—realization made her turn away from the nefarious earl and look instead to the man he had dispatched to carry out his ignoble deed. The man responsible for the decimation of her traveling party and her subsequent capture.

The man tethered to her by a short length of leather cord.

"Griffin?" she asked, stunned, shaking her head. "No. No, I don't believe it."

But looking at him now, Isabel wondered how she had not seen it before. In truth, standing in the stark light of morning, she realized that he had not changed so much at all. Save that the noble boy she recalled and had revered as a hero for nigh on a decade was the selfsame man who had delivered her into captivity for the sake of a few silver pieces. Her heart shattered as she gazed upon him now. The stunning green-gold eyes she remembered so fondly were still that beautiful shade, but colder, flashing at her when she said his name, not with charm and kindness, but with something unreadable. Something cold and dangerous.

"Griffin of Droghallow," she breathed, aghast. "It *is* you."

Chapter Four

"You don't remember me," Isabel said, an absurd accusation when she stood shackled to him, a prisoner captured for reasons she dared not imagine.

He said nothing; under the harsh slash of his brows, his eyes registered only the vaguest confusion, and she thought, perhaps a measure of mild annoyance that he was unable to place her. He cut her loose from him without a word as Dominic descended the steps that led down to the courtyard. Droghallow's dark lord was smiling as he strode forth to where Isabel stood, cursing herself for feeling so wounded.

"What's this, another female heart broken?" Dom asked, chuckling. "My foster brother has quite a way with the fair sex; you're doubtless not the first chit he's forgotten." His assessing gaze traveled over Isabel before sliding to Felice. "Which of you two lovely ladies would be betrothed to Sebastian of Montborne?"

"She is," Felice volunteered eagerly, pointing.

Dom pivoted his head to Isabel, brows smugly arched. "Excellent," he remarked. "You're going to make me a very wealthy man, my lady."

"I suppose it should not surprise me to find that you are behind this," Isabel said, refusing to cower under Dom's arrogance. "Droghallow's heir always was an ignoble bully, utterly lacking in honor. 'Tis not so far a stretch to think that he would stoop to building his future on bride stealing and ransoms."

"Ransom?" Dom chuckled. "I assure you, I haven't the interest in trifling with something as pedestrian as that. Suffice it to say that for reasons of his own, someone of great influence preferred that your wedding to Montborne did not take place. I am merely the tool by which that feat was accomplished, and I expect to be handsomely rewarded for it."

"As do I," Griffin interjected, his cold gaze narrow and fixed on Dom.

Isabel was unsure which chilled her more: the unknown fate that awaited her at Dom's hand, or the mercenary undercurrent in Griffin's voice. She could sense the air of challenge in him, could feel the tension permeate from where he stood behind her, a lion, poised to kill and ready to strike.

At Isabel's side, evidently oblivious to the weight of their present situation, Felice daintily cleared her throat. "My lord," she said, pleasantly addressing Dom, "as it appears to me that I am here only by a chance—and highly misfortunate—association, perhaps you would be kind enough to release me now and see me safely transported back to London."

Dom paused, breaking from Griffin's steely gaze to regard Felice over his shoulder. She was smiling hopefully, blinking at him with every ounce of charm she possessed. "What is your name, my pretty, prattling little dove?" he asked.

"Felice, my lord. Lady Felice of Rathburn, grand-niece to William de Longchamp." She curtsied as if presented before the palace court, her deep, graceful dip somewhat undermined by her wrecked coif and rumpled state of attire.

Dom seemed not to notice. "Fascinating," he purred around a throaty chuckle, giving her an appreciative head-to-toe glance. "Your uncle refused to have audience with me on my last trip to London. Terribly rude of him, wouldn't you say? Especially considering the fact that he was perfectly willing to keep my bribe. I wonder what the pompous dwarf will have to say when he hears that you are now a guest of mine here at Droghallow."

Felice's bright smile faltered. "M-my lord?"

"Take the ladies to the tower cell and lock them in," he ordered of his guards. Then he raised his finger in hesitation. "On second thought, split them up. Put the blonde in the chamber adjoining mine."

When two men moved forward to seize the women, Griffin placed his hand on Isabel's arm, possessively holding her back. "My payment, Dom. Where is it?"

"In time," Dom replied in an affable tone. "Certain arrangements will have to be made before either of us sees our reward. Have a little patience, brother."

But Griffin's grip remained firm on Isabel; the look he gave the guard who would have taken her in hand at that moment was warning enough to make the man retreat a healthy pace. "I've delivered you the Montborne bride as promised. You said nothing about waiting for payment."

"Yes," Dom conceded with a sigh. "I suppose you are right. I didn't. But tell me you would have been willing to undertake this little errand had you known your compensation would not be immediate."

"I wouldn't and you know it," came the rumbling growl from beside Isabel. "And I'm not about to surrender your prize until I have what is owed me."

"Come now, Griffin. You've seen the sorry state of Droghallow's coffers of late. The bulk of my wealth is tied up in London and abroad. I need this boon every bit as much as you do." He grinned suddenly, his eyes gleaming with malice. "You needn't worry. I'll see that you get what's coming to you. Then you can be gone from Droghallow, as is your plan."

Isabel sensed a new tension in the air. Though his grip on her remained solid, Griffin's body had gone utterly still at her side; indeed, she could scarcely hear him breathing in that moment.

"What's the matter, Sergeant? I daresay you seem surprised to hear me say it. Of course I know you've been plotting to leave Droghallow. Scrimping and saving every last farthing to buy your way out of here and finally make something of yourself." The earl's chuckle was as cruel as any blade. Even Isabel flinched to feel its cutting edge. "Old dreams die hard, don't they, *brother?*"

Isabel ventured a sidelong glance at Griffin. He stood unmoving, his hard gaze narrowed on Dom, nostrils flared, his mouth set in a grim line. If looks alone were capable of slaying a person, then the Earl of Droghallow would surely have been struck dead in that moment, his black heart ripped wide open by the anger burning in Griffin's eyes. But Griffin made no move to act on the violence that was so apparent in his gaze, and Isabel knew that he was far more dangerous in his calm than he would have been had he raged and bellowed and beat Dom into submission.

The earl must have come to the same conclusion, for all at once he adopted a less smug expression, his voice taking on a friendly, if somewhat placating tone. "My apologies for this little inconvenience, Griffin. I should like to make it up to you if I can. Perhaps you would be willing to accept a token of my good faith? Something to soothe your churlish mood?" He grinned, nodding in Isabel's direction. "She's passably attractive after all, and spirited, in a simmering sort of way. I wager she'll make entertaining enough bed sport." He pursed his lips and gave a careless shrug. "God knows, she will have no need of her virtue where she is going."

Isabel's breath caught in her throat. At her side, Griffin swore an oath, but to her horror, he finally released his grip on her arm when Dom motioned again for the guards to take the women to the keep. Tears pricked her eyes as she was led away, but she refused to let them fall. She would give neither of them the satisfaction of seeing her break. Instead, she ground her heels into the hard-packed earth of the bailey, pulling against the guard's hold, but her resistance was to no avail. She and Felice were walked up the steps none too gently and pushed into the entryway to the castle. Dom followed close at their heels.

"Think on it, Griff," he said, pausing in the tower doorway to toss the jovial offer over his shoulder. "She's yours for the night if you want her. You need only say the word."

Griffin stared at the dark, yawning mouth of Droghallow's tower keep for some long moments after Dom and his two prisoners had disappeared within, unable to purge the image of the lady's face when she heard Dom's plans for her. The look of fear in her eyes, her tiny gasp, her obvious struggle to maintain her dignity in light of this terrible circumstance. All of it haunted him.

That she seemed to know him—that she would call him by name, seemingly hurt that he did not recall her—was particularly niggling. Had he known her at one time? He did not think he could have. She had been cloistered for most of her life, and even had she not, Griff felt certain he would have never forgotten an exquisite beauty like her.

He stood there in the bailey, trying to reconcile in his mind what he had become this day. A kidnapper, certainly; bride stealing, the most cowardly form. Bad enough that an innocent be torn from her sheltered life and left to wait for ransom in some dank prison cell, but what Dom had suggested for the Montborne bride was something verily more nefarious.

Someone of great influence wanted her out of the way, he had said.

For what purposes, Griff did not know. But there was no reason to guess at who that influential someone was:

Prince John, the king's treacherous younger brother. Dom had been currying the prince's favor in secret for some time now, feigning allegiance to King Richard so long as Droghallow's bribes won him the lands and titles he wanted, yet making it clear to John that given proper incentive, the prince would have a certain ally in him. This latest task was clearly a further test of that alliance. Griff could only imagine what Dom stood to gain for the misdeed.

And he was not fool enough to believe that his foster brother intended to surrender any of his pending boon to him—now or at a later date.

Dom was toying with him somehow, and Griff had little tolerance left for his continual games. Not that he'd ever had much. For too long he had banked his scorn of the arrogant lord, carrying out his orders and tempering his own disapproval because he pitied the weak-hearted, sickly boy Dom had been and he understood the bitter man he had become. Indeed, Griffin reflected for what had not been the first time, he may well have been to blame for some of Dom's viperous nature. Dominic had long resented Griffin's presence at Droghallow—and made no secret of the fact that he would have preferred him gone, though surely no more than Griffin himself had come to want that very thing.

But to leave would have been to break a vow, a promise made to Dom's father, Robert, the old earl. Sir Robert was a hard man and a strict lord, but Griffin had respected him as he would his own sire. If not for him and the gentle-hearted Lady Alys, Griff would have had nothing at all in this life. He would likely have been dead if not for the benevolence of the noble couple who took him into their home when his own kin had deserted him to the charity of strangers.

Sir Robert loved his son, but Dominic was a source of frequent strife and constant concern. Though he tried to school his sole heir in the ways of responsibility and honor, on many occasions, Droghallow's earl expressed his fears to Griffin that Dominic might never be fit to rule his demesne. He had stunned Griffin the day he made him swear to stay on after he was gone. Griff's assurances that Sir Robert would have a good many years before that was an issue that seemed to fall on deaf ears. In an uncustomarily bleak mood, the earl made him vow then and there to look after his interests and see that Dom did not make a mockery of his good name.

That pledge, spoken before Griffin could really know what he would be giving up—and put to the test when Sir Robert died later that year—had kept Griffin's feet rooted firmly in Droghallow's soil. It had kept him from pursuing his own dreams, from seeking answers to questions that had plagued him his entire life. Who was he? Where did he come from? Where did he belong?

Griffin did not recall the precise moment that he finally decided it was time to find out. All he knew was that one day he was staring at a pot full of hard-earned silver— more than two years' wages—and he suddenly knew why he was saving it. He was leaving Droghallow. He would collect enough money to afford him a decent start somewhere else and then he would go. This last task for Dom, odious as it was, would have ensured the commencement of that new life. And now, despite Dom's assurances, Griff was certain that inside the castle his foster brother was gleefully maneuvering a way to cheat him out of the chance at freedom he so desired.

Incensed that he had trusted Dom's word in the first place, Griff ground out an oath and shouted for one of Droghallow's squires to stable the horses stolen from the caravan. It took no coaxing at all for him to join Odo and the other men at the village tavern, where he proceeded for the next few hours to drink himself into a wicked black haze.

He guessed it to be somewhere around midnight when

he finally decided he'd had enough. He was drunk, but he was not about to let Dom's present manipulation go unmet. Downing the dregs of his ale, he pushed himself away from the table and stalked across the tavern's earthen floor.

"Something wrong, Griff?" Odo called from around the neck of a serving wench who had seated herself in his lap. "Where ye goin'?"

"To collect on what's owed me," he replied, and let the door slam behind him.

Chapter Five

The night was half expired before exhaustion finally claimed Isabel, but despite her fatigue, she slept restlessly, jolted awake in stark fear by every bump and movement that sounded in the corridor beyond her locked chamber door. Every voice that echoed through the tower keep made her sit bolt upright on the cell's crude bed, listening, waiting in dread for the nightmare of this new existence to truly begin.

Whatever fate Dom had in store for her, whatever reason he had for ordering her kidnapped—and for whom— Isabel was certain of one thing: her life now was as good as forfeit. And of all the people in this world, Griffin had been the man who delivered her here. It was too horrible to contemplate, too terrifyingly real to acknowledge.

She heard the heavy fall of footsteps nearing the other side of her door and rose up off the thin, down-filled mattress of the bed. The guard Dominic had posted outside hailed the person who approached with a chuckle and a friendly greeting.

"Come to take Dom up on his offer of the wench, have ye?" he asked knowingly. "Can't says I would've turned it down either."

"Shut up and open the door," the visitor ordered in a gruff drawl as he approached, his voice heavy and slurred with drink.

It was Griffin, Isabel realized in horror. A tremor of

disbelief snaked its way down her spine as the lock bar slid out of its sleeve and the door to her chamber swung wide. She scrambled to the edge of the bed, not at all certain what she meant to do, knowing there was nowhere to hide, no means of escape.

"Someone here to see ye, m'lady," the guard laughed.

He stepped aside and Griffin's silhouette filled the doorway. He looked even bigger to her than he had before, grim and ominous, now that she was seeing him in this new, truer, light. His dark mantle swirled around his muscled calves as he stepped over the threshold, the spurs on his boot heels gleaming in the torchlight that spilled in from the corridor behind him. There was a feral look about him, a hard gleam in his eyes as he stared at Isabel from across the short span of floor that separated them. His tawny hair was windblown, hanging in reckless spikes over her brow and shoulders. His sculpted mouth was set in a line of grim determination, his squared jaw tight and unforgiving.

Even from where she stood, her slippered feet crushing the dried rushes on the floor, the backs of her thighs pressed against the bed, Isabel could sense the air of resolve that radiated off of him in waves. Heaven help her, but she was looking at a man capable—and fully certain—of getting precisely what he wanted. She swallowed hard and sidled a wary step to her left.

"Leave us," he instructed the guard.

Isabel flinched at his calmly voiced command. The door closed with a soft groan, sealing Isabel in to meet her fate like a helpless Daniel, alone in the lion's den.

"W-what do you want?" she stammered, her voice rising in fear. "Why have you come here?"

"Shh," Griffin hissed. "Don't be frightened." He spread his arms as he came toward her, his feet a trifle sluggish, palms exposed in a seeming show of peace. "I'm not going to hurt you."

Isabel's heart was pounding like a drum. Had he come

to take his use of her as Dom had offered? she wondered, panic rising in her breast. No. Her mind struggled to deny the terrible thought. Griffin would never hurt her. He would never stoop to something so vile as rape.

But this was not the Griffin she thought she once knew, she reminded herself, her feet inching away from him of their own accord. This was not the same person she had idolized as a hero—the one person whose honor she had believed in all these years.

She did not know him now, this man who reeked of ale and smoldering anger. He was a stranger to her. Worse than a stranger, he was her enemy, no less a threat to her well-being now than Dom himself. Perhaps more, because her heart so dearly wanted to trust him, even now.

"You have nothing to fear, my lady. Just do as I tell you and everything will be all right."

He nodded slowly, as if he had no doubt that she would obey, and stepped closer. Then he reached for her. Isabel turned on her heel as he seized her by the shoulder, his big hand clamping down on her like a vise. She cried out and lunged away sharply, but he held firm, curling his strong fingers into the neckline of her gown. The seams of the fine silk garment popped under the strain, tearing open at the neck and sleeve. He was undaunted. In the space of a heartbeat he had changed his grip, latching onto her arm and pulling her to him with a firm tug.

"Damnation, woman, stop fighting me!" he grated harshly beside her ear.

But Isabel screamed instead and threw herself forward. Blessedly, his grasp gave way, drink no doubt hindering his ability. Freed of his hold, Isabel fell to the floor on her knees in the rushes. Behind her the door to her cell creaked open.

"Help me, please!" she cried in desperation, but it was only Dom's guard, a hard-eyed man who glanced in dispassionate silence from where she sat, trying to hold together the rent shoulder of her gown, then to Griffin, who stood over her, breathing hard, fists clenched, a solid wall of dark intent.

"Do you mind, man?" Griffin growled at the soldier. "I think I can manage to do this on my own. Why don't you take a walk for a couple of hours? I'll fetch you back to your post when I'm through here."

The guard grinned appreciatively and closed the door. His booted footfalls retreated down the corridor, and Griffin turned his attention back to Isabel. He held out his hand. "Come up off the floor, my lady."

Isabel shook her head. "Stay away from me."

"We haven't a lot of time to waste," he told her matter-of-factly when she refused to budge. "The less difficult you make this, the better."

She could hardly believe her ears! That he would stand there so arrogantly, advising her to cooperate with him while he defiled her, outraged Isabel beyond comprehension. "I would rather die first," she declared, then vaulted to her feet and made a headlong break for the unguarded door.

He caught her around the waist and flung her backward onto the bed. The sudden impact of hitting the mattress stunned her, but not nearly so much as the feel of Griffin's body when he placed himself atop her in that next moment, trapping her beneath him.

"Mayhap you'd prefer to sulk in this chamber until Dom is ready to ship you off to God only knows where," he suggested tightly, his eyes flashing in the dim light of the candle that sputtered at her bedside. Isabel scarcely registered his comment. She struggled under Griffin's pinning weight, fighting with all she had, even though she could sense the futility of her efforts in every hard plane of muscle and bone that held her prisoner against the mattress.

"Dom promised me a healthy reward for you," he

drawled, his voice low and full of resolve. "If he won't deliver on that vow, then I shall collect it through another means instead."

"No! Don't touch me!" Isabel cried, bucking and thrashing. He held both her wrists locked in his steely fist, leaving her few defenses to use against what was certain to be a brutal, degrading attack. But when she expected him to descend on her with the full drunken force of his lust and violence, he began to ease off of her. He stilled suddenly, staring at her exposed neck and heaving bosom.

"What the devil?"

She flinched as if struck when he reached down, frowning, distracted now by something he saw. The medallion, she realized, feeling the weight of the cold metal where it lay against her flushed skin. Panting, still tensed for flight, Isabel watched Griffin's expression change as he lifted the bronze half-moon-shaped disc up toward his face, his reaction going from surprise, to confusion . . . to recognition.

"Izzy?"

His momentary hesitation was all the opportunity she needed. Teeth clenched, lips flattened in a sneer he might have mistaken for a smile, Isabel arched her back off the mattress and, with every ounce of fury she could muster, kneed him squarely in the groin.

He drew in his breath sharply and collapsed atop her, his face diving into the space of mattress above her shoulder. With surprisingly little effort, Isabel pushed him over onto his back and scrambled away, triumphant as her feet touched the rush-strewn floor and carried her swiftly across the room toward the door.

He groaned on the bed behind her, muttering an incoherent oath. "Izzy," he gasped, his hand feebly groping for her and catching only a handful of air. "Isabel, please. Wait."

"Why?" she shot back with a haughty bark of sarcasm. "To give you another chance to molest me?"

"God's wounds, lady," he croaked, still doubled over in apparent misery and struggling to drag himself up off the bed. "It wasn't my intent to steal your virtue—I came to take you out of here! I mean to take you to Montborne."

Chapter Six

Head swimming with pain-induced, spinning shards of blinding light, Griff peeled open one eye and saw that the lady actually had paused. Standing at the door, hands fisted at her sides, she stared over her shoulder at him, frowning. "Why should I believe you?"

He levered himself to a sitting position, wincing when the more tender part of his anatomy shifted with the movement. "What other choice do you have?" he hissed.

Her answering laugh was filled with scorn and a good measure of suspicion. "I am to trust that you came up here tonight because you had a change of heart? That now you suddenly wish to help me get safely to Montborne? I am not so great a fool."

" 'Tis as I told you," he said, regaining the normal use of his voice now that his pain was finally subsiding from piercing agony to a dull throb. "Dom reneged on his word to me. I was to be paid for my efforts and now I have every reason to suspect that is not going to happen."

She threw him a haughty glare. "You will pardon me if I do not sympathize with your apparent dilemma, my lord."

Griff chuckled at her spunk, albeit somewhat weakly, for it brought a jolt of renewed pain to his body. "If Dom won't reward me for your capture," he told her, "surely your betrothed will do so for your return."

"The only suitable reward for a rogue of your ilk is a trip to the gibbet," she retorted smartly.

"Perhaps," Griff admitted. "But I think once Montborne hears how I delivered you out of Dom's clutches, he'll be more than willing to see me compensated."

"How can you be so sure?" she challenged. "For all you know, he may find you no less a criminal than Dom himself. How do you mean to convince him to absolve you?"

"I won't have to convince him, my lady. You will."

"I will do no such thing!" she gasped, facing him now in her outrage, hands on her hips. "I will not aid you in this further plan of extortion!"

Griffin got to his feet, serious now. "Aye, my lady. You will." She backed toward the door, one hand slipping behind her, no doubt searching for the latch. He shook his head knowingly. "Even if I allow you to flee this chamber, do not be so foolish as to expect to escape the castle on your own. You'll never make it out of here without me, let alone make it to Montborne."

She was breathing hard, lip caught between her teeth, brow pinched as she contemplated her options. Griff watched her like a hawk, anticipating her every movement, ready to spring if she made even the slightest overture to run. She stared at him, wounded, her gaze blazing in plain contempt. "I despise you, Griffin of Droghallow. I wish I'd never laid eyes on you."

He shrugged as if her declaration did not sting him in the least. "Have we an agreement, Izzy?"

"Don't call me that," she told him quietly. "You haven't the right to call me familiar."

Standing there in the dim light of the chamber, petite and trembling, she was once more the sweet, terrified girl Griffin had rescued from danger some ten years before. Except that now she did not tremble out of fear for a raging forest beast, but out of fear and loathing for him. He tamped down the queer feeling that realization brought with it, telling himself it should not matter what she thought of him. She meant nothing more than a means to an end, his passage to a boon that would be the foundation of his future.

"I am going to take you out of here," he told her sternly as he met her at the door. "And unless you'd prefer to deal with Dom, you are going to do precisely what I tell you to do—without question. Understand?"

The fact that she did not refuse him outright was consent enough. Griff took her by the hand and opened the door a crack. He peered out to make sure the corridor was clear, then stepped over the threshold with Isabel in tow.

As late as it was, the tower stairwell and labyrinth of hallways were empty, most of the castle folk having hours before taken to their pallets. But the implication of safety did not slow Griffin's pace. Indeed, it only made him move all the faster, using the fortunate circumstance to its fullest advantage. He guided Isabel down to the main floor of the keep, past the great hall with its sea of occupants; the trestle tables that lined the chamber during the day were now stacked against the walls, clearing the floor for the bulk of the garrison and dozens of servants who slept there each night on thin pallets of straw.

A few of those common folk stirred, some taking their pleasure with each other despite the lack of privacy. Griff hastened past the wide arched entryway, tugging Isabel's arm when she peered inside and paused, letting out a shocked little gasp at the mingled groans of carnal pleasure that sounded from within. They were nearly to the keep's exit when Griff heard footsteps pad along the corridor in front of them. With no time to spare, he turned to Isabel and grasped her by the shoulders, pushing her into a shadowy alcove of the hallway.

Then he kissed her.

It was a deep kiss, accompanied by the full press of his body, a maneuver primarily meant to conceal the both of them from whomever approached. Griff was not prepared for the bolt of lust that shot through him the instant their

lips met. Nor, it seemed, was Isabel. Her startled cry of
protest when he seized her had dissolved into a soft,
throaty mewl as his mouth brushed over hers, the resisting
push of her hands at his chest all but melting away, her fingers now curling into the loose fabric of his tunic.

She was sweetness and untried passion in his arms, an
intoxicating mix that his body responded to with swift, urgent need. He dragged her further into his embrace, covering her lips with his, all but lost in the sensual pleasure of
the moment.

Through the fevered thud of his pulse, he heard the approaching footsteps, closer now, as the person padding
down the hallway rounded the corner and drew up short.

"Sir Griffin?" a female voice gasped. "Saints, milord!
'Tis late to find you down here."

With more reluctance than he cared to admit, Griff
broke the kiss. He said nothing at first, did not even acknowledge the interruption, his mind too rattled to conjure
any manner of reply. He stared down at Isabel, unsure what
had just passed between them even though his every fiber
and muscle was taut with keen and certain awareness. He
nearly had to shake himself to focus on his surroundings,
to wrestle sense enough to deal with the present situation.

That present situation came a few paces forward, at-
tempting to peer around Griff's shoulder in curiosity.
"Who's that with you—is it Tess from the kitchens?" She
gave a saucy little giggle. "Mayhap milord would be better
pleased with the both of us together."

"To your pallet, Meg," Griff ordered gruffly, his voice
coarse and thick with arousal, his head still bent to hide Isabel from prying eyes, his gaze fixed on her and hungry
with want.

The servant girl obeyed with nothing more than a disappointed sounding huff. Griff listened as her feet scuffed
down the corridor toward the great hall. He waited to hear
they were alone once more, willing his heart to cease

pounding in his head so he could think of something other than the compellingly moist invitation of Isabel's mouth.

"Let's go," he said, taking her by the hand.

Satisfied that the keep had fallen back into silence, he resumed their flight, his brisk stride chewing up the remaining space of corridor that separated them from escape.

Outside, the bailey was quiet, the wall-walk vacant save for the handful of guards on night watch. With a measured air of purpose that dared anyone to question him, Griff descended the stairs leading down into the courtyard. Isabel followed along, forced to take two quick steps to every one of his. He led her to the stables, silencing the old horse master with a pointed stare and a dismissive nod of greeting.

Griff's destrier was stabled in one of the far stalls. The huge gray steed neighed and tossed his head when he saw his master approach, the beast's nostrils flaring as if he smelled insurrection on the wind. With a warning to Isabel to mind her distance from the animal, Griff saddled him and led him out of the berth.

"What about Felice?" she whispered suddenly. "I can't just leave her here."

Griff doubted very much that, were the tables turned, Isabel would receive the same consideration. "The woman is none of my concern, but if you see fit, make arrangements to fetch her once you are safe at Montborne."

She seemed mollified somewhat by the suggestion, nodding as she followed him out of the stables. "Shouldn't we take two horses?" she asked. "We might make better time riding separately."

Griffin shook his head. "Taking one mount out at this hour will cause suspicion enough. Besides, I think it wiser if we rode together."

He did not miss her look of disappointment, despite the fact that she tried to hide it under her scowl. Would she have tried to abandon him on the road? He hoped not, for a woman traveling alone on remote northern byways would not get far without inviting trouble.

At the moment, they had trouble enough of their own, he decided as he mounted the gray, then hoisted Isabel up into the saddle with him. On the battlements near Droghallow's gates, one of the guards took notice of their presence in the bailey. Lance in hand, he said something to the man watching the yard with him, waking the knight with an ungentle nudge.

"Open the gate, Roger," Griffin commanded, turning Isabel's head into his chest and wrapping the edge of his mantle around her shoulders. "Don't show them your face," he whispered in a voice only she would hear.

"Is that you, Griff?" the gatekeeper asked, peering down from his perch.

"It is. Open the gate, will you?"

"Dom gave orders that no one was to leave tonight without his say-so," the guard replied, looking somewhat unsure in his refusal, yet making no move to comply.

Before him, clutching his waist in a death grip, Isabel drew in her breath. Griffin could feel her anxiety, and in truth, he shared it. The only way out was through those gates. Staring up at the guards, he cursed vividly. "Dom said no one was to pass?" he said, more accusation than question.

"That he did, Griff."

"Well, would that he had mentioned that fact before he woke me with orders to deliver this woman back to her cottage in the village before her husband found her missing." He noted the guard's reaction, seeing the look of doubt come over the man's face. Griff pulled his mount's reins and made to wheel it around and head back to the stables. "Fine by me," he said with arrogant disregard. "Let Dom ferry his own whores to and from his bed."

"Wait," the guard called, after a moment. "I wager Dom would trust you before anyone else in his service. If you say he sent you out, that's good enough for me, Griff. I'll open the gates."

" 'Tis about time," Griffin drawled as the portcullis was raised, and he and Isabel rode beneath the heavy iron grid.

He rode in the direction of the village only until he was certain the guards on watch could no longer see him, then he veered his destrier off the road, headed toward the dark cover of the woods. Griff noticed that the horse's gait had begun to falter slightly after they traversed a rocky patch of ground. He slowed the beast to investigate the trouble, bringing him to a halt once they were safely ensconced in the forest.

"What is it?" Isabel asked as he dismounted and pulled her from the saddle.

Griff took up each of the horse's feet in turn, then found the source of the problem. "He picked up a stone," he explained, working the pebble out of the horse's hoof with the tip of his dagger. "There you are, boy, that should feel better now."

Behind him, Isabel's feet crunched in the dry pine needles that littered the ground. "How far do you suppose we are from Montborne?"

"About three days' ride," Griff told her, patting the destrier's flank as he released its foot and made sure the beast could stand.

"Which direction?"

Griff wondered at her questioning interest, sensing that the wheels of conspiracy had begun to turn in her pretty head. Mayhap they had never stopped. "That way," he answered, waving his hand in the general direction of the forest path.

"Oh," she answered, her soft reply punctuated by more movement at his back. "Three days isn't so terribly far. I think I can make it."

Griff realized his mistake a mere heartbeat before it hit him—literally hit him—for Isabel, the sweet girl he had rescued ten years prior and sought to rescue again tonight, had found herself a hard and rather useful length of oak. Griff acknowledged the makeshift weapon as he turned his head to the side and saw her raise it.

She brought it down on him like a hammer, dropping him quite efficiently on the forest floor. The last thing Griff saw before darkness began to crowd his vision was Isabel, tossing aside her bludgeon and peering down at him as if to ascertain whether or not she had killed him.

He half wondered the very same thing as his heavy eyelids drifted closed and a thick, fuzzy silence engulfed him.

Chapter Seven

"I am truly sorry, Griffin," Isabel whispered as she blinked down at his big, sprawling form. "But I fear you left me no choice in this."

He groaned slightly, not quite a response, but enough to ease her mind with the knowledge that he was alive. She had not meant to kill him after all, merely distract him, until she was able to get away on her own. He certainly seemed distracted now. She did not want to think about how furious he would rightfully be once he woke. Indeed, the more distance she could put between herself and his sore head, the better. Three days separated her from Montborne; she had better get started.

Isabel took a couple of steps toward the waiting gray stallion, trying to ignore the prickle of guilt that began to needle her. Could she simply leave Griffin like this, unconscious in Droghallow's woods? He was sure to be found by Dom's soldiers; how could he explain his part in stealing Isabel out of the keep? Would he be punished—tortured—for her escape?

She really should not worry over him, she reasoned sternly, trying to shake herself into the same brand of disregard for others that he seemed to employ. Griffin of Droghallow was her abductor. A heartless knave, utterly lacking in honor. If he later sought to free her from the terrible situation it was only to use her further for his own gain. She owed him no consideration now. Indeed, she owed him nothing at all.

Well, perhaps that was not quite true.

Isabel paused to regard him over her shoulder, then walked back to where he lay. She took off the pendant she had worn for the past decade, his white lion medallion, a symbol of chivalry and courage that she could no longer believe in. She knelt down and slipped the chain over his head.

"I can't keep this anymore," she told him. "It belongs to you. I've been meaning to return it for a long time; I just never imagined it would be like this."

That was as much of a good-bye as she would allow herself. Isabel stood up and turned away from him. With gentling words for his mount, who seemed to stare at her in silent scorn, Isabel took the reins and stepped into the stirrup, positioning herself astride in the saddle. The beast fidgeted beneath her, agitated with her slight weight, but she was pleased to find he cooperated well enough when she clucked her tongue and gave him a meaningful nudge with her heels.

"Let's away now, horse," she said to the ghost-colored steed, and started off on the path Griffin had indicated would take her to Montborne.

Isabel urged the destrier into a gallop, speeding along the moonlit trail with a buoying sense of renewed control. The forest was quiet, save for the steady pound of the horse's hooves, and the night air was brisk and fragrant with the fresh, heady smells of pine, moss, and freedom. Isabel breathed it all in, drawing strength from her passing surroundings, never before feeling quite so confident, so devoid of doubt and fear.

It felt good to hold her destiny in her hands.

Indeed, if the past day had taught her anything at all, Isabel supposed it was that she could rely on no one, save herself. Not that she ever could. It was a disappointment she fully intended to spare her little sister. Maura would never know the hurt of betrayal. She would never see the ugliness of the world they lived in or know the aching void of loneliness. Where her parents and everyone else she knew had failed her, Isabel would not fail Maura.

It was a vow she had made in earnest. A vow she clung to with steely tenacity as the hours of travel spun off in her wake and night made way for morn.

Despite the weight of her present obligations, Isabel found it difficult not to think about Griffin. It was hard not to picture him crumpled in the fallen leaves and abandoned. Impossible not to revisit the entirely-too-pleasing press of his lips on hers when he had kissed her so unexpectedly in the shadowy corridor of Droghallow's tower keep. Indeed, her mouth still burned from the contact; her body still tingled with a confusion of feelings she could hardly make sense of: astonishment, outrage, and something more elusive—an enigmatic sensation of traveling warmth that seemed to move and breathe inside of her like a living thing, long-slumbering and now awakened by Griffin's sensual kiss.

He had meant nothing by it; she knew better than to think otherwise, of course. It had been merely a clever means of shielding them from discovery. Another example of his willingness to use her in whatever way he saw fit so long as it advanced his selfish goals. If he was not above plundering her mouth to suit his purposes, what more would Griffin dare if he deemed it necessary?

It was fortunate for her that she had disencumbered herself of him, for she did not think she could bear to find out. And the urge to understand this queer feeling he had roused inside of her—despite the certain danger it would involve—was far too compelling for her peace of mind.

Yes, Isabel decided with complete resolve, it was fortunate, indeed, that she was rid of Griffin of Droghallow. She could only hope to remain so . . . forever.

With the first rays of dawn stretching over the horizon, Isabel turned her attention once more to her surroundings. The forest path seemed to have no end, spreading out before her as far as her eyes could see, an infinite ribbon of softly trod earth. She would have expected to reach the edge of the woods by now, or perhaps see a glimpse of open field or a distant village somewhere along the way—anything to indicate her progress. But the hours of travel had yielded no such signs of success. Indeed, for as long as she had been riding, Isabel wondered if she would be spending all three days of her journey to Montborne on this very track.

And something else began to nag at her senses now.

It was a vague feeling that the forest had eyes, that as she guided her stolen mount over a rocky patch of ground, she was being watched.

She paused suddenly, pivoting in the saddle to check the trail at her back. It was empty. No one creeping up behind her. No cause for worry. She let out a nervous little laugh and shook her head in relief, ready to resume her trek.

"Good morn, Isabel."

She knew the source of the deep voice without looking, but nevertheless, Isabel nearly tumbled out of the saddle to find Griffin standing in the woods to her left, leaning against the trunk of a gnarled old oak. He did not seem surprised to see her, nor did he seem overly pleased.

"You!" she gasped in utter astonishment. "How did you catch up to me? I've been riding for hours and you were on foot!"

"Actually, I've been on my arse most of the night, thanks to the blow you dealt me."

She frowned at him in confusion. "I don't understand."

"You followed the forest path," he answered with a shrug.

"It led toward Montborne, you said."

Griffin shook his head. "The path is used for hunting. It leads in a wide circle."

"You lied!"

"No, lady," he said calmly. "Montborne does, indeed, lie in the direction I told you. But this path will not get you there. I, however, can."

"I don't need your help," she told him, incensed with his arrogance and disgusted with herself for wasting precious hours in folly.

When she would have given the gray stallion her heels, Griffin snapped his fingers and called out the beast's name. To her dismay, the horse merely shifted beneath her, ignoring her instructions entirely to walk instead toward its true master.

"It's morning now," Griffin told her as he took the reins from her hands. "Dom is sure to be missing us in a short while. Do you wish to be sitting here arguing with me when he finds us, or do you wish me to see us on our way to Montborne?"

Isabel stared down at him in mute frustration, every bit of her pride urging her to refuse him, despite the fact that he seemed her only hope now. More than anything, she wanted to deny his help, to deny the notion that she might need Griffin, even a little bit. But logic won out over dignity.

Through gritted teeth, she said, "Very well. As I have no other choice, I suppose you should take me to Montborne."

"A sensible decision, my lady," Griffin said as he stepped into the stirrup and climbed up.

He seated himself behind her, the hard planes of his chest and thighs much too close for Isabel's comfort. She might have protested his overprotective hold on her, but in that next instant, he spurred his mount and they were off, thundering along on the beginnings of a journey Isabel sensed would change her forever.

• • •

Dominic of Droghallow was none too pleased with the early morning knock that sounded on his chamber door a couple of hours later. The incessant rapping woke him from a heavy sleep, a sleep spent drunk and physically sated, blissfully entangled in the soft limbs of his pretty blond bed partner. Longchamp's grand-niece had been a delightful surprise, a virgin, charming and spirited, yet perfectly willing to surrender her virtue to him once she learned of his many holdings purchased from the crown in exchange for funds for the crusade. Dom had half a mind to sue for the chit's hand once his deal with Prince John was settled.

The king's brother was building alliances with Prince Philip of France, making covert arrangements to hand over strategic holdings across the realm in exchange for the French ruler's support once Richard was distracted by his interests abroad. John had offered Philip a presence on England's marches, tempting him with a number of border estates, among them the holdings recently inherited by Isabel de Lamere and nearly lost through her sudden, promised marriage to Sebastian of Montborne. Prince John had made it clear to Dom that should he ensure the permanent delay of that marriage—by whatever means necessary—there would be much to gain for Droghallow's ambitious lord.

Dom could hardly wait to collect.

The pounding on his door sounded again, louder this time, accompanied by the urgent voice of one of his guards. "My lord, are you awake?"

"I am now," he growled, sweeping aside Felice's arms and watching in rapt appreciation as she yawned and stretched cat-like beside him. "Don't move," he told her as he sat up and extricated himself from the tangled bed sheets.

Dom retrieved his braies from the floor and gathered the

linen undergarment around his hips, fumbling to hold them up as he opened the door. "What is it?" he demanded of the big knight standing at the threshold.

" 'Tis the woman, my lord. The Montborne bride."

"What of her?"

"Well, she's gone, my lord."

Dom narrowed his gaze, certain he had not heard aright. "Gone? What do you mean, gone?"

"Sh-she's not here, my lord." The guard cleared his throat as if what he was about to say next refused to come to his tongue. "She's just gone. Sir Griffin went to see her late last eve. He gave me leave to quit my post, said he would send for me once he finished with her, but he never came to get me."

"What are you telling me, man," Dom said, not at all as calm as his voice made him seem.

The knight shook his head helplessly. "I must have fallen asleep in the hall, but when I returned to my post this morn, she was gone. Her chamber was empty."

"Jesu!" Dom slammed his palm against the door frame, his head spinning with rage. "How could this have happened?"

"I-I don't know, my lord."

"Fetch my foster brother," Dom ordered. "Tell him I want to see him immediately. And have him assemble the garrison. The woman can't have gone far—tell Griffin I want her found and I want her found now."

But the guard did not move. He merely stared at Dom, blinking dumbly. "Er, my lord . . . Sir Griffin is gone, too. The night watch said he left the castle around midnight. He had a woman with him, my lord. Said he was taking her to the village on your orders."

Dom chuckled like a man suddenly gone mad. "That conniving bastard. If I needed a reason to see him dead, I wager this is as good as any." He turned the full measure of his angry gaze on the knight standing before him, taking great satisfaction in the way the big man blanched. "Inform the garrison that Griffin of Droghallow is now a wanted man. Tell the guards I'll pay a thousand marks for the woman, twice that for him. And I don't care if you have to kill him to bring him in, just bring him in."

Chapter Eight

They traveled hard for the better part of the day, maintaining as brisk a pace as they dared through the dense woods and leaf-strewn bramble that was their road. Isabel's body was aching from the jostling, laborious ride. Her throat was parched, stomach empty and gnawing with hunger, but she did not dare ask Griffin to stop. She would not admit weakness to him; she doubted very much that he would care.

For his part, Griffin seemed unfazed by the day's taxing journey, fully intent to press on ceaselessly to Montborne. She should be happy for that, Isabel supposed. The sooner they made it to Montborne, the sooner she could be away from Griffin of Droghallow.

The sooner she could banish the memory of him to the farthest reaches of her heart.

It was a feat that seemed impossible so long as she was pressed against the hard planes of his chest, feeling the thundering rhythm of the horse's hooves reverberate through his body and into hers, feeling his arm wrapped tight around her waist. It was easier to imagine spending all her days with him, knowing the warmth of his touch, the strength of his embrace.

When he finally slowed his mount some hours later, pausing near a small brook and murmuring that the beast needed to rest and refresh, Isabel was only mildly relieved. When he then released his hold on her to dismount, against

all logic and reason, she found that she missed the contact.
Despite her contempt for his purpose, she missed his pos-
sessive, protecting presence.

And that, surely, made her the veriest sort of fool.

She tried to act indifferent, tossing him a haughty look
as he reached up and helped her from the saddle and gently
set her feet on the ground.

"We can't afford to tarry for long," he said, unfastening
a leather saddle pack and handing it to her. "You'll find
some bread and cheese and a skin of wine in there. Take of
it what you want. I'll get us more supplies when we stop
for the night."

He did not wait for her response. Taking his destrier's
reins, he led the gray stallion to the edge of the stream and
stroked its thick neck and mane as it bent to drink. Isabel
heard the low rumble of Griffin's voice as he spoke to the
animal, heard the plain affection in his timbre. That he was
gentle with his horse intrigued her somewhat, even as it
confused her. She could not help staring at him as he returned to the embankment where she had seated herself on
a patch of soft moss.

"You and that disagreeable beast are well suited," she remarked, munching on a crust of dark bread. "Indeed, you
seem to prefer his company to that of persons, my lord."

"I generally do," he answered.

There was no pretense in his blunt reply, only frank hon-
esty. And, to Isabel's astonishment, she sensed the slightest
hint of loneliness. She well understood that feeling, difficult as it was for her to admit any affinity of emotion with
the hard man now staring down at her.

She brushed her sympathy aside and offered Griffin
some food and wine, not at all surprised when he declined
to share it with her. He remained standing, positioning
himself several paces to her side, his back leaned against a
tall pine—a solitary man, distant, aloof.

He tipped his chin up and looked to the sky, but whether

he sought to gauge the hour or change the subject, Isabel could not be sure. When he spoke, it was as if he spoke to himself, as if she was not there at all. "The day is half gone. Dom's guards will have been on our trail for some time now. 'Twill be difficult to outpace them when we have just the one horse." He shook his head slightly and let out a thoughtful sigh. "Would that we had taken two instead."

Isabel stopped chewing and glared at him, recalling her very suggestion—the one he had refused to consider and rejected out of hand—when they were preparing to flee Droghallow. "Would that I had struck you harder with that tree branch," she muttered under her breath.

He pivoted his head to look at her, idly bringing a finger to his temple as if he could still feel the blow. "I wouldn't remind me too often of that incident if I were you, my lady. Nor the prior attack you made on another part of my anatomy. Two attempts on my life in one day is more than I can willingly abide." He considered her for a moment, then asked, "Where was it you learned to defend yourself so ably? I trust you employed no such deadly skills against anyone in the convent."

There was a glimmer of humor in his eyes as he said it, but it was fleeting and more than a trifle rusty. Nevertheless, Isabel felt a reluctant smile curl her lips. She glanced down at her hands, busying her fingers with a crumbly piece of bread. "No," she said. "My life at the abbey was peaceful enough. 'Twas before, when I lived at home—at Lamere—that I often had to fight using something more than words. The squires and pages who fostered with us used to tease me relentlessly about one thing or another: my hair, my freckles, my awkwardness." She shrugged. "I had become long used to their jests and gibes, but when they turned their cruelty on the younger children of the castle, well, I suppose 'twas more than I could stand."

"So, my Izzy became a courtyard defender, taking on the bullies she once fled." Isabel met his gaze, startled to hear him refer to her as "my Izzy." He seemed equally surprised by the idea, though he masked it well enough under a careless chuckle and a wry lift of his brow. " 'Tis better to do unto others, before they have the chance to do unto you, I say."

Isabel frowned. She did not like his sudden, callous tone of voice. "That sounds to me more like something Dominic of Droghallow would say. Although I must admit I am finding it hard to tell the both of you apart now." She watched his stony expression, the way he stared at her, a grim shadow of the bright, chivalric lad she recalled so fondly. "What happened to you, Griffin? How did you become like this?"

"Like what, my lady?"

It was a challenge, that simple, emotionless question. Isabel knew he was trying to intimidate her, but she could not help herself from asking, from demanding to know what had happened to the youth she had once adored. The boy whose courage had inspired in Isabel her own.

"Where is your honor?" she asked him pointedly. "You once told me you meant to be a great knight. A man of honor, you said. How did a youth who would look death in the eye to rescue a helpless girl turn into the rogue I see now: a mercenary fueled by greed, a common bride thief?"

He hesitated to answer, as if he were actually giving it some thought. "Slowly, I imagine . . . day by day." His shrug was casual, negligent. "As for honor, my lady, I have found it to be somewhat overrated. That's not to say I don't subscribe to my own notions of right and wrong."

"The very reason you would bring me to Montborne," Isabel suggested. "To right the wrong of Dom's cheating you out of your reward for my capture?"

He gave her a slight, assenting nod.

"There is nothing honorable in that," she told him. "What you seem to subscribe to is greed and revenge, a blackguard's brand of justice. I thought you were above such criminal behavior. I thought you were . . . different."

"A criminal, did you say?" he tossed back at her. "Ah, I see. And what excuse do you offer for the crime of stealing my medallion that day in Droghallow's woods?"

"Stealing it!" She gasped, then saw from the glint of humor in his eyes that his accusation was meant in jest. Against her will, Isabel found herself returning his smile, then quickly glanced away embarrassed. "I did not steal your medallion. I found it lying on the ground after you left. There was a weak link in the chain—that's why you lost it, I suppose. But I was able to repair it. A goldsmith would have done a better job I'm sure, but still, I've taken care of it as best I can, and it's held up well these past ten years. I've been meaning to return it to you all this time . . . hoping, actually, that I would have the chance one day."

She was rambling now, chattering on mindlessly because she could not bear the knowledge that he was watching her. She felt his scrutiny like a physical caress, knew his gaze was too astute to miss the rising color in her cheeks, her bottom lip caught between her teeth to keep herself from prattling on any further.

"Ten years," he remarked quietly. " 'Tis no wonder I did not recognize you on sight. The girl I recall was a plump ball of butter, a wide-eyed, freckle-faced child without the good sense to know when she was wandering headlong into danger." She glanced up, just in time to see him give her an appreciative smile. It was a gesture that irritated her beyond toleration for the way she greedily soaked up even the most dubious scrap of his attention. "You have changed—and in some rather dramatic ways, at that—my lady."

"So have you, my lord," she retorted in a less-than-flattering tone of voice. "I expect the man I see before me now would let that boar gore me to shreds before he stepped forth to offer his aid."

Griffin tilted his head and regarded her with a wry twist of his lip. "Quite the contrary, demoiselle. It would sorely aggrieve me to see you meet with harm, now as ever. I can only guess, but I'm fairly certain your bridegroom's anticipated show of appreciation would discount significantly were his bride to be delivered to him in multiple pieces."

Isabel glared at him, appalled and fuming, at an utter loss for words.

"My thanks, incidentally, for the return of my medallion," he offered, lifting the small half disc of bronze into the sunlight as if to appraise it. "I suspect I might be able to get at least a few deniers for it at market somewhere."

That he would even think to sell the amulet after all it had meant to her—after all she had done to keep it safe for the past decade—incensed Isabel beyond measure. "God rot you *and* your bloody medallion," she shot back at him, one of the few times in her cloistered life that she had ever allowed a curse to cross her lips. She swallowed down the lump of hurt and anger that lodged itself in her throat. She would not rail at him. Heaven help her, she would not give him the satisfaction of goading her. She stared at him, forcing herself to hold his hard gaze. "You're a beast, Griffin of Droghallow. A lowly scoundrel and a common thief. To think for all these years I have—"

Adored you, she thought, thankful that she was able to bite back the damning words before they further condemned her.

If she had not known it before, she well knew the truth now. The boy she had practically worshiped for his honor and goodness was gone. Evidently many years gone, though what might have happened to him, Isabel could not be sure. Nor did she think she wanted to let herself get close enough to this stranger who bore his name to find out.

No, the boy she had loved for so long was dead. And Griffin had buried him deep, Isabel realized suddenly.

She could only stare at him now, angered at him for embroiling her in this profound confusion and furious with herself for allowing him to so affect her. She was unsure of what to say in that moment, unsure what to think of him now. She wanted to hate him.

She wanted to, but heaven help her, she could not.

Unable to abide the snarl of confusion that twisted inside her when she thought of him, Isabel stood up and brushed some of the leaves and forest debris from her skirts. When she started to take a step away from the camp, Griffin reached out and grabbed her by the arm. She pulled free of his grasp with an offended scoff. "I suppose it would be too much to ask for a few moments of privacy, sirrah?"

He did not answer, nor did he deny her. And from the glint of warning in his eyes, she knew better than to even consider trying to escape him again.

"A few moments," he said finally. "No more, demoiselle."

Griffin watched her storm off into the woods, her slender spine held rigid as a lance. He knew he had upset her, knew her wanting to be away from him probably had more to do with her offended principles than it did with answering nature's call. It didn't really matter, so long as she would not be foolish enough to use his permission as a chance to slip away. He rather doubted she would. As odious as she likely found him, she needed him if she was going to make it to Montborne and her betrothed.

And he needed her betrothed's reward if he was ever going to get away from what he had allowed himself to become during the past few years at Droghallow.

Isabel had been right when she said it was difficult to tell him apart from Dom. He had been coming to that conclusion himself in recent days, though he had not paused to give it much thought until now. Not until Isabel had so justly accused him of a lack of honor.

He thought about Lady Alys now, too, and Sir Robert. How disappointed they both would be to see him now, how rightly appalled. He and all his talk of chivalry and greatness and worthy, noble quests. It was nothing more than youthful nonsense, the shattered dreams of a man whose hands had since been stained with blood and villainy. Considering it now, he wasn't entirely sure that any amount of silver would change what he had become in his heart: a mercenary knight with less virtue than a back alley whore.

The morose direction of his thoughts was diverted when he heard movement coming from the area of the brook. He had left his haughty little hostage alone for ample time to relieve herself; perhaps she had decided to take to the stream and make her escape after all. Tossing aside his cup of wine, Griff stalked down the embankment and past his mount, his eyes trained to spot Isabel's pale green gown and copper pate amongst the similarly resplendent palette of the autumn woods.

He caught sight of her a few short yards down from their camp, where a large granite boulder thrust out of the bramble and into the stream, creating a bend in the water's flow, and a flat dry surface on which she sat. She had rinsed her face and was now in the process of plaiting her hair; the long auburn tresses hung over the front of her shoulder in damp waves, their shade nearly burgundy having been wetted from the stream. She combed through the silken mass with her fingers, her face turned up to the sun, eyes closed.

Griff wondered how often she had been able to enjoy the simplicity of a pleasant afternoon spent outdoors, how often her head had been bared to the sun since she had been sent to live in the convent. The girl he recalled seemed the sort to relish freedom and the ability to follow her whims; there was an unspoken sadness about the woman he saw before him now, as if she had somehow come to understand that freedom and fancy had their price.

He supposed he had already done a great deal to prove

the fact in the few hours they had unwillingly spent together.

Watching the smooth line of her throat, the delicate arc of her neck as she stretched to feel the full warmth of the sun's rays, Griff wondered what else he might be tempted to prove in the days—and nights—that were yet to come between here and Montborne. Hungrily, his eyes drifted lower, to the rise of her breasts, the bodice of her seafoam-colored bliaut wet in places from her dripping hair. The water must have been cold, for her nipples had risen to hard buds beneath her gown, two perfect pearls that hinted at the loveliness of her firm round breasts. She moved with the innate grace of a feline, her arms lithe and slender, her elegant white fingers rhythmically stroking her hair as she weaved it into a thick plaited rope, unaware of the predatory gaze fixed on her across the way.

Griff's blood quickened while he stood there, intruding on her privacy and stealing this glimpse of her like the base thief she had accused him of being. Lust pooled swift and heavy in his loins when she finished off her braid and leaned back on the boulder, propped on her elbows in a position that called to everything that was elemental and wild in him.

He wanted her, and in the past that had usually been enough. He had never stooped to rape; seduction had always proven far more sporting. But when he looked at Isabel in that moment, something primal stirred inside him, something that whispered insidiously of how he truly was no better than Dom. No less an animal in so many other ways, so why not this?

Though he did not move, could hardly breathe for the torment of his own thoughts, Isabel suddenly sat up. Her eyes flew open to meet his heated stare. Griffin said nothing, his every muscle tense. His senses measured the moment, noting the way her lips parted to suck in a gasp of air, her fingers trembled as she brought them down into her lap. She watched him, her gaze uncertain and not a little fearful. Then she slid off the rock and stood against it, looking small and cornered and far too innocent for the indecent bent of his thinking.

"We've delayed here long enough," he growled when the wary silence stretched out between them. "I know of a village a few hours out where we can find shelter and supplies. We'd best be on our way."

Isabel said nothing as she hastened past him, her eyes downcast, hands gathered protectively at her neck. She said nothing to him for the rest of that day's ride, either, their collective mood as heavy as the dark rain clouds that were beginning to bunch in overhead, creeping down from the northern sky.

Chapter Nine

A cold, sprinkling rain followed them well until dusk. Griff considered the inclement weather to be something of a blessing, for it kept the roads and woodland trails they traveled all but deserted. Only a few straggling peasants remained in their fields when he and Isabel arrived at the village where Griff hoped to find shelter for the night.

The tiny hamlet crouched along Droghallow's northernmost border, comprising little more than a handful of cottages and a humble tavern, a way station that Griff and his men had used on occasion when business for Dom brought them to the area. Though he doubted the simple folk would recognize him without his retinue of soldiers, as Griff guided his mount along the village road, he kept his head low, his face turned away as if to shield himself from the spitting drizzle. Isabel was nestled against him as she had been for most of the day's trek, presently obscured from view by the wide edge of Griffin's mantle tucked around her shoulders.

They attracted scarcely the mildest of interest as they passed, the villeins more focused on returning their goats and cattle to their pens for the eve than they were on the bedraggled pair of pilgrims. Nor did anyone take notice when, near the outskirts of the retiring burgh, Griff slowed his mount and walked it off the road toward one of the village's storage barns.

"Where are you going?" Isabel asked quietly as he dismounted, the first words she had spoken to him since they had stopped earlier in the day. "Are we to stay here for the night?"

" 'Tis as good a place as any," Griff answered as he pulled her from the saddle.

He tried the door of the outbuilding and was pleased to find it unlatched. Inside, the large shed was dark and warm. It smelled invitingly of fresh hay and fleece, the vague oily-musky scent wafting off the bales of wool that were stored there from the last shearing. The spacious barn held ample room for the both of them and Griff's horse, a fine alternative indeed to spending the night in the rain.

"Come," he said to Isabel when she hesitated outside. "We'll be safe here."

She followed him in, seating herself on a plump sack of fleece as Griff led his mount past and began to remove the gray's saddle and riding gear. He heard her yawn behind him and by the time he turned to offer her a blanket, he found that she was already fast asleep, curled up and slumbering like a babe.

Griff strode over and covered her with his mantle, taking care not to wake her. She would need her rest, for tomorrow they would have to make haste; the more distance they could put between them and Droghallow, the better. Indeed, he thought wryly, and the more distance he could put between himself and lovely Isabel, the better. Despite efforts to convince himself otherwise, she was fast becoming pure temptation, a distraction he damned well did not need—not when a careless inattention could cost both of them their lives.

He supposed that that determination had been at the root of his behavior earlier in the glade, when he had knowingly, deliberately, provoked her anger. He did not want her to look upon him with favor or fond regard, and so he had mocked her, from the harsh exaggeration of his initial impression of her as a halfwit little girl wandering lost in

Droghallow's woods, to his scorn of the kindhearted young woman who had painstakingly restored, preserved, and borne around her own delicate neck the misplaced medallion of a boy she knew nothing about and would, had fate not intervened, likely never see again. Even now, with the small bronze half disc lying cold and solid against his chest, Griffin could scarcely believe he had it back.

At last.

After ten long years of scouring every inch of the woods in vain, a decade spent regretting the cherished pendant's loss, finally, he had it back. It was all he had of his true family, the only tangible bit of evidence existing in this world to give him even a hint of who he was. He would never part with it; his flippant statement that he would pawn it on first chance had been a bald-faced lie intended to mask what it actually meant to him—what it meant to him to know that Isabel had cared for the amulet on his behalf all this time. He could scarcely reconcile his good fortune, no more than he could fathom the intriguing woman who had brought it to him after so many years.

Lady Alys, second wife to Robert of Droghallow and the only mother Griffin had ever known, once said to him that nobility was something a person carried in his heart, not hung about his neck like a chain of gold. At the time, Griffin had thought it to be just a pretty saying intended to soothe the feelings of a dejected young boy who had lost the only thing of value he had ever possessed, but now, looking at Isabel, he had to wonder.

For what had not been the first time, he pictured her reclining on the rock near the stream, instead imagining her lying there unclothed, welcoming. He relived the moment he had kissed her in Droghallow's keep, as well, remembering all too vividly the sensual meeting of their mouths, the savage quickening of his blood, the keen response of his body to hers. He wanted to know that feeling again—knew he would, in fact, if given half a chance. While carnal pleasure was a pursuit he seldom shied away from, defiling doe-eyed virgins had never been to his taste. And only a man with fool's lack of sense would risk any portion of his anticipated reward by delivering the Earl of Montborne's affianced in a condition even so much as a shade less than healthy, hale, and wholly untouched.

Griff had been called many unflattering things in his life, but never a fool. He had no intention of forfeiting any chance at his boon, but still, it didn't stop him from wondering. It didn't stop him from wanting.

He did not know how many hours he remained awake, watching Isabel sleep, contemplating the road that lay ahead of him now that he had turned his back on Droghallow. Griff had let the night pass in thoughtful silence, allowing himself to close his eyes for short snatches of time at most, too restless for sleep, too aware of the precariousness of their circumstances to let down his guard. It was not until the first traces of dawn began to filter in through the cracks in the barn's warped wooden walls that Griff decided to see about procuring them some supplies for the rest of their journey. Trusting that Isabel would be more secure secreted away in the shed than out in the open with him, Griff buckled on his sword belt and headed outside.

He had taken with him all the money he saved at Droghallow, collected in a leather pouch he wore on his baldric. A few of the coins were sufficient to bribe the tavern keeper out of bed and purchase food enough to last Isabel and him for at least two days of travel. Griff's stomach began to growl as he waited for the stout old man to pack up his goods: a full skin of wine, a hank of cold mutton and two loaves of black bread. With a murmured thanks, he took the bounty under his arm and stepped out into the crisp, dewy morning.

Though he saw no one about, Griff sensed he was being watched. He walked along the road, taking care to look casual, even as his gaze scanned every croft and cottage for lurking signs of attack. He felt movement shift and pause around him, knew with a warrior's certainty that he was being followed. Immediately, his concern flew to Isabel: Where was she? Had she remained in the barn? Was she safe?

His protective instincts flared, but Griffin willed his feet to keep moving at an easy gait, forced them to walk in the direction opposite the wool shed once he had stepped off the road and headed for the village outbuildings. He waited for signs that whoever shadowed him was still on his heels, unwittingly following him some yards away from Isabel's hiding place.

Confirmation of his suspicions came an instant later, communicated by way of a sword being freed from its scabbard behind him.

Griff tossed down his bundle of foodstuffs and met the confrontation with equal menace, drawing his blade and wheeling on his attacker.

"I expected I might find you here, Griff."

Odo grinned at him from the other end of his blade, but his weapon remained level, unwavering and poised for action.

"Where is the rest of the guard?" Griffin asked, trying to ascertain his chances now that it appeared he was as good as caught. He could only hope he was not too terribly outnumbered. "Don't tell me Dom dispatched but one man out to apprehend me."

Odo shook his head. "He's sent the bulk of the garrison after you, but while they took the road north, I took a shorter path. Figured I'd catch up to you sooner or later."

So, it was just Odo he had to contend with at the moment. Griff battened down his instant sense of relief; he had seen the big knight in action on many occasions, often enough to know that Odo was every bit as apt as any three of Droghallow's other guards put together.

"You shouldn't have done it, Griff. This thing Dom's hatching is serious business. It may even involve London, if the hasty message he sent to Prince John is any indication." When Griffin did not respond, Odo added, "Dom's put a thousand marks on the woman's head—double on yours. A man could do a lot with that much silver."

Griffin chuckled, not at all surprised by the news that Dom had offered a bounty for his capture. "Don't count your reward so soon," he told Odo. "You're a long way from collecting."

The lieutenant tilted his huge head, his unruly beard splitting with his humorless smile. He took a careful step sideways, his grip tightening visibly on his weapon in preparation for combat. Griffin mirrored the action, beginning a wary circle of move and countermove as each man sized up the other and weighed his chances of winning.

"Let's not make this into a war between friends," Odo said, firming his stance in the mud-slicked yard. "After all, I've naught against you, Griff. In fact, I'd be willing to let you walk away. Just give me the woman."

Griff snorted. "Forget it."

The big knight seemed to consider for a moment. "We could split the money," he suggested. "What say you? 'Twould be an easy five hundred apiece."

"The woman stays with me," Griffin said.

"I should warn you," Odo growled, "I'm in a piss poor mood from riding all night in the rain. I haven't the head for games. I came here to get the Montborne wench, and I'm not leaving without her."

Griffin shook his head. "You'll have to go through me first."

"Very well," Odo answered with a nod.

He let his blade relax slightly as if he meant to back down, then, in the next heartbeat, he raised it high and swung at Griffin. The two weapons clashed against each other, the grating sound of metal on metal ringing out and slicing through the tranquility of the waking morn. Odo charged again with lethal force and relentless determination, cleaving the air with his broadsword and hitting Griffin's blade with a jarring series of heavy, solid blows.

A few peasants came out of their huts amid the ruckus, opening doors and poking heads out from window shutters to peer about, only to scurry back inside like timid mice when their sleepy eyes lit on the combat underway.

At first, Griff could only strive to defend against the attacks, deflecting Odo's thrusts with the flat of his weapon while each hammering strike sent him back a pace, his feet squishing and slipping in the muddy yards of the village. A careless stumble over a rut gave Odo the upper hand and cost Griffin a gash on his arm. It was more of an annoyance than a threat to his life, but the metallic smell of blood and the searing pain of sliced flesh served to bring his senses— and his battle rage—into clear focus.

Odo was grinning as he came at Griffin once more, driving him backward with a full body press of his blade. Griff pushed against him, then spun away in the next instant, using the big knight's momentum to his own advantage and sending the guard pitching forward. Whirling to face Odo's snarling return, Griffin raised his sword and brought it down hard. The two blades crashed against each other, sparking with the contact. Odo's curse was vivid, a guttural snarl that left no doubt he was out for blood. With murder flashing in his eyes, the bearlike knight barreled forward.

Though he was a fairly equal match for Droghallow's lieutenant, it was all Griffin could do to meet the thrusts delivered upon him. For every pace he advanced on Odo, the guard forced him back two more, cleaving and hacking from all sides, relentless in his apparent intent to see Griffin skewered on his blade. Chickens squawked and scattered around them as the fight moved farther into the village commons. Rain spat down in icy needles from the char-gray sky, sluicing off Griff's brow and dripping into his eyes as he fought to deflect the onslaught of hammering blows. Before he realized it, his spine came up against the unyielding mass of a cottar's hut. Odo's blade flashed in the dim morning sunlight an instant before it bit into the wattle-and-daub exterior next to Griffin's head, only narrowly missing its mark.

Griff dodged the blow and ducked down low while the guard worked to free his weapon. He made good use of Odo's momentary distraction, plowing into the big knight's gut with his shoulder and knocking him to the ground on his back. Without a moment wasted on pity, Griff raised his sword and sent it home, driving the blade deep into Odo's barrel chest. Odo sucked in a broken gasp of air, then breathed his last through a pained grimace, his eyes wide with shock but still blazing with malice. Griff waited to withdraw his blade until those flinty eyes turned sightless, unblinking as the rain pattered down into them.

The death of the man who had served with Griff for nigh on a decade brought him no measure of satisfaction, nor did it bring much relief. The road ahead was a long one, and now that Dom was offering so steep a reward for their capture, they would find little peace along the way. They were on their own as never before, and time would quickly become their enemy.

With a handful of peasants looking on from the relative safety of their huts, Griff gathered up the bundle of food he had bought from the tavern and headed back for the wool shed to rouse Isabel. He noticed Odo's waiting mount tethered near the road and freed the brown destrier to take it with him. Now he and Isabel had two horses for their journey.

Griff had a feeling they were going to need all the help they could get in making it to Montborne before Dom's machinations—or his royal allies in London—caught up to them.

Chapter Ten

Isabel had been awake for a short while, feeding Griffin's mount a handful of carrots from out of the saddle packs and wondering where its master might have gone. She did not have to wonder long, for in the next instant the door of the wool barn swung open and in rushed Griffin.

"We must go now, my lady," he told her in an urgent tone as he strode past her to ready his horse.

"What's wrong? What happened to you?" Isabel asked, taking in his disheveled appearance with a quick, worrisome glance. He looked like a ragged tomcat, his clothing soiled and torn, his tawny hair sweat-soaked and tousled, his face marred by grime and fresh bruises. "You're bleeding," she gasped when she caught sight of his left arm, the ugly crimson stains and sliced linen sleeve clearly the work of an enemy's blade.

He seemed entirely unfazed by her concern or his injuries. Having saddled the gray, Griffin then unhitched the reins and led the beast forward. "We've been found," he told her simply, as he grasped her hand in his and ushered her out of the barn to where another horse stood waiting.

Isabel saw the Droghallow crest on the brown destrier's saddle blanket and stopped dead in her tracks, frozen by a sudden jolt of panic.

Griffin must have sensed her worry, for he squeezed her hand a little tighter and urged her forward. " 'Tis all right. I took care of the guard who rode it."

"Dom's men have caught up to us already?"

"Only the one for now," Griffin answered as he helped her up onto his mount. "The rest of the garrison will follow soon enough, I wager. They have ample incentive, as Dom has sent word of our flight to Prince John and put a bounty on our return."

"A bounty? For both of us?"

Griffin handed her the gray's reins. "A thousand marks for you, two for me."

"Mother Mary," Isabel gasped, astonished at the price.

A thousand marks was a small fortune, but twice that sum? She could hardly fathom it. How deeply Dom must hate Griffin for betraying his trust. If he would pay so much to have him returned to Droghallow, Isabel could only guess at what tortures Griffin would suffer at Dom's hands. Would Dom kill him? It certainly seemed a logical assumption, given the circumstances.

Isabel watched as Griffin loosened the saddle of the other horse and pulled off the blanket. The square of wool bearing the Droghallow crest was pitched in a heap on the ground. Griffin's face schooled to a calm, even expression, while Isabel fairly trembled with outright fear at the thought of their being hunted fugitives. "Are you certain you wish to do this, Griffin?" she asked him softly as he readjusted the saddle and mounted up. "I assure you I will understand if you were to reconsider. I have a horse now; just point me toward Montborne and I will go alone."

He all but ignored her offer. "We can't risk taking the direct route to Montborne now that Dom's guards are in pursuit. I know of an alternate way, but it will mean a longer ride. It will cost us a few more days, but it seems our best chance."

Isabel met his serious gaze, bolstered by his confidence. He was going to take her to Montborne, despite the personal risks. Perhaps he was doing so for his own selfish reasons, but in that moment, Isabel could not help feeling somewhat selfish herself. She was terrified now more than ever, and the last thing she wanted was to be left alone, even when the most sensible thing for Griffin to do was to abandon her and instead concentrate on saving his own neck.

She wondered how many men would do likewise. She also wondered how long it would take Griffin to decide that perhaps she was not worth the trouble after all. Secretly relieved for his companionship, broody as it generally was, Isabel followed Griffin's galloping mount out of the village and onto the northbound road.

It was raining again. What had started off as an annoying sprinkle had become an earnest downpour by midafternoon. Griffin's clothing was soaked, the heavy wet wool a wearisome weight that chilled him to the bone and drew out the ache of old battle wounds he had thought long forgotten. But it was Isabel that concerned him more. She rode along at his side, wrapped in his mantle and shivering from the cold. Twice in the last hour he had asked her if she wished to stop; twice she had refused, stating that she was well enough to continue and wanted to make all due haste for Montborne.

The news that Dom had issued bounties and dispatched his guards to apprehend them had frightened Isabel, that much was plain. She no longer seemed preoccupied with anger or thoughts of escaping him, but rather focused her energies on cooperation, compelling Griff to press on when even he would have preferred to pause for rest.

He found her stubborn tenacity endearing, particularly now that it was better aligned with his own interests. Ordinarily, Griff was a man who had no patience for a woman's willfulness, but he had to admit that with Isabel it was different. Her strength of spirit intrigued him, perhaps more so than the considerable beauty of her person. He looked at her, a convent-raised dove with a falcon's stout heart, and found himself wanting to know her thoughts. He was curious to understand how her mind worked, to learn what mattered to her.

Clearly, she wanted to wed Sebastian of Montborne. But why? That the earl was rich, handsome, and well-favored by the king was reason enough for any woman to leap at the chance to be his wife. Was it enough for Isabel? She had said that her vow to God was what compelled her, not any measure of esteem or attraction for her betrothed. She had said Griff would not understand her reasons for wishing to marry the earl of Montborne. What did she seek to hide? Was there a stain on her sterling honor? Would she risk her life merely for a chance to buy her way out of ignominy?

Griff nearly chuckled aloud on the heels of that thought. How ironic for him to disapprove of Isabel's motives when he was guilty of the very same intention. Perhaps she was more like him than he might have guessed. One thing was for certain: before their journey ended, Griff meant to find out.

Up ahead, less than a half league away, he spied the knotted outline of a village and overlooking castle perched at the top of a sloping hill. Isabel saw it, too. She raised her head and stared through the rain, her gaze fixed on the inviting glow of torches that lined the village's curtain wall and fortress tower. Without direction from its rider, the gray destrier paused on the path. Sensing that Isabel no longer followed, Griff slowed Odo's mount to a halt and pivoted in the saddle to look behind him.

"It has been a long day. Shall we stop, my lady?"

She gave a weak shake of her head. He wondered if the cold rain had robbed her of her tongue, as well as her sense, for her lips were blue, her cheeks sallow and pale. Beneath his drenched mantle, her shoulders shook; her fingers trembled as she tried to hold on to the gray's reins. When she sneezed, Griff cursed and wheeled his steed around.

"Come, Isabel, before you fall off the blasted beast."

Griffin took the reins from her hands with little effort and led her mount behind him, making sure she remained upright as he negotiated the muddy fields and gullies standing between them and dry lodging. Along the way, he manufactured a lie that he hoped would gain them entrance to the gated town. Getting in would be simple enough for a traveling husband and wife, but Griff knew a woman of Isabel's beauty and obvious gentility would stir overmuch interest. Even bedraggled and sodden she could not be mistaken for a common pilgrim. If they were to hide in plain sight as Griff intended, they would have to blend in with the rest of the folk seeking shelter for the evening. And that meant Isabel would have to don some manner of disguise.

Griff lit on an idea as they approached a tavern on the outskirts of the village. Set away from the other huts and outbuildings, it was clear that the business of this establishment was of questionable character—disreputable, and, Griff hoped, passably discreet. He stopped outside the tavern and instructed Isabel to wait there while he ran in. He returned a few moments later, having made arrangements to purchase what he required. Head down to shield herself from the relentless rain, Isabel scarcely looked up as Griffin took the leads of both horses and guided them around to the back of the thatch-roofed building. A whore of middling age stood at the rear door, holding it open while Griff helped Isabel down from his mount.

"What is this place?" she asked weakly as he ushered her inside. "Where are we?"

The whore took it upon herself to answer. "Ye're at Hexford, love. Four leagues west of Nottingham."

Isabel seized Griffin's arm. "Nottingham?" she gasped. "But Prince John is often in that shire!"

Griff chuckled, giving Isabel's hand an indulgent pat when the whore turned a curious look on them. "My lady was raised in the country," he explained smoothly. "The notion of glimpsing a member of the royal family is a source of great excitement for her."

The whore snorted. "Well, ye won't be seeing Lackland around here. Word has it that the prince has been in London all the past month."

Much relieved for that bit of news, Griff wrapped his arm around Isabel's shoulders and guided her down the short corridor where the whore led. She brought them to a small, dank room, devoid of comforts except for a matted straw pallet and a single chair, over which was slung a dark wool kirtle. She picked up the garment and held it out to Griffin. "Here ye are, m'lord, just like ye asked. Though I wager 'twill be a speck large for yer lady."

"It will do," Griff said as he placed a coin in the whore's open palm and took the gown from her. When he realized how earnestly she peered at Isabel, trying to get a look at her from around Griff's shoulder, he deliberately stepped into her line of sight. "My wife and I are weary from our travels. We would appreciate a moment of privacy."

The whore scowled and began a reluctant shuffle toward the open door. "Don't tarry overlong, m'lord. Mind ye, this room is my business."

Griff nodded, waiting only long enough for the woman to cross the threshold before he closed the rickety oak panel on her heels. Behind him, Isabel shivered and blew out a quavery sigh.

"Here, my lady," he said to her, turning and offering her the whore's kirtle. "Let us get you out of those wet clothes."

Isabel's gaze snapped to him in shock. "Disrobe?"

"You're soaked and freezing, and it would be foolhardy to let you walk into the castle keep in a noblewoman's silk gown when for all we know half the countryside could be searching for a lady of your description. We will draw less attention garbed as common pilgrims."

"Oh . . . of course, you are right." She took the gown from him and held it to her breast, but made no immediate move to comply. It took a long moment of expectant silence for Griff to realize that she was waiting for him to leave the room.

"We've no time for modesty," he told her, his tone more impatient than he had intended. He was tired, cold, hungry, and aching, none of which helped his present mood. And he still had to secure them a space in the castle. If they delayed much longer, the gates could close and they would be forced to seek shelter elsewhere or spend the night outdoors. It was a prospect Griff did not particularly relish. "Change quickly, my lady. I will turn my back until you are finished."

He positioned himself near the door, while behind him, Isabel began to undress. He heard her unfasten the clasp on his mantle, heard the heavy wet fabric slide down the length of her and crush softly on the floor. Her teeth were chattering, her breath shallow and tremulous as she set to work on her gown, gathering up the skirt and pulling the sodden green silk up over her head. An instant later, it, too, fell to the floor.

Griff concentrated on what his eyes could see, counting the knots in the warped oak panels before him, trying to judge the age of the ancient leather hinges—anything to keep from imagining Isabel standing behind him wearing naught but a rain-drenched chemise. The very thought sent a bolt of lust shooting through him. Griffin clamped his jaw tight, willing away this unwanted awareness.

Isabel, thankfully, seemed wholly oblivious to his discomfort. She was making little progress suddenly, struggling now with something on her chemise. Finally, she let out a huff of frustration. "Griffin?" she asked, her voice soft and hesitant. "Will you . . . I can't untie the laces . . ."

Griff felt his every muscle clench taut as a bowstring in reaction to her innocent plea for help. Slowly, he turned around to face her. If he thought himself tense with want before, it was nothing compared to what he felt when his eyes lit on Isabel in that moment.

The flimsy chemise clung indecently to every curve and swell of her body, hugging her breasts and hips and thighs like a glove of wet linen. The drenched fabric hinted at the dusky hue of her nipples, perfect pearls, puckered beneath their sodden veil. Griff noted with an appreciative eye how flat and soft her abdomen was, the sweet indentation of her navel, her flawless skin pale against the nearly transparent undergarment and a pleasing contrast to the dark, enticing shadow of her femininity. His arousal stirred swiftly, an inopportune, if inevitable, reaction to the vision standing before him. He nearly had to shake himself to keep from staring.

Isabel had crossed her arms over her breasts, rubbing her shoulders and still shivering, though whether it was from cold or the hungry look Griffin had likely turned on her, he could not be sure.

"I think I have managed to snarl the laces at my back," she said as he stalked toward her.

Griff came up behind her without a word. He had not realized his hands were clenched into fists until he reached up to sweep aside Isabel's mass of hair. This close, he could tell that she had recently washed her hair in rosewater; the scent lingered on her as he gathered up the thick auburn tresses and draped them over her shoulder. It was all he could do to resist the urge to touch the lily-fair skin of her bare neck, to place his lips against her delicate nape to see if she tasted as sweet as she looked.

Instead, he turned his attention to the knotted laces of her chemise, cursing when his big fingers only worsened the tangled ties. He worked at the knots relentlessly, until at last, they loosened and fell away. Griff pulled apart the zigzagging closure of the undergarment, then stepped away before he was tempted to help Isabel out of it entirely.

"Thank you," she murmured, to which Griffin could only growl.

He turned away once more, waiting impatiently as she stripped off the chemise and donned the dry gown. Her sigh of pleasure as the warm wool covered her body was pure torture to him, a satisfied exhalation that was all too easy to imagine in another setting, issuing forth from another cause.

"Very well, I am dressed," she said, speaking more brightly than he had heard her in the past couple of days. Already the benefit of dry clothing and warmth had renewed her; it would take a lot more than that to soothe Griff's mood. "You may turn around now."

" 'Tis about time," he drawled sullenly.

"Have you a plan for getting us into the castle?" she asked as he turned to face her. "What will you tell the guards to gain us access?"

"That we are husband and wife," Griff answered. "Common folk, en route to your family in the north when we were caught in the rain."

He did not miss her slight flinch when he said they were to pose as a married couple. Did she find the idea intriguing or repulsive? He could not be sure, but even in the candlelight he could see the tint of color rise into her cheeks. To her credit, she said nothing of her obvious discomfort with his plan. Instead she turned a thoughtful frown on him. "How do you expect to explain away your own appearance, my lord?"

"My own—"

Isabel gestured toward his face and left side in explanation, and Griffin cursed. He had all but forgotten about the injuries he had received in his skirmish with Odo. He looked down at his arm, inspecting the torn, bloodied sleeve and the messy gash beneath it.

"Here," Isabel said gently. "Let me have a look."

Before he realized it, she was at his side. Carefully, she

gathered up the fabric of his sleeve and raised it past the place where Odo's sword had taken a bite of him. Using the edge of her damp chemise, she dabbed at the dried blood that was now crusted around the wound, her fingers light, tender. In truth, she need not have been so delicate for the cut hardly pained him. But Griff was loath to tell her so; he was enjoying her attention far more than he should have.

Indeed, if the idea of posing as his wife was unpleasant to her, she would have been appalled to know the increasingly illicit path his thoughts had begun to take. The memory of her exquisite body shrouded in wet linen, the feel of her hands on his skin as she touched him now, her unbound hair cascading over her slim shoulders and down the graceful curve of her back—all of it twined together into a potent spell that had him imagining what it might be like to be her wedded husband.

To be the man who would bed her for the first time and teach her about the endless wonders of pleasure and passion.

It was a ludicrous musing—the very last thing he needed to be thinking about—but that did not make the wanting cease. In that moment, as Isabel's innocent ministrations went from the gash on his arm to the bruises that marred his cheek and jaw, Griffin knew a keen and unabating desire.

She rubbed the soft linen of her makeshift cloth over his brow and cheek, then touched it to the corner of his mouth, blotting away the grime and blood left from the morning's violence. Her hand seemed to linger there, long enough that Griffin entertained the very compelling notion of reaching up and taking her by the wrist to pull her closer to him. He could tell her he did it as part of their ruse, that to be convincing as man and wife they would have to be willing to touch, to embrace, to kiss, like two people accustomed to intimacy. He could tell her that it was all part of their game, that she had to trust him. That she had no choice.

He could manufacture a hundred reasons to convince her of his need to feel her body pressed against his, a thousand lies to cover the truth of how he burned for her . . .

Isabel glanced up suddenly and met his gaze. For a heartbeat, a moment filled with silence and certain, shared awareness, she held his unblinking stare. But then, as if she sensed the danger of his thoughts, she sucked in a small breath and drew back from him. Her gaze darted away, shuttered by the sweep of long lashes. "That should do well enough," she said in a rush of words. "You don't look quite so dreadful now."

Griff chuckled, but his blood was still thrumming in his veins. "Dreadful looking, am I?"

Isabel threw him a shy glance. "No. Not so much . . . now."

"Well, I am glad to hear you say it, *wife,*" he teased, surprised at how easily the false endearment tumbled off his tongue. "After all, it would not do to have my bride recoiling each time she looks upon me."

The moment lost, Griffin pushed up his right sleeve to match the length of the left while Isabel turned away and busied herself on the other side of the small room, folding up her soiled chemise and green silk gown. "Do you really think your plan will get us into the castle?" she asked, her brows drawn together.

"Getting in will not be the difficult part. But keeping our identity secret once we are there may well pose a problem. I suppose it would be too much to hope for that we be left to ourselves the entire time."

Isabel glanced up from what she was doing. "I could pretend to be sick. We could say I am ill from the weather. No one will bother a woman beleaguered with ague."

"No one will house her," Griff corrected. "No, there

must be another way to explain our want for solitude without raising suspicions."

He glanced at the folded bulk of Isabel's gown and suddenly had an idea. He strode over and picked it up, rolling it into a round bundle, which he then presented to Isabel. "Place this under your skirt. Your girdle should hold it in place at your waist."

She gave him a skeptical look as she accepted the ball of rumpled silk. "Very well, but I don't understand how my being plump will serve us."

Griff shook his head. "Not plump, Isabel. Pregnant. Sick with our first child."

Without affording her the chance to protest, he grasped her by the hand and hauled her out of the room, ready to begin their ruse and praying they would be able to pull it off.

Chapter Eleven

Griffin was right about the ease with which they gained access to the castle. His story, along with a silver coin passed discreetly to the gatekeeper, earned them a stall for their horses and space among the folk in the castle's great hall. They were directed up the wide motte that led to the tower keep, instructed to follow the other travelers seeking shelter there that eve. Rain still slanted down from the darkening skies, turning the path to mud and slowing the group's ascent to the castle.

Warm and dry under Griffin's mantle, Isabel hardly noticed the continuing deluge.

Her mind swam with anxiety for the many untold perils that likely yet awaited them on this journey. This stop for shelter was but a pause before they would be back on the road, a short reprieve before they would be back on the run from Droghallow's men. And there was another danger worrying Isabel, too.

The danger of what she was starting to feel for Griffin.

As much as she tried to hold on to her anger and wariness, Isabel had to admit her mistrust of him was beginning to thaw. Indeed, when she thought of him, she felt as if her whole body was slowly melting from somewhere deep inside, warming to the man she should despise.

Heaven help her, but whenever he was near, she experienced the queerest sensation in her belly, a fluttery anticipation, a mad sense of hopeful expectation that Griffin might find her attractive, that he might want to touch her. When she'd found herself staring into his eyes in the seclusion of the tavern's back room, she'd had the unshakable feeling that he might have wanted to kiss her.

But he had not, and she knew she should be relieved.

She should be thinking of Sebastian of Montborne, of her sister's welfare, not contemplating her growing attraction to her captor and enemy. Except Griffin was feeling less of an enemy with each passing hour. Now that they were both declared fugitives, he seemed more of a partner in some strange way, and she his witting accomplice.

More vexing to Isabel's mind was the fact that she found it entirely too easy to pretend to be his wife. It took precious little effort to imagine them partners in life, to make believe that the ruse of her pregnancy was instead real, that her belly swelled with their child and not a bundle of damp silk.

Chagrined for her sinful, wayward thoughts, Isabel lowered her head, pulling the hood of Griffin's mantle low over her brow.

"We're almost there," he said softly beside her, startling her when he reached over and placed his hand on hers in a soothing gesture. "I'll have you out of this rain as soon as I can."

She could not help smiling at his consideration. That he would be concerned for her well-being when he was still soaked to the bone confused her as much as it comforted her. Or was this sudden kindness part of his act? she wondered. Was he merely beginning their ruse of man and wife before they entered the keep? If he pretended now, he did so without the benefit of an audience, for no one in the group of pilgrims traveling with them on the path to the castle paid them any mind. Isabel glanced from his reassuring expression to their joined hands, which were wet from the rain but warm for their mingled contact.

Far more belatedly than was prudent, she felt guilty for

enjoying the polite intimacy of his touch and withdrew her fingers from his grasp. From the corner of her eye, she watched as he slowly retracted his hand and settled back on his mount, his gaze finally leaving her, returning to the flinty coolness she had first known.

His mood remained brooding and aloof even after they settled into the great hall of Hexford Castle. At a trestle table near the back of the enormous chamber, Isabel and Griffin took their places among the common folk. The room buzzed with activity and conversation, a scene as welcoming to Isabel as a thick wool blanket after several days on the run.

Torches burned in black iron sconces affixed to the walls no more than ten paces apart. In the hearth at the center of the hall a fire blazed, its warm glow and radiant heat chasing away the persistent chill of the damp outdoors. If the comfortable climate inside the hall was not enough to make one forget their troubles for a while, the aromas of roasting meat and fresh baked bread being borne to the tables on large platters certainly was. Isabel's stomach growled as the food and wine was served to the high table and then the rest of the hall. She could hardly wait to partake of the steaming viands, her eyes widening in delight as she and Griffin were given a trencher filled with lamb stew and boiled cabbage. They shared their meal and drank from the same cup of wine, observing the eating custom that was commonplace among married couples of all ranks.

While Griffin's grim countenance dissuaded anyone from engaging him in conversation, Isabel was not so fortunate. The other ladies at their table chattered on about one thing or another, making every attempt to include Isabel in their gossip and idle talk. Isabel obliged as courteously as she dared, nodding and smiling when appropriate and keeping her own comments limited to the awful weather and compliments for the hearty fare presented them by Lord and Lady Hexford.

The titled couple sat at the dais, flanked at the high table by their children and an elderly priest from a neighboring parish, who said sacrament over the meal. Throughout the supper, Isabel found herself staring at the Hexfords' little daughter, a cheerful, freckle-faced waif of perhaps six summers. She laughed easily, charming everyone in the hall with her gaiety and bubbly demeanor. Isabel giggled aloud when the girl stole a cherry from the old priest's dessert and popped it in her mouth. When he realized his plate had been vandalized, the white-haired clergy merely slanted a chiding look at the impish thief and wagged his finger at her in mild reproach.

"That one's going to be trouble," one of the women at Isabel and Griffin's table remarked.

"Aye, she's a handful already," another agreed. "Pray ye don't have a girl, leastwise not as yer first child. Boys are much easier to raise."

It took a moment for Isabel to realize that the woman was speaking to her. "Oh," she said finally, glancing down at the still-surprising bulge of her stomach. "I'm sure it will make no difference whatsoever. I will be happy either way."

She made the mistake of looking at Griffin as she said it and felt herself grow warm all the way to her scalp. He was staring at her intensely, his green-gold eyes unreadable and impossibly steady, refusing to release her gaze. Isabel wondered what he was thinking in that moment, wondered what to make of his serious expression and the hard, contemplative set of his mouth. Did he feel as awkward as she? He certainly did not seem uncomfortable, staring at her so pointedly, almost indecently. Isabel's face flamed an even deeper shade of red.

The women seated around them began to titter with amusement.

"Heavy with child and still blushing like a virgin," a

middle-aged woman seated across from Isabel commented. "Isn't that the sweetest thing ye've ever seen?"

The man beside her chuckled. " 'Twas not so long ago that ye were a winsome bride yerself, Gert. And I can still make ye blush on occasion. Especially when I do that thing with yer—" He whispered something in his wife's ear and the matron burst out in a flurry of scandalized giggles.

"Beast!" she gasped, slapping him playfully on the shoulder.

The table dissolved into a round of shared jests and good humor, but Isabel scarcely noticed. She finished the rest of her meal quickly, feeling terribly conspicuous as Griffin fed her from his poniard. She shared his goblet of wine, drinking more than she was accustomed to in her sudden thirst and continued state of anxiety.

The mellow warmth of the mulled wine and the droning buzz of mingled conversations in the hall made Isabel grow reflective. The community of her surroundings made her think about the life she once knew, a life outside the isolation of the abbey and not so unlike the one Hexford's lord and lady enjoyed with their family and friends. She could recall gatherings such as this, with her mother and father seated at the dais, laughing, sharing drink and company with the many people who would come to call. She recalled other, quieter gatherings, too, when she and her parents would retire to the family's private chambers for prayer and storytelling.

It had all been lost in a flash, yanked away just as quickly as the floor was pulled from beneath her father's feet when he stood on the gallows in London, an aging traitor seized by Henry II's soldiers and sentenced to die for his old crimes. That Richard Plantagenet was now king— one of William de Lamere's chief co-conspirators in his treason against the crown—seemed as salt ground into a wound still raw and festering. Her father's death had been such a waste. Nothing would ever make it right, not even the king's apparent gesture of sympathy that would join her with one of his most trusted vassals.

"You are quiet of a sudden," Griffin remarked from beside her, startling her with his nearness and the intimacy of his voice, pitched low for her ears only. "Are you tired, my lady?"

Isabel shook her head, hoping her sudden melancholy did not show in her face. "Just thinking," she answered.

"About Montborne?"

"Nay, Lamere. I was thinking about home . . . and my family."

"You have been away from your kin for a long time?"

"Too long. Though now 'tis just my younger sister and me remaining. I mean to send for her as soon as I am settled at Montborne."

He gave an understanding nod. "She is fortunate to have such a generous sibling."

"In truth, I do it for myself as much as her," Isabel confessed. "I have missed her terribly all these many years."

"Does she yet reside at Lamere?"

"No. None of my family stayed on at Lamere after my father died. My mother took quite ill and returned to her relatives in France to convalesce. Meanwhile, Maura and I were sent to separate convents. She was but two years old when last I saw her. 'Tis hard to believe that she could be eight now. I wonder if I would even recognize her." Isabel pulled at a loose thread in her homespun gown, unable to hold Griffin's probing gaze. "What about you?" she asked, eager to turn the focus on him. "You cannot return to Droghallow after all of this. Won't you miss your home?"

"Droghallow hasn't been my home for a long time. If it ever was."

She thought about what Dom had said when Griffin had demanded his payment for her abduction, his assertion that Griffin had been saving his wages because he wanted to escape Droghallow. She could still see the malice in Dom's eyes, the delight he seemed to take in thwarting Griffin's plans. "Is that why you meant to leave Droghallow?" she asked carefully. "Because you felt you didn't belong there?"

He slid her a wry sidelong glance. "More or less."

More, she suspected, but thought better than to say so. "Perhaps something awaits you elsewhere," she suggested when Griffin turned away to pour himself more wine from the ewer left on their table. "Have you a lady pining for you somewhere, my lord?"

"A strange thing to ask, coming from my 'wife,' " he drawled, a teasing glint in his eyes.

"Well, if you'd been planning to leave Droghallow, you must have had some idea of what you meant to do once you were gone."

He gave her a casual shrug. "Perhaps I had designs on a rather wicked life spent in pursuit of debauchery and plunder."

His grin was as devilish as his suggestion and Isabel laughed in spite of her earlier somber mood. "I hardly think you would need a bride's ransom to accomplish that."

"Indeed, demoiselle," he acquiesced. "No more than I need said bride delving into my personal affairs."

He saluted her with his goblet, then tipped the cup to his lips and drained it of its contents, an obvious attempt to dissuade her further inquiries into his motives. But Isabel would not let him dismiss her so easily. She wanted to know more about him, a curiosity she had been denying quite aptly until now, the wine she had consumed with the meal giving her a measure of courage and loosening her tongue.

"Why did you stay, Griffin? If you were unhappy at Droghallow, why didn't you leave . . . before?"

The cup came away from his mouth slowly. He looked at her as if he debated answering, his brows drawn, his lips pursed wryly, ready to offer glib comment or ready denial. Then, for reasons she could only guess at, he relented. "I stayed because I gave my word that I would."

"To Dom?"

"No," he said, exhaling a quiet breath. "To his father."

"The old earl wanted you to stay?"

Griffin nodded, studying his chipped goblet. "He and I were close, as close as any true father and son I suppose. We hunted together, trained together—did all the things that fathers and sons do."

"Dom couldn't have liked that—sharing his father's attention," Isabel suggested.

Griffin shook his head. "I warrant he didn't. Dom was born with a weak constitution—cursed with it, Sir Robert used to say. He was frequently sick as a child, and easily taxed. Sir Robert feared for his health, so he tended to leave Dom to his own pursuits. Unfortunately, those pursuits usually led to one brand of trouble or another."

He hesitated and Isabel saw a muscle work in his jaw. "What sort of trouble?"

"When he was young, it was generally pranks and bullying, but as he got older . . ." Griffin let the comment drift off as he reached for the flagon and poured himself another cup of wine. "One spring a few years ago, word came up from Droghallow's village that a daughter of one of the peasants had been attacked. Sir Robert went down immediately to look after the situation. He was shocked—sickened, no doubt—to find it was the reeve's girl who'd been battered and violated. She was a sweet young woman, soon to marry a respected man of the village. Sir Robert did not count many men as his friends, but the reeve was one of his most trusted folk and he considered the crime against the man's daughter to be a personal affront to him as well."

"Who attacked the girl?" Isabel asked, but in her heart she already knew the answer . . . Dominic.

"The woman wouldn't say who did it. She had been

beaten severely—her face ruined by bruises and scrapes she had to wear to her wedding later that week—but she was too terrified to tell anyone who was responsible. Sir Robert vowed to the reeve that he would get to the bottom of it. He questioned everyone in the village and castle alike, but nobody knew a thing. Finally, he questioned Dom."

"Did he admit what he had done?"

Griffin's smile was sardonic. "Actually, he attempted to put the blame on me."

"He said you had raped the girl?" Isabel gasped, appalled at the very idea. "Surely Sir Robert did not believe him?"

"No, he didn't. He told me what Dom had said, but he never asked me to refute it. And he never looked at Dom the same again. Sir Robert was too ashamed to admit to the reeve that his son was capable of such a heinous crime, so instead he offered to support the young woman and her husband for the rest of their days at Droghallow. He had a cottage built for them, and he provided for their every need. He never told Dom what he had done to make repairs. Dom didn't find out until . . . later . . . after his father was dead."

A strange distance had crept into Griffin's voice. Isabel watched him, seeing the hauntedness in his eyes as he lifted his cup and took a long swallow. "Was that why you promised Sir Robert that you would stay at Droghallow? To help clean up any of Dom's further messes?"

Griffin tilted his head, not quite a shrug. "Sir Robert had never been confident of his son's ability to manage a fief. This last transgression likely convinced him of the fact. That same day, he called me to his solar and made me pledge to remain at Droghallow after he was gone, to do my best to see that Dom would not destroy everything he had worked so hard to build. In truth, I didn't expect that I would have to make good on my vow. Sir Robert was a robust man, scarcely into his forties. I thought he would live forever. He died later that year."

"So you stayed," Isabel said, respect and sorrow twining together when she thought of the sacrifice Griffin had made. "Despite that you had plans of your own—dreams of your own—you stayed."

"For all the good it did," he drawled, draining his goblet and setting it down with a hollow-sounding thud.

"Perhaps things will work out for the better now," she said, softening to him now that she knew some of his past. She hated that she had made him think of those awful times and knew a sudden want to help him find a brighter future. "Droghallow is behind you now, Griffin. You might use your newfound freedom to look for your own kin."

"My kin?" he asked, his head pivoting toward her, his gaze suddenly piercing and narrowed. "What know you of that matter, my lady?"

She hastened to explain. "Only what you told me when first we met—that you were orphaned as a babe and found nearby Droghallow's gates. That Dom's stepmother—Lady Alys, I believe—recovered you, and she and Sir Robert took you in as their own."

He grunted. "You have a good memory, to recall so much that was said so long ago."

She didn't tell him that there was nothing about their meeting that she had forgotten. She remembered the day as if it were but a few hours past, not a full decade behind them. Nor did she tell him how often she had thought of him in the time since. How often she had prayed for him. Dreamt of him.

"Have you never wondered in all this time, Griffin? Have you never thought you might have family somewhere?"

"I used to question the idea," he admitted after a long moment's consideration. "When I was young, I used to imagine that Alys knew something more than she was saying about my arrival at Droghallow—a secret that she was keeping from me and everyone else." He shook his head, staring into his empty cup. "When she was dying of fever a few winters ago, she told me that I would have all the answers I needed once she was gone. She said I need only look around me and I would find them."

Isabel frowned. "What did she mean?"

"Would that I knew. She was in and out of wakefulness by the time she summoned me to her chamber. I suspect it was merely the fever talking, for if there was a key to the riddle, she took it with her to her grave."

"Perhaps you can solve it even without her help. Perhaps we can solve it together."

He shrugged, giving her a careless chuckle. "It doesn't matter. If I have any living relations, they have made no attempts to find me. Why should I seek them out?"

"Because family is all that matters," she answered, astonished that he could even ask such a question, especially after all he had been through at Droghallow. "Family is all we have in this world. Everything else—wealth, title, property—is merely incidental. Meaningless."

Her impassioned avowal earned her a snort from the cynic seated beside her. "I wager that's easy to say when one is in possession of all those meaningless incidentals. As for myself, I'll gladly take silver over siblings any day."

She frowned to hear him say it, but he afforded her no opportunity to reply, leaving her to help the other men prepare the hall for the night. Trestle tables were stacked against the walls, where they would remain until the morning, the rush-strewn floor to be used as a sleeping quarters for the castle folk and assorted lodgers. Lady Hexford offered up a down coverlet and whatever blankets she could spare, instructing her servants to make sure the brazier remained burning so that everyone would stay warm and be able to dry some of their belongings.

Isabel was pleased when Griffin secured them a pallet

close to the fire, instead of favoring a more secluded spot away from the other people. As important as it was to be discreet so long as they stayed at Hexford, Isabel could think of nothing more inviting than the lure of a warm bed. She tried not to think about the fact that Griffin would be sharing it with her, all but dismissing the thought from her mind until he was situated beside her, the front of his body pressing against the back of hers.

"Are you comfortable?" he asked, stating the question so glibly that Isabel had to wonder if sleeping thus with a woman was something he did every night.

In truth, Isabel was not sure if she was comfortable. Although she was exhausted, sated from the filling meal and heady red wine, her every fiber and bone now seemed alive and fully awake. She could feel Griffin's heart beating against her spine, could feel his warmth, the hard planes of his chest and thighs, his breath tickling the fine hairs at her nape.

"Isabel," he said again, his voice little more than a deep rumble beside her ear. "Are you all right?"

Was she all right? she wondered. The last time they had slept like this, not even a knotted tether was enough to make her want to stay at his side. Now all that held her in place was the warmth of Griffin's body, the comforting weight of his arm slung over her protectively, holding her snugly against him. Now she found herself nestling into his embrace, telling herself it meant nothing, when all the while her heart fluttered in her chest like a caged bird.

"Yes," she whispered a trifle breathlessly. "I'm fine."

Indeed, though it was the worst sort of madness, at the moment she could think of no place else she would rather be.

Chapter Twelve

Thunderstorms kept everyone indoors the next day, the inclement weather convincing many of Hexford's lodgers to stay another night, Isabel and Griffin among them. They spent the morning in the great hall with the rest of the folk, breaking their fast and taking dinner, then passing the bulk of the day being entertained by Hexford's bard.

The lanky singer regaled them all with chansons and bawdy verse, each of his ballads a wonder to Isabel, whose imagination had been fed on naught but Scripture and Bible tales while she lived at the convent. She delighted in the poems he sang about love and romance, hanging on every colorful word, rejoicing when the tales ended happily and groaning her disapproval with the rest of the ladies when fate proved unkind to the lovers in the songs.

She could scarcely breathe when the next ballad sung told of a young woman, betrothed to a man of her father's choosing while her heart pined for a simple knight whom she had long adored. Isabel could not help casting a thoughtful, sidelong glance at Griffin as the bard sang his sad song. Griffin had left the table some time ago, seeming uninterested in the day's entertainment. Instead, he busied himself with checking their supplies, all but ignoring the bard and the rest of the folk as he tied up his satchel and placed it on top of his folded mantle.

Now, as she had so many times since their arrival at Hexford Castle, Isabel surreptitiously watched the man who pretended to be her husband. It was unseemly, this compulsion she had to look upon him, to study him, to know him. It was sinful the way she relived the memory of his touch, letting her thoughts return time and again to the kiss he gave her at Droghallow, that false display of affection that should not have made her burn so then, nor all these days later. It was madness to think that any measure of his tenderness toward her had been based in truth.

Like Isabel's thoughts, the bard's tune had taken a bitter turn. He sang on about the doomed pair, his crooning voice speaking for the poor maid, duty-bound to wed a stranger. A woman who, in one final act of devotion, gave herself to the knight she loved, vowing never to forget him, to hold him in her heart forever. Isabel could only listen in dread and sorrow as the terrible tale continued and the lovers were torn apart, the knight sent into service for his lord, the lady sent away to wed. True to her promise, the woman never forgot her love, and when she learned of his death some years later, she collapsed and perished on the spot, her heart simply ceasing to beat now that her beloved knight was gone.

"They both died?" one of the ladies seated at the table remarked. "Ugh, what an awful tale!"

"Nay, 'tis so romantic!" a younger woman declared. She sighed and propped her chin in her palm. "Oh, to know that sort of love. What is it like, I wonder?"

"Ask her," replied a matron who gestured to Isabel. " 'Tis hard to miss the way ye look upon yer man," she continued knowingly. "The glow that comes over ye when ye gaze upon him tells the tale well enough. Consider yerself fortunate to have found a love so true."

"Oh, I don't—" Isabel began, startled by the observation and ready to deny that she loved Griffin.

But of course these women must assume she did, for they also assumed she was his wife and soon to be the mother of his child. She looked into the half dozen female faces that now blinked at her in expectation, evidently waiting to hear her expound on the virtues of true love. She grasped about for something appropriate to say, but then remained mute for fear that she would only end up stammering.

"Have you and your husband been wed a long time?" the young woman who had so enjoyed the last ballad asked.

"No," Isabel answered, unable to hold the woman's inquisitive gaze. "No, not long at all."

"Newly wed and by the looks of it, already six months bred," another woman commented with a wink and a chuckle. "Beware of love, girl. 'Twill keep ye fat with child for the rest of yer days. I ought to know—bore twelve babes before I was thirty and would have surely had a dozen more if my dear Henry hadn't gone and died, God rest his wicked soul."

Someone else grinned at Isabel, and chimed in with, "Wed to a husband as handsome as yours, no woman with eyes in her head would ever turn him away!"

Assenting remarks and feminine laughter traveled around the table. The jocularity was stifling to Isabel, the weight of her falsehoods and the risk of getting tangled in them pressing in on her, making her anxious to escape the sudden attention. "Will you excuse me, please?" she asked, trying to act casual and failing, if the concerned looks she received were any indication.

"Oh, poor dear! Are ye ill?"

"She has grown rather piqued."

"No, I'm all right," Isabel replied as she rose from the table, cradling the bundle at her waist to keep it in place as she got to her feet.

"Are you going to be sick?" the young woman across from her asked. "Shall I show you to the garderobe?"

Isabel shook her head vehemently. "No. I'm fine, really. I-I think I just need a bit of air."

Several of the ladies clucked their tongues in sympathy, then began sharing stories of their own pregnancies. Isabel left the chatter in her wake, hastening out of the great hall as if on winged feet. She did not stop walking until she was more than two-score paces down the corridor, ensconced in the dim solitude of the drafty hallway. Resting her back against the cool stone she willed her heart to slow, her gaze lighting on a beautiful tapestry that hung on the opposite wall.

It was a colorful rendering of a woodland scene, lush with dark green trees and variegated leaves. Red deer grazed in one section of the piece, while in another a clutch of winged fairies held hands and danced atop spotted mushrooms as a snow-white unicorn looked on. The picture had an instant, calming effect on Isabel, making her recall happier, less complicated times in her life. Times when she actually believed in wood nymphs and mythical beasts. And true love.

How long ago those days seemed to her now. How complicated things had become in the past few days. Not just her life, but her thoughts, her feelings. It was but a few days ago that she had been kidnapped from her caravan, a few days ago that she had found out her captor was Griffin. A few days ago she had despised him, wanted nothing more than to be delivered away from him as far and as fast as possible. And now . . .

Now, Isabel did not know how she felt. With each passing hour, with each step closer to Montborne, she found she was becoming more confused. Conflicted, no longer sure what she believed in. No longer sure what she wanted.

She sighed, thinking it probably wise to return to the hall, when she thought she saw the tapestry move slightly. Suspicious, she looked down and realized that the weaving had a rumple in it. It also had feet. Two small, pink silk slippers stuck out from below the tapestry's fringed edging, betraying the hiding place of a sprite of decidedly mortal stock. Isabel was about to call the imp out when approaching footsteps sounded in the corridor. A harried nursemaid trundled into view, dabbing at her brow and wearing a look of complete exasperation.

"Good morrow, goodwife. I don't suppose you happened to see a rather willful young girl pass this way in the last few minutes?"

"No," Isabel answered truthfully. "No one has passed me here at all."

"Oh, confound it," the maid grumbled. "I fear Father Aldon will not be happy about this one bit. 'Tis the third time this week little Marian has managed to escape her catechism. To think the child's parents actually have a mind to wed her to the church one day!" she exclaimed, woefully shaking her head as she crossed herself.

Without waiting for any sort of reply from Isabel, the nurse stormed off once more on her fruitless chase, disappearing down the snaking corridor in a flourish of swishing skirts and unintelligible mutterings.

" 'Tis all right," Isabel said to the tapestry after she was gone. "You can come out now."

From behind the thick weaving, the Hexfords' daughter appeared. She glanced down the hallway, then turned a frown on Isabel. "How'd you know where I was?"

"Why, the fairies told me, of course," she answered, gesturing to the circle of embroidered imps.

"Nuh-uh," little Marian said, shaking her head even though her eyes sparkled with intrigue. "You're jus' teasing. Fairies don't talk."

Isabel raised her brows in mock surprise. "No? Well, they certainly did when I was your age. Mayhap if we are very quiet, and concentrate very hard, we'll hear them."

She pressed her ear against the tapestry and pretended to listen intently. It did not take long for Marian to do likewise, smiling up at Isabel as if the two of them shared a wonderful secret.

"Come here," the little girl said, slipping her pudgy fingers into Isabel's hand. "I'll show you something."

Isabel spared the noise of the hall but a moment's pause before happily following Marian along the corridor and up the tower steps. There was a chamber at the top of the spiral staircase, a child's playroom by the looks of it, with a rocking pony and a miniature table and chairs carved out of birch and peopled with a collection of stuffed cloth dolls, each one wearing a different colored gown, all of them equally elaborate.

But it was not until Isabel stood in the center of the room that she noticed the true wonder of the place. Painted on the whitewashed stone walls was a continuing panel of changing scenery, so incredibly lovely it fair stole her breath. On each of the four walls was a depiction of the seasons in turn: spring, with its new green leaves and blossoms, baby animals peering innocent and wide-eyed from behind tree trunks and lush ferns; summer, awash with flowers and sunny skies; autumn, resplendent with jewel-rich hues of warm gold, red, and orange; even winter was a sight to behold, with white frosted pine trees and snowflakes falling from an indigo sky, the sliver of a pale blue moon illuminating a perfect rendition of Hexford Castle, spangled with garlands of holly and dripping icicles.

When Isabel could only stare in awe, little Marian pulled her toward the arrow-slit window where sat a chest of some sort. It was a cage, Isabel realized, hunkering down beside the girl to peer inside the woven wire walls. Fresh grass lined the bottom in a blanket of green, and atop it sat an assortment of small pots containing fragrant flowering plants of all varieties. Fluttering about this pleasant little prison were nearly a dozen butterflies, their happy colors and spritelike behavior wringing a giggle from both Isabel and her new friend.

"They're beautiful," Isabel said, smiling warmly, the very sight of these creatures gladdening her heart.

"My papa brings me one each time he goes away," little Marian replied. "Want to hold one?"

She lifted the lid on the cage and instantly the butterflies took flight, pouring up into the chamber like leaves caught on the wind. Isabel gasped, horrified that all of Marian's pets were escaping so easily. But the little girl did not seem worried in the least.

"Stand still," she instructed Isabel. "Like this."

Spreading her short arms wide and gazing up at the rainbow of color fluttering above her head, she waited quietly, moving not a muscle, a feat that seemed next to impossible in a person of such boundless energy. But her patience soon paid off. In moments, one of the butterflies alighted on her sleeve, then another followed, and another. Marian giggled and turned to Isabel, beaming.

"Now you try."

Isabel mimicked the little girl's stance, tipping her head up and delighting in the dizzying cloud of butterflies dancing in the rafters. She bit her lip, waiting breathlessly for the first to land. A set of orange-and-black wings spiraled down and perched on her upturned palm. Next, a pale butter-colored beauty floated haphazardly toward her, settling on her shoulder. To Isabel's delight, several more landed in similar fashion, peppering both her and Marian in splotches of beating, living color.

Isabel could not stifle her joy. She laughed in wonderment, so caught up in the moment she scarcely heard the heavy footsteps ascending the tower stairs. Marian heard it well enough, her startled gaze snapping to Isabel.

"Oh, no! 'Tis my nurse!" she whispered in alarm. A quick shake of her arms sent her butterflies scattering, and, without another word, the child dashed out of the chamber.

"Wait!" Isabel took a hasty step forward, but it was too late. Marian was gone, little more than a rush of pattering feet retreating down the opposite wing of the hallway.

Left to her own defenses, Isabel tried to gather the

swarm of escaping insects, cursing herself for following this whim and not at all sure how she could explain herself to the child's keeper. She attempted to shoo a couple of butterflies into their cage before the nurse reached the door, but it was no use. The stubborn creatures tumbled on the air, spinning away from her like mischievous pixies. Isabel heard the footsteps halt at the chamber's threshold.

"I can explain this," she offered hopelessly, and whirled around to face the nurse.

But little Marian's maid was not the person standing there, glaring at her in thunderous silence.

It was Griffin.

His gaze slowly raking her from head to toe, he stepped inside and closed the door.

Chapter Thirteen

Griff had been more than a bit concerned when he found Isabel missing from the great hall a few moments before. A hasty search of the garderobe had met without success, as did his thorough patrol of the corridors. He had been scouring every corner for signs of her, growing angry with himself for not keeping a better watch, when suddenly, inexplicably, from down the high tower steps floated a butterfly. Then he heard it—the sweet sound of Isabel's laughter coming from somewhere abovestairs.

Storming up the steps two at a time, he had been prepared to greet her with every ounce of his mounting fury. He crested the top of the stairwell and drew up short at the threshold to the chamber, fully intending to scold her for her recklessness. To demand an explanation for making him fret over her disappearance.

But Griffin could think of nothing to explain the vision he beheld in that moment.

Against a backdrop of painted daisies and wild summer orchids, surrounded by a dazzling cloud of butterflies, Isabel stood across the room from him like an enchantress stepped out of a dream—beautiful, bewitching, a fantasy of earth and air and sweet temptation. A provocative version of the waif he had first met in Droghallow's woods a decade past.

"Griffin," she said breathlessly, regarding him with a look of mingled repentance and surprise. "Thank heaven 'tis you! You must help me put these butterflies back in their cage before someone else finds us here."

His gaze locked on her, Griff stepped farther into the room, not the least interested in retrieving the wayward insects. He watched her stretch, biting her lip and reaching up with her open palm as if to catch a raindrop. Two paces carried Griff directly behind her, close enough to touch her as she gently placed a butterfly atop a flower and closed the lid. She turned around and drew in her breath, clearly startled to find him crowding her so deliberately.

"Th-the Hexford child was playing a game—hiding from her nurse," she stammered. "I did not see the harm . . ."

Her voice trailed off as Griff reached out and brushed the backs of his fingers down the silky waves of her hair, tracing the delicate outline of her face with the edge of his hand as he gently dislodged a topaz-colored butterfly that clung to her fiery auburn tresses.

"Oh," Isabel gasped, giving a nervous-sounding laugh as he brought the jewel-toned insect away on his finger and presented it to her. She took it, then turned and set it in the cage with the other, replacing the lid without a sound.

When she did not face him again, when she stood there in tense silence, her back to him, her slender spine rigid, Griffin slowly, tenderly, placed his hands on her shoulders. He heard her soft intake of breath, felt her fine bones quiver as his palms settled lightly atop her arms. Her head tipped back as he caressed her, tentatively at first, scarcely touching her, almost afraid that if he moved too boldly, that if he clutched her too tightly, the sweet illusion would dissolve like mist burned away in the morning sunshine. He feared that if she knew how badly he wanted her, how tormented he was becoming by the very thought of her, she would pull away and run.

But she did not pull away.

God help him, she did not run.

"Oh, Griffin," she said in a broken, barely audible whisper. "What are we doing?"

He answered her truthfully, slowly shaking his head in a state of hopeless, helpless confusion. "I don't know."

As he said it, he swept aside the glossy mass of her hair, then leaned forward and pressed his lips against her nape, satisfying the curiosity that had been plaguing him since the tavern two days ago. As he knew it would be, Isabel's skin was warm, soft as velvet and sweet as cream. She melted into his arms even while she trembled, tucking her cheek to her shoulder and granting him full access to the delicate column of her neck, the tender lobe of her ear.

Her soft mewl of pleasure made him hungry to taste her mouth. He slipped his fingertips under her slim jaw and gently coaxed her around, tilting her face up to meet his. For a moment, he could only look at her, mesmerized by the beauty of her face, ensnared by the depth of emotion glittering in her smoky topaz gaze.

She trusted him.

It was there in her eyes—a hopefulness, a belief in him that Griff himself could hardly fathom.

Not at all sure he wanted that burden of responsibility, Griffin dipped his head and claimed her mouth in a savage kiss. He pulled her into his embrace, testing the seam of her lips with his tongue, an insistent pressure that she yielded to with little resistance. When she parted to let him within, he nipped at her lower lip, catching the plump flesh between his teeth, then ravishing her with a languorous, sensual mating of their mouths.

All the hunger he had felt for her these past hours—nay, these past torturous, maddening days—poured out of him as he crushed her lips with his. He wanted to be gentle. He meant to sample her kiss and be done with it, to appease the maddening urge and think no more about wanting her. God curse him, he had not the will to be gentle, nor to walk away. Not when she was clinging to him so deliciously, her

body echoing the fevered wanting of his own, her mouth
open for his plunder, her soft gasps of surprise and pleasure like a siren's song at his ear, luring him into dangerous
waters.

She said his name and he waded farther into the roiling
tide, leaving the satiny sweetness of her mouth to kiss a descending path along the velvety line of her jaw and neck.
His hand came up between them, seeking her breast. He
cupped the pert mound through her gown, kneading it,
wanting to tear away the offending barrier of her bodice so
he could see her, so he could feel the tight bud of her nipple bead like a pearl between his fingers. Splendor of God,
but if her kiss intoxicated him so, the smallest taste of her
sweet body would surely send him into mindless oblivion.

Nay, he was already there, he realized. His desire for her
in that moment was unlike any he had ever felt—quicksil-
ver, molten. Consuming all reason in a swift conflagration
of pure, primal need. Without a thought for what he was
inviting, Griffin skimmed his hands down the outline of her
slender form, his callused palms rasping against the rough-
spun fabric of the commoner's gown she wore. Just past
her hips, he curled his fingers into the skirts, gathering up
the thick folds of wool to permit his hands beneath. She
sucked in her breath when he touched the bare skin of her
thigh, a startled gasp that he caught with another hungry
meeting of their mouths.

She was quaking in his arms, her limbs aquiver as he
smoothed his hands over her velvety skin, up the lithe muscle of her flank. She moaned as he dragged her skirts
higher, seeking the supple, round curve of her bottom.
Then, vaguely, through the haze of want clouding his
senses, Griffin realized that her hands were no longer
twined in his hair, but in between them now, pressing flat
against his chest in resistance.

"Griffin, no," she gasped against his mouth, turning her
head away from him. "We mustn't . . . I can't . . ."

"Don't be afraid. I'm not going to hurt you," he soothed against her ear, and although he meant it, the rough sound of his voice was surely enough to convince her otherwise. He released her skirts, letting them fall back down around her ankles as he reached up and cupped her face in his hands. He kissed her, staring hard into her darting, anxious eyes. "I won't do anything you don't want me to do," he murmured against her mouth.

"But we should not be here like this together. We should not be doing this." Her breath hitched, shuddering out of her on a quavery sigh even as her head tipped back in pleasure. "Oh, God . . . Griffin, this isn't right."

"Does it feel right?" he demanded roughly, knowing how unjust it was to ask, but too needful of her to be fair. He kissed away any weak reply she might have made, smoothing his hands down her back and gripping the swell of her buttocks in his hands. He drew her up onto her toes, pressing her pelvis against his straining arousal, grinding into her with the force of his desire, the full measure of his passion. She squirmed with virginal frustration, her fingers curled into the shoulders of his tunic, clenching at his biceps, her slender thighs quivering where they met the solid length of his own. "Tell me anything has ever felt more right to you than this maddening hunger, this torturous heaven."

"Please," she gasped, more breathless sigh than protest. "Oh, God . . . Please . . ."

Griff bent his head to hers, sucking at the tender flesh below her ear and taking wicked pleasure in the way her back arched, her breasts flattened against his chest, her breath all but robbed by his ruthless assault on her senses. "Tell me that this fierce longing is mine alone and I will rein it in," he rasped, his mouth partially open where it still touched her neck. "Tell me, sweet Isabel, that my touch doesn't please you, and I swear, this is the last you will feel it."

"Oh, Griffin," she sighed, dropping her forehead to rest against his breastbone, her body still warm and trembling in his arms.

With the edge of his fist, Griffin tipped her chin up, forcing her to meet his gaze. "Can you look me in the eye and tell me that you do not want me as much as I want you?"

She stared up at him in mute torment, her jaw quivering, mouth trembling but giving him neither confession nor denial. Finally, she shook her head. "No," she said, and Griffin watched in humbled amazement as a single tear rolled down her cheek. She backed out of his arms, eyes glistening with a well of damning, heartsick tears. "Heaven help me," she whispered, "but I cannot tell you nay."

Pressing the back of her hand to her kiss-bruised lips, she pivoted on her heel and ran to the door, flinging it open and nearly stumbling down the stairwell in her haste to flee him.

Chapter Fourteen

What was she thinking? Mother Mary, what had she done?

Shamed by her actions, horrified by her terrible admission to Griffin, Isabel could not run away fast enough. She descended the tower stairs and fled down the snaking corridor, heading in no particular direction, not caring where it led. She needed solitude. She needed guidance.

Following the dimly-lit passage around one corner and the next, Isabel let the dark artery carry her deeper into the heart of the castle, beyond the hall, beyond the solar and common rooms—anywhere, so long as it carried her far from Griffin. She could not face him now. She could not face a soul now, not when her lips still burned from Griffin's kiss, her throat yet constricted with tears and this new, profound humiliation.

What sort of woman was she to invite such a breach of honor? What sort of wanton would let a man kiss her so brazenly—let him touch her so illicitly—when she was pledged to another? What sort of fool would forsake a solemn vow for a few moments of bliss when it would mean certain heartache, certain and duly deserved condemnation?

Isabel was reminded at once of the hopeless lady in the bard's tragic ballad. Heaven help her, but she would not follow that same path. She would not give herself to a man she could never have, a man who would use her and toss her aside for a handful of silver. If she possessed even so much as an ounce of will, she would not give her heart to Griffin of Droghallow.

She would not love him—she could not.

That phrase became her prayer, a silent, desperate plea as she navigated the gloomy corridor, breath hitching, heart hammering in her breast. Finally her feet simply stopped moving, her legs refusing to carry her any farther. Disoriented, uncertain precisely where she was, Isabel looked around and realized she had paused outside the keep's chapel. It did not surprise her that even without design she would end up there.

So often during her time at the abbey, she had sought solace and answers in the peaceful silence of the chapel. Hexford's chapel was smaller than the one at the abbey of St. Winifred, but its whitewashed walls and flickering altar candles promised the same sanctuary—a holy place that smelled of incense and tradition and merciful absolution, a haven far removed from the bustle of the castle and the churning confusion of her thoughts.

Isabel entered, breathing an inward sigh of relief to find no one else about. Her leather-soled shoes padded lightly on the stone floor when she advanced toward the nave, her soft scuffs and the hiss and pop of melting wax the only sounds to disturb the quiet of the vacant chamber.

Alone with God and the weight of her recent sins, Isabel sank to her knees before the altar and bowed her head in prayer. She did not know how long she was there, asking for strength and guidance and forgiveness. She prayed for relief from her feelings for Griffin, for fair weather and clear roads that would deliver her in all haste to Montborne before temptation claimed her again.

They were selfish prayers, all of them, but she was desperate.

Was this queer confusion she felt merely a woman's desire, or was it something deeper? What was it that made her yearn to be near Griffin yet made her tremble in his presence? Why did it seem so natural to let him touch her, to let him kiss her and hold her, when everything she knew, everything she had learned in this life, proclaimed it to be wrong, to be a sin?

This thing she felt for Griffin was like the devil's own temptation, a test of honor that Isabel was failing miserably. He had asked her if his kiss felt right to her, if it pleased her to have him touch her, if she shared any measure of what he so aptly called a fierce longing.

Even now, on her knees in the house of God, with the crucifix and Holy Mother staring down at her in mute judgment, Isabel could not deny it. She longed for Griffin. She yearned to feel his warm caress, his strong embrace . . . his sensual, dizzying kiss. She wanted all of this and more. She wanted his heart.

Though it was wrong—a sin to so much as think it—she wanted his love.

"Please," she whispered beseechingly through fresh tears, her fingers twined together before her and held tight as a vise. "Please, Lord, I beg you. I don't want to feel this . . . show me what I am to do."

A sound at the back of the chapel startled her: the shuffle of footsteps, the swish of long silk robes. Isabel quickly dashed away the wetness from her cheeks and pivoted her head over her shoulder to see who had entered.

"Oh. Forgive me, my child," Father Aldon, Hexford's visiting old priest, said when his gaze lit on her. "I'm afraid I did not see you there. Please, do not let me disturb your prayer."

" 'Tis all right, Father. I had finished; I was just about to leave."

She started to rise and found that her legs were slow to cooperate, having been folded beneath her and pinned against the damp stone floor. The priest saw her struggle and hastened forward, offering his hand to help her up. His wrinkled skin was cool and thin against Isabel's fingers, but his smile was gentle as he assisted her to her feet. His expression muted to concern the longer he looked at her.

"You've been weeping, child," he said in a sympathetic tone, retaining his feeble grasp on her hand. "Perhaps you would like to tell me what troubles you?"

Isabel shook her head and casually slid her fingers out of his hold. "Thank you, but no."

"You know, daughter, a burden shared is a burden lifted."

She forced a smile. "I was feeling a bit melancholy but my time in chapel helped. I am fine, Father, really."

To say that she was fine was an outright lie. She hoped Father Aldon would believe her, that he would accept her casual dismissal, give her blessing and bid her good day. But he only seemed to study her more closely, his silvery eyes lingering on her face as if he could see her pain. As if he could see right through her to the lies and sin that corrupted her wicked soul.

Isabel found she could not hold that wizened gaze. She glanced down at her hands, clasped together now at her waist—a waist that bulged awkwardly with further evidence of her mendacity. Calculating the distance between herself and the door, she looked up and started to give the priest her excuses to leave. "I have been here overlong, Father. By your leave, I should like to return to the hall and let you get back to what you were doing."

But the old clergyman seemed more interested in her now. "You are not of the flock here at Hexford," he remarked thoughtfully after a long moment. "A pilgrim, are you, my lady? Recently come to take shelter through the worst of the weather?"

Isabel nodded. "That's right, Father."

"Yes," he mused, wagging a finger at her in recognition. "Now that I look upon you, I do recall seeing you and your husband at sup last eve. Traveling from somewhere in the north, I believe someone said?"

"To the north," she corrected, guilt making her reply a bit too hastily, a bit too urgently. "We are on our way north . . . to visit with my family."

"Ah, journeying home for the birth of your babe, then?" he suggested. "I wager 'twas an arduous enough prospect without the beleaguering rains. Your husband was wise to stop and wait out the storms. After all, you're carrying precious cargo, are you not?"

"Yes . . . of course," she answered, scarcely able to get the deception past her tongue because of the false smile she struggled to muster at the same time. She felt herself blush and for once she welcomed the tendency. Perhaps Father Aldon would think her stammering and awkwardness merely the outward abashment of a shy new bride.

"My sister lives in the northern country, outside of Yorkshire," the priest said, seeming intent on engaging Isabel in friendly conversation. "Lovely area. And neighboring Rievaulx Abbey is a sight to behold. Have you ever seen the place, my child?"

She shook her head and Father Aldon went on to describe his last visit to the large Cistercian foundation, regaling her with his impressions of the nearly six hundred monks, lay brothers, and servants who lived at the abbey, a massive population that was of late turning its combined efforts toward the lucrative new venture of sheep farming. Isabel listened patiently to the priest's report, even though she was growing anxious to be out of his company.

She felt conspicuous in Father Aldon's presence, as if his casual talk was merely a means for him to delay her, to observe her a while longer, his gray eyes keen and watchful. She wondered if her shame still showed in her face, wondered if the priest could read her thoughts, if he could read the sin and worry that she was trying so hard to conceal.

"I take it you have been long away from home, my child."

"Forever," Isabel answered. After all, it was true enough. She blinked past her pang of sadness to offer Father Aldon a smile. "I suppose I have been here in chapel overlong as well. My husband will begin to worry about me if I do not soon return to the hall."

"Protective of you, is he?"

"A bit," Isabel answered.

"Well, that is understandable, I expect, given the circumstances."

Isabel looked up suddenly, caught off guard by the comment. Too late to call back her startled expression, she realized only belatedly that he was referring to her presumed delicate condition. The breath she exhaled in relief sounded a trifle shaky, even to her own ears. "Will you excuse me, Father? I really must be going."

She took a step to leave and Father Aldon reached out to her, placing his hand on her arm. "Are you certain there is nothing troubling you, my child? Nothing you wish to confess before you go?"

Isabel's gaze snapped to him. "Confess?"

He tilted his chin down, his lips pressed together in a knowing smile. "I suspect that things are not quite as they seem between you and that man . . . are they?"

"W-what?" she asked, taken aback, fretful to hear him suddenly refer to Griffin as *that man*. She attempted a look of mild confusion. "I'm afraid I don't know what you mean, Father."

"Do you not, child?" He asked the question gently, but the look he pinned her with was unyielding. "He is not your husband, is he? The both of you are masquerading for some reason, pretending to be wed. And you are pretending something more, are you not?"

Isabel blanched under Father Aldon's unwavering stare. She knew full well what he was insinuating. Of their own accord, her hands drifted down, settling atop the rumpled gown she concealed beneath her dress, a deception that felt so false, so wrong in this place of truth.

"Does he pose some manner of threat to you?" Father Aldon pressed, his voice careful but probing. "Are you in some sort of danger with this man, my lady?"

"No," Isabel denied at once, shaking her head vehemently and shocked that he had been able to unearth so much of her guile from just a few moments in her presence. "No, he poses no danger to me at all. I appreciate your concern, Father, but I assure you, all is well. I am fine."

But it seemed he believed it no more now than he had the first time she had tried to convince him of that fact.

"Why don't you tell me what this is about," he suggested kindly. "Perhaps there is some way that I can help you."

Isabel's first reaction was to refuse. She need not divulge any of her troubles to the father; while he had divined a portion of the tale on his own, to willingly share the rest could be a mistake. Indeed, it might very well put her in jeopardy. She and Griffin would be on their way as soon as the weather cleared, which surely could not be long.

And then what? she wondered. Several more days of running, of hiding. Several more nights of being alone with Griffin.

Far too much opportunity for temptation.

She knew it was only a matter of time before she gave in to this thing she felt for Griffin, this burning, wicked thing that made her crave his kiss, made her loins tremble with sinful longing. The shame of what she had nearly done with him, the knowledge of all that she might have forsaken for the bliss of his touch, pressed down on her in that moment like a weight too cumbersome to bear. She was a weak woman; if she had not known it before, there could be no denying it now, when the mere thought of Griffin's caress still beckoned, making her yearn to be back in his arms though the only safe thing—indeed, the only sane thing—to do was to deliver herself as far away from him as she could.

"Child," Father Aldon said, "you needn't shoulder your troubles alone. Let me help."

Isabel stared into the priest's smiling face, uncertain of where to turn. Should she confide in him? Griffin had warned her to trust no one save himself, but now she questioned if he had done so to protect her or, rather, his own interests. Had he said it to keep her dependent on him alone, to ensure that she did not seek help from someone else, thereby denying him his chance to demand a reward from Sebastian? Would she not be safer under the protection of the church?

And what of Griffin? He was an outlaw now, hunted for his involvement with her. If Dom's men caught up to them on the road, they would surely punish him, perhaps kill him without delay. Despite all that had happened between them—moreover, because of all they had shared thus far—Isabel could not bear the thought of Griffin's meeting with harm. Even worse, she could not bear the fact that she would be the cause.

Had she not asked God to help her? Had she not asked Him to show her a way out of her pain and confusion? Perhaps, she thought, this was it. Perhaps this exposure of her lies to Father Aldon—and his offer of intervention—was in fact God's way of answering her prayers. Perhaps the safest path to Montborne was one she must travel alone now, in faith.

Without Griffin.

Swallowing past a new onslaught of emotion, past the knot of guilt and trepidation that lodged itself in her throat for what she was about to do, Isabel met the priest's expec-

tant gaze. "I must get to the northern demesne of Montborne, Father—my life may well depend on it. Can you assure me the church's protection until I am delivered there?"

"Yes, of course, my dear child." Father Aldon nodded
and took her hand in his. "You've made the right decision,"
he assured her, smiling, the very picture of benevolence
and gentle understanding. "I will make all the necessary
arrangements at once."

Griffin's head was still reeling some time after Isabel
had fled their encounter in the tower. Unable to face her
rightful scorn and outrage, he had quit the castle and gone
to the stables. He shook off the rain and threw a gruff nod
of greeting to two squires who sat tending some of the
Hexford knights' gear. He stalked past them to where his
and Isabel's mounts were stabled, pleased to find them near
the back for he sorely needed the space and quiet.

He needed time to think, to try to reconcile what he was
feeling and, more to the point, what he intended to do
about it. He had been horribly cruel to Isabel, behaving
like a brute, pawing her like a lust-crazed youth, not ceasing until she was reduced to tears. Around her, he seemed
to have no control. She commanded his thoughts, his
moods, his actions. More troublesome was the fact that she
was also beginning to command his heart, something no
other woman had managed to do before. Of course, Isabel
was hardly just another woman.

It was easy to forget that she belonged to someone else.
Easier still to forget she was a virgin, untried and innocent.

He would never in the rest of his days be able to purge
from his mind the image of her standing before him in that
Edenlike setting of the tower chamber, framed by a garden
of painted flowers and wreathed in butterflies. For a moment, he had almost believed that she was his wife in truth,
that the blush in her cheeks when she saw him was affec-

tion, not surprise, that the swell of her waist was due to his child—their child—slumbering peacefully beneath its mother's heart.

Even now, the memory brought with it a swift surge of possessiveness.

It was a feeling he had no right to claim. Despite the breathless admission he had coerced from her with kisses and blatant manipulation, if Isabel felt anything for him, he supposed she should feel contempt. Given a chance to re- flect on what he had done, Isabel would likely despise him now more than ever. Perhaps it would be better for both of them if she did. It would make it all the easier to keep his distance from her, something he would strive to do if he had even a shred of honor left in his scoundrel's heart.

Taking a brush down from a shelf beside the gray's stall, Griffin stepped inside and began to curry the destrier's coat and mane. Over the rhythmic scrape of brush against hide, he could hear the two squires talking. They spoke of trivial things: tourneys and horses, games and festivals. Griff could hardly remember what it was like to be so young, so pure of heart.

How long would it be before these boys lost some of their zeal? he wondered. How many years of knighting would it take before they learned what it was truly like to make a living by one's sword, forever serving the whims of another man, fighting not because they believed in some- thing but because it was their duty?

How many nights would they drink themselves into mind-numbing oblivion, trying to wash away the gritty taste of smoke and ash and infamy, trying to drown the man they had somehow allowed themselves to become?

Griff scoffed to himself and tuned out the boys' chatter, marshaling his thoughts around matters he still had some measure of control over, like what his best strategy was for getting Isabel safely delivered to Montborne. Strange how it was becoming harder and harder for him to imagine that day. When he had set out on this journey, his plan had been so clear, so straightforward. Deliver the woman, demand his reward, then leave and never look back.

He was not sure when his focus had begun to shift, but now it did not seem so simple as that. Nothing did anymore. He was coming to know Isabel, and it was changing him somehow, affecting him beyond his attraction to her. Beyond reason. No, this fierce emotion he had for her was something he'd had no experience with before, something that terrified him as much as it seduced him.

"Jesus," he sighed in astonishment, feeling the startling impact of what he was about to admit to himself . . .

Was he falling in love with her?

The stunning realization was intruded on by the approach of someone outside. Running footsteps sloshed in the puddled yard, then clomped into the stable. "Did you hear the news?" a breathless, youthful voice asked. "There is an outlaw on the loose and thought to be somewhere in our area!"

The hair on the back of Griff's neck prickled to attention. His hand stilled, the brush falling idle midway down the gray's shoulder as he waited in dread of this condemning information.

"An outlaw?" another boy exclaimed, his question rising with excitement. A jingle of dropped tack rang out as the young grooms both threw down their work to hear more. "Is it true?"

"Aye. Lord Hexford's brother came to visit this morn and brought the word. He said that soldiers from a demesne some days to our south arrived at an inn where he stayed the night. They searched the place from top to bottom, he said, inquiring after a rogue knight who has stolen a woman from her betrothed. The soldiers warned all to beware, for the cur has already killed one man who tried to apprehend him."

"God's eyes," the third boy breathed in apparent awe.

"An outlaw and a murderer! Do you think he will be hanged if caught?"

"Oh, I wager so."

"I saw a man hanged in Derby last spring," one of the youths volunteered. "His neck snapped like a dried twig!"

"I heard that sometimes ye don't die right away," another said. "A man can swing for hours before he breathes his last."

"Just as well for the knave loose on our county," a different lad commented, his youthful chivalry evidently offended. "Only the worst sort of rogue would kidnap an innocent maid. He's got no honor at all, that one."

Griff did not need to hear anything else. He set down the brush and casually left the stall, then walked purposefully toward the trio of zealous knights-in-training, risking no more than the slightest sidelong glance as he left in case the guards had furnished a description of him. He need not have been concerned; the boys were too engrossed in the morbid new focus of their discussion to pay him any mind.

"Does this blackguard have a name?" one of them asked as Griff passed.

"Droghallow," he heard the first youth answer behind him, spitting it as if it were poison on his tongue. "They say his name is Griffin of Droghallow."

Griff cursed under his breath and stalked out into the muddy bailey. If Dom's men were scouring the nearby areas, it could not be long before they arrived at Hexford. He had to find Isabel at once. Although it was sure to send her into a state of understandable panic, he had to tell her of this latest setback so they could take swift measures to avoid a potential confrontation. They certainly could not afford to be sitting in Hexford's hall when an army of Droghallow guards rode through the gates to beg a search.

They would have to leave first thing on the morrow— perhaps tonight if at all possible. Yes, tonight, he decided, checking the skies and seeing that the storm front appeared to be moving off at last. They would take one final meal to tide them over, then slip out of the castle before the hall was cleared. No one would suspect they had gone until they were already hours away.

Though Griffin doubted he was given this portent of danger through any brand of divine intervention, nevertheless, he sent a quick word of thanks heavenward. Even if the news of Dom's search party had traveled the entire keep, he and Isabel were still relatively safe from discovery, for now at least. The guards were looking for a knight and his noble lady hostage, not a common man and his expecting wife.

So long as they continued their facade for the few hours they would remain at Hexford, so long as they hid behind their cloak of anonymity, he was certain they would make it.

Chapter Fifteen

Griff entered the castle nearly at a dead run, his booted footfalls sounding hollow and urgent in the torchlit corridor, his mind fixed on a single thought: Isabel. His purposeful strides chewed up the stone floor beneath him, sending cresset flames to waggling in his wake as he rounded a bend and stalked inside the great hall.

He scanned the crowded chamber for her face, for a glimpse of her burnished copper mane among the masses, and let out an oath. There was no sign of her; no one had seen her for at least an hour, he was told by a clutch of women, not since the both of them had quit the hall after the midday meal. Griffin had to struggle to keep his concern from showing in his expression.

Mayhap Isabel was more upset than he realized by what had transpired between them in the tower. He could not blame her, he thought, feeling a renewed prick of guilt for his brutish behavior.

He was just about to turn away when one of the women tapped his arm and pointed toward the arched entryway to the hall. "There she is, love."

Escorted by the priest called Aldon, Isabel stood paused outside the great hall. It appeared she had been crying recently, her tears dried but her cheeks still flushed, eyes yet rimmed in red. The old clergyman said something to her— something reassuring by the looks of it, for Isabel nodded and gave him a weak smile.

"You'll see, 'twill all work out as it should, my child," the priest was saying as Griff strode up and interrupted the exchange with his very presence.

"My lady," he said with forced mildness. "Your absence was beginning to worry me."

He did not miss the strangely condemning glint in the old man's eyes, but he dismissed it as pious arrogance and took Isabel's hand in his, pressing a chaste kiss to her palm. It was a calculated move that would have afforded him the opportunity to pull her into the protective circle of his arm had she not withdrawn, looking away as if she could not bear to meet his eyes.

"I have been looking for you," he said evenly, though it unnerved him by the way she seemed to shrink back from him. He didn't like the fact that she would not lift her gaze, that she seemed so shuttered, so full of tension.

Wary of him.

He shifted slightly and cleared his throat. "We must talk, my lady."

"Yes, Griffin," she answered in a quiet, distant-sounding voice. "We must."

And then, at last, she looked up.

Griffin had never seen such sorrow, such terrible regret. It tore at him, the sadness he saw shimmering in her gaze; it rent something asunder inside of him. Had he done this to her? He gritted his teeth, wanting to kick himself for causing her even a moment's distress.

But before he could beg her forgiveness, before he could reach out, pull her into his arms, and vow never to hurt her again, Isabel blurted out something that seemed to suck the very air from his lungs.

"I've asked Father Aldon to help me get to Mont-borne."

Dazed—uncertain he had heard aright—Griff threw a wild glance at the old priest. "You what?"

"The good father has offered to give me the church's

protection until I am safely arrived at Montborne, and I
have agreed. I will be leaving with him in the morn."

Griffin ground out a rather vivid oath and seized Isabel
by the arm. "I don't think you understand what you are
doing."

"No, sir knight," the priest interjected. " 'Tis you who
does not understand. This lady has begged sanctuary with
the church. To interfere in this is to go against God."

"Damn the church. And damn you," Griff growled,
whirling on the old man and sending him back a pace with
the ferocity of his glare.

Isabel gasped, but she did not fight him when he took
her firmly in hand and stalked away from the priest, searching for somewhere private to speak with her. He found it in
a windowed antechamber adjacent to the great hall. Haul-
ing Isabel around before him, Griff turned and kicked the
door shut with a solid bang.

"Griffin," she said softly. "I'm sorry. I didn't know what
else to do."

"Are you mad?" he demanded. "Do you want to get us
both killed?"

"No!" she gasped. "This is the best way to avoid that
eventuality. The surest means to save us both."

"By involving someone you've just met? Do you actually trust him—a man you know nothing about—more than
you trust me?"

"He's a man of God," she reminded him, as if that
should make a difference.

Griff exhaled sharply and ran a hand through his hair.
"What have you told him?"

"I didn't have to tell him much." She rushed on, nervously picking at a loose thread on her gown. "He came
upon me in the chapel, saw that I was crying. I guess he
could tell I was hiding something. He said he suspected I
was in danger, that he knew we were not married—"

"Jesus," Griff swore. "What else does he know?"

"I didn't tell him about Dom or anything else, if that's what you mean. I told him only that I needed to get to Montborne, that my life depended on it."

"And what about me?"

Isabel shrugged, giving a slow shake of her head. "I told him that I had hired you to take me there, but now I feel that it is time we go our separate ways."

"Do you?" he asked.

She did not answer.

"Dom's guards are in the area," he told her, more calmly than he might have thought he could. At her look of alarm, he went on to explain what he had heard in the stables, about the soldiers' search of the nearby inn and the likelihood that they would soon be nosing around at Hexford. "The rains are starting to clear," he said. "If we leave tonight, we should be able to put a good distance between ourselves and the search party."

"Griffin," Isabel said gently. "Don't you see? This is just all the more reason why we should part now, the sooner the better. The knights from Droghallow are not going to give up until they have us."

"I won't let them near you," he averred. "I'm taking you to Montborne, my lady. Dom is not going to win in this."

Her smile was a trifle sad as she tilted her head down, then regarded him from under her lashes. "Are you sure that's not all you're concerned about—making certain Dom doesn't win?" she asked carefully. "How much does your want to see me to Montborne have to do with your stated intent to demand payment for my return?"

Griff scowled, oddly insulted by the accusation. Money had been at the root of his plan, of course, but at the moment he had not given a thought to what he might stand to gain in delivering Isabel to Montborne. Indeed, his concerns of late had become more centered on what he stood to lose. Namely her. That she could think him so base, so greedy and self-serving, after everything that had passed between them, burned him more than he cared to admit.

"You think I'm using you," he said, holding that haughty gaze.

"Aren't you?"

"You mean the way you intend to use your betrothed, my lady?" The question shot out of his mouth before he could bite it back. Now he could only stare at her, watching as she went from surprised to outraged.

"Using him?" she repeated. "The king has decreed that I wed Sebastian. Lest you think otherwise, you should know that I have no choice in this. It is my duty."

"A happy convenience," Griff tossed back. "I wonder if you would be so determined to marry were your groom a less accomplished man, less able to provide you with the comforts of wealth and title that you profess so self-righteously not to need."

"That isn't fair," she argued. "My family's lands need to be protected. I promised myself years ago that I would look after my sister if I could. This marriage will give me that chance."

"And what about you, Isabel?" He advanced on her, slowly crossing the space that separated them. "What will make you happy?"

She shrugged, though her face showed her distress. "My heart will be glad enough."

"Married to a man you don't love," he challenged, ruthless in his provocation of her.

"Why do you force me to defend myself, Griffin? I have to do this."

"You don't love him."

"I made a vow," she insisted.

Griff took another step toward her, near enough to touch her now. "You don't love him."

"I pledged my honor!" she choked, her hands fisting in her skirts. "My honor is all I have left."

Griff's sharp bark of laughter sounded strained, cruel, even to his own ears. "Honor," he snarled. "Is that what you'll cling to when you find yourself lying beneath your husband and thinking of me?"

He wasn't surprised when she slapped him.

He well deserved it, after all. The sting of her palm against his cheek actually served to bring him to his senses. It made him realize the foolishness of where he had been heading, the futility of what he might have said to her in that moment, if given half a chance.

He stared at her, at those shimmering topaz eyes and the trembling mouth he so wanted to kiss, knowing that depending on what he said next, he might never see her again. Perhaps that truly was what she wanted. "Very well," he said with curt finality. "Go with your priest then. And keep your precious honor. I sure as hell have no bloody use for it."

"Griffin," she said, but he was already three strides across the room. "Oh, Griffin. Wait."

But he did not wait. Throwing open the door, he stormed out of the solar and past the startled priest who had evidently positioned himself just outside in a blatant attempt to eavesdrop on their private conversation. He had likely gotten an earful, Griff thought sullenly, cutting a dark glare at him as he stalked off down the corridor.

Thank God he was done with this fool's mission. Thank God he was relieved of his obligation to the woman, relieved of her maddening presence. Let someone else worry about keeping her safe and warm and fed; he would do well enough to guard his own neck. Let someone else deliver her into her husband's waiting arms; he could think of far better things to do. Yes, he thought, his footsteps hard and angry in the passageway, thank God this was the last he would have to concern himself with Isabel de Lamere.

And thank God for the slimmest thread of sanity that kept him from voicing the invitation that was still too close to the tip of his tongue for his current peace of mind. An invitation that would have begged Isabel to forget about Sebastian of Montborne, to simply turn her back on all of this mess and run away with him instead.

Father Aldon poked his head into the solar where Isabel stood trying to compose herself after Griffin's angry departure. "What a terrible, beastly man," he remarked with unchristian-like disdain. "He didn't hurt you, did he, my child?"

"No," she answered, but in truth she had never hurt so badly in all her life. She could hardly believe that he was gone, that in the morning she would be leaving, likely never to see Griffin again. She should have been relieved. Instead she felt as if a piece of her heart had broken off and fallen away, leaving a void that would never again be filled.

She let the old priest show her out of the solar and up the castle stairs, only half listening as he explained that he had arranged a room for her away from the hall, where a bath and a change of clothes awaited her, a private chamber where she could get a good night's rest before they headed out in the morning. He wanted her to look her best, he told her, for he had arranged for special escort to meet them personally and see Isabel delivered to where she belonged.

He showed her to her chamber, then bade her good eve with a kind smile and a warm blessing. Isabel collapsed at once into the soft coverlet of the bed, burying her face in the bolster, too exhausted to think.

Too distressed to notice that on the other side of her closed door, Father Aldon had quietly turned a key and locked her in.

Chapter Sixteen

Griffin reached for the flagon sitting in front of him on the trestle table and poured what was left of the spiced wine into his cup. He had been sitting alone in a far-flung corner of Hexford's great hall for hours now, pursuing total inebriation with a vengeance and a good deal of success.

At first, after his conversation—and ultimate parting—with Isabel, Griff had thought he would simply leave Hexford, carry out his plan to elude the imminent arrival of Dom's guards by heading out immediately. After all, she had no use for him now. She'd had no trouble letting him know she no longer needed his help.

But he had not even made it out of the castle before he realized he could not go. Not yet.

If he had any sort of pride, he would not waste another thought on Isabel de Lamere, let alone sit brooding in a darkened corner, waiting . . . for what? The chance to see her one more time? Another opportunity for him to make a fool of himself before her? Before everyone in the castle?

Was this what love did to an otherwise sane person?

If so, Griffin decided that he wanted none of it. If love was to blame for the ache he felt inside, for the foolish urge he felt to knock down every door in the keep until he found the one that Isabel now hid behind, then Griffin would gladly do without it. If love was what compelled him to let her go to another man when all he wanted to do was beg her to stay with him, then Griffin would gladly leave the bloody emotion to the bards.

As it was, not even Hexford's accomplished troubadour could make love sound appealing. For the third time this eve, while strolling the hall and plucking his lute, the minstrel lapsed into a pitiful song about the ill-fated romance between a noblewoman and a simple knight, an affair destined for tragedy due to the lady's betrothal to another, wealthier, man. Griff had thought the ballad ridiculous and morose when he had first heard it a couple of nights ago, but now each verse seemed torn from his own experience. He took a long swallow of wine as the bard approached his table, strumming slowly as he reached the end of the song, his dulcet voice lingering on the final dramatic note.

The folk in the hall burst into effusive cheers and applause.

"Again!" came a collective shout from some of the women. "Sing it again!"

Griffin caught the troubadour's eye with a sidelong look of warning. "One more round of that maudlin tune," he growled under his breath, "and you'll be wearing your lute around your neck."

The bard blinked in startlement, swallowing hard. Then he took a careful step back. "P-perhaps a jauntier song instead," he suggested to the crowd, dashing away as if he could not leave Griff's table fast enough.

He took the advice to heart, keeping to a repertoire of bawdy verse and soldiers' ballads, which blurred to a din of wordless background noise the deeper into his cups Griffin became. He didn't know how long he had been sitting there, nor when precisely his forehead had dropped to the table, but through the haze of voices, smoke, and wine, he sensed he was no longer alone in his corner of the hall.

"Griffin of Droghallow."

Without thinking, his mind too numbed with drink to react with any measure of caution, Griff lifted his head off the table. Through bleary, squinted eyes, he saw the torchlit outlines of two Hexford knights, their broad, mail-clad shoulders and gleaming weapons pinning him in where he sat. He should have known this was coming. He should have reached for his sword. He should have kicked away from the table, laced them both open before they knew what hit them, and ran.

Instead, he laughed.

"How'd you find me?" he drawled, his tongue thick and unwieldy in his mouth. "Did the good father tell you who I was, or did the lady?" He cursed then, and shook his head. "Never mind. It doesn't matter."

"Griffin of Droghallow," the larger of the duo repeated. "It is our duty to inform you that you are under arrest for the crimes of kidnap and murder."

"Come along peaceably now," the second man advised. "You've nowhere left to go."

Griff had to admit there was more than a bit of accuracy in that statement. He didn't have anywhere to go, not in that next instant, certainly. Perhaps not ever. God's truth, but he was almost relieved to be found out.

He exhaled a mirthless chuckle, then lifted his cup and drained it.

"Get up," the first guard ordered. He stepped forward and made a grab for Griffin's arm.

Griff jerked away, shaking off the forcible assistance and pushing to his feet of his own accord. His glare seemed enough to keep both knights at bay, though he did not miss the fact that neither looked overly reluctant to run him through if they deemed it necessary. The two men parted to let him pass between them, then fell in at his sides, flanking him with swords at the ready.

They escorted him out of the hall, leading him past the gaping troubadour and the whispering folk, and down to the castle's underbelly. He made no move to resist, hardly flinching as he was brought to a barred cell and shoved inside, stripped of his weapons, the heavy iron slats firmly separating him from any hope of escape. But they need not have bothered with all of that. He wasn't thinking about self-preservation. He didn't particularly care about his own inevitable fate.

Surely the wine had something to do with his present state of apathy, but what truly kept Griff calm as the guards locked him in the cell and walked away was the thought that Isabel would be taken care of. What kept him sane as the lightless prison fell into black and utter silence was the idea that despite what was likely to happen to him now, Isabel was soon to be on her way to Montborne, safe from Dom under the sheltering arm of the church.

It was enough for him to know that she was protected. She was out of danger, better off without him. And that would have to be enough for him.

Isabel had thought she had felt like a fraud before, pretending to be married to Griffin and heavy with his child, but it was nothing compared to how she felt that next morning, bathed in rosewater and dressed in a beautiful gown of creamy white silk. Father Aldon had roused her just after dawn, sending in three serving girls to see to her toilette and informing her that he would await her below-stairs with the guards, who would provide an added measure of protection for them on the road.

Isabel felt guilty that he was going to so much trouble on her behalf, but the old priest seemed happy enough to be escorting her from Hexford. Indeed, she thought, he seemed nearly giddy to have been given the task.

For her part, Isabel was anything but happy. She should have been grateful that she no longer had to run in fear from Dominic of Droghallow, that she would soon be at Montborne. She should have been appreciative of all Father Aldon was doing for her, not secretly wishing she had never involved him in her plight.

Not feeling with every beat of her heart that walking away from Griffin was to be the greatest regret of her life.

But it was too late to turn back now. Father Aldon was waiting. Her duty as Lady Montborne was waiting. Her life was waiting, and to second-guess it in this final hour was only to delay the inevitable. There was nothing to be gained by it.

Isabel marshaled her courage as the maids helped her don a dark wool traveling cloak. It took all the strength she had to quit the chamber and descend the stairs, to exit the castle and step out into the bailey where the priest and her escorts stood. No fanfare marked her departure and for that she was grateful. Not even Lord and Lady Hexford had risen to see her off; all that greeted her as she slowly crossed the courtyard was Father Aldon's eager smile and the watchful gazes of the two knights who would ride with them, their mounts shifting on the damp ground and blowing steam into the dawning morn.

Foolishly, knowing it was futile, Isabel paused and made a quick scan of the bailey, looking about for some sign of Griffin. Hoping beyond all reason that she would see him.

But he was not there.

No. Of course, he wasn't. He would not have stayed. Not after their terrible conversation yesterday afternoon. Not after she pushed him away like she had. Not after she struck him.

Dear Lord, how she wished she could take it back. He had not deserved that humiliation; nothing he had said to her was untrue. And that was what had terrified her most of all. She could not deny that she felt nothing for Sebastian of Montborne; she had never so much as met him. But even if she had known the earl forever, Isabel knew he would pale next to Griffin.

Her heart would never belong to Sebastian because it already belonged to Griffin of Droghallow.

And now he was gone.

"My lady, if you will," Father Aldon said in a commanding tone when her feet seemed unwilling to move. "We haven't all day."

No sooner was Isabel seated on her mount did the priest give the order to open the gates. Her horse followed the others, setting off at a hard gallop down Hexford's motte, the relentless beat of thundering hooves filling her head and drowning out the sound of her breaking heart.

Chapter Seventeen

The echoing tick of spurs on stone roused Griffin from a thick, drink-induced sleep. He did not bother to move when he heard the heavy door to the prison creak open, the blinding light of the guards' pitch torches searing his eyes as the duo of the night before stepped inside and faced him from the other side of the iron grate.

"Time to get up, cur," one of them growled. "On your feet. Now."

Griff levered himself off the floor, tossing a smirk at the knights. "And here I had just gotten comfortable."

Neither guard seemed remotely amused by his sarcasm. The larger of the two unfastened a coil of rope from his baldric and approached the cell. "Step forward. Put your hands together and stick them between the bars."

Griff presented himself as requested, chuckling when the guards jerked his arms farther out and quickly bound him at the wrists. Once tied, they shoved him back into the cell and unlocked the grate. The two knights seized him, one at each elbow. "Are we going somewhere, boys?"

"You are," the big one answered with a sneer as they walked him out of the prison and began the trek up the dark, dank stairs. "I wager you'll be off to the hangman later this morn."

"Aye," the second added. "After ye fetch a pretty purse for m'lord Hexford, that is. Five thousand marks ought to see you swing good and long on the gibbet."

Griffin's head was clearing quickly, but he wasn't quite sure he heard this last comment aright. "Five thousand," he considered aloud as the guards brought him out of the castle. "Dom must be desperate to see me dead if he's upped my bounty to that rich sum."

The knights exchanged a look of wry amusement, leading him to where his horse and two others waited, saddled for travel. "Droghallow will have the pleasure of hanging ye, but someone else was just as eager to see it done," one of them said.

"Indeed." His companion chuckled. "Ye should feel right honored, cur. The prince himself has offered his own silver for yer head."

"Oh? I thought Lackland was in London," Griff said, a queasy feeling begin to churn in his gut.

"Derbyshire as of late," the guard corrected. "Father Aldon rides to see him as we speak."

Christ's bones, Griff thought, panic rising to his throat and nearly cutting off his breath.

Isabel.

She was walking into a trap!

Griff's mind was racing, blood pounding, body numb with dread as the guards pushed him up onto his mount. One man had his horse's lead; the other was already swinging up onto the destrier behind and checking his tack. "Open the gates," the man ordered, and the portcullis cranked upward.

"Not so cocksure suddenly, are ye?" scoffed the knight holding his reins.

Griff stared down at him in furious contempt, all the while trying the bonds at his wrists and calculating how quickly he might be able to reach the dagger he kept in his saddlebag. But the rope held tight. Once he set off with the guards, his chances of escape would only further diminish.

He had to get out of there now. He had to reach Isabel before Aldon delivered her directly into Lackland's hands.

His mind latching onto an idea, he shot a covert glance over his shoulder, then leaned forward to speak to the knight standing below. "Mayhap you and I could strike our own deal," he suggested conspiratorially.

The man sneered but his eyes narrowed in consideration. "What sort of deal?"

His hands looped around the pommel of his saddle, Griff waited patiently as the knight drew in. His foot slipped out of the stirrup without the man's notice.

"I'm listening, cur," the guard growled.

"Closer," Griff instructed. "Unless you want your friend to hear."

The knight advanced until he stood directly below. "Very well. Let's have this deal."

Griffin smiled. "Here's my offer," he said finally. "Give me a blade to cut these ropes from my wrists, and I won't kill you when I make my escape."

"What?" the knight choked. "You're mad!"

It was all the warning Griffin afforded him. Pressing back, using the pommel as a lever, he bent his leg and planted his boot squarely in the knight's face. The blow sent the guard sprawling backward.

"Christ Jesus!" the other shouted at Griffin's back.

But the alarm went up too late. Griff kicked his destrier into action, his urgent yell propelling the beast into a full gallop. The gray shot out of the open gates and down the motte, speeding at Griff's command toward the edge of the surrounding forest like an arrow. Griffin could only hold on for his life, trusting his mount to understand his guidance, maneuvering the destrier with only the nudge and pressure of his knees and thighs.

In the distance behind him, Griffin could hear a number of Hexford's guards spill into the woods. They were gaining on him. He would never get to Isabel before they caught up to him; his only hope was to lose them. Griff slowed his mount slightly and looked over his shoulder.

"There he is!" one of his pursuers called. "This way, men!"

Griff turned off the path he meant to follow and instead plunged deeper into the thicket, pleased to hear the knights follow soon after. He dodged low-hanging boughs and jumped fallen logs, keeping himself just far enough ahead that he would be seen intermittently but not caught. A short distance before him, he spied a crevice wedged between a broken ledge of granite. Riding toward it, he called his mount to a halt and leapt off, his jump cushioned by the blanket of moss and loamy ground of the forest floor. A soft command and a meaningful elbow to the gray's flank sent it trotting away from him while Griff ran for the cover of the rocks. He scarcely had time to conceal himself before the Hexford knights thundered into the area, some drawing up, others cantering on blindly.

"I swear I saw him ride through here," someone said.

"Well, he won't get far now that he's off the path."

"Ahead!" another shouted, pointing in the direction Griff had sent his destrier. "I just saw the bastard's mount up ahead!"

Griffin breathed a sigh of relief as the men resumed their chase. He waited until he no longer heard their riding gear, then cautiously came out of his hiding place. Hands tied before him, he could only pray that the knights would not return, for he had no real means of defending himself. Running low to the ground, careful to keep his head down, his eyes and ears trained for signs of attack, Griffin negotiated his way through the bracken and thorny underbrush.

He wasn't sure how the last Hexford guard caught up to him.

One moment he was coming around a thick pine, the next he had a sword point biting into the muscle bunched tightly between his shoulder blades.

"Turn around, cur, or I'll run ye through where ye stand."

Griff slowly obeyed, pivoting to confront this inconvenient obstacle. The uglier half of his gaoler duo glared at him from behind his weapon, his nose fat and bloodied from Griffin's assault, eyes burning with malice.

"I don't suppose you're here because you've reconsidered my offer," Griff drawled.

The knight jerked his head in the direction of his waiting mount. "Try anything foolish and ye're as good as dead."

Griffin didn't bother to point out that if Dom or the prince had their way, he was already good as dead. Instead, he walked toward the guard's roan stallion, wondering if the man would be stupid enough to trust putting him on the beast. He wasn't. Keeping the blade leveled on his prisoner, the Hexford knight grabbed a length of rope from his saddle and shook it out. "Loop this around yer hands and let the ends fall to the ground," he ordered Griffin.

"My deal still stands," Griff told him as he picked up the rope tether and did as instructed. "Cut me loose, and I'll let you live."

The knight chuckled. "Ye must take me for God's own fool, cur."

Griff shrugged, staring hard, watching, waiting as the guard took a careful step forward and bent to retrieve the rope. Then he sprang. One swift kick knocked the sword out of the knight's hand. A lunge and a quick twist brought his arms down over the man's head, locking him in a lethal embrace. The soldier coughed, choked, writhed to get free, but Griff held tight.

"P-please . . . Don't—"

"You had your chance," Griffin told him, long past mercy.

Using the combined strength of his linked hands, he squeezed his arm around the guard's neck, cutting off precious air. The knight clawed at him in futile struggle. He sputtered, gurgled, then, finally, went utterly limp. Griffin released him to retrieve a dagger that was sheathed on the man's belt. He maneuvered the thin blade into place and sliced through the bonds at his wrists, then grabbed up the knight's sword and mount as well.

With the rest of the Hexford guards gone some time in the opposite direction, Griff headed back toward the path and sped off, determined to catch up to Isabel and the duplicitous Father Aldon.

The sun was nearly at its zenith before Father Aldon finally called for the first rest. They had traveled all morn, a dogged trek that carried them some leagues away from Hexford, following a westbound course of the priest's own design. Though Isabel welcomed the reprieve from her saddle's hard seat, the longer they tarried at their refreshment and rest, the more anxious she became. She was exhausted and emotionally drained, simply eager to be done with the journey. Eager to be done with all of this.

She had spent the past few hours trying to convince herself that she had made the right decision, that parting company with Griffin was the best thing to do for both of them. The safest, most sensible solution. Indeed, it was the only solution. For if her heart ached for losing him now, what might it have done if they had completed the trip to Montborne together, then faced the inevitability of parting? She did not think she could have borne that brand of pain.

As it was, she could hardly keep her thoughts from straying to Griffin, to wondering where he had gone after they spoke so heatedly, and as well, what he would do now that he was no longer burdened with her. She tried to busy herself with thoughts of Montborne, thoughts of Maura and their reunion that was soon to come. But none of that, not even Father Aldon's studious, queerly condemning stare could dissaude her mind from returning to thoughts of Griffin. She could not stop herself from missing him.

"You should eat something, my lady," the priest said,

those silvery eyes watching her like a falcon sizing up a field mouse. "I daresay you look a trifle pallid."

"I am merely . . . tired," Isabel answered, searching for a word that would explain her prolonged sullenness.

"Very well, eat or rest," he told her with a dismissive flick of his wrist. "Whatever will put some color back into your cheeks."

At that moment, one of their armed escorts from Hexford strode up to where Isabel and the priest sat. "The horses will need an hour or so before we continue on to Derby, Father. The weather looks clear, so if all goes well we should reach the shire before nightfall."

"Excellent," he replied.

Isabel watched the knight walk away, then she faced Father Aldon. "What is in Derbyshire?" she asked, this being the first she had heard of the apparent planned stop.

"Nothing you need fret about, my child."

She did not trust his subtly patronizing tone, or the strange little smile he tried to hide behind the rim of his cup as he took a sip of his wine. Suddenly, Griffin's words of caution in Hexford's solar came back to her . . .

You trust him—a man you know nothing about—more than you trust me?

Looking at Father Aldon now, Isabel was not sure she trusted him at all. He had seemed so kind in Hexford's chapel, so understanding. So willing to help.

Too willing, Isabel was beginning to think.

She considered the gown of fine sendal that the priest had insisted she wear for the ride, the dove-white color and delicate gold braiding at the hem and neckline seeming more fit for court than travel. Even her shoes winked with shiny metallic threads. She had been made to dress like a bride on her way to the altar, an observation that did not seem so alarming before, but now, in light of where she was heading—to Derbyshire, a favored lair of Prince John—Isabel weathered a prickle of ice-cold anxiety.

Was she garbed as a bride . . . or a sacrifice?

"You mentioned last eve that you had arranged a special escort for me, Father," Isabel said, interrupting the old priest's enjoyment of a chunk of aromatic cheese. "Does this escort await in Derbyshire?"

He looked up from his food, his wiry brows rising on his forehead. "Yes, child. We will be met there, just as I said."

"By whom?" she questioned, heedless of her challenging tone. "Dominic of Droghallow, or Prince John himself?"

Father Aldon nearly choked on his mouthful of crumbly cheese. He started coughing, his lined face turning red, his hand clawing out to clutch his cup of wine. He took a long swallow, then, when it appeared that he could breathe again, he leveled a watery-eyed glare on Isabel. "I am pledged to serve my liege, my lady. I must act in accordance with the prince's best interests."

"The prince's best interests? I thought you were pledged to serve God."

The old priest merely chuckled at her hot retort. "Perhaps the horses are rested enough to continue on after all," he remarked casually, snapping his fingers to call forth one of the knights. "The lady is growing fatigued with our company, I fear. Saddle our mounts so that we may be on our way, will you?"

The soldier obeyed without question, carrying out Father Aldon's orders as if he knew the priest's commands came on higher authority. Isabel watched the guardsmen prepare the horses, mentally berating herself for not seeing Father Aldon's duplicity sooner. Cursing herself for placing her trust in anyone besides Griffin.

Dieu, and what of Griffin? Isabel thought with a sudden, sinking dread. Had her foolishness endangered him as well? She prayed not. Hopefully he was leagues away from Hexford by now, well out of Dom's reach and following his own path. Just as she would have to follow hers, by way of Derbyshire, it would seem.

She mounted up as directed, being careful to appear somewhat cooperative while inwardly she watched her escorts' every move and plotted her best odds of escape. With three of them against her, two of them armed to the teeth, she would never elude them on the road. And to wait until they arrived at Derbyshire would be the gravest folly.

Factoring out and discarding nearly a half dozen hazardous plans, Isabel had all but given up hope when suddenly she heard something that made her pause. Someone was calling her name. It was a distant sound, so faint she wondered if she had really heard it at all. She turned to look behind her and then she saw him.

Griffin.

He was riding toward them at breakneck speed—a more welcome sight Isabel had never seen in all her days. Her heart elated, relieved beyond words, she bit her lip to keep from crying out her joy.

Father Aldon was far less enthused. He hissed a surprisingly vivid curse the instant his gaze lit on Griffin. "Get rid of him," he ordered the Hexford guards. "Now!"

"No!" Isabel cried. She turned to see the priest's savage expression, horrified by the murderous intent she saw gleaming in his eyes.

"Damn it," he growled. "What are you idiots waiting for? Somebody kill the bastard already!"

One of the knights reached for his crossbow and began to load it.

Isabel's heart lurched when she realized the guard's intent. "No!" she cried. "Oh, God, no! Leave him alone! Don't hurt him, I beg you!"

"Do it!" Father Aldon commanded.

"He's too far away," the bowman complained as he took aim on Griffin's approaching form. "That's it, keep coming, ye bastard. He'll be close enough in a moment."

"Griffin, no!" Isabel shouted, pivoting back to face him and heartsick to see him galloping forward so urgently. "No, stay back!"

"Shut her up," the priest ordered.

When the other guard moved to knit her in, Isabel jerked her horse's reins and wheeled the beast around. The knight made a grab for her, but she eluded his reach, dodging away when he swung his arm out to snag her.

"Griffin!" she cried. "Turn around! You must go back!"

With a burst of sheer determination, Isabel broke out of the guards' tight ranks. She slapped the reins against her palfrey's flank, sending the horse into a dead run.

"Get her!" Father Aldon bellowed. "God's blood, get the both of them, damn you!"

Isabel rode as if her very life depended on it. In truth, it did. If anything were to happen to Griffin, she would simply die. She had to save him. "Griffin, go back!" she screamed, panicked to the depths of her soul.

Behind her some untold yards, she heard the Hexford knight's dooming words: "He's close enough. I've got him now!"

Isabel's heart was in her throat as her palfrey sped on. She kicked her mount into a hard gallop, feeling the landscape whiz past her in a breezy blur of color and eerie, expectant silence. Ahead of her, Griffin had finally hauled on the reins and pulled his mount to a halt.

But he did not turn away.

Heaven help him, but now he was just standing there, watching Isabel ride toward him. "Griffin, go back!" She rode harder, determined to reach him. Determined to spare him in whatever way she could.

Distantly, she heard the guard release the trigger, the staccato snap of the crossbow being discharged ringing like a clap of thunder in her ears.

She begged her horse to run faster, pleaded with God to deliver Griffin from the bolt's lethal path.

Suddenly, she saw Griffin glance past her, saw his expression freeze and turn to stark alarm. She thought she heard him call her name, thought she heard him tell her to watch out. But she was not concerned for herself. He was all that mattered. She had to reach him in time.

Heaven help her, she had to.

Isabel raced on, close enough to see his face clearly now, close enough to see his fear, close enough to hear him say, "My lady! Oh, God, Isabel! No!"

She felt something strike her from behind, a breath-stealing jolt that knocked her forward against her palfrey's neck. She felt the searing burn of torn flesh, the liquid heat of blood seeping out of her, trickling down her side. She felt her world tilt crazily, felt the ground come up beneath her, enveloping her in a blanket of fluffy, soundless darkness.

And then she felt nothing at all.

Chapter Eighteen

"No!" Griffin's anguished, animal roar tore out of him like a living thing when Isabel lurched forward and fell from her saddle. He could not believe what he was seeing, could not accept what had just happened in that terrible moment.

Isabel had been struck.

The stunning horror of that realization took hold of him with icy talons as he spurred the roan and raced to the spot where she lay. He jerked back on the horse's reins, staring down in fury and helpless despair at Isabel's crumpled form as his mount reared beside her.

"Isabel!"

He said her name again—his voice strangled, urgent—but she did not so much as stir. She was so still. So lifeless. A dark, wet stain had begun to soak the grassy earth beneath her.

Blood.

Isabel's blood, spilled to save him.

Damnation, she had done this—she had knowingly put herself in the arrow's path—for him!

Griffin's self-loathing was matched in that moment only by his profane contempt for Father Aldon, the man who had pledged his protection, then delivered Isabel into peril. Griff's angry gaze snapped up, locking on the old priest. Aldon must have sensed the heat of that murderous stare across the distance of the field, for he immediately wheeled his mount around and gave it his heels, pausing only long enough to shout an order to the two Hexford guards to finish Griffin off.

While the bowman nocked another bolt and took aim, Griffin charged forward. His stolen Hexford mount had the benefit of its dead owner's shield fastened to its saddle; Griff made good use of the boon, yanking the kite of leather-bound wood free and raising it—just in time to deflect the arrow's swift assault. He shouted a war cry as he drew his sword and bore down on his attackers.

The bowman who shot Isabel fell first. Griff smashed the crossbow up with the flat of his blade while the knight struggled to reload. The guard then fumbled for his sword, but it was an effort made too late to save himself. Griffin brought the razor-sharp edge of his weapon down hard into the man's side, nearly cleaving him in two.

The second knight was on Griff at the same time, coming at him from his left, less than an arm's length away, weapon slicing toward him. Griffin caught the movement in the corner of his eye and pivoted in his saddle, meeting the first blow with the broad face of the Hexford shield. The heavy blade skidded off the shield and narrowly missed biting into Griff's thigh, an irritation that only heightened his rage. While the knight made to strike again, Griffin brought his sword around and thrust it forward, an unforgiving jab to the guard's midsection. The Hexford soldier froze in shock, then toppled off his horse with a pained gurgle, likely dead even before he hit the ground.

The two knights dispatched to the hereafter, Griffin wheeled his huffing mount around and headed after the fast-retreating Father Aldon. It did not take long to catch up. The priest's flowing mantle billowed behind him like a red velvet sail, and he threw a quick glance over his shoulder as Griffin gained on him. Griff leaned in, blood pounding furiously as he approached and came up alongside. He reached out, latching ahold of the rippling waves of

Aldon's cloak and jerking the old man out of his saddle.
Griff threw him down, then reined in his mount and leaped
to the ground.

"Stay away," the priest gasped as he rolled to his back
and faced Griffin's wrathful expression. He crossed himself, then held up his skinned, trembling palms in surrender. "Stay away, I say! I am a man of God!"

"Then prepare to meet Him." Towering over the panic-
stricken clergyman, Griff withdrew his dagger.

Eyes bulging, Father Aldon let out a shriek of terror.
When he tried to scrabble away, Griffin placed his boot
firmly on the edge of his robes, pinning him to the spot.
"P-please, sir!" Aldon sputtered. "Have mercy—I beg
you!"

Griff fisted his hand in the old man's vestments and
wrenched him to his feet. The dagger's slim blade rested flat
against the father's jaw. He swallowed hard, his knobby
throat scraping the edge of the knife. One flick of his wrist,
Griff thought, and the treacherous priest would join Isabel's
other assailants. Aldon had earned his death, to be sure.

"Please," Father Aldon sobbed. "Please. Have mercy."
He was shaking now, voice robbed by fear, mouthing the
word "please" over and over again.

Griffin stared at him in disgust, this weak man with a
heart so vile, so corrupt, he could turn it against an innocent woman for his own selfish gain. It struck him that the
same could have easily been said of him. The thought sickened him. Sobered him.

Who was he to judge this man? Who was he to judge
anyone? Isabel's blood was on his hands just as much as it
was on Father Aldon's. Perhaps more so.

Griffin let out a sigh and relaxed his hold, letting the
dagger slowly fall away from Aldon's neck. "Be gone."

"M-my lord?"

"Get out of my sight, priest," Griff ordered coolly. "Tell

Lackland you failed him in this. Ask *him* for mercy and see how far it will take you."

The priest stumbled back a pace, but his eyes remained wide and fearful, his panic only seeming to deepen as Griffin's offer sunk in. He no doubt knew that being granted his freedom now was merely another sort of death sentence. One to be meted out by Prince John's own order if the father was fool enough to return to Derbyshire without his prize. Griffin doubted the cagey old priest would be so naïve about the prospect of his own welfare. Either way, he was certain this would be the last he would see of Father Aldon.

Griff hardly noticed when the priest turned and ran. His thoughts focused entirely on Isabel, he swung back onto his horse and hastened to her side, praying for the best and dreading what he might find.

She had not moved in the slightest, but was still in the place where she had fallen, looking so small and fragile. So lifeless. Griff jumped off his mount and rushed to where she lay, dropping to his knees in the grass beside her and gingerly turning her over. His hand came away sticky and crimson red.

"My lady," he whispered. "Ah, God."

So much blood. It covered most of her left arm and spread in a deep, ugly stain across the front of her creamy white gown. He lifted the edge of her mantle and carefully laid the fabric aside. Isabel moaned as he gathered her up to inspect the damage wrought by the crossbow bolt, the faint sound and weak breath she drew into her lungs flooding Griffin with profound relief.

She was alive, at least. Thank God for that.

Lying in his arms, Isabel began to stir. She sucked in a broken breath of air, her eyelids fluttering open weakly. "Griffin," she gasped, then said his name again, her voice thready, urgent.

"Shh, my lady," he said softly, taking her hand in his when she reached out for him. "I am here."

"Did they . . . hurt . . ." She swallowed, blinked slowly, and tried with obvious effort to force the breath out of her lungs once more. "Tried to . . . save you."

"I know." Griff shook his head, humbled as he gazed down at her. "I know what you did, brave little fool."

"I'm very tired," she said in a small voice, her eyelids drifting closed. "I'm just . . . so . . . very tired."

Shock was descending on her quickly. Griff knew he had to act with haste. He had to get her wound cleaned and bound and get her warm. "Don't worry," he told her softly. "Don't worry, Isabel. I'm going to take care of you. I promise."

Scooping her up into his arms, Griffin got to his feet and carried Isabel to his waiting mount. She hardly roused as he shifted her weight to one arm and stepped into the stirrup, settling her onto his lap atop the roan's broad back. Holding her limp body against him, he smoothed a damp tendril of hair from her brow and placed his lips to her cool skin. "You're going to be all right, Isabel," he whispered, his voice rough and fierce with raw emotion. He had to clear his throat to dislodge the lump of pain that threatened to choke him.

"Please, God," he begged of the heavens above him. "Let her be all right."

Chapter Nineteen

"I thought you said he was your puppet, Droghallow."

John Plantagenet leaned back in his wide, ornately carved and cushioned chair at the high table of his residence in Derby and eyed Dom over his short, steepled fingers. "Your puppet, you said, and yet your foster brother seems to be the one pulling all the strings in this recent debacle of yours."

Dom weathered the criticism with a look of polite, if unfazed, confidence. He was none too pleased to have been summoned to a royal scolding with the prince, particularly when it called him away from the rousing bedsport he had been enjoying with Felice at Droghallow. "He has eluded capture thus far," he admitted, "but we will find him, Your Grace. My men are searching every corner of the realm as we speak. He won't get far."

Lackland looked less than convinced. "Would that I had not allowed you to persuade me to let you choose the man for this job," he complained, his dark wiry brows furrowing into a scowl. "I warned you that he was too arrogant, too brash to be entrusted with a matter of this importance. I warrant you have let your hatred for him cloud your judgment, Droghallow."

Mayhap he had, Dom reflected as he stared at the king's brother. Although John Plantagenet surely knew what it was like to despise his own kin, Dom doubted anyone would understand the seething contempt he harbored for

Griffin, the orphaned nobody who had been found at Droghallow's gates when Dom was just five years old. He was golden even then—a brawny, smiling babe with sparkling green eyes and a crown of bright curls.

Dom had hated him on sight.

He could still remember his outrage when his stepmother brought the swaddled infant into the castle early one summer morn. Dom had been pleading unsuccessfully with his father to take him on the day's hunt when Alys and two of her maids burst into the solar, full of giggling female excitement. At the sight of his beloved new bride, Robert of Droghallow all but ignored his son, eagerly turning his attention to the three chattering women and the strange little bundle that Alys carried in her arms. Dom had glanced up with sullen irritation, not at all interested in what new wonder might have had his young stepmother so lit up.

Until he saw a plump pink fist thrust upward from the loosened wrappings.

"A baby, my lord!" Alys had told her husband in breathless awe. "I found him lying just outside the gates when I went to deliver alms to the village. I think he's been abandoned, poor dearling. Is he not the most precious thing you've ever seen?"

Dom thought he was probably just a peasant's castoff, a commoner's leavings, not so unlike the mangy runt pup he had tried to take in that spring past, only to be refused by his father who worried that the mongrel would bring his disease and filth into Droghallow. Instead of gaining a boy's first pet, Dom had been made to toss the pup in a grain sack filled with stones and drown it in the river. He had not dared disobey his father's cruel orders, no matter how it destroyed him to have to carry them out. For months afterward—in truth, at times, even still—Dominic heard those helpless, muffled whimpers in his dreams.

"How sad to think this little angel might be without a home," Alys had said in her gentle, compassionate voice.

Dom saw the hope in her eyes, sensed with budding alarm the direction of her thinking. "He's likely just lost," he interjected, scowling furiously when the babe gurgled and cooed in Alys's arms. "Someone might be looking for him. He must belong somewhere."

Alys's understanding smile only angered him further. She looked to her husband then, something warm and unreadable in her gaze. "Perhaps we should keep him here, my lord," she suggested, "until we can be sure."

Standing in the sunlit center of his father's solar, Dom had waited for Robert of Droghallow to refuse Alys's plea, to toss out her rescued whelp with equal impassivity. He waited to see the stern scowl he knew so well turned for once on his pretty stepmother. He waited to hear the hard impatience in his father's tone as he told his wife to take the child and its likely troubles away from his castle.

Dom had waited, but Robert of Droghallow's refusal did not come. Instead, he lovingly reached out and cupped his bride's face in his palm. He kissed her brow, then looked down to inspect her squirming bundle, his mouth beginning to quirk into a slight, rare grin.

Then, to Dom's complete and utter fury, Robert of Droghallow nodded his head.

"If it pleases you, my lady," he had said to Alys in a tender voice, "it pleases me."

"No! You can't! This isn't fair!" Dom had actually shouted his disbelief, the first time he had ever raised his voice in his father's presence. His outburst shocked himself as much as it shocked everyone else in the room. And it had earned him a severe cuff aside his head when his father whirled on him in that next moment.

"Enough, Dominic," Robert of Droghallow growled, jabbing a hard finger at him. "No son of mine will whine and wail before me like a little girl."

"Robert, please," Alys had chided softly when Dom's tears welled and began to fall. "He's just a boy. He can't help how he feels. Give him time, my lord, he'll understand."

But Dom did not understand. Resenting his foster brother from the start, he prayed the boy's kin would come and take him back. He prayed he would simply vanish from Droghallow, and when the weeks he stayed turned into years, Dom did everything he could to destroy Griffin, beginning with the subtle yet unrelenting sabotage of his relationship with Lord Robert, a sabotage that did not end until the earl was dead of a failed heart at the age of forty-two.

Robert of Droghallow had been hunting with Griffin earlier that day, enjoying a brisk autumn excursion while Dom nursed a head cold in his chamber. His father had come back laughing, but pale and exhausted, complaining of indigestion as he took to his bed to rest a while.

Alys had been worried. While Griffin was stabling the horses and delivering the day's bounty to Droghallow's butcher, Alys ran to fetch Dom. "Your father is not well," she told him. "Come quickly."

Dom had raced to the lord's chamber where Robert of Droghallow lay, fully clothed and unmoving atop the fur coverlet of his large bed. He looked strangely small in that moment, Dom recalled, a pallid shadow of the boisterous, masculine giant his son had long feared and revered. Dom went to his side and clasped his hand around his father's big sun-browned fingers.

"He's so cold," Dom had said to Alys, who stood at his back, her jaw quivering, gentle eyes filling with tears. "We must do something!"

"I'll go get the priest," she whispered brokenly, then hastened out of the chamber, leaving the two men alone.

Dom had nearly jumped out of his skin when he turned back and heard his father rasp out a single, incomprehensible word from between his white lips. "Shh, Father," he said, squeezing the limp hand he held so tightly in his own. "Rest easy now."

The earl's eyelids fluttered slightly as a small spasm seized him. "Griffin," he breathed, and Dom's blood seemed to freeze to ice in his veins. "Griffin . . . is that you, my boy?"

"It's me, Father," Dom whispered, pained beyond measure. "It's me, your son."

But Robert of Droghallow likely did not hear him, for in that next instant, he sucked in a shallow breath and his entire body went rigid. A moment later, that thready gasp of breath and all the air that yet remained inside of his lungs leaked out on a queer, prolonged rattle that marked the ebb of the man's life.

Just like that, he was gone.

Alys and the chaplain arrived not long after, Griffin racing in but a few steps behind them. Dom released his father's dead hand as his stepmother threw herself over her husband's body, weeping with sorrow. The priest crossed himself and murmured a prayer for Robert's soul. Griffin stood in the doorway, his sandy hair still wind-tousled, his cheeks still ruddy from the day spent outdoors. His eyes were as sad as any grief-stricken son's, his strong jaw clamped tight, a sixteen-year-old man too proud to cry.

"I can't believe he's gone," he said, shaking his head as Dom approached him. "He seemed well enough all morn—robust as ever I've seen him, jesting about a dozen different things. There was no hint at all that he was ill." Dom felt his hatred coil a little tighter when he pictured his father riding beside Griffin, clapping him on the shoulder, making jokes, bonding as he never had with his own flesh-and-blood son. "Would that I had known," Griffin was saying. "Would that I had been here. Did he say anything to you, Dom? Anything at all before he passed?"

Dominic had met Griffin's searching gaze and held it, choosing his words with cool deliberation. "Yes, actually. He did say something," he replied evenly. "He said that he was glad I was at his side. He said he was proud to have me—*his son*—beside him in his final moments on this earth."

Dom did not understand Griffin's quiet acceptance of the lie. He did not understand why he chose to stay on at Droghallow after Dom became earl, a position that allowed him to lord over his foster brother and the rest of the folk as he had always dreamed, ruling with a demanding, unforgiving nature that would have—perhaps, at last—made his father proud.

Dom easily could have turned Griffin out of the keep and never thought twice about it. Alys would have protested, surely, but he could have ignored her, and soon enough she was dead anyway, perished of ague the winter after her husband's death. Dom instead had decided it would be more amusing to keep Griffin on at Droghallow, to have the idealistic golden boy serve him as captain of the guard. Dom had worked hard to corrupt him, charging him with the most unpleasant of tasks and watching with private glee as slowly, day by day, year by year, Griffin's damnable sense of honor lost more and more of its luster.

The sad truth was, Griffin was a born leader. Even through his blinding animosity for him, Dom could see that plain fact. In another place, under other circumstances, Griffin might have been a great man, capable of great things. But he'd had the misfortune of arriving on Droghallow's doorstep twenty-five years ago, and if anyone was to blame for what became of him while there, Dom was of the mind that it was Alys, not him, who should have shouldered that guilt. After all, it was she who took him in. She who pretended to know nothing of his origins when in fact he was blood kin to her—the son of a highborn cousin, a babe sent away in secret to be raised by the barren Alys and her devoted husband.

This knowledge came to Dom quite by chance, upon his discovery of a cache of correspondence hidden away by his stepmother and not unearthed until a few weeks after her death. Dom had ordered her chamber cleared of all belongings, a task nearly completed when a maid came to him with a small coffer she had found hidden behind a loose stone in Alys's chamber wall.

"I don't know how I missed it until now," the maid had said when Dom broke open the box to see what it contained. "Lady Alys must have kept it hidden there all along, right under our noses."

Dom expected to find some manner of treasure secreted inside, something to warrant Alys's care in concealing the sturdy wooden container. Though he had not discovered gold, he had found a boon of another sort, for inside was a collection of letters. Hundreds of them. One for each month that Griffin was at Droghallow, lovingly penned by a mother who missed her son and lived each day with the guilt of sending him away.

Dom wasn't sure if his father had been aware of Griffin's true parentage. He rather doubted the old man would have cared. Griffin was all the son that Dom could never be: strong and hale, equally adept with both sword and wit. If he had not died so unexpectedly, Robert of Droghallow might have been tempted to take steps to entrust Griffin with his properties instead of Dom. Just thinking on that likely prospect was enough to cause Dom's blood to boil anew.

The way Dom saw it, Griffin had robbed him of his father's affection. If not for his arrival, the earl might have been able to eventually find room in his heart for the weakling son of his first wife. He might have been able to take some measure of pride in him, might have been able to love him just a little. By design or nay, Griffin had stolen Dom's place in his own household, and for too long, Dom had been seeking repairs for that offense.

He had gained some satisfaction toward that end by reading every letter Griffin's mother had written. It had taken hours to wade through them all and when he was fin-

ished, Dom burned them that very same day, knowingly
denying Griffin the information, confident that he would
find a use for it one day on his own.

And so he had, the day he learned of Prince John's want
to stop a certain noble marriage.

This last task—the kidnap of the Montborne bride—
would have all but evened the score. Indeed, when Dom
had first heard about the pending union, and Prince John's
want to thwart it, he could not have offered his services
fast enough. Griffin was his natural choice—his only
choice—for the mission.

"You have my word," Dom told the prince now, breaking
out of his reflection to meet the cold gray stare of John
Plantagenet. "Griffin and the woman will be apprehended.
There is no one who is more determined to see this deed
through to fruition than myself."

Not even you, he amended silently as he bowed before
his royal conspirator and was granted his leave.

Chapter Twenty

Isabel remained mercifully unconscious for the time it took Griffin to find them feasible shelter so he could look after her wound. The only asylum to be had was in the woods outside Derbyshire, in a deep cavern notched between two massive slabs of lichen-covered granite. Adequate at best, but well hidden. Griff dismounted to make a quick check of the place, then, satisfied with its state of total vacancy, he went back to his waiting mount to fetch Isabel.

Carrying her in his arms, his horse's lead in one hand, Griff ventured into the cave. A flat expanse of dry rock would have to serve as Isabel's pallet as he tended her. Griff set her down as gently as he could, positioning her where there was the best light. This far back in the cavern, sunlight was a meager, fleeting thing. It squeezed in through the cave's narrow mouth, stretching in like a hag's finger, a milky nimbus that would be all but vanished in a matter of an hour.

Griff made haste to use his time to best advantage, bringing together what few tools he had to work with and returning to kneel at Isabel's side.

Even in the dim light of the cavern, he could see the grim evidence of the bolt's damage. Isabel's blood stained the deep blue wool of her mantle where the torn fabric pressed against her injured arm, a thickening patch of wet blackness that set a knot of fear in Griffin's throat. With

care not to disturb her, he lifted the edge of the cloak away,
then grasped the sleeve of Isabel's gown as gingerly as he
could and rent it at the shoulder seams.

His breath hissed out of him when he saw the ravaged
patch of skin laid bare.

It seemed such a heinous violation, so incongruous, that
terrible, ragged ugliness marring the pale perfection of her
skin. At least the arrow had only grazed her. Had she
leaped any farther into its path, the bolt would have impaled her upper arm, a grim thought Griff refused to pon-
der for long. Steeling himself to what must be done, he
reached over to retrieve his saddle pack from the floor beside him.

He pulled a wineskin from within the pouch, cursing
when he realized it could contain no more than a couple of
swallows. Better than none at all, he decided, but he still
needed a length of cloth with which to bind her arm once it
was cleaned. He grabbed up the hem of her rumpled mantle then threw it aside in frustration. Wool would only
breed festering; the best bandage would be of breathable
fabric.

Griff's gaze slid back to the fine silk gown Isabel wore.
The voluminous skirts were soiled and torn from her fall,
but beneath the mantle clasped together at her throat, the
bodice of the dress was still a pristine white. It would have
to suffice. Griff knelt down and untied the laces that bound
the garment's neckline together above Isabel's breasts, then
paused. There would be no easy way to get her out of the
gown without jostling her and he was loathe to add to her
discomfort. Left no other choice, he drew a dagger from a
sheath on his belt, slipped the blade beneath the thin fabric
and efficiently sliced the bliaut open from neck to hem.

How different it was to look upon her nudity now, he
thought. The sight of her naked body inspired an ache in
him that went deeper than lust or wanting. What he felt
when he looked upon her in that moment was nothing short

of a burning, heartsick brand of guilt. A profound humility. Raw emotions, so foreign to him that he found it hard to keep from turning away from her. But he forced himself to remain unflinching as he reached out and lifted her arm out to the side where he could better work on her wound.

He uncorked his wineskin and poured a small portion of the claret over the worst part of the gash. Isabel jerked the instant the wine touched her skin. She gave an incoherent whimper, her closed eyelids fluttering. Griff knew the pain he was inflicting on her; he had tended his own battle injuries often enough to know the fiery kiss of wine on an open wound. But it was a necessary measure, and he could only pray that Isabel's senses would remain mercifully dulled for a while longer as he finished.

Waiting for her fretful stirring to subside, he grasped her wrist to steady her arm as he applied a second dose to the cut. This time Isabel cried out in earnest.

Her eyes flew open, wide with fright and glossy with disorientation. "Please . . . nooo," she moaned. Her wounded arm went tight in Griffin's grasp, her outflung hand fisting, her fingernails sinking into the fleshy pinkness of her palm. The wiry tendons in her wrist strained beneath her skin as she struggled against Griffin's firm hold.

"Shh," he whispered, placing his free hand gently against her brow when her head began to thrash from side to side. " 'Tis all right, Isabel, I promise."

"It hurts," she hissed through a grimace of agony.

"I know it does, but I'm almost done." He swept aside a lock of damp hair that fell onto her brow, wishing he could as easily sweep aside her pain. "Close your eyes," he told her gently. "Try to sleep, angel."

Griff was unsure where the endearment came from—he had never been the sort of man to bother with sweet words or meaningless courtly gestures—but hearing it seemed to soothe Isabel, and so he said it again, repeating his soft command and stroking her hair until her eyelids finally drooped closed once more. He finished dressing her arm as quickly as he could, completing the process with a strip of clean silk taken from her bodice and wrapped around the cut to bind it and staunch the bleeding. He tied off the ends of the bandage and sat back on his heels, his spine pressed against the stone wall of the cavern, watching as she fell into an exhausted slumber.

For what seemed the thousandth time, Griffin relived the moment Isabel had delivered herself into the arrow's path. Too late, he had seen it heading straight for him, a speeding blur of hard wood and razor-sharp steel—certain death. And then Isabel had suddenly cut into the line of fire, a deliberate act that placed herself between him and the bowman's bolt.

Griff still could hardly believe it. He had never seen such courage in all his days . . .

Not true, his conscience chided. There had been a time, once before, when he had witnessed the sort of courage and honor that Isabel displayed. And he had destroyed it.

At Hexford, when he told Isabel about the reeve's daughter and what Dom had done to her, he had been careful to leave out the events that came next, some few short months later, after Sir Robert was dead and Dom had been made earl. He didn't tell her about the day Dominic found out about his father's gesture of kindness to the woman and her new husband. He didn't tell her how irate Dom had been to learn that some of Droghallow's money—now his money—was being used to support a couple of commoners.

Griffin didn't tell Isabel that as captain of the garrison, he was enlisted to accompany his lord to the village when Dom decided to eject the couple from their cottage and burn it down in spite. Nor did he tell her that when Dom attempted to seize the woman bodily, and her husband stepped in to protect her, it was he, Griffin, who was obligated to draw his weapon in defense of his lord. It was he who stood between the man and Dom, he who held him off when the cottar drew a knife and lunged for his wife's assailant.

And it was he, Griffin, who slayed that good man, killing for the first time. He had been physically sick with the act, knowing that he had just murdered a man whose only crime was acting out of courage and honor to come to the aid of someone he loved. The sacrifice had been such a waste; it had not spared his wife from Dom in the end.

So often Griff wished that he had turned his blade on Dom instead. But he hadn't, and he'd spent the rest of his years at Droghallow regretting that failure. Because of his pledge to Sir Robert, he stayed at Droghallow, carrying out his tasks as head of the guard in a state of emotional numbness, an apathy that had thoroughly consumed him . . . until the day he was reunited with Isabel. She made him feel again. She made him hope. Being with her made him better somehow.

Looking at the blood that stained his hands and tunic from her wound—blood spilled because of her own courage and honor—he could not help acknowledging how completely he was failing her. No more, he vowed. She had trusted in him once. She had believed in him. He meant to prove to her that she could do so again. Her sacrifice would not be for naught.

Griffin eyed her bandaged arm with a judicious eye. The wound was going to require another dressing in a few hours and he had no wine left to clean it. He had a source of fresh water; somewhere outside the cavern, a stream rushed and gurgled. But they needed wine and they needed food, for Isabel's injury would surely delay them from traveling for a couple of days. He would be damned if he would let her weather the discomfort of hunger along with

her other pains. As soon as night fell, he would venture out
and find a town where he could get them some supplies.

Isabel was still sleeping when Griffin ducked out of the
cave some hours later. He drew the hood of his mantle up
over his head and mounted up, breathing in the cold night
air and letting the crisp chill of autumn fill his lungs. With
a nudge to his destrier's sides, he guided the roan toward
the edge of the night-dark woods and onto a hard-packed
strip of road.

The beast's hooves clopped at an easy canter, adding a
strange counter beat to the faintly tenor sounds of chanting
coming from somewhere in the distance. Smoke from a
scattering of hearth fires wafted on the late evening breeze
as Griff spurred the horse up an incline, the crest overlooking a village nestled in the valley below. Torchlight glowed
from a handful of crude domiciles and a large, thatch-
roofed tavern inn situated on a small rise near the elbow of
the main road.

Griff clucked his tongue at the destrier and headed
down.

At least a dozen horses stood tethered outside the public
house, some of them clearly knights' mounts, others the
bulky, swaybacked beasts belonging to mercenaries and
men of lesser means who had come to drink or lodge for
the night. Griff swung down from the saddle and added the
Hexford roan to the rest of the waiting mounts, then
walked toward the noise-filled tavern. The door to the establishment flew open as he approached and a drunken
farmer stumbled out into the night, mumbling a hail to
Griffin and staggering to the edge of the building, where he
then untied his hose and proceeded to relieve himself. Griff
kept his head low as he grabbed the open door and stepped
inside the inn, the smell of smoke and tallow, sweat and
ale, assailing his nostrils as the warped oak panel creaked
closed behind him.

The innkeeper nodded a greeting at Griffin as a serving wench trundled past with six filled tankards in her hands. She slid him an appreciative sidelong glance. "Be right with ye, deary," she purred through a sparsely toothed grin.

Assessing his surroundings with a warrior's eye for trouble, Griff took up an empty space at the end of the pub's counter. The common men standing nearby paid him little mind as he strode past them to claim the vacant spot, all of them too engrossed in conversation and drink to care that he had joined their little group uninvited. Griff did not much notice his tablemates either; his gaze was fixed on a clutch of soldiers who occupied the back of the tavern—a motley assemblage of knights and rootless warriors. The group was loud, deep into their cups, trading war stories and playing at dice, the lot of them restless with an undercurrent of feral aggression that often hung about fighting men imbued with too much ale and idle time.

Griffin did not miss the fact that more than one pair of eyes stared through the haze of the busy room to glance in his direction. He kept his gaze trained on them, his hand sliding under his mantle to rest surreptitiously upon the pommel of his sword. The serving wench came around a moment later, leaning her bosom across the scarred counter to inquire after his order.

"I could use some food and drink for the road," Griff said, handing her his empty wineskin.

"Passing through, are ye, love?"

"That's right."

"What a shame," she remarked, her gaze lingering overlong. "And I warrant 'tis not the best night for travel, either. There's brigands on the prowl, from what I hear. See those men over there?" She indicated the crowd of soldiers at the back of the tavern. "They say a murderer is loose in Derbyshire and now two knights and a local priest have gone missing."

"Is that so?" Griffin replied, schooling his expression to

one of suitable concern. "My thanks for the warning. I shall keep an eye out for danger on the road as I go."

"Mayhap ye'll be wanting to wait out the morn instead," she suggested. "I've got a pallet in the back I could let ye have. If ye don't mind sharing it with me, that is."

"A tempting offer," Griff lied pleasantly, "but I cannot delay."

"Pity," she sighed, heaving a shrug and tossing him a disappointed pout. "Can I bring ye a cup of ale while ye wait on yer food, love?"

Griff nodded. Although he had no mind to drink, he supposed he would blend in more readily from behind the rim of a tankard. He paid the woman when she returned, his attention more focused on the knot of armed men across the room. They had evidently decided he was of no particular consequence; the noisy group had since returned to their talk and gaming, affording him no more regard than anyone else in the crowded public room.

Only a few sober heads lifted when the tavern door opened a moment later, ushering in a draft of cold night air that set the table lanterns to wavering and stirring the meager scattering of old rushes that littered the earthen floor. Griff cast a glance over his shoulder to where four men now entered the establishment: a nobleman flanked by three knights who bore the standard and colors he knew all too well.

Dominic of Droghallow paused just past the threshold and stripped off his riding gloves, tucking them into the leather strap of his baldric. His dark head pivoted slowly, eyes narrow as he scanned the packed tavern.

The innkeeper nodded to the new arrivals. "Good eve, m'lord. Gentlemen."

Dom ignored the greeting and strode forward to lean his elbow against the tavern counter. Continuing his appraisal of the inn's patrons, he hooked the edge of his mantle around the hilt of his sheathed sword and motioned to one of his guards. "Check the back rooms." The knight and another advanced toward the rear of the establishment while Dom waited at the bar in arrogant, watchful silence.

"Can I help ye with something, m'lord?" the tavern keeper inquired.

"I am looking for an outlaw knight and the lady he has abducted from her betrothed. They were last spotted in the area just outside Derbyshire."

From where he sat in the corner of the busy room, Griffin hunched down, hanging his head over his cup of ale and grateful for the deep shadows of his mantle's cowl.

"This man is dangerous," Dom continued, his voice rising over the ruckus of conversation and gaming. When the noise scarcely lessened, the earl of Droghallow's tone turned shrill with impatience. "This man I seek is a murderer and a traitor to the crown. Anyone with information regarding his whereabouts will be handsomely rewarded."

"How handsomely?" someone shouted from the back of the room where the knights were seated.

"Aye," another chimed. "What are ye willin' to pay fer this bride thief, 'lord?"

"Ten thousand silver marks."

Dom's answer hung in the air like the haze of smoke that filled the rafters of the tavern. Dice games ceased; conversations halted midsentence. One of the men seated at Griffin's side hissed an oath of astonishment, a reaction Griff himself was inclined to share. Ten thousand marks was a fortune in silver, more wealth than any of these men might hope to see in a lifetime, himself included. Time had never been on his side in this risky venture, but it was fast becoming his worst enemy. Dom and the scheming prince seemed intent to rouse the entire county of Derbyshire to apprehend them.

Griffin was hugely relieved to see the serving wench headed his way at last, a parcel of wrapped viands tucked under her arm. She brought a foamy tankard to one table then passed the place where Dom stood, having since launched into detailed descriptions of both Griffin and his lady hostage, right down to the crescent scar on Griff's chin, a mark left by Dom's careless blade when they were boys.

"The miscreant will be hard to miss," Dominic was telling his rapt audience. "He is taller than most, and deadlier. Should he be located, I advise you to take all necessary precautions in his capture. I care not whether he is delivered to me dead or alive."

"There ye are," the tavern wench said as she set the wineskin and bundle of foodstuffs down before Griffin. "I packed ye some venison and cheese and a loaf of dark bread. It should keep ye fed for a couple of days on the road."

"My thanks," Griff murmured, retrieving a handful of coins from his purse. He put them on the counter to avoid further interaction, but the saucy woman would not be so easily dismissed. She gathered up the coins then leaned over his shoulder, her face beside his.

"Ye sure ye won't change yer mind about stayin' the night, love?"

"Mayhap another time," Griff drawled.

He felt something change in her demeanor, sensed a sudden air of startlement about the woman even before she drew back and sucked in a quick breath. He turned his head slightly and met her wide-eyed gaze, realizing his mistake a moment too late. She stared at him as if seeing him for the first time, her focus rooted on his mouth—at the falcate scar that cut into his chin and betrayed him as the criminal in question.

Griffin waited in tense dread for her to cry out in alarm. He would stand no chance of escape with so many men assembled in the small tavern—a score of warriors and at least as many common men fueled with ale and now this most recent promise of unfathomable wealth. He stared at the woman who now held his fate in her work-worn hands.

"Please," he whispered nearly inaudibly and gave a small shake of his head.

The tavern wench swallowed hard and took a step away from him, her eyes never leaving his face. Though she said nothing, her expression was blanched, pale, as if she stared into the visage of the devil himself. Her hands trembled and she wiped them on her apron, nervously fisting her fingers into the soiled square of white linen.

"Willa!" the innkeeper called, his harsh shout making her jump to attention. He gestured toward Dominic, who was watching as his dispatched guards returned from the back rooms emptyhanded. "Bring this fine gentleman refreshment before he perishes, why don't ye?"

With one lingering look at Griffin, the serving woman hurried away to carry out the order. Griff, meanwhile, took the opportunity to gather his things and move from his place at the counter. Though Willa had not called attention to him right away, he did not plan to tarry long enough for her to change her mind. While she waddled back to the bar, Griffin pulled his hood a little lower on his head and took three prudent steps toward the tavern door.

Dom's blade whisked out of its scabbard with a rasp of warning before coming to rest squarely in Griffin's path, stopping him in his tracks.

"No one quits this place tonight without my leave."

Griff paused, every muscle going tense inside him. Instinctively, beneath the cover of his cloak, his hand crept down to grip the hilt of his sword. Fighting his way out of there would be a futile effort, but one he intended to make nevertheless. Or die trying.

"Remove your hood and turn around, man," Dom ordered.

Griffin noted the subtle advance of two Droghallow

guards, saw his chances of escape begin to dwindle down
to nothing. The door was within arm's reach, but trapped
on the other side of Dom's bare blade, it may well have
been a league away.

"I said, turn around," Dom repeated, a brittle, wary edge
to his voice.

Griff drew in a steadying breath and prepared himself
for the bloody fight that was sure to follow. Hand clenched
on his sword, he pivoted his head to the side and raised his
eyes to look upon his foster brother, the man who now
wanted him dead and might well succeed.

But Dom did not have a chance to peer into the shadows
that concealed Griffin's face from view. Before the earl
could demand to see who stood before him, Willa burst
forth with a sloshing tankard of ale. She stumbled as if
pushed from behind, her squawk of alarm drawing Dominic's attention away from Griff for one crucial moment.
Pitching forward, the serving wench reached out to grab
one of Dom's knights in an effort to steady herself, while
the cup of ale in her other hand went flying, its contents
projecting out in an amber arc that doused a startled Dominic from head to toe.

"You clumsy idiot!" he cried, wiping at the dripping
mess that soaked his silk tunic and fine leather boots.

In the momentary chaos that followed, Griff sidled for
the door, pausing only long enough to see Willa scramble
up to wipe at the earl's fine clothing with her apron.
Through a string of apologies for her carelessness, she met
Griff's glance over Dom's shoulder and shot him a knowing wink before the Droghallow guards seized her and
pulled her off of their sputtering, outraged lord.

Griffin dashed out of the smoky tavern and into the cool,
dark night, his package of wine and foodstuffs tucked securely under his arm. He untethered his mount and leapt
into the saddle, spurring the beast into a gallop and sending

a mental word of thanks to the unlikely ally named Willa
who had just saved him from a date with certain death.

Dominic of Droghallow was so infuriated he could
hardly see straight. His guards had finally managed to dis-
entangle him from the witless woman who had drenched
him in ale, then proceeded to further soil him by attempt-
ing to wipe him down with her filthy apron. He had a mind
to throttle the wench for her clumsiness, however, he had
other more pressing matters to attend. The tavern keeper
rushed forward to assist, but Dom dismissed him with an
impatient flick of his wrist, then turned his attention back
to the cloaked man he had stopped at the door.

The man who was no longer there.

"Where is he?" he demanded of his guards. "The man in
the hooded cloak. Which one of you let him go?"

The knights said nothing, offering no excuse save the
exchange of sheepish looks that sent Dom into a further
rage. Cursing vividly, he shoved them out of his way and
lunged out the open tavern door, skidding to a halt under
the slim awning of the building's thatched roof. A gust of
cold wind swooped down from the black night sky and buf-
feted him, snatching up the edges of his mantle and whip-
ping it about his legs.

Dom peered into the darkness, scenting treachery ripe
in the air, but seeing nothing to substantiate his suspicions.
Nothing but a sliver of moonlight peeking through the
heavy cover of night clouds and a ribbon of empty road
stretching out in both directions.

The two soldiers came out of the tavern on his heels,
weapons at the ready.

"Where were the both of you when I could have used
your help?" he drawled sarcastically. He gave an arrogant
sniff and brushed at his wet sleeve. "Fetch my mount. I've
had my fill of Derbyshire; I'm heading back to Droghallow.

The rest of you shall remain here on search until Griffin and the Montborne woman are found and taken in. I don't want to see any of you before then, understand?"

The knights nodded obediently and raced off to gather their lord's mount. Dominic brought his hands up and pressed his fingers to his temples, willing away a headache that was beginning to pound behind his eyelids. His dealings with John Lackland were making him sorely tired; his constant aggravation was making him edgy, making him jump at phantoms. He was sick to death of thinking about Griffin, sick of contemplating the grim future that lay ahead of him if he failed the prince in this traitorous scheme.

There would be time enough to fret over his troublesome foster brother once the bastard was captured, he reasoned. Let his men and the bounty hunters of Derbyshire deal with apprehending him. Dom was on to more appealing pursuits that awaited him elsewhere, pursuits he was eager to resume in his bed with Felice at Droghallow.

Chapter Twenty-one

A queer and total darkness surrounded Isabel even after she opened her eyes. For some time, she had been hearing the constant drip of water echoing from somewhere beyond her conscious mind, the intermittent *plerk, plerk,* nagging her toward wakefulness. She did not know where she was. It was a cool, musty place, ripe with the tang of moss and damp stone.

Was it a cell? she wondered through her dazed senses. Had Father Aldon taken her to Derbyshire and Prince John after all?

Too weak to summon any measure of panic for what might have become of her, Isabel blinked into the crowding darkness and tried to make sense of where she was, of what had happened. Her head felt light, fuzzy; her mouth was thick and parched. Her limbs were too heavy to move under the pressing weight of her mantle. The hard cold surface upon which she lay had given her an ache in her back, but the discomfort paled next to the fiery pain that burned at her shoulder.

Suddenly the day's events came speeding back to her, almost as swift as the bolt that had ripped through the afternoon sky on Father Aldon's command. She remembered the bowman's shout that Griffin was in his sights. She remembered her terror, her desperation to thwart the horrible prospect of Griffin being harmed. She remembered hearing the arrow fly, remembered steering her horse into its path.

She remembered being struck from behind as if by lightning, remembered Griffin's cry of alarm. She remembered falling, falling . . .

Dear God, had she failed?

Heart clenched in fear, Isabel peered into the endless darkness above her. She had to see Griffin, had to know that he was alive.

"Gri—" she called out, unable to gather air enough to say his whole name, her voice little better than a faint croak. She tried to sit up, but could barely lift her head. "Griffin?"

A strong hand cupped the base of her skull, warm fingers threading through her hair. A gentle arm eased her back down. "I'm here, Isabel. Be quiet now. You're all right."

"Oh, Griffin," she gasped, so relieved to hear his voice. So glad to know he was at her side.

Her eyes beginning to adjust to the gloom, she could see him now, his face taking shape through the dark—just the barest hint of the harsh planes of his cheeks, his stern jaw and chin, his mouth, set in a grim line of concern. The rest of him was nearly obscured by the blackness of the place, but he was there.

He was whole and hale.

And he was with her.

Isabel settled at once, breathing a heavy sigh as her limbs and heart relaxed, her fear slowly dissipating so long as Griffin was there beside her. "Where are . . ." she said, then swallowed and tried again. "What is this place? Were we captured?"

"No," Griffin whispered. He smoothed her brow with the backs of his knuckles, a tender gesture that was there and gone much too soon for her liking. "We're safe," he told her, an odd distance creeping into his voice as he withdrew his touch and sat back on his heels next to her. "We're in a forest cave on the outskirts of Derbyshire. No one will find us here."

"Are you sure?"

"I am. This cave has had no inhabitants for centuries, by the looks of it. I doubt I would have seen it myself if my mount had not been startled by a darting hare just outside." She felt movement next to her as he lifted something and brought it toward her face. "Open your mouth," he instructed. "It's water. Drink."

Isabel parted her lips and let the cool liquid pass between her teeth. It tasted as crisp and clean as the spring he must have taken it from, a welcome draught that immediately quenched and soothed her dry throat.

"Easy," Griffin whispered, but in her thrist she took too much, too fast, and ended up coughing. The jarring of her body sent a stab of pain through her wounded arm. She winced, sucking in a sharp hiss of air. Griffin set the cup aside and held her head up until the spasm subsided. "Are you all right?" he asked.

Isabel nodded faintly and reached for his hand. She caught his fingers in hers and held them before he could withdraw from her again. "Griffin, I'm sorry. The things I said to you at Hexford . . . I should have never—"

"My lady," he interrupted softly. "Don't apologize."

But Isabel ignored his polite dismissal, determined to say what was on her mind. "I do apologize, for everything. And I thank you. I don't know what I would have done had you not come after me."

He exhaled a wry-sounding laugh. "I nearly didn't have the chance, truth be told. It seems Aldon had heard we were being sought by Dom and Prince John. He had plans to turn me over to Droghallow's soldiers while he took you directly to Lackland."

"What a fool I was to trust him," Isabel replied, heartsick to think he would have suffered on her account.

"No, you didn't know," he answered, forgiving when he surely had every right to be furious with her. "You could not have known, Isabel."

She frowned, chagrined, and shook her head. "You tried to warn me, but I didn't want to see it. I was so confused, I suppose I was not thinking rationally. I wasn't at all surprised to find that you had already gone when I left Hexford with Father Aldon this morning."

"I was there," Griffin replied. "There more or less, that is. I spent the night in Hexford's gaol, courtesy of the good father and a couple of enthusiastic castle guards."

She could hear the wry humor in his voice, but Isabel was only further appalled with her own naïvete. "He had you gaoled? Griffin, I'm sorry . . . I had no idea. I looked for you in the bailey this morning, and when I didn't see you, I just thought . . ."

He stared down at her, his gaze searching. "What did you think?"

She glanced away from him, to the dark wall of granite that curved high over their heads. "You were so angry after what happened between us yesterday afternoon, I suppose I thought . . . that you had left me."

"No."

That one simple word filled her with a queer sort of elation, a flooding sense of relief that she surely had no right to feel. She stared up into his eyes, their golden-green depths made unreadable in the gloom of the cavern, and wondered if he could see the joy in her face. She wondered if he could see the swell of emotions churning inside of her, her sudden want to hold him close, now that he was once again at her side, and never let him go.

A strange silence stretched out between them, unfurling slow and heavy, an unspoken awareness of the intimacy of their present position, the physical closeness they suddenly shared in that moment, their hands yet entwined in the dark with naught but the sounds of their mingled breathing to separate them. Griffin's fingers curled around hers, warm and strong, comforting. "I didn't leave you, Isabel," he said, his voice soft, husky. "I would not have left you, not even in anger."

He gave a slow shake of his head and gently released her hand. "In any event, I should be the one thanking you, my lady. You saved my life back there. Though God only knows what was going through your pretty head at the time to make you take such a risk."

Heaven help her, but she almost told him. Looking up at his intense expression, the handsome planes of his cheeks drawn taut with concern and some other, unreadable emotion, Isabel was only a hairsbreadth away from telling Griffin what had gone through her mind—what had gone through her heart—when she saw the deadly arrow flying toward him . . .

She loved him.

It was there, on the tip of her tongue, a confession that would have damned her as surely as it would have freed her soul. Dear God, she loved him.

Perhaps she always had, from that first encounter more than a decade past. But that was merely adoration, she realized suddenly; a little girl's infatuation with a heroic image, perfect and unattainable. The love she felt now was for this man who knelt at her side—this gruff, flawed human being who seemed intent to bar her from his heart. This man she could never have, even if by some miracle he would want her.

Isabel bit her lip to keep from blurting out the words she ached to tell him, watching with an odd mixture of regret and relief as he pushed himself up off the cavern floor to stand, putting a measure of space between them.

"Now that you're awake," he said, "I'll start a fire and have another look at your arm. I've brought you some food and wine. You should eat. The wine will keep you warm."

He helped her sit, then left her to sample the bundle of

viands he had unwrapped at her side while he busied himself gathering up some dry twigs that lay scattered about the cave. Isabel tore off a piece of roast venison, washing it down with the rich red wine as Griffin put together a small pile of kindling. It took only a half dozen strikes of his flint to light the ancient wood and soon enough a modest fire crackled at the center of their stone shelter.

Isabel watched the flames come to life, gazing in quiet fascination as they played over Griffin's features, illuminating his mane of wild tawny hair and gilding his handsome face with a warm, golden glow. He found a cracked old log and added it to the pyre, then tipped his head back to watch as a curling tendril of smoke spiraled up toward the roof of the cave and caught on a fresh draft of air coming in from the cavern's narrow mouth. The thin, chilly breeze ushered the sooty ribbon of ash up and away from the fire, carrying it deep into the night.

"How long do you expect we should stay here?" Isabel asked him over the soft snap and hiss of the small blaze.

He lifted his shoulder in a shrug as he glanced back at her. "Until you are well enough to travel. A couple of days, perhaps more."

She could see the guardedness in his features, could sense his underlying contemplation of their vulnerability now that they were hobbled by her injury. "But it's too dangerous for us to delay," she told him, shifting in a weak attempt to sit up. "We must keep moving. I am sore, but I warrant I am fine to travel."

She did not so much as press her hand to the floor to shift her position before a fresh jab of pain lanced through her. Isabel sucked in her breath through gritted teeth and fell back against the wall of the cave. A rush of perspiration instantly needled her brow, trickling along the fine hairs at her temple.

Griffin abandoned the fire and was at her side in a heartbeat. "Fine to travel, did you say?" He shook his head, frowning at her in apparent frustration. "I will tell you when you're fine enough to travel. Let me see your arm."

Though his tone was gruff, he took her in tender hands, a strong warrior with a touch so light, Isabel could only marvel at the powerful fingers holding her now, inspecting her wound with such care. It seemed strange that a man so adept at violence and battle could, in turn, be so gentle. But then Griffin of Droghallow, this man with the face of a fallen angel and the devil's own smile, was a myriad of contrasts, having once been her hero, then her enemy. Her hired abductor, mercenary escort, and now her . . .

What?

He was her protector, certainly, but that was merely the simplest of definitions for a relationship that had become anything but simple. What she felt for him was complicated, more complicated than anything she had ever felt before. It was love, that much she was certain, but it went beyond that somehow. The connection she felt to him went soul deep, a connection that seemed a part of her every fiber and feeling.

To Isabel's mind, there remained only one simplicity in the chaos of her current existence, a sole truth that she would be a fool to deny: whatever she and Griffin might share on this journey—whatever bonds they might form—would come to an end the moment they reached Montborne.

It was that sobering fact that kept her from reaching out to him now, kept her hand at her side when all she wanted to do was cup his strong jaw in her palm and caress the proud slope of his beard-grizzled cheek. Knowing that the heartache she felt now would only deepen the closer she allowed herself to get to him was all that kept her from telling him how confused she was, how frightened she was.

How desperately she needed him to hold her, just hold her.

An involuntary shudder swept over her and Griffin looked up to meet her gaze. "I am hurting you."

Isabel shook her head. "No."

"Here," he said, holding the wineskin up to her lips. "Drink what you can. It will help ease the pain."

" 'Tis not entirely unbearable," she insisted after swallowing a mouthful of the bitter wine. "Really, Griffin. It does not pain me overmuch."

"Mayhap not now, but I have to clean the wound. I will be as gentle as I can, but the duller your senses, the better." He pressed the lip of the wineskin to her mouth. "Drink, my lady."

Seeing the gravity of his expression and trusting that he knew more about such things than she did, Isabel obeyed. She tipped the wineskin up to her lips and drank what seemed like half of its contents. The wine seared her throat as it slid down, but then, as she swallowed more great gulps of the stuff, it slowly mellowed, generating a heat of its own that warmed her from the inside out. She sighed and handed the container back to Griffin.

"I think I'm feeling rather tingly."

He gave her a small smile. "That's a good start. Try to relax for a moment while I prepare some fresh bandages."

Grabbing a length of snowy-white silk from a pile of similarly shredded swatches that lay beside her makeshift pallet, Griffin then withdrew his dagger and sliced the cloth in half, creating two wide streamers. The edge of one glinted with threads of gold, the metallic embroidery sparkling in the firelight. It was the dress Father Aldon had made her wear that morning, she realized, suddenly becoming acutely aware of the scratchiness of the wool mantle rubbing against her bare skin.

"I'm sorry about your gown," Griffin said when he returned. "I didn't . . . I fear I had no other choice."

" 'Tis of no great consequence," Isabel said, feeling shy

for her nudity but trusting him implicitly. "Perhaps between here and Montborne we will be fortunate enough to find an alewife with an old kirtle to spare."

Griffin chuckled at her jest, but his expression remained serious. "No more old kirtles for you, my lady. I shall buy you the finest gown in England at first opportunity. You'll arrive at Montborne looking like a queen."

Isabel smiled wistfully, half hoping that day would never come.

"Lie back," Griffin instructed her, taking her hand and stretching her arm out so he could dress it. "I'm going to take off the old bandages, then clean the wound with the wine. You'll let me know if the pain is too much?"

"Yes. I am in your hands, my lord."

She had not expected the unwrapping to burn like it did. Although it was clear that Griffin took extra care to be gentle, Isabel's arm felt afire as Griffin stripped off the last layer of bindings. She sunk her teeth into the sides of her mouth through the worst of it, keeping up a brave front while Griffin worked expediently to undress and wash the wound. A second dose of wine was applied, and then a third, the pain dulling to an achy sort of heat by the time he paused to blot the wound dry. He looked up at her, his eyes tender with concern.

"How are you faring so far?"

Isabel managed a weak smile, knowing he only did what was necessary to make her better. "I vow I would fare no better under the care of the abbess of St. Winifred herself, and people traveled many leagues for the benefit of her skills."

"I am no healer," Griffin said, dismissing her praise as he reached for the ribbons of torn silk and began to carefully wrap the bindings around her arm. "I have tended my own battle injuries, but never another's. Never a lady's. Your skin is so delicate, and the bolt was . . . unforgiving.

God's blood, Isabel, when I think what you did . . ." His voice trailed off, his gaze sliding askance to meet hers. "You might have been killed."

"I wasn't," she replied, unable to keep from smiling up at him if only to reassure him. "Besides, I warrant I owed you as much. You saved my life once; now I have saved yours. We are finally even, my lord."

"Even?" he scoffed mildly, looking both annoyed and tortured by her remark. "There was no score between us to settle, my lady. You owed me nothing."

"I couldn't let them harm you," she said, her voice soft but steady. "No matter what might have happened."

Instead of warming to her earnest declaration, he scowled and went back to work on her arm, finishing the first wrapping and looping the outer bandage around to secure it in place. "You should not have risked it. It was madness, Isabel."

"Perhaps," she admitted quietly. "But I would do it again, and without a moment's regret."

He tied off the ends of the last bandage and his fingers went suddenly still in their ministrations. He pivoted his head to regard her, firelight dancing in gay contrast across the stern, stark angles of his face.

"I would take a thousand arrows for you, Griffin. I swear it."

Something flickered in his hooded gaze, an elusive spark of emotion that was there for an instant and gone, vanished under the deepening slash of his brows. His mouth curved slightly, but Isabel saw more anguish in the effort than she did elation. "You're speaking nonsense. The wine has gone to your head, making you say things you don't mean. Things you may later regret."

"It's not the wine, Griffin. I know exactly what I'm saying."

His gaze intensified as he looked upon her in the lengthening silence, the muscles in his jaw growing taut. His eyes seemed to look into the depths of her very soul, his face naught but a scant few inches from hers.

"My lady." His voice was a deep masculine growl, his breath warm against her cheek. Slowly, almost tentatively, he leaned in and placed a tender kiss on her mouth. It was sweet and heady and much too brief, a chaste meeting of their lips that still managed to make Isabel melt inside. Griffin kept his face close to hers even after he ended their kiss, his forehead pressed against hers, his hand woven into the hair at her nape, cupping her skull and drawing her close. His lips brushed her mouth as he spoke. "Never have I known such fear as I did in that moment you turned into the arrow's path. And I don't ever want to know it again, do you understand?"

He moved away from her then, a distance Isabel immediately mourned. "Besides," he added, his voice quiet, oddly reflective, "I'm not worth what you did. No one— nothing in this world—is worth the price you might have paid today. Honor is for fools, Isabel, trust me. The sooner you learn it, the better."

She shook her head. "I don't believe that and neither do you."

His answer was swift, brittle. "Don't I? Mayhap you should tell that to all the men I've killed in service to Dom. Tell it to their wives and children, or the folk I've made homeless in the villages I've helped to sack." Isabel felt herself shrink away from him a little, not sure what to make of the darkness that had begun to creep into his eyes. Her timid reaction did not seem to surprise him; he gave a harsh, almost sad laugh. "My hands have been bloodied hundreds of times with the sacrifice of decent, noble men. They did what their honor commanded them to do, but they're still dead."

"You can't hold yourself responsible for what you did at Droghallow," she told him gently. "You were only doing what you had to do. There's no dishonor in that."

"No? I expect the daughter of Droghallow's reeve would beg to differ with you on that score, my lady."

Isabel frowned. "You mean the woman Dom attacked?"

"I didn't tell you everything that happened," he said, his voice too level for the heavy burden that showed in his eyes. "When we spoke of it at Hexford that night, there were things I left out. Things I am ashamed to tell you, even now."

Although she feared what he might say, Isabel reached out her hand to him. "You can tell me anything, Griffin."

To her relief, he did not pull away. He wouldn't look at her, but he caught her fingers and held them, his grasp firm, needful somehow. His thumb idly stroked the back of her knuckles as he spoke, staring at their clasped hands. "You remember how Sir Robert had made provisions for the woman and her new husband?"

"Yes. He wanted to make up for what Dom had done."

Griffin sighed, his chest lifting as he drew another breath and continued. "When the earl died later that year, Dom immediately called for a strict accounting of his assets. He wanted to know where all of his money was going and to whom. Upon learning of Sir Robert's arrangement, he flew into a rage. I was ordered to accompany him down to the village and help him eject the couple from their cottage. I suppose I thought he would turn them both out of Droghallow and let the matter go." He made a dry sound in the back of his throat. "Dom had other plans."

Isabel swallowed a sudden knot of dread. "What did he do?"

"It was noontide when we got there. The woman and her husband had just sat down to share a meal before continuing on with their day's tasks. Dom demanded entry, and of course, as their overlord, they could not refuse him. He drew his sword and cleared their table with a long sweep of his arm, telling them that as he had paid for the food, it was his to ruin. He had similar words for the woman."

"They must have been so terrified," Isabel whispered, finding it easy to put herself in their place, at the mercy of a cruel lord's whims with nowhere to run.

"She was crying, pleading for mercy as Dom advanced on her. Her husband tried to intervene, but I stood between him and Dom. He was cursing us both, snarling as he fought to get past me and help his wife. He slipped on some of the debris scattered on the floor of the hut, and when he got back to his feet, he had a small knife in his hand. Dom was too preoccupied to notice the threat, but I saw the blade plain enough, and I knew the cottar intended to use it." Griffin was frowning, likely reliving the painful moment in his mind. He blinked, then finally turned his gaze on Isabel. "I couldn't let him do it."

"Griffin . . ." she said softly, feeling the burden of his guilt.

"I had promised I would look after Dom, and despite my loathing for him in that instant, I could not stand aside and let him be killed. So I struck first. I murdered that young man when all he wanted to do was spare his wife from a second degradation at Dom's hands." Griffin exhaled a shaky breath. "He had to know he would die, but it didn't stop him from acting, from doing what was right. I admired his honor, but it didn't save him or his home. And it didn't save his wife, either."

"Mother Mary," she sighed, heartsick. "Have you carried this with you all these years?"

"I should have turned my blade on Dom instead," he replied, not hearing her, too caught up in the pain of old memories to see that she did not condemn him for what he had done. "Maybe now you better understand who I am. Maybe now you see how wrong you were to try to save me."

"No," she said. "This doesn't change anything. It doesn't change the way I think about you . . . it doesn't change the way I feel."

"It damned well should," he scoffed. "You should be scheming a way to be rid of me at first chance."

"I never want to be rid of you, Griffin," she answered without hesitation. "I think I would go with you to the ends of the earth if you asked me to."

He went suddenly still as he looked at her then, searching her gaze as if confused by her gesture of understanding, confused by the depth of her acceptance of him in that moment. When she brought his hand to her mouth and kissed his battle-hardened fingers, he swore a soft oath. "My lady," he whispered, part question, part warning.

Isabel said nothing, holding his pained stare as she turned her face into his palm and kissed its warm, callused center. Griffin's brows crashed together, a tormented frown that bespoke of his inner turmoil. His eyes penetrated through the gloom of the cavern, searching hers, hungry yet uncertain, no doubt a reflection of her own gaze. He said her name and then he was moving closer to her, catching her mouth with his.

They kissed with a desperation neither could deny, their lips meeting, parting, then meeting again, hands touching, twining, trembling in their quest for contact. Isabel had never felt so alive, so willing to let go of everything so long as she was clinging to Griffin. She took all that he gave her in that moment, welcoming the sensual invasion of his tongue, letting his hands close over her naked breasts that so ached for his touch. She opened to him wherever he wanted her to, holding him close.

Wanting him closer.

When she would have wrapped her arms around him tighter, instead he started to back away. "No," he said, his voice thick, strangled-sounding. "I don't want to hurt you, Isabel."

Lovingly, she stroked his cheek. "You're not."

"Yes, I am. I will. This isn't fair to you. I promised myself—" He broke off abruptly, shaking his head. "I can't do this to you. I won't." Behind him, the fire popped and shifted, the last of the kindling fading to embers. He reached out, drawing the mantle tighter around her shoulders. "The fire will be out soon. You should try to sleep before it starts to get cold in here."

She didn't bother to argue because in that next moment, Griffin moved beside her and gathered her into his arms. His embrace was now more nurturing than sensual, and while her body still sang with his kiss, his wondrous touch, Isabel found herself snuggling into him like a kitten nesting in a basket of warm fleece. She buried her face in the solid comfort of his chest, breathing in the scent of him, that sublime mix of woodsmoke, night air, and man. Her palm rested over his heart, the steady thud of his pulse soothing her, easing her into a state of total tranquility and peace.

Her eyelids drifted closed almost immediately, and soon she was drifting off, succumbing to the weightlessness of a deep, black sleep that seemed to pull her under like the tide.

Chapter Twenty-two

He must have fallen asleep, though for how long Griff could not be certain. The fire had long since burnt to ash; morning was dawning damp and chilly beyond the cave, the cold air permeating the curve of rock at his back and seeping through his tunic and into his bones. Griffin pulled the edge of his mantle a little higher around Isabel, who slept soundly in his arms, quiet as a babe. He moved gently, loath to wake her as he reached down to tuck the soft wool under her chin.

Refreshed from sleep, his body responded easily to the feel of her draped over him in languorous slumber, their legs entwined beneath the cover of the cloak, her hip propped against his, her slender torso and firm, full breasts nestled enticingly into his chest. She was warm and soft in his arms, an angel fell from heaven on broken wings, wounded, trusting him to take care of her.

All too willingly, Griffin's mind returned to the intimacy they had shared last night, her tender understanding of his shame, her infinite goodness. His mind returned to the kiss they shared, as well, to the searing passion he had felt in Isabel's embrace, the hunger he had scarcely been able to control. God help him, he felt those savage stirrings come to life again just looking at her, just recalling the sweetness of her touch, her innocent sensuality. Of its own accord, his hand came up to caress the soft waves of her unbound hair, which tumbled down her back and onto him in a warm cloud of auburn silk. For a long moment, he tipped his head back and allowed himself to savor the quiet of the moment. He allowed himself to simply savor the feel of her, tracing his fingers idly through her hair.

Though it went against all logic and reason, Griffin wondered what it might be like for the two of them without the threat of Dominic or John Lackland. He wondered what it would be like without the royal order of Isabel's marriage to Sebastian of Montborne. How much silver would it take, he wondered, for the both of them to run away from all of this madness? How feasible might it be to disappear from England, to flee to someplace where they could be safe together? Someplace where they would never be found.

Although he doubted there existed such a place, it did not keep Griffin from thinking on it, from wishing for a solution to the impossible situation that held them pinned between two unbearable outcomes, each to result in their inevitable separation.

I think I would go with you to the ends of the earth if you asked me to.

That earnest if not slightly drunken confession continued to haunt him all these hours later. God rot him, but when she said it, he had nearly swept her up and taken her away on the spot. He was tempted to do so even now. Particularly now, before she woke up sober and clearheaded enough to recant her foolish offer.

"My sweet Izzy," Griff whispered as he stroked the lean curve of her arm. "What are we to do, you and I?" Tenderly, he swept aside the mass of flame-colored waves that had fallen into her face, then bent his head down to press his lips to her brow.

All the blood in his veins seemed to freeze the moment his mouth touched her skin.

Her forehead burned like fire against his mouth; her skin was flushed pink and hot to the touch.

Dear God, Griffin realized in sudden, sweeping alarm. She was fevered.

"Isabel?" he said on a harsh, indrawn breath. "Isabel, wake up."

But she did not so much as stir. Her lifeless form sprawled atop him like a child's doll, limp, unmoving, unhearing. Terrifyingly still.

"Isabel," he repeated, his voice stern, strangled with budding panic. He gave her a little shake, but it did nothing to rouse her. He felt her cheeks with the back of his hand, pressed his ear to her pale, parched lips to listen for signs of life. The shallow breath of air she drew into her lungs gave him hope, but when he then pulled away the coverlet and hastily removed the bandage from her arm, he knew a swift and heart-wrenching twist of dread.

The wound had become infected. Thready fingers of redness trailed out from the center of the gash in all directions, poison creeping insidiously under her creamy skin. The light in the cave was too dim to tell how far the danger had advanced. Praying it was not as bad as he feared, Griffin carefully rolled Isabel into his arms and got to his feet. The mantle she was wrapped in trailed behind him, rustling on the earthen floor and then through the fallen leaves as he carried her out of the cavern, ducking under the low overhang of ivy-covered granite and bringing her into the pale light of the new morn.

Dawn proved to be as cruel as it was honest. In the pinkish glow of the autumn sunrise, Isabel's wound bloomed red and angry at her shoulder, fanning out in a jagged starburst shape toward her breast and lower arm, the infection seeming to spread almost before Griffin's eyes. God's blood, he should have known. He had been too late with the wine, too late cleaning the injury. He stared down at the fiery wound, cursing himself for her pain. He had promised to take care of her, had sworn to her that she would be all right.

Damnation, but she had trusted him. He could not fail her; he had to make it right somehow. He had to get her fever down before she slipped away entirely, had to find a way to cool her heated brow and body.

Heading toward the trickling rush of the nearby stream, Griffin carried Isabel through the forest bracken and down the gentle slope of the riverbed. His boots slipped on the muck and dew-slicked rocks as he brought her to the water's edge and waded in. The icy brook soaked his hose and boots, the bracing cold drenching him to the waist, chilling him to the bone. He held Isabel in his arms, using his free hand to gather water and anoint her forehead as the current swirled and churned around them.

His teeth were chattering, limbs growing numb, but he hardly noticed. Over and over, he scooped up handfuls of water and fed it to her fever, praying it would help, praying she would respond. God help him, he had never felt so helpless, so inept. He did not know what to do, nor where he could take her. He was alone with her in these woods, alone with the responsibility of making her better, for he could not bring her into town and risk certain capture the moment they ventured into the open streets. Their allies—and, indeed, their choices—had been few before and were dwindling fast now that their bounty price had gone so high.

They had no one to turn to, nowhere to go.

And so Griffin simply started running, knee-deep in the freezing cold water of the stream. The weight of the current pushed against him with every stride, making his steps heavy, dragging. Sunlight slanted down from the treetops to dance on the surface of the brook, shattering like crystal as he crashed through it. Above him, high in the canopy of branches, a flock of starlings screeched at the intrusion and took flight. Somewhere, up ahead in the distance, Griffin heard the faint hum of voices raised in mournful song.

Monks' voices, he realized, chanting their Latin prayers.

The vaguely familiar, low-tenor, haunting tone caught his ear at once, drawing him toward the sound like a beacon in a storm. He trudged out of the water and up the bank, his feet dragging in the leaves and pine needles that blanketed the loamy ground, his breath huffing out of his straining lungs and misting in the chill forest air. He saw nothing ahead to indicate his progress toward the monastery; his ears alone guided him through the gorse and bracken that clawed at his boots and snagged on Isabel's trailing, sodden mantle. He traversed one rock-strewn gully and then a next, half stumbling in his haste, his panic, commanding his legs to keep going, pleading with Isabel to hang on, that it could not be far now.

And it wasn't, thank God.

At last, the dark shadows of the monastery came into view through the trees. A low curtain wall of river rock and stacked wedges of granite circled a clutch of ancient buildings that seemed to rely more on their remoteness for protection than they did the barrier of their gate or stone enclosure. Griff pivoted his hip against the thigh-high fence and slung his legs over one at a time, taking care not to jostle Isabel as he jumped to the ground on the other side and ran across the space of the small courtyard.

"Please!" he shouted as he neared the tight huddle of buildings. "Someone! We need help!"

The drone of chanting was the only reply. Griffin followed the sound past the stables and almonry, then down a trellis-enclosed, narrow walkway lined with climbing rosebushes and worn from the treads of countless sandaled feet that had made the short trek toward the chapel at its end. Griff's heels dug into the hard-packed earth, his boots and spurs chewing up the path with each long stride.

He ran the last few steps to the chapel door and scarcely paused before kicking it open. The old oak panel swung wide, banging against the wall. Daylight poured inside, illuminating the windowless, candlelit chapel peopled with more than a score of kneeling monks, their tonsured heads bowed in prayerful chant but a moment ago and now turned on the stranger who filled the doorway of their private sanctuary. A stranger who stood before them dripping wet, panting, face taut with worry, holding a half-naked, unconscious woman in his arms.

"This lady has been injured," Griffin said to the slack-jawed, gaping assembly of holy men, too grim to trifle with apologies for disrupting the assembly. "Please. She needs help."

For a long moment, no one moved. Then the monk at the head of the group gave a nod to one of the brothers and a slim cleric rose in silence from his place on the floor. Head bowed, the young monk walked toward Griffin and motioned for him to follow. Griff fell in behind, carrying Isabel down one winding corridor and then another, until finally the novice stopped and indicated a small chamber off the hallway.

He pointed to a modest pallet situated inside. Griffin carried Isabel in and laid her gently on the thin straw mattress. As an afterthought, he tugged the mantle together to cover her, as if the wet wool was any source of warmth. As if it could hide the fact that he had brought her there naked, half dying as a result of his inadequate care. Shamed, Griffin turned back to face the young monk.

"She was hit by a crossbow bolt yesterday. It grazed her arm," he said, gesturing to her and feeling a stab of anguish for how small and pale she looked on the humble bed. "I did what I could to clean and bind it, but this morning . . ." He shook his head, swallowing past a knot of dread that clogged his throat. "I don't know how long she's been fevered. A few hours, perhaps. But the wound is festering."

The novice's gaze was sympathetic, devoid of condemnation. Still, Griffin found it hard not to blame himself for Isabel's condition. He should have sought help immediately. He had seen enough soldiers die in fevered agony from injuries less severe than Isabel's; he never should have risked trying to tend her on his own. If she died . . . God's love, if she died, he did not think he could bear it.

"Can you help her?" he demanded of the silent cleric, watching in helpless frustration as the monk knelt down beside the pallet and gingerly inspected Isabel's arm. "I must know if you can help her."

A moment passed without response, a moment during which Griffin could only close his eyes and plead with God to show him some scrap of mercy. The monk came up off the floor in a faint rustle of robes, his expression placid, maddeningly indiscernible. With one hand outstretched, he nodded to Griffin, indicating the open door.

"No. I'm not leaving her," Griff growled. "Heal her, but heal her where I can watch you."

The young monk stared apologetically but maintained his stance. He blinked slowly at Griffin, waiting patiently for him to accept the terms of his help.

"My son," a gentle voice called from the corridor outside. Griff turned to find the elder monk standing at the threshold, his hands tucked into the wide bells of his sleeves. "Time is fleeting. We should leave the good brother to his work."

Griffin cast a final glance at Isabel, then reluctantly allowed himself to be walked to the door. Once outside, the oak panel sealing him off from the room, Griff turned, pressing his head and splayed palms against the rough wood, idly watching as water dripped from his wet hair and tunic to splash on the floor at his feet.

"Have you a scribe here?" he asked the monk with whom he shared the cramped space of the hallway.

"Of course. Most of our brothers are skilled with letters."

"I need to send a message," Griffin said, deciding then and there what he had to do for Isabel. It was the only thing he could do for her now. "I need to send word to Sebastian,

Earl of Montborne. He should know that his betrothed is here . . . that she is ill and in need of escort home."

"Very well." The monk's voice was gentle beside him. "Consider it done, my son."

"Thank you."

"Brother Ronan is a good healer," the old monk offered, placing his hand on Griffin's shoulder. "If there is aught to be done for your lady, he will see to it with his herbs and God's help."

"I pray you are right, Father." Griff released the weight of his thoughts in his heavy, heartsick sigh. "I pray you are right."

"Come," the monk said. "We will pray together, my son."

Chapter Twenty-three

It had taken three days. Three days before Isabel gave the first indication that she might survive. Brother Ronan had kept her arm wrapped with a series of herbal pastes and poultices, all of them sickly colored and foul smelling. Griffin asked on several occasions what the nasty concoctions were made of and how they were working, but his questions earned him only a bland smile or a cryptic shrug from the infirmarer monk. Brother Ronan would not tell him how Isabel fared nor how long she might remain asleep, his silence subjecting Griffin to a prolonged and maddening state of ignorance and utter helplessness.

He had told himself that he would send his message to Montborne, then go, leaving Isabel in the monastery's care. But his urgent missive was long gone, and he still could not leave. Not without knowing that she would be all right, not without seeing her well with his own eyes.

And so Griffin had stayed for the duration, holding cold compresses to Isabel's brow, cleaning soiled bandages, making new ones as Brother Ronan required them, helping in whatever ways he could. He did not eat or sleep, leaving Isabel's side only when he had to, and returning always with the same hopeful question: "Any change?"

Finally, around dusk of the third day, her fever broke.

Griff waited in tense anticipation for Brother Ronan to confirm his suspicions. At last, his hand on Isabel's brow, the monk turned to Griffin and nodded, the uncustomary width of his smile telling him that the worst was over. But still, Isabel did not wake.

As dusk dragged on toward midnight with no further sign that Isabel was on the mend, Griffin wondered if this seeming improvement had been but a false omen, the cruel trick of a vengeful God who had every reason to scorn him. Weary, some long hours into another night's vigil, Griffin let his head drop, resting his forehead on his bent elbow.

"Gri . . . Griffin?"

It was such a quiet sound, the barest thread of a whisper, that Griff thought at first his ears had deceived him. He raised his head, almost afraid to look at her and find her still asleep, still separated from the rest of the living world. But then she stirred slightly. Her pale lips parted and she said his name again, stronger this time as her eyes slowly opened. "Griffin . . ."

"I'm here," he whispered. "I'm here."

He left her side just long enough to go to the door and call for Brother Ronan to come to the room, then returned to the pallet where she lay and hunkered down at her side. Isabel blinked several times, her eyes growing brighter in the dim candlelit room, more alert as she peered up at him, then slowly took in her surroundings. Griffin squeezed her hand, scarcely able to rein in his urge to sweep her into his arms. "You've had me so worried, my lady. Thank God you are awake at last. How do you feel?"

She blinked up at him, then frowned. "Starving."

Griff's answering shout of laughter was thick with joy and deep relief. "Starving," he chuckled, smoothing the hair from her brow. He turned at the sound of Brother Ronan's sandals padding softly into the room. "My lady is awake, and she's hungry," he told the silent, smiling monk. "Will you fetch her something from the kitchens? Some bread and wine, perhaps a wedge of cheese?"

"Turnips," Isabel murmured sleepily. "I should like some boiled turnips, I think."

Griffin brought her fingers to his lips and kissed them. "Anything you want. If there are none in the kitchens, I'll go to the gardens and dig some up myself."

Brother Ronan returned a short while later with Isabel's requested meal. He placed the tray of steaming food on the pallet near her feet and left as quietly as he came, as if he sensed the intimacy of the moment and knew it was not his to share. Griffin helped Isabel sit up, propping the bolsters at her back. He fed her, held her cup while she drank, and when she was finished and too exhausted to stay awake past her last bite, he settled her back under the covers and watched as she slept.

Griffin was tired beyond measure himself, but he found no solace in that moment, for now that Isabel was whole and hale, he knew that he would soon have to find the words to tell her good-bye.

Food was foremost on Isabel's mind the following morning, as well. After allowing her privacy for her morning toilette and a fresh dressing for her arm, Griffin was back at her bedside, pleased to see her sitting up on her own. She whispered her thanks to Brother Ronan as he brought in a steaming bowl of fish stew and a loaf of bread, heartier fare than any of the monks would take to break their fast, but they seemed happy enough to feed their ravenous little stray.

"I'm glad to see you're feeling better," Griffin said, taking the bowl when she struggled to balance it on her lap.

She had been given a dark brown habit to wear, a boxy, crudely cut garment that hung off her slim shoulders like a grain sack. But above the plain collar, her cheeks were pink, her eyes clear and bright, and Griffin had never seen a more welcome sight in all his years.

God, how he wanted to embrace her, tell her how scared he had been that he might never see her thus again. If not for Brother Ronan, collecting his things from the table at

Isabel's bedside, Griffin might have acted on his urge. Instead, he waited, watching as the young monk arranged his jars of herbs and laid out a supply of fresh bandages. Finally, with a nod to both of them, he padded quietly out of the room.

No sooner did he close the door, than Isabel reached over and scratched at the binding on her arm, trying to dig her fingers under the knots.

"Let it be," Griffin chided, grabbing her hand.

"But it itches."

"It's healing."

She peered down at the bandage and wrinkled her nose. "It stinks."

"Brother Ronan is no perfumer, but his poultices work. Besides, you'll grow used to the smell, just as I have these past few days."

"Thank you," she said. At his look of confusion, she offered him a warm smile. "Thank you for staying with me the whole time. Brother Ronan told me how concerned you were."

"Brother Ronan told you?" He scowled, letting the spoon fall back into the bowl with an exclaimed bark of disbelief. "Three days in the same room with nothing but each other for company and he never deigned to utter a single word to me. Not even when I was ranting at him in frustration. I swear I took the man for a deaf mute."

"Oh, he hears, but he doesn't speak," Isabel hastened to correct him. "Not with words, anyway. He has taken a vow of silence. He speaks with his eyes."

Griffin grunted, spooning up a bit of broth and holding it out to Isabel. When she didn't take it, he glanced up and met her gaze.

"Your eyes are telling me something as well, my lord."

"Oh?" he asked, not at all as casual as he tried to sound.

"Yes, they are. Something is troubling you. What is it?"

He shrugged. "I've been worried about you for a good

many days. I still am, truth be told. Now why don't you finish your stew and concentrate on getting well?"

"You're keeping something from me, Griffin, I can tell.
If you're concerned that Dominic's men will find us here,
you needn't worry—"

"That's not it, Isabel."

"—because from what I understand, this monastery has
been here in seclusion for nigh on a century. We're the first
outsiders Brother Ronan has ever seen. Why, I expect we
could live here until we were old and gray and no one
would ever know."

"We can't—" Griff exhaled sharply, shaking his head.
"We can't live here, Isabel."

He didn't say any more than that. In truth, there was no
need. She understood. She had a life waiting for her somewhere else, promises she had to keep. He wasn't going to
take that away from her, no matter how it might tear him up
to let her go.

"We can't stay here," he said again, needing to convince
himself as much as her.

Isabel's gaze was soft, knowing; her small smile wistful.
"Can we pretend, then?" she asked quietly. "Maybe for a
little while?"

Griffin stared at her, feeling the same ache in his chest
now that he felt when she lay unconscious in her bed. The
ache of loss, of loneliness without her in his life. As unfair
as it was to her, he didn't want to feel that ache. Not now.
Not any sooner than he had to.

"Eat," he said, handing her the bowl and giving her
cheek a brief caress. "Try to rest. I'll come back and check
on you again a bit later."

Chapter Twenty-four

Isabel spent the rest of the morning dozing off and on in her small room, listening each time she heard footsteps in the hallway, hoping each time her door opened and Brother Ronan came in to check her dressings that it would be Griffin instead. He had stayed away from her for hours. Indeed, she had not so much as heard his voice since his first visit with her earlier that day, when she had carelessly reminded him of their troubles with Dom, then foolishly asked him to make believe those troubles did not exist.

Of course he could not pretend they were out of danger. It had been selfish of her to ask. After all, the responsibility of getting her delivered to Montborne rested squarely on his shoulders. It was easy to forget that it was he who had to provide for them, he who risked his neck every moment they spent on the run, he who bore the burden of looking after her and his own well-being, as well.

It was easy to forget about her own responsibilities, too. To her king, her house, her sister—and to her betrothed. She had made commitments. Promises. Consecrated vows. To put her heart—to put her woman's longings—before all of those obligations would be the worst sort of dishonor.

And then, there was Griffin. She could not forget how much he needed Sebastian's reward for her return. Though he had not made mention of it lately, Isabel knew it was all he had to hold onto—the hope that when this madness was ended, there would be some sort of future waiting for him.

It broke her heart to think that future did not include her, but she didn't see how it could, and she didn't know how she was going to bear it once he was gone from her life forever.

She sighed, blinking back the sadness that began to well in her eyes at the very thought, her ear drawn to noises in the hall. Outside in the corridor came the sound of footsteps, the familiar, measured stride much too purposeful to belong to any of the brethren. Her heart gladdening as the door swung open, she met Griffin's entry with an uncontained, happy smile.

"You're awake," he said, grinning. He held out his hand. "Walk with me."

Isabel nodded, tossing aside her coverlet and slinging her legs over the edge of the pallet. She lifted the hem of her borrowed habit and scuffed into the sandals she had been given by the monks, meeting Griffin at the door, her spirits buoyed by his very presence.

She didn't ask where they were going, merely let him lead her along one winding passageway and the next, happy just to be with him. He took her hand in his as he turned and walked down a narrow hall, pausing to smile at her over his shoulder as he braced his hand against a dark oak panel and opened the door on a glorious courtyard garden.

A trellis of roses formed a canopied archway into the Eden-like setting, a hedge-enclosed feast for the senses, awash with color and fragrance and warm autumn sunshine. Isabel stepped past Griffin to enter the garden, tipping her head back to breathe in the mingled scents of juniper, rose, and sweet bay. A bird twittered from a branch of an apple tree ripe with fruit, its song carrying on the gentle, cooling breeze that sifted through the hedges like the soft sigh of an angel.

"This is heaven," Isabel whispered, beaming her joy at Griffin.

"Come," he said, and led her further within.

Her hand ensconced in his, he brought her to the heart of the garden, to a private shady alcove where a turf-covered bench sat overlooking a small reflection pool. Nearby, spread upon the grass, was a blanket bearing a tempting assortment of things to eat: a loaf of bread, a wedge of yellow cheese, three bright red apples—even a bowl of boiled turnips.

"You did this for me?" she asked, laughing as she dropped down onto the blanket and grabbed one of the apples.

Griffin removed his sword belt and sat himself next to her, resting his elbows on his up-drawn knees. "You've been so long in bed, I thought you might enjoy a day outside."

"It's perfect."

She bit into the apple and leaned forward to investigate the rest of their food when a queer rumple in the blanket caught her eye. Something was tucked underneath it—a cloth package, square-shaped and about the width of her chest, wrapped in linen and tied with a strand of red ribbon. "What's this?" she asked, pulling the parcel from its hiding place.

Griffin snatched it back from her and held it behind him. "You'll find out later."

"What is it?" she asked, her curiosity piqued. "Is it a package of tarts? Sweetmeats?"

"Not quite," he said with a chuckle. His eyes were smiling still, but his expression grew serious as he brought the bundle around and handed it to her. "It's for you."

Isabel tossed aside her half-eaten apple and took this new prize, her heart suddenly fluttering in her chest. She brought the soft, wrapped parcel onto her lap and frowned up at him in hesitation. "For me?" At his nod, she carefully untied the ribbon that held the package closed, unfolding the linen wrapping to unveil what it contained.

What she saw stole her breath away.

Inside was a creamy linen chainse and a gown of the finest sky-blue silk, cut to the height of fashion, its sleeves dropping down to elongated points, its bodice fitted and yoked above yards of diaphanous skirts. But if the gown was exquisite for its design, it fell nothing short of extraordinary for the delicate needlework that adorned it. For embroidered at the neckline and hem was a chain of tiny, beautifully rendered butterflies in every color of the rainbow, their jewel-toned hues picking up the sun's rays and reflecting them back like diamonds. A pair of matching silk slippers tumbled out as she held the dress up to look at it more closely. Isabel had never seen anything so amazing, so extraordinary, in all her life.

"I told you I'd have you arriving at Montborne looking like a queen," Griffin said when she could manage no reply. His smile was wistful, his eyes watching her as if he thought he might be looking on her for the last time. "Mayhap you'll let me see it on you later."

"Of course," she exclaimed, still awestruck by its beauty. "But how did you—where did you get it?"

"I found it at a shop in Derbyshire. The tailor had made it for a noblewoman in town but my price was fair and he was willing to sell it to me."

"Is that where you were all morning?" Isabel gasped, astonished that he would go to the trouble—and the risk—for her. In fact, the longer she considered the notion, the more upset she became. "Griffin, you should not have done this. What if Dominic's men had spied you in town? What if they'd captured you?"

His answering grin was sardonic, reckless. "Obviously, they didn't."

"And this dress is so beautiful—" She picked it up again, marveling at its loveliness. "Griffin, it must have cost a fortune."

He shrugged off her disbelief, leaning back on the blanket to watch her in enigmatic silence. She stared at his self-satisfied expression, his lazy smile, her gaze drifting over the long, athletic lines of his body . . . and she suddenly realized that his coin purse was missing. The purse that held everything he owned, the months' worth of wages he had been saving at Droghallow to help him start his new life. He had spent it all.

"It was worth it," he said, answering her question before she could summon her own voice to ask it. "You are worth it."

For a long moment, she could only stare at the gown, wondering how she would ever be able to wear it without thinking of Griffin, without reflecting on everything he meant to her and always would. "Thank you," she said at last, feeble words, her voice sounding so very small, shaky with emotion. She set his amazing gift aside and leaned forward to press a kiss to Griffin's mouth.

She had meant it to be a chaste meeting of their lips, a kiss bestowed in thanks on a cherished friend, but when she opened her eyes Griffin was holding himself so still, staring at her, his gaze hooded, smoldering. Filled with the same heat, the same need, she felt swelling to life in her.

"I'm going to miss you," she whispered breathlessly, confessing her thoughts without thinking, without caring if it was right or wrong. "Oh, Griffin . . . how will I ever live without you?"

Griffin's eyes fell to her mouth as she said it; his jaw clenched, breath rasping out of him. And then he was kissing her. A growl curled low and deep within him as their lips crushed together in a desperate joining. He brought his hands up to frame her face, his strong fingers trembling, wading into her hair to clench possessively at the base of her neck, pulling her close. He shifted to bend himself over her, easing her down onto the blanket as if he could not help himself, kissing her with a savageness that nearly made her want to weep.

Over and over, she whispered his name, breathing it like a prayer against his mouth, his cheek, his neck. His hands swept down the front of her and she arched into them, arching into his body like a supplicant come to worship at a holy altar.

But the need she felt for him was anything but holy. It burned like the devil's own fire, a swift, consuming blaze of heat and longing that flared hotter, more ravenous, with every sensual thrust of Griffin's tongue, every hungered nip of his mouth, every rush of warm breath that rasped against her sensitive flesh. It made her greedy for more of him, this wicked burning, commanding her past humility, past the lonely part of her that answered to duty and honor. All she knew was she needed him. Needed to feel his touch everywhere, needed to feel his skin against hers.

She could scarcely bite back her cry of pleasure when he reached down and cupped her breast, kneading her flesh to a sweet, aching tautness. His palm rasped against the rough fabric of her habit, the heat of his touch searing through the heavy linen weave as he traced a path of exquisite fire over her ribs, her abdomen, and down, to that place that burned the hottest for him. She squirmed beneath him as he caressed her there, panted in helpless wonder as he smoothed his hand over the quivering mound, stirring her blood to a delicious, dizzying frenzy.

"Ah, God . . . Isabel," he swore against her neck, his voice thick, reverent. Too soon, he dragged his hand away, bringing it up to catch her own as he seized her lips in another fevered, open-mouthed kiss. "Touch me, Isabel. I need you to touch me."

Their hands entwined, he guided her under his tunic, pressing her fingers to the warm skin of his bare chest as their tongues clashed and quested in a sensual mating. She felt his heart pound hard and heavy against her palm, felt the solid heat of him, so strong, so powerful, his muscles bunched and tight, his skin soft as the richest velvet. Isabel let her fingers see what her eyes could not, tracing the thick-hewn sinew at his shoulders, the solid line of his breastbone, her palm smoothing across the wide, flat discs of his chest, rubbing over the tight nipple at their center.

Griffin groaned when she allowed her hand to skim lower, her fingernails raking lightly down the firm ridges of his belly. He was propped up on one elbow as he kissed her, affording her the full breadth of his torso, his groin a rigid and insistent pressure at her hip. Although it was shameful, Isabel had the sudden want to feel that part of him that was so mysterious, so potently male. She reached down between them, tentatively at first, unsure what to do. As if he sensed her uncertainty, Griffin shifted beside her, filling her splayed palm with the solid length of his arousal. When she could only hold her hand there, marveling at the impossible strength of what swelled tighter beneath the layers of his hose and braies, he began to move against her, guiding her touch, showing her how to please him.

"I need to touch you, too," he whispered roughly.

Isabel's reply was little more than a breathless plea: "Yes."

She felt a sudden, delicious shiver sweep up the length of her and realized somewhat dazedly that the hem of her habit was being lifted, baring her legs to the cool autumn breeze. Baring her skin to Griffin's touch. He stroked the length of her leg, his battle-hardened fingers warm against her calf, tender against the sensitive length of her inner thigh. She could scarcely breathe as his hand traveled higher, his palm skidding along the curve of her hip, into the concave hollow and thatch of curls nestled low between the bones of her pelvis.

Although he moved slowly, his fingers wading gently into the moist cleft of her thighs, her body flinched with an instinctual urge to bar the sensual intrusion, her legs jerking suddenly, coming together. Everything that was prudent and sane in her warned that this was wrong, that she should not crave something so wicked, that she should not invite this shameless brand of intimacy. But all it took was a soft brush of Griffin's thumb, the vaguest pressure of his hand and her legs fell open to him, granting him entry to that sacred, most private place that burned for him.

If she thought herself lost to his kiss, if she thought herself mad with desire for his touch, it was nothing compared to the mindless bliss he stoked within her in that moment. His palm was hot, firm against her mons, his caress coaxing her to arch into him, her body weeping, yearning for something she needed desperately but could not name. In her rapture, she felt his fingers slip between the petals of her body; she writhed in anguished pleasure when he found the pearl of her womanhood and stroked it to a tight, quivering bead of raw sensation.

"Oh, Griffin," she gasped, something strange and swelling starting to build deep inside of her with every brazen caress of his hand. She squeezed her eyes shut, raising her hips up off the blanket to meet the oncoming wave of fire, Griffin's touch growing wilder, more demanding, his fingers blunt and questing between her thighs. Though she craved the wickedness of his touch, she was distracted by a sudden pinch as he pressed deeper, a surprising, sharp jolt of pain that stabbed through her veil of mounting pleasure. She clutched him tighter, but was unable to bite back her pained little whimper. Griffin stopped at once and broke away, his head rearing up, a curse raw in his throat.

"Isabel. God—I'm sorry."

She shook her head. "It's all right."

"No," he said tersely. "I swear to you, this wasn't my intention."

"It's all right," she repeated, flustered and embarrassed to have ruined what had been so special, so exquisite between them. "I didn't mean to . . . please don't stop."

He turned his head out of her kiss when she raised up to him. "We're not going to do this."

Isabel reached for him, but he was already moving off of her, rolling onto his back on the blanket and leaving her lying cold and empty beside him. She shifted toward him, hating to think that her inexperience could be so disappointing, so displeasing to him. "Show me what you want," she whispered, desperate to reclaim the moment, yet knowing in her heart that it was already lost. "Won't you tell me what to do? Show me what you want, Griffin."

He shook his head, his arm slung over his forehead. He closed his eyes as if he could not bear to look at her. His sigh was heavy, regretful. "I want . . . I want you to go, Isabel. Please . . . leave me now. Just take your things and go back to your chamber before someone finds us here."

She didn't know what to say. She didn't know how to fix what she had done wrong, and so she simply did what he asked her, retrieving her gown and slippers and rushing out of the garden before she broke down and wept in front of him.

Chapter Twenty-five

The monastery quieted as the brethren went to chapel for their evening mass. Their procession having passed his way some moments before, Griffin now stood in one of the openwork corridors that overlooked the gardens, staring into the encroaching night and contemplating the many mistakes he had made since embarking on his journey with Isabel. The mistakes he was making even now, in letting himself be near her, in not telling her about the message he had sent to Montborne.

Truth to tell, he would call the missive back if he could, but it would have easily reached its destination by now. It was much too late for second thoughts, and the sooner he delivered Isabel to her betrothed, the better. Their encounter in the garden that afternoon had been proof enough of that. Even now, some hours later, he still shook with his want for her. He filled his lungs with the crisp night air and he could smell her, the subtle perfume of her hair, her skin, her sweet essence. He closed his eyes and he could see her, her head thrown back in pleasure, her mouth open, lips flushed and glistening from his kiss.

God help him, but he could still feel her, could still feel the silky dew of her body and the tremors of her waking passion, the innocent surrender that had so unmanned him, turning him into a beast that would have stolen her virtue in the middle of a monastery courtyard. Would still, he knew, because though the hunger he felt for her was banked, it was burning nonetheless. He swore an oath into the darkness, hoping to shove the unwanted temptation from his head like the puff of misting breath he expelled into the cold moonlit night.

His harsh sigh was answered by a small sound behind him in the arcade. An unsure footstep, a shift in the air. He knew without turning around that it was her. He had come to know her presence the way he knew his own thoughts, and he had to steel himself from turning around to face her.

"You shouldn't be out here, Isabel." She did not heed the warning in his tone; she said nothing, but he heard her take a small step toward him. His scowled deepened. "It's cold tonight, my lady. And it's late."

"I . . . I wanted to see you."

He squeezed his eyes shut to hear the note of fear in her voice, knowing that he had put it there. Jaw clenched, he stood unmoving, listening as she drew nearer. A breeze swept along the cobbled stones of the passageway, sifting through her skirts as it eddied by. He could almost feel the shudder that passed over her. Could imagine her breasts awash in gooseflesh, her nipples puckered and erect beneath the fabric that covered them . . .

He exhaled sharply, then bit off a curse as Isabel took another step forward. From the monastery chapel cradled in the heart of the labyrinthine compound came the low hum of the monks in prayer, their chants drifting softly into the night, the woody tang of incense and candle smoke streaming on the wind. Griffin kept his gaze fixed on the shadowy courtyard, his shoulder propped against a supporting wall of ancient, arched stone. He crossed his arms over his chest, hands fisted to keep from reaching out to her. "You should be in your chamber, my lady."

"No, my lord. Not until you hear what I have to say."

He waited for her to lash out at him for his behavior in the garden that day; surely she had every right to be offended, appalled. He waited for her to demand repairs to her honor, half hoping she would tell him that she wished him gone from the monastery at once. Half expecting she would tell him how she despised him, how she wished him gone from her life forever.

He would understand, of course. Griffin heard her draw a shaky breath behind him, and he waited for the words that were going to shatter his heart.

"I was barely twelve years old when I was sent to live at the abbey," she said quietly. "My father, whom I adored, had been accused of treason—a word I didn't fully understand, save that the very mention of it seemed to shake our house to its foundation. My father had betrayed his king some years before, you see, allying himself with men who would place the crown on the head of another."

"Richard," Griff supplied, well aware of the familial struggles for power that had occurred while Henry Plantagenet ruled England. Ironically, those struggles continued even now, with Lionheart on the throne and his younger brother already scheming to see him ousted.

"It was an old crime," Isabel said. "The failed rebellion was no longer as relevant with Henry near his death, but when the king heard rumors of his vassal's part in the betrayal, he demanded an answer. He sent his soldiers to Lamere to question my father and obtain either his confession or denial." Isabel gave a sad little laugh. "He could have said it wasn't true. Henry was fond of him; he would have taken my father at his word. My mother pleaded with him to deny the accusations, warning him what it would cost if he did not refute the allegations. Everything would be forfeit: his title, his holdings, quite possibly his life . . . but he would not listen. It was as if none of that—none of us—mattered. When the sheriff and royal guards arrived to read the charges, my father calmly listened, and when the last of it was said, he simply stood up and let the soldiers take him away."

Griffin swore under his breath, unable to imagine the weight of that day, the hurt it must have caused the child who had to watch as her family was rent asunder.

"I hated him for it," Isabel whispered. "I hated that he could be so selfish, that he could care so little for me, or for my mother and Maura. I couldn't comprehend how he could throw all of us away. And when my mother wept over his traitor's grave, sick in her heart and soon in her mind, I swore I would make it right if I could."

And so was born a young woman's sense of honor and noble duty, Griffin realized with a pang of regret. If he had not understood her conviction to family before, he well did now. His chest ached for the pain she had endured at so young an age, the pain she bore even now. It was all he could do to keep from turning around to catch her in his arms. But it wasn't his place to console her; he would not assume she wanted his sympathy.

"I didn't think I would ever be willing to turn my back on my commitments," she said after a long, thoughtful pause. "I didn't think anything could ever matter more to me than the promises I made that day."

Every particle of Griffin's being stilled as the words tumbled off her tongue. He did not draw breath, could only stand there, staring into the dark, listening to the heavy thud of his heart and Isabel's soft voice a few short paces at his back.

"I know now what my father must have been going through. How he must have struggled with the decision of doing the honorable thing. I thought him selfish and a coward, but in these past few days, I have begun to recognize the same faults in me."

"Not you," Griffin said, knowing himself more by both unfavorable descriptions.

Isabel stood closer to him now; he could feel the heat of her against his spine, their bodies not touching but sharing the same space, warming the air between them, charging it with a tension that coiled tighter each second they remained apart.

"Although it would condemn him, my father had to do what he felt in his heart was right. He couldn't have lived with himself pretending to support a king he did not believe in, knowing he was living a lie, and so he gave it up. All of it. All of us. Now here I am, about to enter a marriage I don't believe in—a relationship that will never be true. If I had a fraction of my father's honor, his courage, I would do the same as he did—"

"No," Griff told her, taking a step away from her, hoping to stop her before she said anything more. He could not let her tell him what she would be willing to give up for him. He couldn't trust himself to deny her. "It would be a mistake, my lady. One I won't let you make."

"Nor would I ever ask you to give up your future," she whispered. "But I feel as if I have this one chance—that I am holding something precious in my hands, something I will never have again. Something that's going to slip away unless I hold it fast, even if just for a moment. If just for one night."

"Isabel," he said, and turned to face her at last. His breath abandoned him on a humbled, ragged sigh. "Ah, God . . . Isabel."

She stood in a moonbeam's slim column, wearing the dress he had given her that afternoon. Without the chainse to line it, the filmy gown was rendered nearly transparent, the pale blue silk skimming her form like a gossamer veil, the skirts wafting around her legs like mist. He knew she would be a vision in the dress, but what he looked upon now was a goddess, an enchanting angel much too lovely for his mortal eyes. And much too sweet for the tears that began to stream down her cheeks.

"My lady," he said as he closed the space between them.

"What you are suggesting . . . I am not worth the price you would pay."

She turned her face into his caress, her voice very small when she finally managed to speak. "I promised myself that I would not beg you, that if you didn't want me—"

"Never," he told her fiercely, tipping her chin up and forcing her to meet his gaze. "Never have I wanted anything more in my life . . ."

Her smile was sad, unsteady. "Then, please . . . Griffin . . . my lord . . . I need you."

Griffin held her face in his hands, searching those glistening topaz eyes for any sign of trepidation, any hint of doubt. There was no uncertainty, rather a wealth of fierce emotion swimming in the tears that swelled and spilled down her cheeks. He swept them away with his thumbs, pressing a tender kiss to her brow, her nose, her mouth. Her arms came up around him in a tentative, needful embrace.

"Please," she sighed against his ear.

Overwhelmed, his throat too constricted for speech, Griffin bent to place his arm under her knees and scooped her off her feet. She clung to him, her face buried in the curve of his neck as he navigated the maze of walkways and corridors that led to her chamber at the infirmary. The climbing voices of the monks at mass surrounded them, the chanted Latin prayers echoing in the high arches of the halls, infusing the night with a sense of reverence. An atmosphere of mystery and sacredness.

"This night is yours," he vowed to Isabel as he opened the door to her small room. He shut it with his boot heel, then carried her to the thin straw pallet, the bedside candle flickering as he placed her atop the humble mattress. He glanced to the pool of tallow with its wobbly flame, then down into Isabel's glowing eyes. "I wish I could give you more," he said, kissing her. "This room should be a palace, this bed fat with feathers and plush with furs."

She pressed her fingers to his lips and gave a small shake of her head. "All I need is you."

Griffin sucked her fingertip into his mouth, then eased himself over her, bracing his weight on his fists, his elbows bent as he leaned down to kiss her again. He moved his lips over hers gently, lavishing her with a slow, worshipful joining of their mouths, and then their tongues. He would not rush her tonight. No matter the depth of his hunger for her, he would stretch the night out, wringing each hour, each minute, of its full measure.

And so he did, making love to her with his mouth, learning her most sensitive places and just how to stir them. He tasted every sigh and whimper that fell from her lips, tasted the velvet softness of her neck, the fluttering pulse at the hollow of her throat. With fingers more clumsy than he would have wished, he untied the laces that bound the bodice of her gown together at her breasts, spreading open the butterfly-adorned neckline to gaze upon her nakedness in wordless, reverent awe.

She was so beautiful, his Isabel, her long auburn hair spread around her like a halo of silken fire, her small breasts proud and firm, tipped with perfect buds that pebbled and peaked against his tongue when he dipped his head to sample their sweetness. She arched against him as he sucked each nipple into his mouth, her back rising off the mattress, aiding him in his want to ease her out of her clothing.

Her torso freed of the gown, Griffin smoothed his palm down the length of her, memorizing the softness of her skin, the delicacy of her breastbone and ribs, the pleasing dip of her belly. He kissed her there, at the sweet indentation of her navel, smiling when she shuddered under the subtle invasion of his tongue, a rush of gooseflesh spreading up her sides.

"It tickles," she gasped, laughing softly.

He gave her a wicked lift of his brow. "I'm going to tickle you some more."

Sliding his hands down her hips, he removed her gown entirely, lifting first one long leg, then the other, from within the tangle of skirts. He draped the kirtle over a faldstool near the pallet, then turned his attention back to Isabel, his breath rasping out of him on a vow. "Mon Dieu, you are exquisite," he whispered, his loins thick with the heat of mounting passion, his arousal straining against the confines of his clothing.

He positioned himself between her legs, reaching over to lift her slender foot in his hand. He leaned down, kissing the fine bones of her ankle, letting his mouth slide up the length of her calf, along the side of her knee, bending forward as he reached the velvet span of her inner thigh. She breathed a voiceless "Oh!" as he sucked a mouthful of the tender flesh between his teeth, teasing her with a playful nip before hooking her bent knee over his shoulder so he could lower himself between her parted legs.

She went rigid the instant his tongue touched her. Her pelvis arched and she started to squirm away, but Griffin held her in place, his hands resting lightly atop her hips, letting her know there was no need for shame, nothing to fear. As he had with the rest of her body, he made love to her slowly here, as well, coaxing her to a writhing frenzy before taking the swollen pearl of her femininity into his mouth and laving it to the point of sudden, shattering release.

Isabel's climax nearly unmanned him. She keened against him, whimpering his name, her reaction so unreserved, so complete, it was all he could do not to strip his clothes off and bury himself deep within her. But he had promised her the night was hers, and so he rode out the wave of her release, easing her back to earth with gentle kisses, soft caresses, murmured endearments.

She reached down for him, her fingers scrabbling for him and twining in his hair. "Please . . . enough . . ."

"Enough?" he chuckled, crawling up the length of her. "My lady, we are only getting started."

Her laugh was breathless, her eyes dark beneath her half-closed lids. "I want to feel you," she whispered, bringing her hand up to stroke his face. "I need to feel your body."

"As you wish." Braced on his knees astride her, Griffin unlaced his tunic and stripped it off. He flung the linen shirt to the floor, pausing to revel in the feel of Isabel's fingers touching his bare skin, his medallion pendant sliding cool against his skin as her hand drifted across the planes of his chest and down along his abdomen. Her gaze lingered where his erection rose thick and throbbing between his legs, stretching the fabric of his hose. "Feel what you do to me," he growled, taking her hand and placing it against his straining flesh. "Feel how much I want you."

With his guidance, she closed her hand around the length of him, her parted lips and smoky gaze telling him that she wanted to know more, that she was ready to experience whatever he would show her. Shaking, exalted, Griffin unfastened the points of his hose and braies, rolling the last of his clothing off his hips and kicking it aside. Isabel made a soft exclamation of surprise as his arousal sprang free of its encumbrances, a guileless reaction that brought a prideful grin to Griffin's lips.

"Does it hurt?" she asked innocently as she gazed upon his swollen member, sounding so concerned he nearly laughed aloud.

"In a way," he admitted. He slid down on the bed, covering her, holding himself above her and teasing her belly with the blunt head of his penis. "It aches for you, my lady."

"I think I ache for it, too," she whispered.

Griffin eased himself between her parted thighs, his shaft slipping deliciously into the cleft of moist curls. The wet heat of her body seared his flesh, soliciting a deep shudder of sensation from within the very core of his being. Instinctively, his hips began to rock against her, his sex shifting into place, impatient to be in her. Her moan of pleasure made him harder as they slid together, not yet joined but melding, yearning, moving as one. She matched his rhythm, clinging to him, her fingernails biting into his back, her legs coming up around his to hold him to her.

When he would have tried to slow down, tried to pace himself, she urged him on with a single word: "Yes . . ."

And then, he was beyond wanting, beyond desire, caressing her breasts, kissing her mouth, grinding against her in an effort to get closer, to bring her back to the brink of ecstasy when the pain of what he would do—what he had to do to answer his own need—would not be so difficult. She was nearly there; her limbs were quaking, breath coming fast and hot against his face.

"I have to be inside you," he murmured, not giving a damn for how needy he sounded in that moment.

She clutched at him, squirming in passionate frustration. "Oh, yes . . ."

He couldn't have waited any longer if his life depended on it. Holding her between his braced elbows, he shifted his pelvis, and with a single, deep thrust, he penetrated the barrier of her maidenhead. She cried out, but already her sheath was convulsing around him, the tight walls of her womb wracked with the force of the climax she had been so close to finding before he entered her. Despite that his body was taut, fevered, trembling with the need for release, Griffin held as still as he could, allowing himself only the smallest of movements while Isabel caught her breath, adjusting to this new, sensual invasion.

He placed a kiss to her damp brow. "That was the worst of it, I promise."

"Well, it wasn't so bad," she whispered shakily. "It hardly hurt at all."

Griffin smiled down at her, his brave little angel. "You're crying."

"Yes," she answered. "Because I'm happy."

Prayerfully, humbled, he kissed the tip of her nose. "So am I, my lady," he said, hoping she wouldn't hear the bittersweet edge to his voice.

With a reverence that deepened every moment he gazed upon her, Griffin began to move within the sweet sanctity of Isabel's body. She accepted him fully, rising up to meet his light, easy thrusts, caressing his back, kissing his chest and shoulders, as he slowly found his pace once more. He rocked against her in a numbing brand of bliss, filling and withdrawing, his tempo growing more urgent as her womb clenched around him, coaxing his release.

Too soon, he felt his climax building, climbing to crescendo. He was lost to the feel of her, the scent and taste of her . . . lost to the very thought of her. He whispered her name, praising her as he filled her with the breadth of his passion, his strokes long and deep, hips pumping, his sex raging toward completion. He wanted to make it last, but he was too hard, too hungry. Too far gone.

His control began to slip, then snap. He lifted her pelvis and impaled her with a final, savage thrust, a hoarse shout tearing from his throat as his seed began a fast, molten rush from his body. Only at the last moment did he find the strength to catch himself, somehow managing to pull out of her silken warmth and roll away before he cost Isabel anything more than her virginity that night.

She turned toward him on the mattress after he left her, placing her head against his chest and stroking him as he shuddered, struggling to find his breath. Her lips were tender on his bare skin, her kisses sweet with concern. "Are you all right?" she whispered.

Griff gave a thick chuckle and wrapped his arms around her. "Oh, yes. I don't think I've ever been better."

He could feel her smile curve where her cheek rested against him. "My White Lion has saved me again," she told him, her voice like a sigh. "I thought I owed you my life for rescuing me the day we met, but now . . . after tonight . . ."

"No," he said, gathering her close. "I was the one in need of rescue, my lady. And you have given it well beyond what I deserve."

She said nothing for a long moment, her fingers stroking idly at his chest. The evening had grown still, the monastery chapel having faded to quiet. Mass was ended; on the table next to the small bed, the candle sputtered and breathed its last. Griffin eyed the bowl of smoking, melted tallow with scorn.

"I shouldn't stay here much longer."

Isabel's reply was soft, regretful. "I know." She toyed with the medallion hanging around his neck, lifting the half-moon of bronze into her palm, rubbing her thumb over the enameled design. "Would you think poorly of me if I told you that it wasn't enough? I thought I could be satisfied with just one night, but it's passing so quickly . . . I'm afraid to let you go."

"My sweet lady." He bent his head and placed a kiss in her hair. "Sometimes we have to do things, even if they scare us."

It wasn't the answer she was looking for, he realized, but he would not give her false hope, not after all she had given him since he had come to know her. In truth, he shared her fears, perhaps more for his understanding of how short their time together now really was. As much as he hoped for her happiness, he could not bear the thought that she might forget him one day. They would always have the memory of this night, but in time another man would bring her pleasure. Another man would give her children, be at her side as she grew old. As unfair as it was for him to despise that man, Griffin found himself nursing a profound contempt, a selfish want to know that Isabel would take something with her from their time together, something to remind her . . . and then he knew.

"I never forgave myself for losing that medallion," he heard himself telling her as she let the amulet fall to rest once more against his skin. "It was my greatest treasure, everything of value that I had as a youth."

"And you said you planned to sell it at first chance," she scolded, slapping her palm down on his stomach in light reprimand.

He chuckled, but there was little humor in his voice. "I never would have sold it. And I should have thanked you for keeping it for me." She started to say something, no doubt ready to deny his appreciation, but her reply cut short when he reached up to remove the medallion from around his neck. He brought it down before her, draping the long chain over her bed-tousled head and letting the pendant settle between her bare breasts. "I want you to have it back."

"Griffin, I can't," she said, meeting his gaze. "You said yourself it's your greatest treasure. It's all you have of your family . . ."

If he had family at all, Griffin supposed that he was looking at it now. If the bond of blood could be as thick and true as what he felt for Isabel, then he need never know any other kin. She was all that mattered to him, and if he had been searching for a place of belonging before, he had surely come to know it with her. He lifted the medallion into his palm, staring at the image of the white lion rampant, the one half of a full circle that seemed somehow complete now that it rested over Isabel's heart.

"This is where it belongs," he said.

And with her sweet, answering sigh, the night became a fragile thing. Too fragile for talk, and so they came together again without words, a joining of lips and hands and bodies, a breathless twining of hearts and souls. Griffin brought Isabel astride his hips and slowly guided her to another climax, watching as she rode him to the precipice of bliss and following her over the edge in the next instant. This time, he could not stop himself from filling her with his essence; he was too desperate to hold onto her, to hold onto the moment.

Together they shattered, their gazes locked, burning. Neither could look away; neither could let go, not even when their bodies collapsed on the bed, spent and sated. Trembling, silent, they clung to each other, unwilling to separate. Unwilling to surrender to their exhaustion, or to acknowledge the threat of the fast-approaching dawn.

Chapter Twenty-six

He was gone when Isabel opened her eyes that next morning. He had left, probably some time after she had finally fallen asleep, but his scent and the memory of last night's splendor remained. She stretched her limbs and rolled to put her face in the thin down bolster, breathing in the arousing muskiness of sweat and leather and man. She could smell him in her hair and on her skin and she thought she might die for the pleasing ache it brought to her soul.

Her body knew a pleasing ache as well, a fullness and a void. Though she had never been so tired, down to the depths of her bones, never had she felt so alive. And she knew that the source of her awakening could be summed up in one word: Griffin. She had to see him. She had to tell him how special last night had been. She had to know if he felt any fraction of the bliss she did for what they had shared.

Scarcely able to breathe for her excitement to start a new day with him, to put herself near him again, Isabel pushed up off the pallet and reached for her clothes. And then she heard it.

The slowing beat of horses' hooves on the approach. The clink and shift of riding gear. The jangle of armor and the low rumble of men's voices. Someone hailed the father abbot in the courtyard with an indiscernible greeting, the tone short, serious. Demanding.

Dear God, was it Dom's men?

Panic rising in her throat like a knot of cold, cutting steel, Isabel threw on her chainse and blue silk gown, her fingers working like mad to lace the bodice, the injury at her arm burning for her haste and lack of care. She shoved her feet into her shoes and lunged for the door to her chamber, frantic to find Griffin. Frantic to warn him that they had been found.

She flung open the panel, dashing out as it banged against the wall, a sound that seemed to echo like a clap of thunder in the corridor. The leather soles of her slippers slapped on the smooth stone floor as she ran through the quiet infirmary building. Isabel headed for the main artery of the maze of halls and passageways, in the hopes that she could flee to the back of the compound before the guards forced their way inside to search for them.

With every pained stretch of her legs, every lurching beat of her heart, she prayed that Griffin was safe somewhere on the monastery grounds. She begged God to keep him hidden from the soldiers in the yard, asked for speed in reaching him before either of them fell into Dom's hands.

Let her be taken if one of them must go, she pleaded as she rounded the last corner, breathless and panting. She half stumbled, her fingers clawing at the rough wall to keep from falling as she pitched into another wild run down another corridor.

Please, Lord, she silently intoned, let her find him before the guards did. She would go with them willingly, so long as she could be certain Griffin would not be harmed . . .

"My lady."

The deep, unfamiliar voice issued forth from behind her, a calm command that stopped her halfway down the wide passageway that would have led to freedom.

"My lady, Isabel de Lamere."

Slowly, making good her bargain with God, she turned to face her fate. A knight stood in the gloom at the end of the main corridor, his large frame blocking out the scant

light at his back, casting him in ominous silhouette. A rich
surcoat of shadowy color fell from his broad shoulders to
his knees, the line broken by a wide belt of leather cinched
at his waist. Though his clothing bespoke his titled rank,
he wore a suit of chain mail armor, as if fully prepared for
the prospect of battle; his sheathed sword a slash of darkness at his hip, his polished steel helm tucked under his
arm.

"It is I, my lady," he said when she made no immediate
reply. "Sebastian, Earl of Montborne. Your betrothed. I
have come to take you home."

Griffin sat on a turf-covered bench in the monastery garden, his elbows resting on his knees, his head dropped low
between his shoulders as he stared sightlessly into the
small reflection pool at his feet. He had gone there for solitude, to find some space to think, having been able to tear
himself away from Isabel's side only a few short hours before. But now, hearing a shuffle of activity within the clois-
ter—the stir of voices, the unmistakable sounds of arriving
soldiers—he knew the true reason he had sought the garden's seclusion: He had gone there to hide.

The day he had been dreading was here . . .

Sebastian of Montborne had arrived, and Isabel was
soon to be leaving.

He supposed he had felt the awful coming of it in his
bones that morning, when he woke up beside her, holding
her with a fierceness that was too gnawing, a contentment
that was too complete, too profound to last. It hurt too
much to hold her knowing he would have to let her go, and
so he had left her. Now that her betrothed was come to
fetch her, Griffin hoped that she would understand his absence. He hoped that she would not regret the beauty of the
night they had shared, that she might know what it had
meant to him . . . what she meant to him, and always
would.

But more than that, his cowardly heart wished—prayed as never before—that she would simply ride away to where she belonged, and spare him the pain of watching her go.

"My lady, did you hear me? You've nothing to fear anymore; you're safe now."

Sebastian of Montborne took a careful step toward her, his free hand extended in a gesture of peace, surely meant to comfort the stranger who was his bride, a woman who stood numb and trembling a few paces away from him. She could not believe what she was hearing, could not make sense of what she was seeing. Not Dom, not a retinue of hard-eyed guards ready to seize her to meet the whims of a scheming lord and a wicked prince . . . but her betrothed.

She should have felt grateful. She should have felt relieved. Instead she felt a deep sickness in her soul, a wretched hopelessness that clawed at her, sucking the breath from her lungs as it sought to sap the strength from her legs.

It had been easy to deny that she was sworn to the earl when he was merely a name flitting about in her head, a guilty feeling of obligation that she had allowed her heart to push aside. But now that he was here, flesh and blood, a man whose only trespass was to be chosen by the king to be her husband, Isabel knew a terrible sense of shame. He had given her no cause to fear him and yet she shook with bone-deep dread as his spurs ticked on the stone floor with his approach.

"P-please," she stammered, unable to stop herself from taking an unsteady step backward. Her heel caught in the train of her skirts, nearly tripping her, but the handsome, dark-haired earl had already closed the space between them, reaching out as if to catch her before she could fall. Isabel flinched away from the firm grip that held her elbow, staring into her affianced's slightly confused, but noncondemning eyes.

There could be no denying him now, no denying what was happening.

She would have to leave the monastery. After all that had occurred, after all that she had been through, now she would have to leave Griffin. Just like that, the small happiness she had known was ended.

"I can't—" she gasped, struggling to speak for the way the ground seemed to be opening up beneath her, the air seeming to close in tight around her. "Oh, God, I . . . I can't . . . can't breathe—"

She backed away, first one step, then another, shaking her head, her voice all but robbed. The earl reached out to her, though not with force, nor did he try to curb her flight. Closing his hand around the empty air where she had been standing, he watched, his dark brows drawn together in a slight scowl as she retreated another pace, then turned on her heel and bolted.

She didn't care if he followed or stayed; she ran along the corridor tunnel without direction now, nearly sobbing, arms crossed over the ache swelling in the pit of her stomach. At the end of the cavernous hallway, she rounded a sharp bend, and crashed into one of the monks, scarcely pausing to acknowledge the startled young brother, her head spinning, heart roiling. Light beckoned from the other side of a door up ahead of her, clear white sunrays outlining the dark shape of the old oak panel. She lunged for it, bracing her palms against the rough wood and pushing it open, staggering into the warm daylight of the garden.

Outside, still running, still sucking in choking gasps of air, Isabel navigated the maze of flower beds and shrubbery, the branches of an alder bush snagging at her skirts and long flowing sleeves as she stumbled past, blind with panic. She came around the alcove where she and Griffin had spent last afternoon, their private corner of the garden.

And, by Mary's sweet mercy, there he was.

"Oh, Griffin!" she cried, throwing herself into his arms as he rose from the turf bench he had been sitting on and turned to face her. She gulped in a fortifying breath and pushed the awful words out in a rush. "It's him . . . Sebastian of Montborne! Oh, God, Griffin—he's here. I don't know how he found us, but he's here. He's come for me and I don't know what to do!"

She felt his arms drop down around her, lightly, as if he was reluctant to embrace her now. Her heart was still racing as she clung to him, her breath still rapid and harsh in her ears, but not so drowning that she did not hear the heavy sigh leak out of Griffin. She sensed his queer stillness, his vague withdrawal.

Sensed his total lack of surprise at this terrible, unexpected news.

"You knew he was coming," she whispered, drawing away from him. Heaven help her, but the truth was there in his eyes. She could hardly find her voice to speak. "Did you . . . my God, did you send for him?"

That he would not reply was answer enough. She pulled out of his weak embrace, stunned, feeling as if she had been physically struck. His face gave her no comfort either; he looked down at her in expressionless silence, the skin seeming tight across his cheeks, his jaw held firm. But he would not deny his betrayal. Isabel was miserable with the idea, hurting someplace deep inside.

"When?" she asked, her voice choked and raw.

It took him a moment to answer. "The day I brought you here. I had one of the brothers scribe a message to Montborne and see that it was delivered. You were so sick . . . I didn't know what else to do." He shook his head and let out a soft curse. "I thought your betrothed had a right to know where you were."

"And what about me?" she scoffed brokenly. "You should have told me you had sent for him. I had a right to know—"

"Yes, you did," he admitted. "In truth, I didn't think it would matter; I hadn't planned to stay. I thought I would leave once I saw that you were better, but then . . ."

"But then I threw myself at your feet and you thought differently," she supplied, a bitter edge to her tone.

"It was nothing like that, Isabel."

"No?" she scoffed. "Well, then, mayhap you stayed to make sure you were able to claim your reward for my return."

He exhaled sharply. "It's not about some damned reward. I don't want anything from Sebastian of Montborne."

"What about me, Griffin? Do you want nothing from me, either?"

"I want you to be happy."

"Liar," she shot back. "You say that while you're standing here breaking my heart."

"We knew this day was coming, didn't we?" he asked matter-of-factly. "We knew the day would come when you would go to Montborne and I would go my own way. All we were doing was delaying the inevitable." He reached out to touch her face, but she turned away from his caress. "I thought it would be easier this way," he said. "For both of us."

She felt a tear slide down her cheek. "I must mean nothing to you at all if you found it so easy to simply turn your back and let me go."

"God, no. You couldn't have it more wrong, my lady." His voice gentled, nearly to the point of a whisper. "Isabel . . . I love you."

It killed her to hear those precious words when her betrothed was but a few hundred yards away in the monastery, preparing to take her with him at any moment. "How dare you say it," she charged bitterly. "How dare you tell me you love me—now, when it's too late for us to do anything about it. When you knew all along that he was coming for me!"

Griffin moved closer. "I love you."

"No," she said, needing to deny it, for it hurt so badly to think he might mean it after all.

"I love you, Isabel, and I always will."

She brought her hand up to slap the words from his lips, but he caught her by the wrist and held her steady, his grip unyielding, his gaze intense with emotion. "Unhand me!" she cried, fisting her free hand and beating his shoulder in a fit of helpless, heartbroken rage. "I hate you! Let me go!"

"The lady said let go, sirrah. I suggest you release her at once."

The growled demand made both of them still, then Griffin slowly freed his hold on her arm. Together, they turned toward the source of the interruption, Isabel's face streaming with tears, Griffin's hard with frustration and something deeper that she could not read. The Earl of Montborne stood before them like an impassive wall of muscle and tight-reined determination, but he was no longer alone as he had been in the corridor with Isabel a few moments ago. Four knights flanked him, two on each side, the lot of them poised to strike and awaiting his command.

"You are Griffin of Droghallow?"

Isabel saw Griffin's vague nod of acknowledgment in the corner of her eye, then glanced up to find the earl's hard gaze fixed on her, his gray-green eyes narrowed in an unwavering stare: cool, assessing . . . knowing. A muscle jerked in his dark-bearded jaw, his nostrils flaring as if he could scent her betrayal. Isabel's ears burned with the depth of her shame, but she struggled to keep her chin high, forced herself to hold his gaze. Sebastian seemed to consider her for a moment in stony silence, then his focus leveled on Griffin.

"Arrest him," he ordered his guards. "We'll take him with us to Montborne to stand trial for his crimes."

Chapter Twenty-seven

The two days spent en route for Montborne were easily among the worst of Isabel's life. Although the earl had taken steps to see to her comfort, having brought her a gentle palfrey outfitted with a soft padded saddle and rich wool blankets to warm her during the journey, Isabel could not recall when she had ever felt so miserable. Riding alongside her betrothed and his caparisoned white charger, flanked at the fore and aft by two pairs of armed knights, it was all she could do to not bolt from the group and flee for the beckoning escape of the distant hills. Instead, she marshaled that urge along with another, equally compelling one: the urge to constantly turn her eyes to the tail of the traveling party, where Griffin rode on a bay gelding, bound and under guard.

As they left the monastery, Sebastian had given Griffin over to two mounted Montborne soldiers; one held the bay's reins, the other held the rope that had been fastened around Griffin's wrists. He was being treated with a modicum of care, but as a criminal nonetheless.

For her part, Isabel, too, felt somewhat the criminal. In her guilt, she could hardly bear to look at her betrothed, and so she stared at the road ahead, unable to offer him more than the weakest of replies when he tried to engage her in polite conversation to pass the time, and eating beside him in awkward, prolonged silence when they stopped to rest and refresh the horses during the trek north.

And all the while, she could feel Griffin's eyes on her.

He had been seated with the company of guards some dozen yards away from Sebastian and her, his tether slackened to afford him space to eat and drink, the opposite end tied around the base of a sturdy ash to ensure he stayed put. Isabel could not tell what he was thinking; his emotionless gaze told her nothing. Did he hate her? He had intended to leave her with Sebastian and set off on his own, but now, because of her, he was arrested and soon to stand trial for his role in her kidnapping. What punishment would he see at Montborne? She was too terrified to so much as think on the prospect.

"Does it pain you terribly, my lady?"

Sebastian's low voice next to her startled Isabel out of her grim musings. She forced her gaze away from Griffin and back to her betrothed, trying to make sense of what he was asking.

"Your arm," he said. "It troubles me to think you are suffering. If the injury pains you overmuch, we could slow our progress so you can rest more frequently. I don't want to tax you any more than you have been already."

Isabel managed a small smile. "Thank you for your concern, my lord."

He poured her a cup of wine from a hard leather decanter and handed it to her. When Isabel tried to take it, his grip resisted slightly, prompting her to look up at him. His gray-green gaze was piercing, unsettling. "We are to be wed soon," he reminded her. "You may call me Sebastian if it pleases you . . . Isabel."

It seemed so odd to hear her name roll off another man's tongue. Odder still to think that what the earl said was true: they were to be wed soon. She looked into the face of her affianced, a noble, handsome face that would make any maiden swoon. Against her will, she found herself comparing him to Griffin, contrasting the two men who were likely the same in age, yet as different in appearance and demeanor as night and day.

Where Griffin was golden and smolderingly intense, Sebastian of Montborne was dark and dynamic, a man whose very presence commanded respect and not a little fear. The earl seemed to crackle with vitality, his keen gaze not quite able to hide its roguish gleam, the wry twist of his mouth hinting at a reckless nature that probably took a great effort to curb. From what Isabel knew of him before and what she had now seen of him these past couple of days, Sebastian of Montborne seemed a good man. Kind yet firm, gentle yet strong. He would make any woman a fine husband . . .

Any woman but her.

She took a sip of her wine, then brought the cup down and stared into the bloodred claret, feeling the weight of a thousand stones settle onto her chest. "My lord," she began hesitantly, "I . . . I think we should talk about our . . . about this marriage arrangement."

She glanced up, half hoping she had not said the words aloud—half hoping she was not sitting there with Sebastian of Montborne, about to tell him that she could not marry him. But she had said the words, and he was there beside her, looking at her with an expectant, almost sympathetic gaze. "I would be lying if I told you I didn't have a few reservations about this marriage myself, my lady. Though I mean no disrespect to you, if I had my choice I would be with my king preparing to join the fight in the Holy Land, not preparing to take a bride. But neither one of us has the luxury of choosing in this matter. Our king wishes to join our lands through marriage, Isabel, and as his subjects we must oblige."

His admission surprised Isabel. She supposed she had been so wrapped up in her own misery that she had not paused to consider Sebastian. That he wanted for other things as well did not make the weight of her regrets lessen, but it did make her feel a certain shared sadness with the youthful earl. He deserved better than she could ever hope to give him as his wife. "I'm sorry, Sebastian," she whispered. "I'm sorry about all of this. I wish it could be different . . . for both of us."

He gave her a gentle nod of acknowledgment. "I am not going to ask what transpired between you and him," he said, his voice lowering to a very private timbre. "Perhaps in time you will decide to tell me on your own. Perhaps in time it will no longer matter. I can't demand your love as my wife, Isabel, but I can demand your fidelity. You should know, here and now, that I will demand that much of you."

When she could only stare at him, fully understanding how right he was to expect her agreement yet somehow unable to voice her pledge, Sebastian set down his cup of wine and rose from his place beside her. "I'll leave you to your thoughts, my lady. Providing you've no objections, I'll tell the men to mount up within the hour. I would prefer to make Montborne before sundown."

Griffin had never seen Montborne, but he had heard of its splendor on occasion through Dom, who had always described it in jealous, spiteful terms, as if in telling Griffin of its majesty Dom was somehow delivering personal insult to him as well. Now, as he rode under the barbican gates and into the large courtyard that lay at the foot of the enormous castle, Griff could understand his foster brother's envy.

Montborne was magnificent.

Easily three times the size of Droghallow's square stone keep, this polygonal tower rose several stories into the evening sky, its parapets and battlements blocking out the slim color of the fading sun and casting long shadows over the bailey. Soldiers and castle folk paused in their activities to look with affection upon their returning lord and his new bride—and stare in scorn at the brigand responsible for her damage and delayed arrival.

Griffin could only watch as Isabel was assisted from her palfrey and shown inside the castle by a clutch of chattering maids. She glanced back at him as they led her up the keep's outer stairs, but her regard was brief and filled with the same sadness and regret he had seen in her eyes during the whole of their journey to Montborne. And there was something else in her eyes in that moment, too, Griff realized.

Resignation.

She was going to marry Sebastian of Montborne. The reality of it—the crushing finality of it—hit him like a lance thrust through his heart. He tried to tell himself it was the plan all along, that he had always known this day was coming. That it was for the best where both of them were concerned. But now he knew the truth: he had been hoping—madly, futilely hoping—that somehow they would have found a way to be together.

It wasn't going to happen.

He had pushed her into Sebastian's arms that awful morning at the monastery, and now it appeared she had decided to stay there. He wanted to scream his anguish over losing her, but he schooled his face to one of cool composure as the earl jumped off his horse and strode over to face him.

"I would have a word with you in private before I send for the sheriff, sir." A look from the dark-haired nobleman sent one of his guards over to help Griff down from his mount. His hands were untied, a gesture of confidence from the earl that Griff had to respect. He acknowledged his appreciation with a slight nod. "We can talk in my solar," Sebastian told him, then turned to lead the way across the bailey and into the keep.

The earl brought Griffin to his private chamber off the great hall and closed the door. He left Griff in the center of the rush-covered floor and walked to the room's large window, standing before the pane of costly glass and staring out at the fiery approach of sunset. "It seems we have some trouble between us, sir knight. You have committed an act of treason in stealing my bride, an act that demands recompense, yet if I do what is right by my king and myself, I shall lose any hope of alliance with the woman I am pledged to marry. It seems to me that whether you live or die, I am doomed to abide your ghost dwelling in my home."

"You have to do what you must," Griff answered from behind him, sounding much more casual than he felt. "As for Isabel—your betrothed—" he corrected hastily "—I'm certain the lady will bear you no ill will for your decision."

The earl of Montborne exhaled a wry chuckle. "You underestimate, sir. She loves you."

"No, she doesn't," Griff replied tersely. "After all I have put her through these past couple of weeks, she despises me. I'm certain of it."

"So. You love her as well," the earl remarked. "Is that why you sent the message from the Derbyshire monastery?"

Griffin shook his head. "She was wounded and very ill. I only wanted to see her safely delivered to where she belonged."

"An odd statement for her abductor to make, don't you think? Would it surprise you to know that your overlord took it upon himself to inform me of my bride's capture some days ago, advising me that you had acted alone in this kidnapping plot?" Sebastian pivoted to regard him over his shoulder. "No, I can see that it doesn't. It didn't surprise me either, frankly. Dominic of Droghallow has never allied himself with Montborne, so I didn't see why he would feel the need to do so now, particularly when half the realm is aware of his recent involvement with Prince John."

"I did act alone," Griffin admitted. "I took the lady from Droghallow with plans to ransom her back to you for a reward."

Sebastian turned. "And now? How much of a reward would it take for you to leave and never come back?"

Griff considered for a moment, thinking back on all his plans, his future, all the hopes that hinged on the promise of a fat ransom. He thought about all those things, then answered the damning truth because after everything he had been through these past few days, the truth—his honor— was all he had left. "I would always come back. So long as she is here, no amount of money—nothing in this world— would keep me away from her."

The earl's smile was grim. "As her husband, I wouldn't have that, you understand."

"I do," Griff replied, for he expected no less.

Sebastian frowned at him, then slowly shook his head. "The sheriff will be here in the morning. When he asks after your involvement in my betrothed's abduction, I will leave it to you to answer in your own defense. In consideration of your returning Isabel to my care, I give you my word as a gentleman that I shall say nothing against you to the king's officer. However, speaking as the man who will take her to wife, neither can I allow myself to say anything on your behalf."

Griff inclined his head in acceptance of the fact. "And I give you my word," he replied, "I will tell the sheriff much the same as I told you here—that I stole your betrothed with the intention of hostaging her for a ransom."

Sebastian's oath was expelled on a harsh breath. "You will be inviting a charge of treason."

"Is that not what I stand guilty of?"

"It brings a sentence of death," the earl warned.

Griff said nothing, for he knew full well the punishment for treason against the crown. He didn't particularly want to die, but he expected he would rather suffer a hangman's noose on the morrow than live the rest of his days without Isabel.

"Very well," Sebastian said after Griffin's extended silence. He opened the door and called for the guards. Two armed knights appeared in the corridor a moment later, ready for their lord's orders. "Take the prisoner belowstairs to await the sheriff."

Chapter Twenty-eight

"Your bath is drawn, my lady. Shall I help you disrobe?"

The maid's question, like most of the previous ones she had asked, went unanswered. The girl shot an anxious look to one of the other attendants assigned to assist their lord's new bride, and was given a helpless shrug. A third servant, older than the others, pushed up her sleeves and approached the lady sitting in sullen silence on the chamber's big bed.

"Come now, my lady. You must be sorely tired; let us get you out of that dress and into some warm water—"

Isabel jumped when the maid's hands settled on her. "No," she snapped, then realized how curt her tone had sounded and made a hasty apology. "Please," she told the group of them, "I would simply like to be left alone for a while."

"Of course," the elder servant replied, bobbing an acquiescent curtsy. "As you wish, my lady."

For the past hour since her arrival at Montborne, Isabel had been sitting on the bed, clutching Griffin's medallion pendant in her fist and staring into the fire that roared in the room's deep hearth, all but ignoring the half-dozen servants who had been flitting in and out trying to make her comfortable. Waiting there idle was driving her mad; not knowing where Griffin was or how he fared was a frustration she could bear no longer.

"Do you know where my lord Sebastian has taken the man who arrived with us today?" she asked the last of the maids as the girl gathered up a couple of empty water buckets.

Nearly to the door, the servant turned. "Why, my lord has sent him to the castle prison, of course."

"The prison," Isabel gasped. "Where is it?"

" 'Tis below the keep, but you needn't worry, my lady. The cells are well guarded, and anyway, my lord is sending for the sheriff to arrive on the morrow—"

Isabel vaulted off the bed before the maid could finish. Without a care for how it looked to the serving girl, she fled the room in a panic and raced down the spiral stairwell that led to the first floor of the castle. Sebastian was standing with a couple of his knights near the entrance to the solar when she skidded to a halt at the base of the steps. The trio of men looked to her disheveled, hasty arrival in surprise.

"My lord," she called to him, out of breath from flight and fear. She worried her skirts in her hands, nervously clutching at the pale blue silk as she attempted a calmer approach toward her betrothed. "Sebastian, please. I must know. What do you mean to do with him?"

With his eyes trained on her, the earl jerked his chin at the guards in dismissal. Isabel stood before him, watching the two men depart and weathering their scrutinous looks as they sidled by to leave Sebastian and her to their privacy.

"I have heard that he is gaoled belowstairs," she said when they were standing alone in the windowed antechamber. "You have sent for the sheriff?"

"I have. My messenger was dispatched a moment ago."

His uncompromising reply seemed to suck all the air out of Isabel's lungs. She closed her eyes, blinking back the flood of cold, numbing dread that swelled inside her. Of its own accord, her hand came up to grasp Griffin's medallion, the white lion talisman that had so often given her strength. Never had she needed that strength more. "On what charges does he stand accused?"

"I think you know," Sebastian answered.

Treason.

The accusation crowded her mind as it strangled her heart, but she could not voice the hated word that would rob her once more of all she held dear. She stared into Sebastian's cool features, this man she was promised to marry, the man who would send her beloved to die on the gallows come the morn. "Sebastian, you must listen," she appealed to him, reaching out to catch his hand, her eyes flooding with tears. "Surely you owe me no consideration in this, but I beg you, do not surrender him to the sheriff. Call your messenger back, please. Release Griffin."

A muscle twitched in the earl's jaw as he stared down at her. "Griffin of Droghallow is a criminal, my lady. He abducted you from your escort here to gain a profit. Whether that profit was to come from the coffers of his traitorous overlord or mine own is inconsequential. By all rights, you should be thanking me for locking the blackguard up, not begging me to set him free."

Isabel saw the unspoken accusation in her betrothed's eyes and she had to force herself not to glance away. "It wasn't the way you're making it sound. 'Tis true Griffin was ordered into the kidnapping, but he changed his mind. He rescued me from Droghallow and sought to bring me here instead. He provided for me, and kept me safe from Dom's men. He protected me—"

The earl grunted. "If the condition of your arm is any indication, demoiselle, I'd say he nearly got you killed."

Isabel blew out a small, defeated sigh, knowing that to explain her actions in taking the bolt for Griffin—to explain any aspect of their time together—would do nothing to sway Sebastian to her cause. Indeed, it might only strengthen his resolve against Griffin, and that was a risk she refused to take. "I know what you must think of me, my lord, but grant me this one thing, I beseech you. Call back your message to the sheriff, release Griffin, and I will ask nothing else of you so long as I live."

"What you ask now is a great deal, Isabel. More than I can grant you." The earl pulled his hand out of her grasp. "This man has wronged me. He has wronged his king— *our king.* As Richard's vassal, I am obliged to demand reparation."

He turned to walk toward the window as if meaning to end their conversation then and there, but Isabel took a half step after him, reaching out to place her hand atop the sleeve of his tunic. He paused, pivoting to face her again. "If you seek reparation," she said, "then demand it of me. You said you would demand my fidelity as your wife, my lord. If you do this to ensure it, I give you my word that I would honor you as my husband without your sending Griffin to the gallows."

"I don't do this as punishment for you or for him, my lady. I do it because my loyalty is to my king. I would ask you to try to understand."

"Please," Isabel whispered brokenly, unable to staunch the tears that welled and spilled down her cheeks. "Please, Sebastian . . . I will do anything you ask, just call back your message to the sheriff."

"The matter is out of my hands," he told her, his raven brows drawn together in a frown. "I'm sorry, Isabel."

"No," she choked, feeling as if she were breaking apart into a thousand tiny pieces. "My lord . . . Sebastian, no . . ."

But the earl's face remained unchanging, impassive. Unrelenting. Nothing she could say would dissuade him from his course, that much was clear. Sick with the idea, Isabel put her face in her hands and pivoted on her heel to take her leave before she broke down in front of him. She managed two steps, then drew up short as a slim figure came to stand before the open chamber door.

"What have I done in offense that I must hear it from my maids that my son's bride is arrived at last?" There was a teasing, affectionate note in the woman's soft scold, a mother's warmth in her smile . . . until her eyes lit upon Isabel's tear-stained face. "Oh, my dear," she said, coming forward to place her arm around Isabel. "Whatever is wrong?"

Isabel could not answer. She turned her face into Lady Montborne's shoulder and wept, needful of the sympathy even if it came from a relative stranger. She needed a mother's soothing embrace even if it came from the dame of her betrothed. Isabel poured out her grief, weeping like a helpless, hurting child.

"Sebastian," Lady Montborne said, "whatever is this about?"

The woman's voice was edged with confusion; she was unaware, evidently, of Isabel's shame. Perhaps she was even unaware of the circumstances in which Isabel had finally come to Montborne. When the earl did not answer forthwith, his mother pulled Isabel out of her arms and blotted her wet cheeks with the long sleeve of her rich samite bliaut. "What is it, child? Coming here to your new home should be a happy occasion, not a cause for so many tears."

She stared at Isabel, her aged face lined with genuine concern, her pale, gentle gaze searching. Lady Montborne gave a little sigh, shaking her head when Isabel's tears would not cease. The lady smoothed a stray lock of hair from Isabel's brow. "Dear, dear," she whispered, "you weep as if your whole world is ending."

"I-I'm sorry," Isabel stammered. She willed herself to composure, reaching down within her to summon a measure of dignity before her betrothed and his lady mother.

How ashamed Griffin would be to see her now, so weak and inconsolable. Her whole world was ending, but her sorrow over it would serve no one now, least of all him. "I'm sorry," she said again. "Please excuse me."

She withdrew from Lady Montborne's arms to take her leave, but the noblewoman's hand suddenly tightened on Isabel's wrist. She looked down from Isabel's face slightly, her delicate silvered brows knit into a frown as she reached out to lift Griffin's medallion pendant into her palm. "Mon Dieu," she gasped. "Where did you . . . ?"

"It's mine," Isabel said quickly. She took the white lion amulet out of the elder woman's slack grasp. "It was a gift."

Lady Montborne stared at Isabel as if she had seen a ghost, her light green eyes haunted, the fine lines of her face seeming to deepen as she stared at the medallion Isabel clutched possessively in her fist. "Who . . . did someone give it to you?" she asked, her face gone ashen. When she tried to take a step toward Isabel, her knees buckled beneath her.

"What is it, Mother?" Sebastian rushed forward to catch her from the fall, holding her up at the elbow. "Good God, you're shaking." He turned his scowling, confused gaze on Isabel. "Let me see that medallion."

But Isabel only clutched it tighter, fearful that if she let him see the amulet now, if she admitted where she had gotten it, she would lose this precious treasure from Griffin. Of their own accord, her feet began to back toward the door. He stared at her for a long moment, but he made no move to force her to his will, and when the earl turned his attention to his distressed mother once more, helping her into a cushioned chair, Isabel took the opportunity and bolted from the room.

In all his five and twenty years, Sebastian of Montborne had never seen his lady mother so distraught. Time had done its share to weaken the once robust woman, but nothing, not even the death of her husband two years past had ever so affected her as had this queer encounter with his betrothed.

He should have warned his mother that Isabel was likely to be upset when she arrived. He should have advised her about the kidnapping, but with the recent decline in her health, he had thought it best to spare her the troubling news. Now, in light of her present state of distress, he had to wonder at the wisdom of that decision.

"How do you suppose she came to have it?" she asked, an abrupt question that made him pause where he stood, pouring her a cup of wine from a decanter on his desk.

"What's that, my lady?" He offered her the drink, but she refused it, idly batting his hand away.

"The medallion. I wonder how she . . . I wonder where she might have gotten it."

Sebastian gave a shrug. He had not noticed the pendant until seeing his mother's strange reaction to it. "In truth, I suspect it was a token given to her by her abductor." At his mother's look of shock and confusion, he hastened to explain. "Perhaps I should have told you, but I did not want to upset you. Lady Isabel was captured by brigands a couple of weeks ago while en route to Montborne."

His mother's brows crashed together. "What?"

"The chief offender—the man to whom that medallion no doubt belongs—is sitting in our gaol awaiting the sheriff as we speak."

"He is—" She swallowed hard and blinked in disbelief. "Mon Dieu, he's here? At Montborne?"

Sebastian nodded. "The blackguard was with her when we found her near Derbyshire. Actually, it was his own message that led me to her. Nevertheless, I've sent for the sheriff; he'll stand trial for his crimes on the morrow."

"Oh, no," she whispered, her hand flying to her mouth, fingers trembling. "Oh, God, no."

"It's all right now," he told her, trying to assuage some of the fear he saw swimming in her eyes. "Everything will be fine, I promise."

"What is his name?" she choked, her voice raw and thready. She reached out, clutching at his sleeve. "His name, Sebastian! What is this man called?"

"Droghallow," he answered. "He is Griffin of Droghallow."

With a cry of unmistakable anguish, she lunged to her feet. She stared at Sebastian, shaking her head, her face awash with torment. "Oh, my God!" she gasped. "Heaven help me, what have I done?"

Without waiting for him to follow, she swept past Sebastian, heading down the corridor toward the castle's prison cells.

Chapter Twenty-nine

Seated on a meager wooden bench in his cell, Griffin lifted his head when he heard the echoing clap of leather-soled slippers fast descending the stairwell that snaked down to the castle's gaol. There was a rush of voices on the other side of the heavy wooden door—one female, the other belonging to his guard—and then a key was turned in the lock and the thick, iron-banded panel yawned open. Griff stood, shielding his eyes as torchlight spilled into his cell from outside.

For a moment, he had thought it might be Isabel come to see him one last time. Instead, from behind the soldier who had been dispatched to the prison for night duty, came another lady, someone Griffin had never seen before. She was aged at least twice his own years, but still noble of face and form, her steel-gray hair plaited and covered with a wine-colored veil, her slender frame draped in a fine bliaut of burgundy samite.

And she was crying.

"Mon Dieu," she whispered as she stepped up to the row of cells, the hem of her skirts rustling in the straw that littered the floor. Settling her gaze on Griffin, she froze. "Unlock his cell."

The knight gaped at her in disbelief. "But my lady, I cannot. This man is a prisoner of the earl—"

"Unlock it. Please."

Sebastian entered the prison area in that next moment,

the bones of his face accentuated by the flickering torch-light and his tightly held expression. "Do as she asks," he commanded the warden, then shot a warning glance at Griffin. "I trust he won't be fool enough to bring harm to my lady mother."

With the earl's permission, the guard went to the iron grate with his key. He opened the cell door and moved aside as Lady Montborne took a hesitant step forward. She pressed her lips together as she stared at Griffin, her pale gaze searching his, studying him. She swallowed as if she wasn't sure she could summon her voice to speak.

"What is your name?" she asked softly, approaching him despite a growl of caution from her son.

"I am Griffin of Droghallow, madam."

"You are." It was more sigh than answer, a breathless whisper of a word that seemed to lift a heavy weight from her features. "Griffin," she repeated, then brought her shaking fingertips up to her lips. She took another step toward him, then another, coming to stand before him in the cell. Something danced in her tear-filled eyes, an emotion not quite recognition but something near it, something deep and unreadable. "You are Griffin of Droghallow."

At his slight nod, the lady bowed her head and let out a broken sob. She reached down, took his hand in hers.

Then sank to her knees before him in the dry blanket of straw.

Griff could only stare, helpless and astonished, as Lady Montborne held his palm against her cheek and wept.

"Forgive me," she said, turning her face up to look at him. "Please . . . forgive me."

Behind her, the earl swore an oath. His disbelieving gaze locked with Griffin's. "What the devil is the meaning of this? I would have an explanation of the madness I see before me."

Griffin could offer no such thing, but Lady Montborne did.

"I cannot let you call for this man's death, my son," she answered, a tear dripping off her chin to splash on Griffin's hand. "You see, Sebastian . . . he is your brother."

Isabel paced her chamber, heartsick with frustration and the terrible helplessness of her situation. She could not bear the thought of Griffin facing charges in the morning, no more than she could bear the thought of living a single day without him. In the hour or more that she had spent alone in her room at Montborne, she had devised at least a dozen plans to fix the disaster her life had become, ridiculous plans of escape and flight with Griffin, plans that would make them fugitives once more if not succeeding in getting them both killed.

Plans that would defy her king's orders and forsake a little girl who was waiting in a lonely convent, counting on Isabel to bring her home.

"Oh, Maura," she sighed into the emptiness of her chamber. "I have made a bigger mess of things than Papa did."

She stared unseeing into the stone fireplace that dominated most of one wall, watching the flames twist and undulate, so lost in her thoughts that she scarcely heard the soft rap on her door. When the panel creaked open, Isabel turned her head, ready to dismiss the maid who had offered earlier that hour to bring her some food and wine from the kitchens. But it wasn't a castle servant; it was her betrothed's mother.

Lady Montborne stood in the wedge of torchlight that poured in from the corridor. She smiled at Isabel, but there was a sadness in her eyes. Even in the dim light, it was plain to see how her regal face was flushed with recently spent emotion; her slender fingers trembled on the latch of the door. "May I come in?" she asked.

"My lady, yes, of course." Isabel offered her the respectful curtsy she had been too distraught to think of when they first met in Sebastian's solar. "Please accept my apologies for the way I behaved before . . . I pray I have not caused you distress."

"No, my dear." Lady Montborne moved gracefully across the room. She placed a warm hand on Isabel's cheek. "You have been through quite an ordeal as I understand it. And these are trying times for us all."

Isabel bowed her head. "Yes, my lady."

"Please," she said, "will you call me Joanna?" At Isabel's nod, the lady smiled. She let out a small sigh then, folding her slim arms one over the other as her gaze traveled the room. "This chamber was mine when I first came to Montborne as a betrothed new bride. I didn't know a soul when I arrived, not even Lord Eustace, the man I was to marry. I was just fourteen at the time, a mere babe in so many ways, and terrified to be so far away from my parents and siblings." She walked to the big curtained bed and reached out to lift one of the tassels that held the heavy silk panels open during the day. "I cried myself to sleep every night I spent in here before my wedding . . . and for several nights afterward as well."

It was easy to imagine a young girl's fear over the idea of marriage to a stranger, but Isabel was a woman grown, and the cause of the tears she had shed in this room had less to do with what she faced than with what she was being forced to leave behind. She glanced away from Lady Joanna, turning her gaze once more to the fire, watching the ash fall away from the glowing embers of the wood and gather beneath the grate.

"Eustace was more than twice my age; I thought him so old and serious when first we met. He had been wed before, you see, but his wife had died in childbirth . . . along with her babes."

Isabel turned her head toward Lady Joanna, frowning in curiosity. "There was more than one child?"

"Twins," the lady confirmed, a sad twist to her lips. "A

rarity of nature, to be sure. Some might call it a miracle from God, but most—including Eustace—understood it to be evidence of a far less celebratory occurrence."

"Adultery," Isabel answered in a whisper. Once, a few years ago, a woman had arrived at the convent, banished there by her husband for the offense of bearing him two babes in their marriage bed. The young mother had vehemently denied the accusations, pleading with her husband to take her back, but he refused. Even some of the nuns seemed to look upon her with a small measure of scorn. Never had it been known to happen, Isabel had often heard it said, that a woman would give birth to two babes at one time—unless two men were the cause of it.

"As you can imagine, castle gossip ran rampant and vicious after the death of Eustace's first wife," Lady Joanna continued. "Indeed, the rumors were still flying upon my arrival at Montborne. The earl was described to me as a jealous man, hard-willed and suspicious of everyone. I learned of his mistrust firsthand when he denied me permission to leave the castle without his escort after we were wed. I was kept a veritable prisoner in this room, removed from other people save my husband and my maids."

A log shifted in the fireplace, cracking apart and shooting up a shower of sparks. Isabel rubbed off a chill, considering how lonely Lady Joanna must have been in her marriage. How sad she must have been in this room all alone.

"Despite his possessiveness, Eustace was not unkind to me. I came to know him, to understand him, and during that first year of our marriage I grew to care for him deeply." Lady Joanna exhaled as she seated herself on the thick down mattress. "I was ecstatic when I learned I was pregnant. I could not wait to share my joy, so I blurted out the news to him over supper that same day."

Isabel heard the hesitation in her voice. She glanced

over her shoulder and saw the aged noblewoman swallow, her delicate white throat working as if to dislodge the words that would not come. "Your husband was not pleased to hear that you were with child?" Isabel asked gently.

"Oh, yes," Lady Joanna replied with a soft, sorrow-filled laugh. "He was thrilled. He showered me with gifts and affection throughout the term of my pregnancy, becoming the sort of husband every maiden dreams of— chivalrous, romantic, so devoted. I had never known such peace and happiness as I did during those precious few months."

Isabel found herself drifting over to the bed as Lady Joanna spoke. She sat beside her without a word, almost afraid to hear more of what she would say, but somehow needing to know what happened to the young woman who once stood in Isabel's place.

"My time came earlier than expected, and my labor was difficult. Eustace worried for me terribly, but there was nothing he could do. The midwives refused him entry to the laying-in room and so he waited on the other side of the door. I could hear the harsh tick of his spurs as he paced the hallway, could hear his fists pounding on the door whenever I cried out in pain. He stayed out there all the while, until very late that night, when it was finally all over.

"I was dozing and nearly faint with exhaustion when Eustace demanded entry to the room. I heard the mid-wives' worried voices as they tried to dissuade him from coming in, heard them rushing about the room, whispering indiscernibly beside the bed. I heard the click of the latch on the door, heard the thud of Eustace's booted feet as he strode in." Lady Joanna took a long breath, then let it out on a shaky sigh. "He came up to the bed, smiling at me, so proud. He kissed my brow, then turned to look upon the cradle on the floor. All the color—all the life—seemed to drain from his face in that moment. His dark brows crushed together; his warm smile hardened into a fierce, bitter line.

"I didn't understand the change in him at first. I tried to sit up, fearful that something was wrong with our babe. I asked him to tell me what was the matter, and when Eustace looked at me again, his eyes were burning with hurt. 'I trusted you,' he hissed at me. Then he stormed out and scarcely spoke to me ever again. You see," Lady Montborne said, tears beginning to well in her eyes, "Eustace thought I betrayed him. He thought I had lain with another man, for when he looked into the cradle, he saw two swaddled babes—twin boys: one light-haired and golden, one dark like him."

"Oh, Joanna," Isabel murmured, reaching out to grasp the older woman's hand in sympathy.

"Eustace was the only man I had ever been with, but nothing I said would convince him. I had expected him to annul our marriage, to cast me out as an adulteress. But he didn't. He was aging and he needed an heir . . . so he made me cast out one of the babes instead."

Isabel's heart lodged in her throat over the cruelty in that order. She could not imagine the terrible grief Lady Joanna must have endured, not only in losing one of her children, but in losing her husband's trust as well.

"Eustace would permit me to keep only one of our sons. Sebastian was second born, but he most resembled my husband. By Eustace's decision, he was to be heir."

"And the other?" Isabel asked, scarcely able to find her voice. "What happened to the other child?"

"I could not trust Eustace in his anger to determine where the first child should go, and so I made arrangements to send him away to live in secret with my cousin—"

"Alys of Droghallow." Isabel started to tremble as she realized what she was hearing. A knot of emotion churned inside of her, a tangle of relief and anguish, confusion and sudden clarity. She shook her head from side to side, meeting Lady Joanna's remorseful gaze. "So Griffin is . . ."

"My son," the lady finished. "That pendant you wear belongs to him. 'Tis one half of my family's crest; Sebastian wears the other side. I placed it in Griffin's swaddling so that Alys would know who he was."

Isabel closed her hand around the white lion medallion that hung suspended over her heart. "He did not know," she said woodenly. "Alys never told him."

Lady Joanna made a sad sound, pressing her lips together. "She wouldn't have. I made her vow to keep the truth from him, for I knew that if he found out he would come here, and I could not predict how my husband might have reacted to seeing him. I couldn't bear the thought of my child's meeting with harm and so I tried to content myself with watching him grow up from afar, relying on Alys's letters to tell me what he was doing, how he fared. She passed away some years ago, but until then we corresponded at least monthly, always about Griffin. I could not have asked for two finer sons than mine."

Isabel's head was spinning. The ramifications of what this meant—her relationship with Griffin, her betrothal to Sebastian . . . the sudden, immutable reality that they were brothers. For Isabel to wed Sebastian before would have been to betray her own heart, but now, according to Holy Law, it would be nothing short of incest. The king himself would be hard-pressed to argue for the match if the church learned of the situation.

"I never dreamed I would see Griffin as a grown man," Lady Joanna murmured, her voice soft and not a little bit sad. "I suppose I didn't dare hope for the chance after what I had done to him. But then, when I saw his medallion around your neck, well, I could not believe my eyes."

"You've got to tell him," Isabel said, twisting her hands

to clasp the elder lady's fingers in a firm hold. "You must let Griffin know who he is. Sebastian must be told whom he has gaoled—"

"Oh, my dear," their mother replied as a fat tear rolled down her cheek. "They know. God help me, but I have told them everything . . . and now I can only pray that I have not lost both my sons."

Chapter Thirty

Griffin stared at Montborne's dark lord—his brother—and could hardly find words to speak. Upon their mother's astonishing disclosure he had been freed at once from his cell and fetters, but in the short time since she had left the two men standing alone in the gaol, neither had managed much more than a guarded glance at the other.

Griff knew what Sebastian was likely thinking; no doubt they both shared similar thoughts. How different would their lives have been had they not gone twenty-five years without knowing about the other? What might have happened had they not been denied the knowledge of each other's existence, denied the kinship, the brotherly bond? Who might both of them be now, had they not spent half a lifetime living a lie?

Griffin counted another thought among the jumble that filled his mind: how bitingly ironic it was to think that had he not been sent to live in anonymity at Droghallow all those years ago, he would be earl of Montborne . . .

And Isabel would be *his* bride.

"It's funny, you know," Sebastian said at last. "All my life I was groomed to be earl. As the sole heir to my father's titles and properties, the responsibility of Montborne—the honor of holding such a prosperous fief—rested squarely on me. Frankly, the mantle never seemed a good fit." He slid a look at Griffin and gave a wry laugh.

"Now I reckon I know why. By rights, it should have been yours."

Griff shook his head. "You are earl in all ways that matter. I begrudge you nothing."

"No?" Sebastian's ebony brow arched. "Not even the hand of your lady love?"

Griff felt the muscles in his jaw tighten at the reference to Isabel. He stared at the flickering flame of a rushlight that burned near the stairwell door, thinking about all he and Isabel had been through together, all they had shared.

He loved her like he would love no other again; that fact he could never deny. Nor could he deny the coil of rage that seared like a brand in his gut when he thought about Dominic of Droghallow, the man who would have bartered Isabel away to the whims of a wicked prince just as easily as he would have used Griffin against his own family in seeking to thwart the joining of the houses of Montborne and Lamere.

Now, when he considered how eager Dom had been to enlist him in the task of kidnapping Sebastian's bride, Griffin suspected Droghallow's lord was fully aware of what he was doing—and to whom.

"We are in an awkward situation that grows all the more so by the moment," Sebastian remarked. "It seems trite to offer you land or silver in exchange for what would have been your birthright, but I pray you take no insult when I say that both are yours if you want them. You are, of course, welcome to stay on at Montborne . . ."

"I won't be staying," Griff answered tersely. Indeed, he could consider no such thing so long as Dominic of Droghallow sat unmet in his great hall, unscathed by the treachery he had sought to stir up. To walk in and challenge Droghallow's lord was likely tantamount to suicide, but in that moment, Griffin knew no other course. He had to return to Droghallow and confront Dom—for the sake of Isabel's honor as well as his own. "There is a matter that demands my immediate attention elsewhere," he said when Sebastian regarded him with a questioning look. "I should like to be away as soon as possible, but I will need a horse and a few days' supplies."

"Consider it done," the earl agreed. "You'll have my finest mount and whatever Cook can provide from the kitchens."

His mind set to this new resolve, Griffin nodded his thanks to Sebastian. "Will you do one more thing for me?"

"Name it."

Paused near the door to the stairwell, Griff swallowed hard and met his brother's gaze. "Give me your assurances that you will take care of Isabel. Marry her. Permit her to send for her young sister, Maura. Make her happy."

"You speak as if you're never to return," Sebastian said, his gray-green eyes steady, narrowed with understanding.

"I am trusting you with all I hold dear in this world," Griff replied. "I need to know that whatever happens to me, Isabel will be safe and well cared for. Will you promise me this?"

The earl of Montborne stared at him for a long moment, saying nothing, then he strode forth and held out his hand. "As your brother, I give you my solemn oath."

"My lady, is anything amiss?"

Speechless from Lady Joanna's shocking revelations, Isabel could only shake her head as she dashed past the castle maid who stood in the corridor with a tray of steaming food. Isabel had left her chamber without waiting for leave, her hasty flight upsetting the torches that flamed from their cressets on the stone walls of the tower stairwell. Her heart hammering in her breast, she flew by curious servants who stared as they stepped aside to let her pass. She found the large iron-banded door that led to the prison cells below the keep and threw it open, slipping on the narrow stairs in her haste to reach the bottom.

A guard stood post on the landing; he merely frowned at Isabel as she ducked past him and into the fetid, musty air of the dark gaol. A single rushlight hissed in its sconce near the door, the slim, wobbling illumination enough to show her that the place was all but deserted. The cells were empty; nothing but vacant quiet greeted her. She stepped farther within, pivoting her head to peer into the darkened corners.

"He's gone." A deep voice issued from behind her. She whirled about, breathless, and found Sebastian sitting on a faldstool in the gloom at her back.

"Where?" she asked.

"He didn't say, my lady."

"Will he . . ." She took a quick breath and worked to keep her voice from breaking. "Will he be back?"

The earl stared at her, sympathy evident in his carefully held expression. "I don't know."

Isabel had to struggle to tamp down the stab of pain that tore through her. Griffin was gone. He had left without a word to her. The very thought was like a wound torn afresh, though why his departure should surprise her, she knew not. He had sought to divest himself of her that day at the monastery; now, given this new chance, it appeared he had succeeded.

"I offered for him to stay . . . given the circumstances, it seemed the least I could do," Sebastian said. "I trust you understand what I am talking about, my lady."

Isabel nodded weakly. "Your mother explained everything to me . . . what had happened, what she had done."

The earl rose from his stool and stalked to the open grate of the prison cell. He gripped the iron bars in his hands, staring up at the granite ceiling and the three solid walls of stone that comprised the rest of the gaol. "For nearly all my life, I have been schooled to enjoy noble, gentlemanly pursuits, guided away from boyish recklessness and a young man's need for adventure because of my obligation to Montborne. I have long felt that I was living another man's life, but I had no idea just how right I'd been." He released the grate with some force and let it bang against the wall. "I may as well have been physically shackled to this keep from the day I was born."

"And now you are shackled to a bride you do not want," Isabel suggested, recalling their conversation en route to Montborne, when Sebastian had confessed that marriage had not been foremost on his mind.

Sebastian regarded her over his shoulder, the rushlight playing over his striking features and setting a glossy sheen to his raven-dark hair. "Ours will be an arrangement in name only, you have my word of honor on that, my lady. I respect your feelings for my . . ." he hesitated as if stumbling over a foreign phrase ". . . for my brother, and will not force myself upon you. If you have his child in the months to come, I shall raise it as my own and bear you no ill will."

"Oh, Sebastian," Isabel said softly, touched by his kindness. "Don't you see? I cannot marry you, not in name only or in truth. My heart belongs to Griffin. It always will." Even if he thought so little of her that he would leave her there at Montborne without so much as a backward glance. And she knew that regardless of that fact, whatever it took, she would find a way to go to him, to tell him how she felt. "I'll gather my things and be ready to leave in the morn. You've been most generous and I've no wish to impose on your goodwill any longer."

She bowed her head in deference to the earl and took a step toward the open door.

"My lady . . . I don't think you understand."

If his voice had not been so gentle, Isabel might have kept walking. But the soft tone spawned a knot of dread in her stomach. Her feet stilled beneath her, and slowly, she turned around to face him. Sebastian's gaze was soft, apologetic. Terrifying in its tenderness.

"It is the king's will, my lady," Sebastian said, "but it is also Griffin's own wish that you and I are wed."

"W-what?" she heard herself whisper. She shook her head from side to side, trying to deny what he said. "His wish that we . . . ? No, that can't be true . . ."

But Sebastian's expression remained firm, unyielding. He spoke slowly, his voice tender even as his words cut into her like a blade. "Before he left, Griffin made me promise him, out of concern for your well-being, that I would take you to wife . . . as our king commands."

The numbing statement hung between them in the semi-darkness, punctuated by the soft pop of the oiled rushes smoldering in their sconce. Isabel stood there in the shadows of the gaol, watching mutely as Sebastian looked down at his boots, then simply walked past her. He paused in the doorway as if he meant to say something more but then perhaps thought better of it. When she glanced up, he was gone, leaving Isabel alone and shaking in the cold, vacant blackness of Montborne's prison.

Chapter Thirty-one

"What will ye have, me love?"

The tavern maid stumbled back on her heels when Griff lifted his head and met her gaze. While the din of the afternoon crowd growing drunk in the Derbyshire public room was raucous, it was not so loud as to drown out the woman's gasp of startlement upon seeing a known outlaw seated within arm's reach of her. Wild-eyed and speechless, she worried her hands in her stained apron, swallowing with an apparent degree of effort.

"Good eve, Willa," Griffin drawled. "Do you suppose a man could get a tankard of ale around here?"

"Oh, my—of course, m'lord," she stammered, bobbing her head and dashing off to serve him.

Griff leaned back on the bench he occupied at a corner table of the tavern. He pressed his spine against the plastered wall of the establishment and let out a heavy sigh. It had been a hard day-and-a-half ride from Montborne to his stop here, where he had last seen Dom and his soldiers. A few questions posed to some of the townsfolk along the way garnered him information that Droghallow's lord had since returned to his keep, though a handful of his men yet prowled the Derbyshire villages for signs of the bride thief they had been ordered to hunt down and retrieve.

Griffin had no intention of waiting around to be apprehended; he would take refreshment here, then find a few hours' rest somewhere away from town before continuing on his way to Droghallow. The mount Sebastian had given him was a robust beast that would make the journey easily, the finest in his stables, just as the earl had promised. Sebastian had also gifted Griffin with another consideration, for along with the food and supplies, secreted in one of his saddle packs had been a satchel fat with silver. Griff had not counted the coins, but he felt their significant weight where the purse now hung from a cord tied to his baldric.

He withdrew a couple of sous to pay for his ale when Willa returned with the cup a moment later. Tipping the tankard to his lips to taste the bitter drink, Griff could not help thinking about all that had transpired in the past few days. He could not help his astonishment over the news he had learned at Montborne . . . the place of his birth. God's blood, but it still staggered him to think that he was brother to the earl. To think that as the eldest, even by scant moments, he had been born the rightful heir.

What he had told Sebastian was the truth: he did not begrudge him Montborne and its title. Nor did he blame his lady mother for sending him away. He had seen the pain in her eyes, heard the torment in her words as she told him of the events leading up to the night of his birth. As hard as it was to reconcile the depth of his father's scorn, Griff harbored no ill regard for him either. The old earl's jealousy and superstition had commanded his will the day he forced his wife to surrender one of their children.

In truth, he almost wished the mystery of his past would never have been solved. The question of who he was, where he belonged, had burned inside him all his life, but now that it was answered he felt more empty than ever before. And it had little to do with envy over lost years or privileges and kinship denied him in his banishment to Droghallow.

No, the hollowness in his heart had everything to do with Isabel.

It had taken all his strength to ride out of Montborne's

gates without seeing her, without going to her and begging for one last embrace, a bittersweet final kiss. More than anything, he had wanted to see her beautiful face again, to feel her arms around him before he left, perhaps forever. But he knew that if he allowed himself to be near her, especially then—knowing that in another place, another time, she might well have been his—he would never have found the will to leave.

With a muttered curse, he cast aside the thought. There would be plenty of time to count his regrets in the days it would take him to reach Droghallow.

Griff drained his cup and set it down on the table. He stood up to take his leave, catching Willa's eye across the room and beckoning her hither with a crook of his finger. She abandoned the tankards she had been swabbing out and bustled over to where he sat.

"Aye, m'lord? Will ye be needin' anything else?"

"Yes," he told her. "Put out your hands."

She gaped at him in frank uncertainty. "Beg pardon, m'lord?"

Griff reached out and seized her by the wrist, turning her hand over and uncurling her gnarled, work-callused fingers. He pulled the satchel of coins free from where it hung on his baldric and deposited it in her upturned palm. "For you," he said, watching her eyes widen at the sound of so much silver clinking together within the pouch.

"B-but m'lord!" she gasped, then looked about and lowered her voice to a private whisper. "I don't understand. What be the meaning of this?"

"Consider it a token of my thanks," he told her. "For coming to my aid the last time I was in town."

She shook her head, blinking at him disbelievingly as she weighed the satchel in her palm. "Saints preserve me—there must be several pounds in here!" She laughed, a sudden bark of joy that she tried to stifle behind her hand. " 'Tis so much money, m'lord!"

Griffin smiled at her ebullient reaction. "I wager it will be plenty enough to take you out of this place."

Willa hugged the purse to her bosom, her cheeks flushing with color. " 'Tis nothing short of a miracle is what this is," she whispered. "Be ye some sort of angel, m'lord? A heavenly body come to answer a poor woman's prayers?"

Griff gave a wry chuckle. "Just a man looking to settle his debts."

Smiling broadly, Willa stepped forward and placed a kiss on Griffin's cheek. "God bless ye, love."

"Go on, now," he told her, dismissing her with a faint scowl and a jerk of his chin. She backed away from him, still grinning, then she sauntered to the bar like a countess, her prize dropped safely into the bodice of her ragged, ale-stained gown.

The silver would surely do her more good than it could him, Griff reflected as he crossed the littered tavern floor and stepped into the bracing cold of the autumn afternoon. Droghallow was less than a week away; fewer than seven days separated him from the battle yet to come with Dom. A battle he truly did not expect to survive.

Even if he made it into the castle undetected, he could not hope to call Dom to arms without a garrison of knights being set upon him in protection of their lord. A small part of him regretted his decision to ride for Droghallow alone, but another part of him, a part he had thought long forgotten, compelled him forward regardless of the danger.

That spurring part of him was honor. Battered and rusty, but honor nonetheless. And if he did not go to Droghallow now, he would lose even this last meager scrap of his self-worth. Dom had stolen a good deal of his life from him, but Griffin would be damned if he would permit him to take what was left of his honor.

Mounting the fine white charger given to him by Sebastian, Griff wheeled the steed about and gave it his heels, steering the beast onto the beaten strip of southern road that would deliver him to Droghallow and whatever fate awaited him there.

October's chill had grown damp with rain by the time Griffin reached his destination. A cold, wet night meant misery to an uncovered rider already long tired of his saddle, but it also meant fewer guards on watch at Droghallow. The company of more than two dozen knights patrolling the castle's battlements had dwindled to a sparse handful as the drizzling night wore on toward dawn.

From the concealment of the woods that fringed Droghallow's broad sloping motte, Griff dismounted and watched the inky silhouettes of the armored soldiers and their spike-tipped lances. He grinned with satisfaction as the dark sky rumbled and shook above them, then opened up with a torrential downpour. While the guards ran to huddle beneath a slim overhang of brickwork, Griff ran for the postern gate located at the far end of Droghallow's soaring curtain wall.

Stealth, and a once inquisitive lad's firsthand knowledge of the keep's secret passageways, led him through the wending bowels of the tower and storerooms, then up a private stairwell that snaked and climbed to the living quarters situated on the floors above. Griff stole along the corridor, past empty castle apartments and anterooms, to the polished oak door that sealed off the lord's chamber from the rest of the keep.

Griff flexed his hand and reached out, wrapping his fingers around the cold iron latch. He squeezed the handle and heard it click softly on the other side. While capable of being locked from within, on this eve Dom had left the door unbarred, an oversight the arrogant earl would no doubt rue in a few short moments. With slow deliberation, Griff pushed the panel open and carefully let himself into the darkened room.

Floor-length brocade curtains were drawn around all

four sides of Dominic's bed, the pale silk panels ruffling
slightly in the evening drafts that whistled in through the
shutters of the chamber's sole window. Dom's deep snores
were underscored by soft feminine breathing, a rustle of
bedsheets as one of the two occupants shifted on the mattress. Having no desire to slay an unarmed man in his
sleep, Griff crossed the lightless chamber and unhooked
the fastener on the shutters, letting the panels swing wide.
Cold air and rain blew in from outdoors, skating across the
rushes on the floor and setting the draperies around the bed
into a violent quiver.

One of the two bed partners roused with the sudden chill.
Griff stepped back into the shadows as the curtain was
parted and a bare white leg was flung over the edge of the
bed. It was the woman—Felice, he realized as she set her
feet on the floor and rose from behind the veil of the drapes.
She weathered a deep shiver that shook her from head to
toe, muttering angrily through her chattering teeth as she
slipped naked from the warmth of the bed. Two paces to the
open window, she looked up and saw him standing there.

Griff cut off her cry of startlement with a grim shake of
his head. "Utter so much as a whimper and you'll fare no
better than him," he warned quietly. He reached over to
pull a tunic from a peg on the wall and tossed it to her to
cover herself. "Go on."

Felice clutched the tunic to her body like a shield, sliding a worried glance toward the bed where Dom had now
begun to shift. When she did not move immediately, Griff
subtly advanced toward her. It was all the coaxing she
needed. Felice scurried out of the chamber like a field
mouse fleeing a hungry barn cat.

With her out of his way, Griffin pulled his dagger from
its sheath and stalked over to where Dom yet rested. He
swept aside the curtain and stared down at the man who
sought to destroy him.

"Felice, close the curtains," Dom murmured against the

bolster beneath his head. "You're letting in a draft, my dove."

Silently, Griff leaned forward. He pressed the flat of his blade against Dom's face, letting the edge of the cold steel bite into the hollow below the earl's beard-grizzled cheekbone. "I'm afraid Felice had to rush off suddenly."

Dom's eyes flew open. "Jesus Christ!" he gasped, staring up in alarm at the slivered, threatening gaze of his foster brother. He braced his palms beneath his chest on the mattress, but froze when it appeared he was unsure if he could manage an escape without losing half his face in the process. Wincing, he let out his breath on a strangled sounding groan.

Griff took an unhealthy amount of pleasure in seeing Dom too stricken to move, pale and sweating under his blade. "I warrant our meeting like this has been a long time coming, has it not, *brother?*"

"Good God, have you gone mad?" Dominic seethed. "You are a dead man! My guards will kill you for this."

Griff chuckled. "I've already considered that likelihood, yet here I am. Perhaps I am mad after all."

"Why?" Dom asked. "Why do you do this, Griffin? Do you mean to kill me? For what purpose—money? Revenge? If you think I am holding a grudge for your taking the woman from me, I assure you, I am not! I could bring you no harm—you are as my own brother!"

Griff scoffed, leaning in a little heavier on his dagger. The sharp edge cut into Dom's flesh, drawing a thin line of blood along the length of the slim blade. How satisfying it would be to turn it toward Dom's neck and drive it home, he thought with a savage burst of ire.

Dom likely sensed the brutality of Griff's thinking, for his words began to spill out of him in a desperate rush. "I have been searching for you across all of England to tell you to come back, Griffin. All I wanted was the woman returned. You must believe me!"

"Is that why you and Lackland put such a handsome
bounty on my head?"

"Prince John called for the bounties, not me!" Dom
wailed. "I swear, I tried to defend you to him—"

"Damn your lies," Griff growled. "Are you so far es-
tranged from the truth that you forget what it is entirely? I
have never asked a thing of you in all the years I lived under this roof," Griff said tightly, "but tonight you will give
me what I demand, Dom. By nails and blood, you will give
me what I am due."

Dominic began to shake, his body's tremors setting the
entire mattress to trembling. "Anything!" he choked.
"Gold. Land. Anything I have! It's yours!"

Griff eased off of him in disgust, taking away the blade
as he rocked back on his heels. "Get up."

At first Dom didn't move. Slowly, he turned his head to
where Griffin stood, his eyes yet wild and frightened, his
breath still rushing out of him, rapid and shallow. He
pushed his torso up off the mattress, then brought his legs
beneath him and sat there staring at Griffin, naked and
shaking. Pathetic.

Griff sheathed his dagger. "Get dressed," he ordered.

Dom crept off the bed, stumbling in the folds of the long
curtains as he went to retrieve the braies and hose that lay
discarded on the floor of the large chamber. He donned
his clothing quickly, if somewhat clumsily, for the continued trembling of his unsteady fingers. Griff kicked a rumpled tunic to him, waiting in stony silence as the earl
shrugged into it and turned to face him.

"What is it you demand of me, Griffin?" he asked, looking thin and wan, very much the weakling youth that Griff
remembered from his early days at Droghallow. "What will
you have?"

Griff walked to where Dom's broadsword sat propped
against the wall in its sheath. "I will have the truth from

you at last," he said as he threw the weapon to him, "or I will have your death."

Dom caught his sword in both hands, his palms slapping against the hard leather that encased it. He held the weapon thus for a moment, quaking, his mouth moving mutely as Griff reached down and calmly drew his own blade. Lightning cracked outside the flapping shutters. The polished length of steel Griff held before him shone silver and deadly in the sharp jag of brightness that illuminated the room. In the dark that followed, Dom began to mumble an incoherent prayer.

"Draw your weapon," Griff instructed him.

"P-please, Griffin. I beg you—"

With a snarl, Griff slashed his sword through the air, bringing it to rest neatly beneath his foster brother's quivering chin. "Your weapon, sirrah."

His neck stretched taut, Dom fumbled to free his blade of its scabbard. Griff brought his hand down, striking at his opponent's wobbly-held sword as he stepped back to give him room to fight. A crash of thunder shook the tower; the rain surged harder, slanting into the room and wetting the rushes beneath Dom's feet.

"How long have you known about me?" Griff asked, his voice low, cold, even to his own ears. "Did you know I was born of Montborne when you charged me with the kidnap of Sebastian's bride?"

Dom feigned a measure of surprise. "What? You, a Montborne! I had no idea—"

Griff put his rage into his answering thrust, a violent blow that nearly knocked Dom's weapon from his grasp. "The truth, damn you, or I'll slay you where you stand."

The earl's throat convulsed. "I might have had my suspicions, but I—"

This time Griffin's jab bit into the fleshy part of Dominic's upper arm.

"All right!" he relented, jumping out of Griff's path as he glanced down to his torn sleeve and the dark stain that seeped into the white linen. "All right . . . I knew."

"How long?"

Dom sniffed, tilting his chin at an arrogant angle as he considered. "Since Alys died. She had some . . . letters. They were written by a highborn cousin of hers—Joanna of Montborne. One of my servants found the box that contained them hidden in Alys's chamber. I read the letters," he said quietly, "and then I burned them."

"Bastard," Griff growled. He swiped at him, but in his fury, his aim was off. The earl feinted to the side and Griffin missed his mark. "You stole my life, Dom. You denied me the information of my birth and then you sought to use it against me by hiring me to steal my own brother's bride. Would you ever have told me?"

"Oh, yes," Dom replied. "Indeed, I had every intention of telling you—"

"After Isabel was delivered to John and you had your payment," Griffin finished for him. His foster brother's flat stare was ample confirmation. "Jesus, Dom. Can you hate me so much?"

"The truth is what you crave?" he asked, his teeth bared in a parody of a smile. "Yes. I hate you that much."

Griff stared at the leering stranger standing before him, the vacant-souled beast he had fought for all these years, protected like his own kin. "You hated me, and so you cared not that your plot against me would have likely sent an innocent woman into a living hell? She nearly died because of your damned orders."

"The chit was merely a means to an end." Dominic chuckled. "It was you I meant to send into a living hell, *brother*." Slyly, he inched his way along the perimeter of the room, his subtle steps carrying him nearer and nearer to the partially open door. "You say I stole your life? Nay. 'Tis you who is the thief—you and Alys both! The two of you conspired to steal my father's affection. No doubt you would have stolen Droghallow from me as well, had my weak-hearted fool of a sire not perished before you could wheedle the demesne out of him."

"I never sought to steal a thing from you," Griffin said, moving closer to the door himself, anticipating Dom's likely flight. "I never wanted to replace you in your father's esteem, nor did I ever have designs on Droghallow."

"Oh, no?" Dom scoffed. "Then why else would you have stayed all this time?"

"Because I made a promise." Griff saw the earl's slight flinch over the statement, the falter in his smug, scornful smile. "Your father asked me to stay here, Dom. He made me swear to him that I would remain at Droghallow in service to you where I could see that you ruled as he would have you do. He didn't want to go to his grave worrying that his son would pander away everything he had worked so hard to build."

"Liar!" Dom blurted angrily.

"I failed him," Griffin said, "but surely no more than you have in your greed and dishonor."

Dominic's gaze narrowed to lethal slits that burned a rage so deep it was visible across the distance of the darkened room. His glance slid beside him to where a water ewer sat atop a sideboard near the door. Griff lunged forward just as Dom hurled the pottery vessel at his head. He ducked, and the ewer shattered against the wall where he had been standing.

The momentary diversion was all the opportunity Dom needed. He bolted out the chamber door and into the corridor, the soles of his bare, wet feet smacking on the stone floor with each hasty step, his untucked tunic flapping around his knees. He slipped and skidded around a bend in the passageway, bellowing for his guards from the top of the spiraling stairwell.

Griff fell in behind and gave chase, ignoring the instinct

that told him to turn instead for the other set of stairs, where he might manage to escape to save his own skin. But his issue with Dom was not yet satisfied. Until it was, he fully intended to play out this confrontation to its end— even if it meant charging headlong into a sea of armed Droghallow guards.

Dom was only a few steps ahead on the winding stairwell. Still screaming for assistance, he half stumbled down the stairs, his sword sparking off the curving stone wall as he fought to keep his balance. He threw a quick glance over his shoulder and saw Griffin behind him, gaining on him.

At the base of the stairs were two tall iron candelabras; Dom deliberately knocked them both over as he passed, throwing the obstacles into Griffin's path. Griff leaped off the last couple of steps with a snarl. Having cleared the flaming mess, his spurs bit into the floor of the landing as he set off down another passageway, fast on Dom's heels.

He kept waiting for a retinue of knights to step into his line of sight, kept waiting to feel the bite of steel in his back, or the sudden jarring impact of a crossbow's bolt. But no interference came from Droghallow's garrison, and in the next moment they would be too late, for Dom was within his reach.

Griff seized him by the scruff of his tunic, pulling him up short. His footing lost, Dominic began to choke. His weapon slipped from his grasp and clattered to the floor. Clawing at the garroting fabric at his throat, Dom sputtered and cursed. But Griff was too far gone in his rage to care; he only pulled the collar tighter. He jerked Dom off his feet and shoved him face first into the stone wall of the corridor. Coming up close behind him, Griff jammed his blade against the earl's spine.

Dom gasped, screwing his eyes shut, his lips dry and bloodless. "Kill me and you'll never get out of here alive," he growled. "You must know that, Griffin. Don't be a fool."

With Dom's warning came the confirming sound of heavy, booted footfalls echoing from the head of the corridor. Several dozen knights were making their way into the keep, armor jangling, spurs clacking with each urgent step. Griffin shook off his hesitation and savagely hauled Dom around, forcing his foster brother to face him. He raised the point of his sword, holding it at Dom's throat. The blade cut in, drawing a bead of blood at the place where his pulse hammered wildly.

The knights were coming closer, nearly to the bend that would deliver them to where Griffin stood, intent and ready to slay their lord. The earl blinked away a trickle of sweat that rolled from his forehead into his eye. One of the guards shouted his name. Dom drew in his breath, then swallowed hard, as if he meant to answer the call, and quickly thought better of it.

Griff brought his arm up, leveling the blade for a lethal thrust. "I warrant you are deserving of a far slower death than the one I give you tonight, Dom."

His hand flexed around the sword's leather grip. Dominic averted his gaze, turning his head so as not to watch the blow that would seal his doom. The guards, meanwhile, had rounded the final corner of the passageway. They were nearly upon them now.

Griff's nostrils flared with the deep breath he took in preparation for what he was about to do.

At his back, he heard the soldiers draw to a halt. There followed a deep, rational voice he had come to recognize in the course of the past few days. "Griffin. He's not worth it, my brother. You are better than this."

"Am I?" he muttered, wanting to spill Dom's blood even though he knew the satisfaction of seeing him dead would be fleeting. Still, he did not back off so much as a fraction, and Dominic's eyes, now open, grew wide with the realization that he might yet die. "I should kill him for what he would have done to Isabel, for what he did to me, and you . . . for everything he's done."

"You no doubt have a thousand good reasons to slay him," Sebastian reasoned calmly as he placed his hand on Griff's shoulder. "But it is not your place to do so, nor is it mine. Surely you do not mean to deny King Richard the pleasure of dealing with this treasonous rabble as he sees fit."

Griffin considered his brother's words, and slowly, he relaxed his hold on Dom. The earl sagged against the wall once Griff brought down his weapon and started to move away from him. A nod from Sebastian sent two of his guards forth to seize the earl bodily, taking hold of him by the arms, while another man bearing an official's scroll stepped forward to address him.

"Dominic of Droghallow," the king's official said. "As sheriff for our lord and king, Richard of England, I hereby arrest and charge you with the counts of kidnap, conspiracy, and treason against the crown. You will stand trial for your crimes by week's end. Meanwhile, your titles, lands, and all your possessions are declared forfeit and shall be surrendered at once."

Dom dropped his head in defeat as the sheriff and guards led him away.

"Richard will be looking for a new lord for Droghallow," Sebastian said as he came up beside Griffin. "Perhaps I will make a recommendation on your behalf when I next have audience with the king."

"No," Griff replied. "I want nothing more to do with this place."

"What of Montborne?"

Griffin turned to regard his brother, frowning at Sebastian's enigmatic smile. "What of it?"

"I have decided to join the king on crusade in the Holy

Land. The call for soldiers and arms has gone up again, and I am going." Sebastian raised a brow, his gaze lighting with a spark of excitement. "I will need to place Montborne under someone's charge while I am away. Someone who could hold the fief, should anything happen—"

Griff swore a curse. "I cannot do it. You must know I cannot . . ."

"I would trust no one else to this."

Griffin stared at him, shaking his head at the enormity of the request. And there was another concern, too. "What about Isabel?"

"Come," Sebastian said. "We can talk on the journey back home."

Chapter Thirty-two

More than a week and a half had passed since the night Griffin left Montborne. By morning Sebastian had been gone as well, accompanied by a retinue of soldiers. While neither man had disclosed their plans of where they were headed, Isabel harbored any number of fears that, somehow, they would both end up at Droghallow.

She knew Griffin too well to think otherwise, certain that no matter his plans for his future, his pride would not allow Dominic's treachery go unchallenged. As for Sebastian, well, she need only know his brother to understand how he, too, would be compelled to take issue with a knave like Dom. But suspecting where they had gone did not ease the worry of what might befall either one of them once they arrived on Droghallow's soil.

Meanwhile, at Montborne, wedding preparations were well underway. Isabel had observed the activity of servants and seamstresses with an odd sense of detachment, as if the ceremony set to take place in a fortnight concerned another woman, not her. She had endured the fitting and hemming of her bridal gown in a state of emotional numbness, unable to look for more than a moment when the maids brought her to stand before a polished glass mirror, unwilling to acknowledge the farce to which she had subscribed.

How would she ever be able to wed Sebastian when her heart yearned for his brother? That he had not repudiated her upon learning of her indiscretion with Griffin bespoke of his honor, but what of her own? How could she allow herself to pledge before God that she would keep Sebastian as her husband, forsaking all others, when she would never stop loving Griffin?

She had posed these very questions to Lady Joanna in the days they had spent together at Montborne, days in which the two women had formed a close bond, each of them waiting for word, worrying for the men who mattered most in their lives. To Isabel's concerns about her pending marriage, Lady Joanna had simply embraced her, advising her to trust in God that everything would work out as it should. Isabel was not so confident.

Retiring to the solace of her chamber after the midday meal, she took up a seat at the small desk situated next to the window. Beside her on the smooth oak writing surface was a folded square of parchment, addressed to a certain convent in France—her letter of apology to Maura, a sister's deep regrets for not being able to send for her after all, for being unable to fulfill her promises to both Maura and her betrothed. Isabel had written the letter in the hours after she had first arrived at Montborne; today she would finally send it on its way.

A beeswax candle burned in an iron holder on the edge of the desk. Isabel reached for it, bringing it over the missive and tipping the shallow metal dish to pour a dollop of melted wax onto the parchment as a seal. She nearly dropped the entire thing when the herald's call sounded from high on the tower's ramparts. The series of staccato blasts rang through the keep, rousing all within earshot to the joyous announcement.

Montborne's lord had returned.

Her heart heavy for the news she would deliver him, Isabel could not bear to look as the bailey filled with the clank of the rising portcullis and the subsequent beat of horses' hooves, thundering through the gates and into the courtyard. There was a flurry of activity below, folk rushing to greet Sebastian and his men. Inside the castle, servants scurried about excitedly.

Isabel rose and moved away from the desk, her letter to Maura clutched in her hand. She hardly had time to gather her resolve before a maid rapped softly on her partially open door.

"My lady? My lord is arrived at last. He requests the favor of your audience in his solar."

"Thank you," Isabel replied. "I shall be right there."

Mustering her courage, she smoothed her skirts, then crossed her chamber and made her way down to the lord's solar. As she approached the door to the chamber, a servant came out carrying a wooden coffer filled with silver tankards, coins, and other objects of value. He bowed to Isabel, then bustled past, calling to another servant to assist him in gathering up a trunk of clothing for their lord.

Isabel frowned in curiosity, then stepped into the doorway of Sebastian's private chamber.

"Come in, my lady," he called from where he sat at his desk. He looked more alive than she had seen him before, leaned back in his chair, his booted foot propped up on the desk. His dark hair was wild and windblown, his cheeks flushed ruddy with color. He gave her a reckless, boyish smile, his pale eyes dancing with unbridled energy. "We must needs talk."

"Yes," she acknowledged softly. "I warrant we must at that, my lord. About our marriage—"

"You should know that I have decided to join King Richard in the war against the infidels, my lady. A ship sails from Portsmouth in a few weeks. I mean to be on it."

"You go to join the crusade?" Isabel gasped. "But, my lord, it's so dangerous—"

Sebastian's grin seemed to indicate that he might actually welcome the idea. "Do not worry for me," he said. "And you needn't worry for yourself or Montborne, either, my lady. I have made arrangements for someone to stay and hold the fief in my stead."

Isabel sensed a sudden shift in the air to her left, a movement in the shadows that sent a current of awareness through her every fiber and left her shaking with anticipation, trembling with a flood of hope. She turned her head and there he was, standing a few paces beside her, all but concealed by the afternoon gloom that stretched into the corner of Sebastian's chamber.

"Griffin," she whispered.

It took every ounce of control she possessed not to close the distance between them and throw herself into his arms. He was bloodied and travel-worn, but whole and hale, and so very handsome. Seeing him before her once again was a sight so heartbreakingly welcome that Isabel could scarcely breathe. She took a step closer to him without realizing it, her feet moving as of their own accord.

"I met up with him at Droghallow," she heard Sebastian say from behind her. "The chivalrous fool might have gotten himself killed if I'd have let him march into Dominic's lair on his own. I saved his noble arse, and now he's agreed to do me this favor and hold Montborne in my absence."

All the while his brother spoke, Griffin's stare remained fixed on Isabel. His gaze was intense and unwavering, but maddeningly unreadable in the murky shadows of the room. She wanted to shout her glee at the prospect of Griffin's staying, but a more reasonable part of her warned that this would be the worst sort of torture, to have him so near when, if she remained as well, she could only do so pledged as Sebastian's wife.

"How soon do you leave, my lord?" she asked the earl quietly.

"As soon as I am packed." As if Sebastian had followed her train of thought, he cleared his throat, and said, "There does exist one slight dilemma, I'm afraid. The king expects to hear that the demesnes of Montborne and Lamere are joined through marriage. I am loath to go to him without being able to assure him that his will is done. So I think it best if the wedding be conducted without delay."

Isabel's heart lurched. "My lord, I fear I cannot—"

Sebastian cut her off with a rakish grin. "I realize he is a poor substitute for me in many ways, my lady . . . but would you consent to take my brother as your husband instead?"

"My lord?" She gasped, utterly astonished. Her limbs lost all feeling; the letter to Maura slipped out of her slack fingers and fluttered to the floor. "W-would I . . . what?"

"Allow me, if you will, brother," Griffin drawled. He stepped forward and took Isabel's hands in his. Then he sank down on his knees before her. "My lady, can you find it in your heart to forgive me for thinking that I could live even one day without you? I realize I am least deserving of the gift of your affection, but I beg it of you now, humbly. You are the love of my life, Isabel de Lamere. You are my heart, my soul, my saving grace. You are my home."

"Oh, Griffin," she whispered. "I have been so lost without you."

He smiled, pressing her palms to his lips, his kiss achingly tender, filled with all the emotion that smoldered in his gaze. "Then will you have me, my lady? Will you marry me?"

"Yes," she answered tearfully. "Yes, my love, I will marry you. Nothing in this world could make me happier."

Epilogue

June, 1190

The sound of a child's laughter caught on the early summer breeze as Griffin of Montborne rode through the open gates of his home. He drew his white charger to a halt in the courtyard, the morning's hunt called short when one of his squires had ridden out to deliver him a letter just arrived from the Holy Land. Though he had not paused to read it, he knew the bold handwriting could only belong to his adventurous brother, gone now some six months on crusade.

He dismounted and headed for the keep to find Isabel. Then he heard the girlish giggle again, echoed this time by the sweet laughter of his lady wife, the lovely sounds coming from the area of the castle garden. Griff tucked the letter into his sword belt and turned away from the keep, rounding the corner of the tower where Montborne's gardens bloomed with fruit blossoms and fragrant summer flowers.

"Look, Isabel—I caught one! I caught one!"

Eight-year-old Maura de Lamere, a red-haired sprite with laughing blue eyes and a cherub's smile, ran from the far side of the enclosed garden to where her elder sister stood clipping roses and dropping them into a basket that hung from her arm. Isabel lifted her head as Maura came up beside her, her hands clasped together carefully as if she held a fragile egg and feared she might break it. Moving slowly, Isabel braced her free hand against the base of her spine and bent down to see Maura's prize.

"Oh, it's beautiful," she said, smiling as she reached out to caress the young girl's cheek.

With a giggle, Maura opened her hands and a tiny yellow butterfly fluttered up into the air. Both of them watched it dance and climb up over their heads, their happiness seeming to beam from their eyes and their lips, filling the garden with a sweetness—a simple yet profound innocence—that Griffin thought he would never get used to. Isabel must have sensed his presence, for in that next moment, she glanced away from the butterfly and turned to meet his gaze.

A look passed between them: part contentment, part longing. They had spent every day and night of the past six months together, but the mere sight of Isabel was still enough to set Griff's blood pounding with desire. She had never been more beautiful. He looked at her and his breath came a little faster; she smiled and his heart squeezed a little tighter. And he could tell from the smoky sparkle in her topaz gaze that she was equally affected by him.

"Maura," she whispered to her sister, her eyes and her slow-spreading smile yet fixed on Griffin. "Run along and ask Cook if I should bring him any peas from the garden, will you?"

The girl bobbed her head and dashed toward the garden gate to carry out the request. She grinned up at Griffin as she approached him and he gave her a wink, reaching down to ruffle her wild red curls as she passed.

"You shouldn't be out of the keep," Griff gently scolded, stepping forth to take his wife's hand and help ease her onto a squat bench near the rose arbor.

Isabel was big with his child, so big, she had been advised by the midwives and Lady Joanna to stay in her bed for the duration of her pregnancy. But she was not the sort of woman to abide orders merely for the sake of obedience, and Griffin rather enjoyed that headstrong streak in her. He leaned in and kissed her, then he kissed her belly, something he did every day with no small measure of love and complete, wordless awe.

"Your babe is active today," she told him when he lifted his head. "Maura got to feel it kick a short while ago. She wanted to know how the babe got in there."

Griffin laughed, positioning himself behind Isabel to support her back as he gathered her into his arms. "What did you tell her?"

"I told her that love put it there."

She tipped her head back and Griff placed a loving kiss on her forehead. He held her against him for a long while, happy just to lose himself in the sound of her breathing, to feel her fingertips softly caressing his arms, her heartbeat pounding in time with his. She smelled of roses and warm woman, the combination made all the more arousing to a man gone some weeks without being able to make love to his wife. Not that they hadn't been creative with the problem of Isabel's condition. They had discovered many highly pleasing and erotic alternatives to satisfy their hunger for each other, and at the moment, Griffin was contemplating several of those alternatives quite seriously.

"You know, my lady," he whispered against the soft skin below her ear, "I would be doing you a great disservice if I were to permit you to remain out here in the garden when you have been ordered to stay in bed."

She drew in her breath when his mouth moved lower on her neck. "Is that so, my lord?"

"Indeed it is." He brought his hand up to brush her breasts, feeling the nipples rise and pucker through her bodice. Heat surged through him when she let out a little moan of pleasure. Already his desire was rampant, needful. She reached between them and placed her hand against his stiff erection, rubbing him with a maddening touch that had become far too expert for his peace of mind. "Oh, yes," he growled, "I think I need to take you to bed at once, my lady."

He felt her hand shift, then heard the soft scrape of parchment as she pulled the letter from beneath his belt. "What's this?" she asked. "It's a letter from Sebastian! Shall I read it?"

"Perhaps later." He scooped her up, lifting her off the bench and into his arms. He carried her out of the garden and into the castle. "My brother can wait," he said with a roguish grin. "I, however, cannot."

Read on for a sneak peek at *Black Lion's Bride*, the next magnificent historical romance from Tina St. John, coming in Spring 2002.

Prologue

Ascalon, in the Kingdom of Jerusalem
May, 1192

Quiet and moonless, the night stretched out over the desert like thick black velvet, a cloak of complicity for the slim figure that moved with catlike grace along the maze of narrow alleyways crisscrossing the heart of Ascalon's slumbering city. Garbed in a form-fitting tunic and hose of ebony silk, head and face masked likewise save for the eyes, it seemed as though night itself had sprouted legs to steal through the war-ravaged, abandoned marketplace.

The figure's pace was brisk but cautious as it rounded the corner of an ancient mosque then continued past a row of merchants' buildings and down another twisting avenue, each step lighting soundlessly on the cobbles and hard-packed sand of the street, the lithe limbs showing no sign of fatigue or uncertainty. The athletic form and flawless stealth indicated none of the strain that yet lingered from the weeklong journey made on foot from the mountain fortress of Masyaf—a journey that had led here, to the desert port of Ascalon.

To what would be a final glory or an ignoble end.

For it was here that the leader of the Frankish infidels, Richard Coeur de Lion, had made his camp, and it was here that the savage king would breathe his last. He had offended many powerful leaders since coming to the Holy Land; there was no telling which of them might have paid to see him eliminated. And to the agent sent out to see the deed was done, the *fida'i* who now crept into position along the city's steep wall to observe the royal pavilion, it mattered not who had bought this death. Like Conrad of Montferrat a fortnight past, Richard of England would soon feel the lethal bite of an Assassin's dagger.

Although the hour was easily closer to dawn than dusk, the king did not sleep. Camped on the plain among the other soldiers, Coeur de Lion's large tent glowed from within, the flicker of a single candle throwing shadows against the striped silk walls, betraying the fact that its occupant was alone, his bulky shoulders hunched over his desk in thoughtful concentration. As if to mock the very notion of danger, no guards stood sentry outside, nor in the immediate area. Richard's fearless arrogance was widely accepted; tonight it would spell his doom.

With no time to waste, the *fida'i* sent a prayer to Allah then reached down to withdraw a virgin dagger crafted especially for this occasion. The curved blade slipped out of its sheath as silently as the footsteps that now carried the Assassin to within a few paces of the king's pavilion. Suddenly, from somewhere in the distance, a dog began to bark. Then the deep rumble of men's voices carried through the night, their Frankish words serious-sounding, but too low to be understood. Two knights had entered the camp from the opposite end, their broad-shouldered outlines barely visible in the dark, their heavy boots crunching in the rubble that littered the ground as they made their way toward Coeur de Lion's tent.

Concealed in the gloomy darkness, the Assassin watched, measuring the distance between victory and defeat, as King Richard lifted his head then started to rise from his chair. There was time enough to strike before the knights reached him. Self-preservation was of no concern; martyrdom was the Assassin's reward. But even more compelling than the promise of awaiting Paradise was the hope that this feat, might at last win the approval of Rashid al-Din Sinan.

Feared by most as the mysterious Old Man of The Mountain, King of the Assassins, to the *fida'i* sent to Ascalon on this mission, Sinan was better known simply as Father. It was his name, not Allah's, that the Assassin whispered before advancing toward the tent that enveloped Coeur de Lion's unarmed silhouette.

"I dinna suppose the king bothered to explain the urgency of this midnight summons, did he?"

Sebastian, Earl of Montborne, and, more recently, officer to King Richard of England in the war against the Muslim infidels, gave a shrug to the soldier walking at his side. "The king is awake and he wishes to have reports of his troops. What more explanation is needed?"

"Ach," grunted his companion, a large Scotsman from the highlands of that wild northern region. "I might have known better than to complain to you, my friend. You and Lionheart seem to forget that we mere mortals require such things as food and rest to gird us for the next day's battle."

Sebastian chuckled. "And here all these months you've been trying to convince me that the Scots' blood ran thicker than the English. I wonder what your bonny bride would say to hear you now, bemoaning the loss of a few hours' sleep?"

"Aye, my sweet Mary," sighed the Scot. "She would

doubtless give me a pretty scowl and and say, 'James Malcolm Logan, I told you you were mad to leave me to chase glory in that accursed place. Now get your fool's arse back home where you belong before I—' "

A movement in the distant darkness caught Sebastian's eye. He stopped walking, silencing his friend with a slight lift of his hand. "Over there," he said when Logan, too, paused. He kept his voice to no more than a whisper. "Something moved behind that row of tents."

Without the moon to offer light to the camp, it was difficult to see anything beyond the pale shapes of the soldiers' tents and the dark, rising swell of Ascalon's crumbling city wall in the immediate background.

Beside him, Logan was peering into the dark and shaking his head. "I see nothing."

"No," Sebastian insisted, certain he was right by the sudden prickle of rising hairs at the back of his neck. "Something—someone—is out there."

And then there was another shift of the darkness up ahead as a slender figure seemed to materialize from out of the gloom. Clad in black from head to toe, the intruder hunched low, creeping toward the center of camp with unmistakable purpose. Sebastian did not have to see the dagger that curved out of one fist like a deadly steel talon to understand what this intruder was . . .

Assassin.

"Blood of Christ!" Sebastian drew his sword and lunged forward. "The king, Logan! Go to the king!"

While the Scotsman raced for the candlelit glow of Richard's pavilion, Sebastian's boots chewed up the space of earth between him and the Syrian agent of death. In the camp, some of the other soldiers had begun to rouse. They tumbled out of their tents and grabbed up weapons, alerted to the situation by Sebastian's shout of alarm.

The ruckus must have taken the Assassin aback, for he paused suddenly as if to assess the pending threat of capture. The hesitation proved costly. Sebastian headed him off and was fast on his heels as the would-be assailant turned and ran for the open city gate. If he let him escape to the labyrinth of Ascalon's streets and alleyways, Sebastian knew he would never find him.

The Assassin was slight of form, but quick. Sebastian was close enough that he could have cut him down with his sword at least twice, but the agile little bastard dodged away each time, scrambling out of his path like a hare fleeing a hound. The Assassin had nearly reached the freedom of Ascalon's arched gate when he suddenly lost his footing, slipping in a patch of loose gravel. One leg skidded from beneath him and he started to fall. Sebastian hurled himself forward, reaching out with his free hand to grab the Assassin's flailing arm.

"Uh—no!" he shrieked, the thready voice pitched higher than Sebastian might have expected.

A stripling youth, then, sent down from the mountains to kill a king? It seemed a ridiculous notion, but Sebastian had no time to consider it further.

Without warning the Assassin spun on him, and, in pure speed of motion, he hit Sebastian in the side. The blow was not the hardest he had ever taken, but it was swift enough to knock all the wind from his lungs. He lost his grasp on the Assassin's arm and the lad broke away in a run. Sebastian followed, but quickly found he could not keep pace. His feet began to drag beneath him; his sword became a weight he could scarcely hold. He took a couple more steps, his boots scuffing in the sand as the Assassin slipped around the corner of the city gate and disappeared.

At his back, Sebastian heard the clank of weapons and the heavy beat of footsteps as a company of soldiers jogged up behind him. He had not realized he'd stopped moving until he felt a hand come to rest on his shoulder.

"Are you all right, Sir?" one of the crusaders asked.

Sebastian nodded his head and pivoted toward his men,

trying not to let the effort that small movement took show in his face. "Lost my . . . breath." Impatiently, he waved off the assisting hand one of the knights offered him, frustrated that he had let the Assassin get away. "The bastard hit me, and I lost my breath. Leave me alone. I'll be fine."

A dozen guards stared at him in mute stupefaction, wide-eyed and astonished beyond words.

"Jesus," a young soldier managed to gasp.

Sebastian looked down to where their gazes were rooted, and acknowledged the source of their concern with a grim laugh. At his waist, a large pool of blood soaked through the fabric of his tunic and down onto his hose, seeping out of him from a wound at his side. The little whoreson had stabbed him—quite efficiently, from the looks of it.

It was no wonder the men gaped at him as if he were a ghost. In a few more hours, he likely would be.